My Fierce Highlander

Vonda Sinclair

My Fierce Highlander

Copyright © 2011 Vonda Sinclair

ALL RIGHTS RESERVED

www.vondasinclair.com

ISBN-13: 978-1469941080
ISBN-10: 1469941082

DEDICATION

To
Celtic Hearts Romance Writers
&
Rebel Romance Writers

ACKNOWLEDGEMENTS

Special thanks to Sharron Gunn, Jody Allen, and Cindy Vallar for helping me translate Gaelic, answering difficult questions and assisting me with research.

The Highland Adventure Series

My Fierce Highlander
My Wild Highlander
My Brave Highlander
My Daring Highlander
My Notorious Highlander
My Rebel Highlander
My Captive Highlander
Highlander Unbroken
Highlander Entangled

෴

The Scottish Treasure Series

Stolen by a Highland Rogue
Defended by a Highland Renegade

CHAPTER ONE

Scottish Highlands, 1618

A stiff breeze carried the scent of bruised grass and blood on its icy breath.

Death.

Gwyneth Carswell dropped into a crouch and peered through brambles at the tartan-clad bodies, a dozen or more, lying in the dusky gloaming. While gathering herbs earlier, she'd heard the sounds of battle—men shouting, steel clanging, horses screaming.

A chill shook her. The men of the MacIrwin clan, her distant kin, lived and died only for a skirmish. Her sheltered upbringing in England had molded her into the person she was, a lover of peace, but she'd been in the Highlands long enough to expect brutality at every turn. Thank God her son had stayed in the cottage with Mora.

"More senseless death," she whispered, yearning to run and hide in the cottage, curl up beneath the blankets, and forget she was a healer. Forget all the drained blood and horrifying wounds that would never heal.

But she must not. She must again face death all around her. Dread and nausea rising within her, she covered her nose with a handkerchief. After peering about to make sure she was alone, she crept onto the soggy moor and forced herself to look at the butchered bodies of her cousins…and their enemies. Who had they been fighting?

Pressing her eyes closed to block out the slit throats and other mutilation, she murmured a prayer, both for their departed souls and for strength that she might keep going.

Please, allow me to save the life of at least one.

A haunting groan floated on the breeze. A sign? Her prayer answered? Gwyneth froze, listening. The groan sounded again, straight ahead.

She rushed to the far edge of the clearing.

Daylight dwindled, but she knew she'd never before seen the injured man, a large warrior with long dark hair, obviously from the enemy clan. She could not tear her gaze from his clean-shaven face, smeared and spattered with blood. Never had she seen such a striking man. But something more captivated her, something she could only sense with her woman's intuition. She yearned for him to open his eyes, but he didn't.

Blood soaked through his white shirt and fine, pale-blue doublet.

Kneeling on the damp ground, she attempted to press her hand against his chest to feel his heartbeat, but a rolled-up parchment lay in her way within his doublet. She removed it and checked his heart. The thump was slow but strong and steady.

Her eyes locked to his face again. Enticing, yes, but still an enemy.

Wary of him and what message he carried, she stripped the ribbon from the missive and flattened the thick paper. In the dim light, she could barely decipher a few of the Gaelic words inscribed in bold letters across the top.

A peace agreement? Had the MacIrwins ambushed them? She stared down at the man again, lifted his hand and found a seal ring on his finger. A chief?

For a second, it seemed the very ground had a pulse. The vibrating sensation disoriented her.

Horses!

Distant hoof-beats grew louder and thundered in her direction—the MacIrwin reinforcements coming to finish off their enemies. Her pulse roared in her ears.

If they discovered this man hanging onto life, they'd cut his throat. Especially if he was a chief who wanted peace. Gwyneth crammed the parchment back inside his doublet and stood.

She grasped the thick leather belt that held the man's *plaide* in place at his waist and struggled to drag him a few feet into the yellow blooming gorse and weeds. Good lord, he was heavy, comprised of honed warrior muscle. Another tug, then she rolled him down a short incline and behind the bushes, praying all this shifting wouldn't worsen his injuries. She spread her dull-colored skirts and plaid *arisaid* over him to conceal the visibility of his light-colored doublet in the dusk.

Her body trembling, she gently bit her knuckle to quiet her chattering teeth. *Please, do not let them find us.* She hardly dared to breathe.

The horses' hooves thumped over the grass, and the riders yelled in Gaelic—mostly vows of revenge against the cursed MacGraths.

Through the bushes and gorse, she watched as they loaded the dead bodies onto horses.

Warmongers!

Several minutes later, the MacIrwin men rode away. After a while, silence descended and naught could be heard but the nearby stream and a faraway owl. Gwyneth calmed by slow degrees.

Taking a deep breath, she rose on shaking legs. The man lying at her feet was so large she couldn't move him again, not alone, uphill, for the strength that had come with fear had ebbed.

She ran up to the stone cottage, her feet tangling in the rocks and low-growing plants.

Breathing hard, Gwyneth burst through the door, the bitter scent of peat smoke and tangy drying herbs replacing that of fresh air. "Mora, did you hear the battle?"

"Aye, I reckon they were fighting the MacGrath. 'Tis always a blood feud betwixt them." Her friend and fellow healer bent over her knitting, her gray head wrapped in a white *kerch*. The fire smoldering in the center of the room provided little light.

"One man still lives. He's been knocked out, but his breathing is strong. We must bring him here and see to his injuries."

"Who is he?" Suspicion laced through Mora's thick brogue.

"I know not."

"One of the enemy?"

"Likely."

"Mmph. I won't be helping the MacGraths."

"A dozen men are dead. For what purpose? All this fighting is madness!"

"Easy for you to say, English. Lived here nigh on six years, you have, and still you ken naught of our Highland ways."

She knew enough about their violent way of life and hated it. Gwyneth glanced at her five-year-old son sleeping in the box bed on the other side of the room and lowered her voice. "I would die before I'd let Rory become one of them, giving up his precious life over a senseless dispute." She had to find a way to take him out of the Highlands before Laird Donald MacIrwin forced him into the ranks of his fighting men. "And you're right, I cannot understand so much bloodshed over nothing."

"'Tis not for naught. The MacGraths killed Donald's brother ten years past. Then there was the time the MacGraths claimed a goodly portion of MacIrwin land. We don't take the stealing of land lightly."

How could her friend be so cold? "This man who yet lives is carrying a peace treaty. He wears a seal ring and appears to be the chief. Aside from that, he's human and we're healers. If I can save a life, I will, whether he is friend, foe or beast."

"Aye, you with your gentle lady's heart. You'll get us killed. What if Donald finds out?"

A chill raced through her at that thought. "He rarely comes here." Though the clan chief was her second cousin on her father's side, no fondness existed between them.

"'Tis a bad feeling I have about this. You'll regret it."

"Do you not think the MacGraths will exact a severe revenge against us all if the MacIrwins kill their chief? He wants peace, as we do."

"Well, this is not the way to go about it. I've been around a few years longer than you have, Sassenach."

"I will drag the big brute up here myself, then." She yanked a blanket off the bed, left the cottage and strode down the hill once again toward the glen. The stones slid and rolled beneath her slippers and bit into her feet. If Mora wouldn't help her, she'd do what she could for the man.

Something all-consuming rose up from her soul and railed, refusing to allow him to lie there and die. Though his body looked powerful, he was helpless now. As helpless as a child, helpless as little Rory. All this man's fearsomeness at her mercy, she was awed by the power she held over him, to help him reclaim his strength and his life…or let it drain away. That would be a sin far worse than any she'd ever committed, of which she had many. The peace treaty and something deep within her proclaimed his life was worth saving a hundred times over.

Gwyneth crouched behind a patch of thistles at the edge of the glen and listened for MacIrwins. The only sound was the wind hissing through the pine needles and the splash of the stream.

A rock clattered down the slope behind her. Startled, she turned

4

to find Mora approaching with a wood and linen litter. "Verra weil, English. I reckon I cannot let you do all the healing by yourself. And we'll be needing this to haul his big arse up the hill."

Gwyneth arose, suppressing a smile. "I thank you for your kind heart, Mora."

"Mmph. Where is the heathen?"

"I hid him in the weeds and bushes so they wouldn't finish him off." She led Mora across the small glen to the MacGrath.

Mora knelt over him. "Aye, his breathing is strong. He may yet survive."

They rolled him onto the litter. Laboring under his considerable weight, they dragged him toward the cottage. Full night had fallen, making their arduous trek up the hillside even more difficult.

"Good heavens, he must weigh twenty stone." Mora huffed and gasped.

"I'm in agreement." Gwyneth's arms and legs ached from her efforts.

"This one didn't starve the winter."

"No, indeed."

Mora started toward the cottage.

"Let's hide him in the cattle byre. 'Twill be safer should Donald come by," Gwyneth said.

Mora narrowed her eyes. "You're being mighty canny of a sudden."

"Well, I know if he finds us hiding his enemy, he'll likely fly into a violent rage."

"Aye, and kill us all," Mora grumbled.

Gwyneth shoved the dread away and ignored her friend's pessimistic view. "We shall hide him well."

They dragged the MacGrath into the stone byre, which stood several yards from the cottage, and rolled him onto a wool blanket on the hard-packed dirt floor.

After a trip to the cottage, Mora lit several fir roots in order to find his wounds.

"A bonny lad, he is," Mora proclaimed.

Lad, indeed. Rory was a lad. This giant was a man full grown. But bonny, yes. In the soft flame-light, his midnight hair, his equally dark brows and thick lashes captured Gwyneth's attention.

Open your eyes.

They would be dark too, would they not? Dark as tempting, dangerous sin in the blackest night. Beard stubble shadowed his authoritative jaw and framed his sensual mouth.

I am going daft, noticing such things at a time like this.

Forcing herself to ignore his face, she unfastened the brass brooch shaped like a falcon that held the upper part of his blue plaid in place over his shoulder, removed the brown leather pouch-like sporran from his waist and dropped the brooch inside.

"Do you not think he's the laird?" Gwyneth raised his strong hand to show Mora the seal ring, the heat of him seeping beyond her skin.

"Aye, I'd wager he is the young laird. I've never laid eyes on the man afore now. Though I recollect hearing of the old laird's passing sometime back, and he does favor him. 'Course all the MacGraths have a certain dark look about them."

Gwyneth tugged the ring from his finger and placed it in the sporran.

"His clothes are of fine material." Mora pushed the doublet open. "And would you look at this." She pulled a gleaming brass-hilted dagger from inside the garment, near his armpit.

She used the sharp weapon to cut his bloody clothing away from his upper body.

Holding her breath, Gwyneth could but gape as each inch of skin and sculpted muscle was revealed. Among the multitude of scars on his chest, two long shallow sword cuts oozed blood. A lead ball from a pistol had grazed his shoulder, leaving a furrow of torn flesh.

She would stitch him up so he would heal, good as new.

A slice in his plaid alerted them to another wound. Mora unhooked his leather belt and eased his kilt down to reveal a cut to the right side of his lean waist close to his pelvic bone.

Wanton excitement stirred within Gwyneth at the sight of this enemy Scot's near-naked body. *I should close my eyes, look away. He is a patient.* Heat seared her from the inside out.

Though she'd attended to many an unclothed man after a skirmish or during sickness, she had never seen a man so beautifully formed. God had certainly smiled upon him.

"'Tis shallow," Mora said. "He's lucky they didn't strike his vitals."

They cleaned his wounds with a wash of royal fern steeped in clean water, stitched up the deeper cuts, then smeared them with a paste of fern and comfrey.

"My, but a fine-looking man he is, aye?" Mora smiled and winked. "Reminds me of my own big Geordie afore he passed on."

6

Indeed, *fine-looking* was too mild a term, in Gwyneth's estimation but she ignored the question. She would not have Mora know of the embarrassing effect the man was having on her.

Most men of her acquaintance were the same—arrogant, cruel, and harsh. Whether fancy English gentlemen or braw Scottish warriors, they only thought of their own superiority and how they might wield power over others. Women were naught but chattel and thralls. By helping to save this one's life, she was gambling, hoping to win peace.

"Och, here's what ails him most." Mora examined the Scot's head. "He's bashed his skull and good."

"Let me see." Gwyneth knelt on the dirt floor above him. His hair was sticky with blood, and a knot swelled on the back of his head. "It seems to have stopped bleeding."

"Aye. Not much to be done for it, anyway."

Nevertheless, Gwyneth cleaned the wound and applied the herbal paste as best she could in his thick hair. She concentrated on her task more intently while Mora covered him with a blanket and worked his plaid out from under him. Gwyneth tried not to think about his nakedness beneath it. Surely it was a sin to hold such thoughts.

"We've done all we can for him. He's in God's hands now. 'Tis off to bed, I am."

Carrying his belongings, Gwyneth walked with Mora back to the cottage and hid his things in a rough wooden chest. She approached the bed where Rory lay. Relieved he'd slept through the commotion, she kissed his forehead and straightened. "I'll go back out and sit with the MacGrath man for a short while."

"Suit yourself. Best take your *sgian dubh* with you, just in case he wakes up none too happy about where he's at."

Gwyneth nodded and touched the dirk hidden in her bodice to be sure it was still there. She hoped she wouldn't have to defend herself against a man she was trying to help. But, the truth was, she didn't know him or what he might do.

Above the dark rounded peaks of the mountains, a quarter moon peeped through the clouds, providing the faintest of light for her to navigate the path to the byre. A whitish-gray mist crawled up from the glen, reminding her of the souls of the recently departed and giving her a chill. She inhaled the scent of rain before entering the tiny building and closing the door.

The handsome stranger lying insensible on the floor drew her gaze. The old plaid blanket did little to conceal his fine form, large and well-trained for battle, hard and heavy with muscle. She hoped she wouldn't regret helping him. If he carried a peace treaty, surely he was a good man. A better man than Donald MacIrwin, at least.

Now, if only this MacGrath would awaken and return to his own lands, she would rest much easier. If he could somehow bring peace, she would be doubly grateful. But she feared there would be no peace as long as Donald MacIrwin drew breath.

Through the door, the haunting, fluted call of a curlew reached her. Gwyneth shivered. Mora had told her more than once that a curlew heard at night was a bad omen.

⁂

Gwyneth startled awake at a low rumbling noise, then realized it was thunder. Stiff and cold from lying on the hard dirt floor of the byre, she pushed herself to a sitting position while pulling her woolen plaid *arisaid* closer around her shoulders. Though 'twas June, the temperature never warmed here in the Highlands as it did in England. Rain pattered on the thatch, and thunder sounded again. At times like this, she missed the featherbed and cozy counterpane of her youth. And she would prefer a roaring fireplace to the single lit fir root which served in place of a costly candle.

The injured Scot shifted and mumbled.

She moved closer, touched his forehead and found his skin hot and dry. The fever had started.

May God protect him.

His recovery would take several days, if he survived the fever at all. He had to. He simply had to survive. She could not see such a strong, well-favored man leaving this life at so young an age. Surely, he was no more than five years older than her own three and twenty.

She pulled the cloth from the bowl of cool water, squeezed it out, and stroked it gently over his face. She wished to brush her bare fingers over his skin instead but squelched the urge. *How silly of me.* The linen snagged against his beard stubble. His dark lashes fluttered above his high cheekbones.

"Leitha," he said, his voice a deep rumble. Though slurred, the word was clear. He jerked his head abruptly. "Nay, I cannot believe it." After turning his face away, he stilled, as if he'd dropped into a deep sleep.

Who was Leitha? His wife? A sliver of envy made her bow her head in shame. The woman was sure to wonder where he was, perhaps even think him dead. Was he a good husband to her, or a rotten one like Baigh Shaw had been to Gwyneth?

She had found it no easy task being demoted from a wealthy English earl's daughter to the wife and thrall of a low-born, violent Highlander almost twice her age with two grown sons who despised her.

Her father couldn't have punished her any more thoroughly for her one unforgivable sin had he tried. All had been stripped from her six years ago. She possessed nothing of material value, no property or inheritance, not even a wedding dowry. Therefore, she had little choice but to stay where she was. Trapped in the godforsaken Highlands.

Thunder cracked overhead, and the MacGrath jerked.

Gwyneth washed his face again, smoothing the cloth over his thick dark brows and stubborn but appealing mouth. What would his lips feel like...? *I should not think of such.* She hated her sinful sensual side; it had already ruined her life.

His next string of slurred words were Gaelic, and the only one she understood was *"athair."* Father. If he was the chief, then his father was surely dead. Was he seeing specters in his fevered dreams?

Near dawn, he became too quiet and still. She checked his breathing. When it didn't seem as strong as before, she froze, then clasped his muscled forearm in her hands and said a prayer.

⸎⸎⸎

Alasdair MacGrath was fair certain he'd never before awakened to such stabbing pain in his head. He loved good sherry and whisky but never overindulged, so it couldn't be the drink banging on his head.

A voice sifted through his agony. A high-pitched, senseless prattle.

"I'll get you, you worthless MacIrwin bastard."

Those words didn't go with that innocent voice.

Another voice, rougher yet still the same growled, "You're a no-good MacGrath coward. I'll run you through."

What the devil is going on? Alasdair cracked one eye open. He lay on the hard-packed earth floor of some sort of dark room that spun around him. Straw and the smell of aged cow dung told him it was a byre. He squinted toward the open doorway, trying to steady his vision. A wee lad with fair hair sat in the patch of brilliant sunshine.

He continued to act out the battle scene between two man-shaped twigs. "Take that, you puny toad-spotted whoreson!"

If not for the piercing ache in his head—in his whole body—

Alasdair would have laughed outright. As it was, he only managed a snort without doing himself in.

The lad sprung up, whirled around, and gaped at him with wide blue eyes. "You've awakened."

"Aye," Alasdair uttered, his throat dry and voice raspy.

"Ma! Ma!" The lad screamed and sprinted from the byre.

A skewer to the ear would've been more pleasant. Alasdair's thoughtless attempt to shield his ears from the child's hellish noise brought gripping pain to his upper body.

By the saints! What happened to me? He groaned and glanced down at himself. A woolen plaid blanket and a pile of straw covered him. He lifted the blanket and the scent of strong medicinal herbs reached his nostrils. *A healer'd had hold of him?* Various cloth bandages littered his torso. Other than that, he was naked.

Where are my clothes?

And where are my sword and dagger? Cold fear settled in his chest.

Someone appeared in the doorway, blocking out the light—the small frame of a woman. Though he couldn't see her well, he felt her staring at him a long moment. "How do you feel?" she asked.

"As if I took a wee tumble from the peak of Ben Nevis. Where am I?"

"MacIrwin land."

In that moment three things occurred to him—she was English, he was back from the dead, and he lay helpless on enemy land with no weapons. *God's bones.*

A flash of returning memory distracted him—he'd thrust his sword at a grizzly, outraged red-haired man. Something, or someone, had hit him on the head. The powerful blow had knocked him from his mount and all went black.

"Does Donald MacIrwin ken I'm here?" His sore muscles tensed. Wincing at the pain, he forced himself to relax.

"No." The dimness hid her expression, but wariness colored her tone.

"Where are my clansmen?" He prayed his cousin, Fergus, and all the others had survived. But he knew that was impossible. He'd seen some of them fall.

"About five or six died on the battlefield. The others must have returned home."

He didn't even know which ones had perished yet. Dear God, not Fergus or Angus. Fortunately, his brother Lachlan had not accompanied them that day.

10

"I don't understand how I came to be here instead of with them."

"After the skirmish, I went to see if I could save the lives of any of my kinsmen, but you were the only man I found alive."

"You're a MacIrwin, then?"

She crossed her arms. "The MacIrwin is my distant cousin. My grandmother and his grandfather were brother and sister."

He'd best tread softly until he determined whether he could trust this relation of his enemy. "You've the speech of a Sassenach."

"I grew up in England, yes."

"Why would a MacIrwin, even an English one, save the life of a MacGrath? We've been enemies for nigh on two hundred years." Alasdair tried to sit up, but a spasm of burning pain latched onto his lower belly. "*Mo chreach!*" He fell back.

"Do not get up." The waif-like woman rushed forward and knelt beside him. The pleasant smell of fresh air and green herbs clung to her.

She placed a cool hand against his upper chest and pressed him back. After shoving aside the straw and lowering the blanket to just below his waist, she examined the stitched wound on his abdomen.

"You've started this bleeding again." She flicked a glare of censure at him from her vivid blue eyes.

"Pray pardon," he said, then wondered why he'd apologized.

She could not have much MacIrwin blood in her veins, else she would've left him to die on the battlefield. She was nothing like Donald MacIrwin. This was the second time the bastard had deceived them, under oath, into thinking he wanted to sign a peace treaty, when in truth he wanted to murder those bearing it. Alasdair craved peace for his people so badly he'd become too trusting.

While the healer examined his injuries, he studied her captivating face. Was her creamy skin as silky as it looked? She frowned as she worked, and some of her light-brown hair escaped the knot at the back of her head. He wanted to wrap the straight, wispy strands around his fingers. Why didn't she wear the *kerch* head-covering favored by married Highland women? Perhaps she wasn't married, though she had a child. A widow, then. No rings adorned her fingers, but that told him naught since Highland women only wore their wedding rings on special occasions.

One thing was sure, she'd undressed him and seen him naked. Wishing he could've been awake for that, he suppressed a grin.

She caught him watching her, and her skin turned pink. Ah, but she was a bonny Sassenach. He smiled. What was she doing here in the Highlands tending his wounds? Mayhap she was an angel or a fairy and not a human woman at all.

Her cool, efficient hands felt soothing on his skin, overheated from the wool blanket. Indeed, soothing, but her touch slowly coaxed a new heat to life within him, a different sort of tingling heat he had suppressed for some time and was surprised to feel now with such strength.

"Are you in much pain?" Her eyes were guarded when they met his, and he pushed his irrational interest in her away. His very life was in danger and he best focus on that.

"Nay." He had endured far worse. Perhaps it was her gentle touch that eased his aches.

She covered him again with the blanket. "You must lie still."

"Aye. Did I not arrive with any weapons?" He felt more naked without those than without his kilt.

"A dagger. I have it well-hidden." She rose.

"I would have it back to defend myself, if you don't mind. If the MacIrwin shows up, I'll be helpless as a wee bairn."

"How do I know you won't use it on me?"

He scowled. "I wouldn't harm you. Are you thinking I'm daft?"

She studied him with intelligent, watchful eyes. "I'll consider it."

He released an impatient breath. "How long have I been here?"

"Since last night."

Not long, but likely his clan thought him dead because Donald MacIrwin didn't take hostages. Lachlan wouldn't relish taking over as chief. He was probably even now cursing Alasdair for being so careless.

"You hit your head on something," the woman said.

Alasdair moved his head on the straw-filled pillow, and a pain shot through his skull. "Or something hit me on the head. I reckon 'twas the broad side of an ax...which I much prefer to the sharp side." He stroked his fingers over the sore lump on the back of his head. "God's bones, 'tis the size of a sheep's hoof." He laid his head back on the pillow and gazed up at her. Surely she was his guardian angel. "You saved my life."

"Most likely." She glanced away as if it were nothing.

"I thank you." It seemed so little to say. How would he ever repay her? "But why would you care if I lived or died?"

Her gaze examined his eyes, dropped to his mouth, his bare shoulder, then lifted again. She shrugged. "I'm a healer. 'Twas the least I could do for a fellow human being."

"What? You don't think me a savage?" He was certain he looked greatly uncivilized to her English eyes…eyes which now gleamed with blue ire.

"No. The only thing savage is this senseless fighting over nothing!"

"Well, I would see it stopped but your clan will not let it be. When we're provoked, we fight as any clan would. The MacIrwins have committed many a crime against us."

"Two hundred years in the past."

"Nay. More than I can recount during my own lifetime. Including murder."

Her gaze locked to his. "What?"

"Aye, your fine cousin—oh, never mind. Why am I telling a woman? I must be on my way." What a waste of time this all was. He must get back to his own clan.

"No!"

Such a forceful command from the wee lass? He couldn't help but gape at her militant expression.

"You shall not get very far with a broken toe," she added.

"Oh, is that all?" He moved his feet and a stabbing pain ricocheted up his left leg. "God's bones!" With a grunt, he ground his teeth and stilled, praying the pain would go back into hiding.

"You see?" She placed her hands on her hips and glared down at him as if he were a wayward lad. "We didn't even know your big toe was broken until it turned black and swelled."

He released his held breath. "Mayhap 'tis but a sprain."

"God willing, you will be so lucky. I cannot understand why men do this to themselves." A spark of anger flashed in her eyes, and this distracted him from his own agony. Her fire had a definite appeal.

"Och, we're lacking a wee bit in the tower." He wanted to tap a finger against his head, but dared not move too much. Instead, he attempted to relax. "What of your husband? Does he ken I'm here?" He prayed no men of the clan knew of his presence, else it could prove his downfall.

"My husband was killed in a skirmish three years ago," she said in a wooden voice.

Without doubt, she was not yet done grieving the loss. He well knew how mourning could linger. Even after two years, he still missed his wife.

13

"I'm sorry to hear it. And he was...?"

The healer's gaze speared him. "I'm certain you didn't know him. What is your name?"

"Angus MacGrath," he lied, thinking she'd likely recognize his real first name.

She frowned, but curtsied nonetheless. "A pleasure. You are chief of the MacGrath clan, are you not?"

How had she figured that out? Mayhap his clothing had given him away. Or his ring—the weight of it was missing from his finger, but he dared not ask her about it. He studied her curious expression. For his own protection and that of his clan, he must seem like an unimportant person. She might deliver him to the MacIrwin if she knew his true identity.

"Nay, I'm the cousin of the chief." Since he had a cousin named Angus MacGrath, he'd simply pretend to be him.

She surveyed him with narrowed eyes.

"Disappointed, are you, that I'm not the earl and chief?"

Gwyneth studied the smirking Scot, unsure whether to believe him. She'd been almost certain he was the chief. He'd had the seal ring, fine clothing and the treaty on expensive parchment. If he were trying to mislead her, she'd let him think he'd succeeded, while she figured out what he was up to. Maybe he feared she'd turn him over to Donald.

The longer Angus MacGrath talked to her, the more flustered she felt. He had a noble, pleasant way about him that should've put her at ease. But it didn't.

His steady eyes were unreadable, penetrating and mysterious. Dark as she'd imagined. And at times amused and gleaming with sensuality. If she had to be in his presence much, such a man would be dangerous to her sanity and soul. Not wanting him to see into her thoughts, she erected that familiar defense wall about herself. The wall that had protected her from Baigh Shaw or any other man who thought to intimidate her.

"I ken you must fear your cousin will find out I'm here," he said. "I owe you my life, so if anything happens, I'll protect you."

What was wrong with the big lout? He couldn't even rise to his feet, much less defend her. "A lot of good that will do me now. If they show up, I'll have to protect you."

"You would do that for me, m'lady?" His dark brown eyes twinkled, teasing yet still suspicious. His strong accent turned lady into *leddy*, an address she'd only been called with a derogatory slur while in the Highlands.

"I'd prefer you not call me that." Though still a lady in truth, she didn't think of herself as such, nor had she for six years.

A grin tugged at the corners of his mouth, shadowed by a new growth of black whiskers. She couldn't gaze at him overlong. His eyes had a look in them she didn't trust, a look of mischief and interest she dared not think about.

He sobered and shifted his gaze away. "Our clan didn't come here to fight. We were to meet with the MacIrwin and establish a peace agreement. He invited us to his home, and then attacked us. His word means naught."

"Are you saying Laird MacGrath wants peace?" She suspected it was true, but she wanted confirmation.

"Aye, m'lady. Above all else, he wants peace for the clan."

A hint of relief flowed through her. "I found the peace agreement in your doublet," she confessed.

"'Tis not worth a wee pebble in the River Spey now. Burn it if you will. 'Haps it will provide fine heat to cook your porridge."

How could he be so pessimistic and give up so easily? "Will you not try again for peace?"

He snorted. "'Tis useless. There is no peace to be had with Donald MacIrwin. They ambushed us—fired pistol shots at us from the cover of the brush, then came out with their swords. As you can see, 'tis the reason we fight. They understand no other language. We must protect what is ours—our clan, our land, and our cattle. We won't let him run roughshod o'er us."

"Of course not." She well knew how ruthless her cousin was. He had always dealt with her in a wretched manner. Without a doubt, if she did something to displease him, he would have no qualms about killing her. That was why she now questioned her judgment in helping a MacGrath.

How many of those tales of the cold-blooded, murdering MacGraths were true? If what this man said was true, Donald and the MacIrwins were the ones who kept the blood feud going. Which meant she was more in danger from her own clan than this enemy.

"You must leave here as soon as you're able."

"Aye, I won't argue about that." He glanced aside. "Come on in, then. Don't be bashful, lad."

She followed his gaze to the door and found her son standing there, white-faced and wide-eyed.

"Rory, please stay in the cottage."

15

"I heard horses—lots of horses coming."
She froze. "Oh, dear God. 'Tis Donald!

CHAPTER TWO

"The MacIrwins will be here in a matter of minutes. I need my dagger." With a growl, MacGrath moved to get up from the dirt floor of the byre. A grimace contorted his features.

Gwyneth rushed to him, icy anxiety knotting her insides. "There is no time, sir. I must hide you. Rory, go stay in the cottage with Mora, and don't say a word. I'll be there in a moment."

Her son sprinted away.

"I won't play the lamb to his slaughter," MacGrath said between clenched teeth, fierce determination emanating off him in waves.

"I'll cover you in straw and they'll not see you, even should they look in here. You must trust me. There is nowhere else for you to hide now." *Please, God, make him listen to me.*

His stark gaze speared hers. "You should've let me keep my dagger."

"Here, take mine." She pulled the small dirk from the busk of her corset and handed it to him.

"This? 'Tis naught but a wee toothpick!"

"That's all I have. Do not move unless you're certain they've found you." Hands trembling, Gwyneth covered MacGrath from the top of his head to his toes with the blanket, then piled more straw over him until the blanket was hidden.

On the way out, she pulled the door closed behind her. Thank God, Donald wasn't in sight yet. She ran toward the cottage. The rhythmic staccato of hoof beats grew loud like her own pulse.

Inside the cottage, she met Mora's worried gaze. Why was Donald paying a visit? Did he suspect something?

May God protect us.

17

"Rory, sit over here and…shhh." She pointed to a short stool, then clasped her trembling hands together. "Remember what I said? Not a word about the man in the byre."

Rory nodded. His rounded eyes told her he knew if he said the wrong thing, something terrible would happen. She hated that her son had to grow up in this harsh way of life.

Pounding hooves drew closer, the sound making her stomach ache. If Donald and his men discovered MacGrath…. Heavens. She didn't want to think of the consequences.

The horses snorted and kicked up rocks outside the cottage. Donald and his men talked in Gaelic as they dismounted.

Inhaling a deep breath, Gwyneth approached the open door and faced her cousin.

"Did you happen to find Robert or Red John in yon glen?" Donald MacIrwin asked in an ill-tempered tone.

"No, we didn't. Why?" The stench from Donald's stocky body forced Gwyneth to breathe through her mouth. His shaggy brown and gray beard contained a few crumbs from his last meal.

"We couldn't find them after the skirmish yester eve. The MacGraths must've took them hostage. Cursed mongrels." He spat upon the ground.

"Why did the MacGraths attack?" Pretending ignorance, she hid her clenched fists in the folds of her skirts.

Donald's mouth turned to a snarl, and she was unsure whether he was disgusted by her bold question or the subject matter.

"Are you thinking they need a reason? Nay! They're outlaws, the lot of them, wanting to steal more of our land." Lowering his bushy brows, Donald stepped across the threshold and glanced about the room, even peered into the two box beds, neatly covered with woolen plaid blankets.

Surely he didn't expect to find his men there. She dared not move a muscle or even breathe too hard.

Donald's gaze lingered a bit too long on Rory where he sat like a tiny gentleman on a stool by the fire in the center of the floor.

"The wee bastard's shooting up like a weed, aye? I'll see to it he starts training with a sword and targe in a year or two. I'll be needing a few more fighting men."

Upon my faith, you will not get your hooks into my son! Gwyneth clenched her teeth until they ached.

Donald turned and left the cottage. "Search yon wood," he yelled to his men and pointed at the forest beyond the byre. "They may've crawled off and died."

One of his men moved toward the byre.

No! Let him pass by. They simply could not find MacGrath or they were all dead.

The man yanked the door open and stuck his head inside.

After a long moment, he closed it and moved on.

Thank you, God. Gwyneth released a breath, her knees threatening to buckle.

She forced herself to go about her outside chores as usual, feeding the chickens and milking the cows, all the while watching for Donald's men from the corner of her eye.

About an hour later, they appeared to have left the area. Concealing her items in a feed bucket, she carried oat porridge, bread and ale into the byre.

"They've gone." She approached the corner where MacGrath lay and set the food on the ground.

"*Mo chreach.*" He pushed the blanket and straw from his head. "I thank you for the use of your wee dirk, but I'm wanting my dagger now." He handed her the weapon.

"I'll bring it to you. But you must eat and regain your strength."

"When I heard them open the door, I was thinking I was a dead man for certain sure."

"We've outsmarted them for now." She placed a rolled-up blanket beneath his head and shoulders so he might sit up a bit. "Careful you don't cause that wound to bleed again."

His direct stare unnerved her. He seemed intent on catching a glimpse of her thoughts—as if he wanted to know her secrets.

"I thank you for your help," he said, his voice low and deep.

"You're welcome."

But he was the enemy, she had to keep reminding herself. An enemy she had given a weapon to, and had it returned. That connection of fledgling trust was something new to her.

Gwyneth knelt beside him, picked up the bowl and scooped a spoonful of oat porridge for him.

"I'm not so maimed I cannot feed myself, m'lady."

Stubborn male pride. "Don't be silly. You're injured, and I would rather you didn't spill porridge all over my blanket." She held the wooden spoon to his mouth. "Open." If she treated him like a lad, mayhap she wouldn't see him as such a tempting man.

He hesitated, but eventually complied. He took the bite, chewed and swallowed. "'Tis verra good." A hint of a smile lightened his expression, but his perceptive gaze remained steady upon her.

"Mora taught me her secret recipe," she said to fill the uncomfortable silence. She was certainly not accustomed to men praising her cooking…or staring at her with such attentiveness.

"Who's Mora?" he asked.

"A good friend and a healer, also. This is her byre, and Rory and I live in her cottage."

"Ah." He accepted another bite and swallowed. "She trained you in the healing arts, then?"

"Indeed."

"Not only are you a good cook and a gifted healer, you're lovely as a spring morn. You ken the kind—when the sky is so brilliant and blue it hurts your eyes." He winked.

Her face felt singed of a sudden. Good heavens! Such extravagant words, she could not credit. The knock on the head had addled him. But a wink from those darkly seductive eyes was captivating and potent. She fed him quickly so he would stop spewing nonsense. Men did not compliment her looks. Certainly not her late husband, Baigh Shaw.

I'm glad he's gone. Time and again, Baigh had mistreated Rory, and her as well. She was thankful they didn't have to suffer any more bruises at his hand.

"Tell me, m'lady, what is your name?" MacGrath's deep voice murmured the words in an intimate tone that sent tingles down her neck. She was not even that close to him. Though she did wonder what it would feel like if he whispered against her ear. He watched her as a cat watches a sparrow before it pounces.

"Mistress Carswell." She hated the Scottish custom in which the wife did not take her husband's last name when she married, but kept her maiden name. The children, at least, took the husband's name. That was the reason she'd agreed to marry Baigh Shaw, so her son would have a name besides her own.

"And your Christian name?" MacGrath asked.

She dropped her gaze to the bowl of lumpy porridge and the spoon she stirred it with. Not near as appealing as his visage, but safe. "It matters not."

He tilted his head. "I but wondered if your name fits you."

She lifted another bite, trying to focus on the spoon and not his enticing mouth. Not the amused quirk.

"And if my name doesn't fit? What am I to do, pick another one?"

He smiled with a flash of strong white teeth. "Aye, and why not?"

A grin formed on her lips, but she squelched it. This was the senseless banter of a flirtation. Ridiculous here, in a Highland byre. This was no dance in a great hall or fine castle. No need to be coy.

"Gwyneth is my name."

"'Tis Welsh, not English."

His astuteness impressed her. "My mother spent a few years of her youth in Wales. She had a close friend by that name."

"'Tis a bonny and fitting name for you as well."

"I thank you." She lifted a small chunk of bread to his mouth. He opened and took it. Her finger grazed his lip, the silkiness and heat intensifying her awareness. Her hand was much less steady as she lowered it.

MacGrath chewed and swallowed. "'Tis you I must thank. I cannot remember when I've had better porridge and bread. Or someone with such a gentle hand to tend my wounds."

He was a charmer in the guise of a whiskered barbarian, and unfortunately, she was not immune.

She gave him the wooden cup of ale, gathered her wooden utensils and stood. "You're welcome. Now, you must rest so you can heal."

He drank, then handed her the empty cup. "I'm hoping you'll hurry back afore long. I'm enjoying your company."

Ignoring his last statement and the engaging look in his eye, she hurriedly said, "I'll bring your supper later, sir."

"And my dagger, too, aye?"

"Yes." Disliking the heated sensation that covered her body, she strode out the door and closed it before he could utter any more sugared compliments. She'd felt this way years ago when a dashing lord had asked for a dance. Now she knew no good could come of it.

Not for her. Not ever for her.

Her two older sisters had been more fortunate and wiser than she, and they'd married well. She didn't yet know whether her three younger sisters were married; she hadn't seen them in six years. She had no doubt her only brother was doing well at university. He was their father's favorite, after all, his heir, and would never want for anything.

Best not to think of her family, England or men. All were beyond her reach. And she was glad she didn't have to bow down to a man's wishes anymore. She now had the greatest measure of freedom she'd ever had, thanks to Mora. If her friend hadn't taken her in, Donald might have married Gwyneth off to another of his wretched friends.

No, she would never marry again and be under a man's command.

⁂

Alasdair shifted, trying to make himself more comfortable on the hard packed floor. With his belly partway full and his mind floating with images of a lovely lass, he was as content as could be expected. His foot, his head, and various other spots pained him, but he tried not to think on it.

Instead, he closed his eyes and forced his thoughts toward his own safety and that of his clansmen. Did they think him dead? Would Donald MacIrwin return?

Something poked his arm, and his eyes sprang open.

The lad jumped back and clutched a weathered wooden sword to his chest. "I thought you were sleeping."

"Not with you poking at me like that."

Rory's sky-blue eyes remained round.

Alasdair smiled, hoping the lad would lose some of his fear. "'Tis a nice sword you have there."

He held it out and looked at it. "I found it in the wood."

"Did you now? That was a bit of luck."

"What's your name?"

"Angus." Alasdair hated to lie to the child, but 'twas safest for him. "And you're Rory?"

"Aye. Are you a warrior?"

"I suppose I am." Though fighting was not something he chose. He would much rather simply lead his clan in peace.

Rory glanced at the door and lowered his voice. "Will you teach me to be a warrior, too?"

"You're a mite young."

"Next month I'll be six." His eyes lit with excitement. "One time I got to watch the laird's men practicing with their swords and pistols and axes. I want to do that. Someday, I'll be a great fighter."

"That you will, lad. I've no doubt of it."

"Watch this." Rory launched into some fancy footwork and thrust his sword about.

Fine entertainment, but Alasdair dared not laugh. He maintained a solemn expression, and when Rory, breathing hard from the exertion, halted and looked to him for reaction, Alasdair

22

nodded. "Well done indeed. I see you already ken a few things."

Rory came forward, curious eyes examining him. "What kind of sword do you have?"

"None at the moment. I'm guessing someone took my favorite sword and made off with it. But I shall get another. A basket-hilted broadsword is a good weapon, for you can wield it one-handed and hold your mount's reins or a targe in the other hand."

"I want a great two-handed Highland sword." Rory stepped back, clasped his small sword in both hands and slung it about as if fighting an invisible enemy.

Alasdair almost laughed. "Aye, another fine weapon when you're wanting to mow down a few dozen of the enemy."

Rory paused, mouth agape. "Have you done that?"

"On occasion."

"How many men have you killed?"

"I didn't keep a count, lad. Doing battle is a lot worse than you're imagining. 'Tis not anything to be happy or excited about. 'Tis simply a sad and gruesome necessity to protect the clan."

"Aye," Rory mimicked his accent and pressed his mouth into a solemn line. "I'm going to protect my ma and Mora from Laird MacIrwin."

A cold frisson ran thorough Alasdair. "Why is that? What would he do to them?"

Rory frowned and thought for a moment. "I don't know. But he's mean."

"Make sure you don't tell the MacIrwin or any of his men I'm here."

"I know. He would kill you on sight."

"That he would." Canny lad. Alasdair wondered whether he might spill the information his mother had denied him. "Tell me, Rory, what was your father's name?"

"My da? Baigh Shaw."

Saints! The man who murdered my father? Alasdair could scarce draw breath for a moment. Surely he'd misheard.

"In truth? Baigh Shaw?" He tried to keep his voice calm, when all he wanted to do was yell.

Rory nodded. "But I don't remember him. He died in battle."

"Rory," Gwyneth scolded from the doorway. "Come out of there at once and leave Master MacGrath alone."

Slumping, Rory shuffled toward the door.

The child was innocent of any crime his father had committed.

But his mother might be a different matter. "He's not bothering me."

"You must rest. Come now, Rory."

"Yes'm."

Alasdair listened to the two walk away even as he pushed himself up. Pain wracked his body but determination made it bearable. He had to get out of his enemy's pocket. Grasping the blanket around his waist, he stood and limped along the byre's stone wall. With each step, his big toe throbbed as if a hammer pounded it. Dizziness almost overwhelmed him, and he staggered. When the blackness abated, he continued onward.

"I must find my clothes and shoes," he muttered to himself.

"What are you doing up?" The demand came from behind him.

Turning halfway, he glared at the woman—Gwyneth. "Your porridge has worked a miracle. I'm near recovered."

"You are not." She stamped forward, treating him as she would Rory. "You must lie down, sir."

"Nay, I don't wish to lie down."

"I knew Rory would upset you."

"I'm not upset!" he growled. Upset? Damnation, he wanted to destroy something.

"Very well." She took several paces back. "I was but trying to help."

He froze, realizing she feared he would hit her. Nay, he would never strike a woman, even when angry. With a deep breath, some of his rage slipped away. "Pray pardon."

She surveyed him with wide eyes for a long moment. "May I examine your wound?"

"And which wound would that be?" He turned fully toward her, holding the blanket in place at his hips. He still couldn't believe it. She was the widow of a murderer, the man who had poisoned Alasdair's father in his own home. Perhaps she had even helped, given that she was a healer who knew about herbs and their properties.

She bent and examined the stitched cut that smarted and burned on his lower abdomen. "As I suspected, you are bleeding again."

He couldn't help but watch her. She was so close to him, her breath fanned against his stomach. His imagination turned wicked and he visualized her brushing her lips over the skin beneath his navel, kissing him, moving lower. No matter that he could barely walk, he felt himself tingling, hardening, wanting her. He had not experienced such keen desire in many a moon.

"Devil take it," he muttered under his breath, hating his uncontrollable reaction to her. She was a woman; he was a man. That was the only explanation. No matter that she might have concocted the poison that killed his father more than five years before.

Indeed, it did matter. He fought back the nausea gripping him.

"Where are my clothes and shoes?"

"Your shirt and doublet were ruined. Your plaid fared better but 'tis still bloody."

"I thank you, but I would have it back now. As well as my shoes, belt, sporran and *sgian dubh*."

"Of course." She frowned. "You are not thinking to leave now, are you?"

"Nay," he lied. "I but wish to have my belongings."

She eyed him suspiciously, then left.

Combating dizziness and disorientation, he limped forward, pain shooting through his foot with each step. He'd walked from many a battlefield more broken up than he was now.

She returned a few minutes later, carrying his possessions. "I suppose you need help with your plaid."

"If you would be so kind." He hated asking for her assistance with anything.

She set his shoes, sporran and dagger aside. He was thankful to have at least one weapon left with which to defend himself.

She laid his wide leather belt on the earth floor, flung out the four-yard-long blue and black plaid on top of it and quickly gathered it into pleats. She had done this before and plenty. For Baigh Shaw, the venomed whoreson.

"There now." She rose. "Can you do the rest yourself?"

"Aye and I thank you." Cursed kilt. He should've worn trews on the day of the battle, but he hadn't expected to be fighting.

When she disappeared out the door, he limped over and lay down naked on the pleated material. No easy task with pain wracking his body. He grasped both sides of the belt and fastened it around his waist. Teeth clenched together, he pushed himself up onto his feet and adjusted the kilt until it hung to his satisfaction. After finding his brooch in his sporran, he fashioned the top ends of his *plaide* into a sash. He wished he had a shirt. He didn't relish going about like a bare-chested barbarian.

Pulling the seal ring from his sporran, he frowned. No doubt

Gwyneth knew its significance, but no time to worry about that now. He replaced it and strapped the pouch around his waist.

Being careful of his broken toe, he slipped on his shoes. His injuries were not severe enough to stop him from escaping this godforsaken place as soon as he could.

Nighttime would be the best time to leave, but he would have a harder time finding his way. How he wished he had a sword.

Gwyneth returned a moment later. Her gaze stroked over his bare chest. He knew it wasn't so appealing with its bruises, cuts and scars. But her face flushed just the same. Did she see him as a man now, since he was dressed, rather than just her patient?

"I see you had no trouble dressing. You are more recovered than I thought."

"Aye. Why did you not tell me Baigh Shaw was your husband?" His question came out harsher than he'd intended.

"You knew him?"

"Indeed."

Her eyes rounded. "Did Rory tell you that?"

"Never mind how I figured it out."

"I take it you were not fond of Baigh."

"Canny lass," Alasdair muttered, then narrowed his eyes, gauging her fearful expression.

She took one step back and clenched her hands before her. "What did he do?"

"I don't wish to speak of it." Hell, why had he said anything.

"Very well. I'll leave you alone then." Her wary gaze remained locked on him until she disappeared out the door.

Long minutes later, Alasdair limped to the door and peered out at the surroundings. The byre and cottage sat in a tiny sheltered cove just off the glen. A stand of black pines grew thick on the sloping hills behind the cottage, and a few shaggy black cattle grazed further down toward the glen. He spied no one around. It was time to take his leave of this place.

Holding onto the rough stone wall of the byre, he limped outside. The fresh air, washed clean with the rain the night before, pushed back a bit of the fogginess in his throbbing head. The sun warmed his face and lightened his mood. He said a prayer of thanks that he had survived. Glancing around, he made sure he was alone.

Pain shot up from his foot with each step, but he continued on his way, hobbling toward the edge of the wood. God's truth, if he was going to limp like an old man, he'd need the staff of an old man.

He would sharpen the top and make a spear. More cumbersome than a sword, but still highly effective for defense.

After choosing a small oak tree to his satisfaction, he whittled at the wood with his dagger. Inhaling the scent of green tree sap, he wondered if Gwyneth could have provided the powdered meadow saffron Shaw had slipped into Alasdair's father's ale. Why, then, had she saved his life? Perhaps she was trying to appease her own guilt.

Since Rory was almost six, obviously she'd been married to Shaw at the time.

His spear sharpened, Alasdair didn't have time to linger and discover the truth. He glanced back to make sure no one watched him. All remained silent and still. He limped deeper into the cool forest, his footsteps releasing the scents of moldering leaves and black dirt.

By the sun, he gauged he was traveling east, toward his own land. He would never be so glad as to see MacGrath sod, and his clan. He listened for the sounds of hidden enemies, but the high-pitched calls of crossbills feeding in the pine branches overhead thwarted his efforts.

Hearing a different sort of bird, this one screeching in the distance, he paused. The MacIrwin call, he would recognize it anywhere. It sounded again, closer this time. Searching out a place to hide, he crept down an embankment, careful not to disturb the brown pine needles, and hid below a gigantic decaying tree stump, one of many that littered the area.

Minutes later, a MacIrwin strode by, humming a ballad, his rawhide shoes padding over the damp leaves. Crouching, Alasdair held his breath and watched. He did not want to kill a man this day.

Once the other man moved on and the sounds of the forest returned to normal, Alasdair crawled from his hideout and continued on his way.

The more steps he took, the more intense the agony from his toe—stabbing pain that shot halfway up his leg. He ground his teeth. The exertion spiked the aching in his head as well.

The trees thinned and gave way to scrubby bushes and tall gorse. He paused at the edge of a moor swathed in heather and other short vegetation. Only a couple boulders and larger bushes dotting the land would provide any sort of cover. Crossing without being seen would prove a hellish task.

Perhaps he should wait for nightfall before attempting it.

Keeping a close watch on the landscape spread out before him, he rested for a spell between gooseberry bushes.

The gash on his abdomen smarted and burned. He glanced down and found it bleeding again despite the fine stitches. The bonny healer would've scolded him over that.

He'd never gotten the chance to ask her what an English lady was doing here in the Highlands. Likely, she wouldn't have told him anyway. And it was just as likely he'd never see her again. He didn't care for the feel of that, despite her possible guilt.

Something about her had held his attention, not just her clear, vivid blue eyes that met his with courage and intelligence. She was a wee, slight thing but appeared to possess the hidden strength of a mighty oak. Perhaps he had enjoyed too much making her blush with his compliments. He glanced back in the direction of the woods and her cottage, some small aching spot within his chest making him yearn to see her one more time. To thank her again for saving his life.

Sometime later, thick gloaming settled over the land along with a faint gray mist. Surely it was murky enough that he wouldn't be seen easily. His predominately blue and black tartan was dull in color, and he wore no light-colored shirt that would glow at a distance in the twilight.

His gaze scanning the deserted moor, he stood and limped forward. Though he had to be careful where he stepped among the rocks and heather so as not to further injure his toe, he made good progress across the damp ground until a distant noise met his ears. Hoof beats.

He turned. A horse and rider approached at a trot from behind. God's bones! He'd been spotted. Glancing about for cover, he found no bushes nearby. Only a large rock. Teeth gritted against the piercing pain in his foot, he limped forward and crouched behind the rock.

"Who are you?" the rider called out in Gaelic. Too close, the man drew up, but Alasdair dared not peer out.

The horse clomped closer. A sword swished from a sheath in a metallic hiss.

CHAPTER THREE

After returning from a visit to a sick clanswoman, Gwyneth stepped inside the byre and found it empty.

Good lord! Where was MacGrath?

She darted outside again and surveyed her surroundings. Nothing moved but the cattle and sheep. Had Donald captured MacGrath while she, Mora and Rory had been gone? Or had he left? Surely if Donald had come, he or his men would have tracked her down and asked questions. Or worse.

Since there was no sign of a struggle, MacGrath must have left on his own power. How could he journey with a broken toe? He was a madman to think he could cross that many hills and moors without a MacIrwin seeing him. She and Mora might have saved his life, only to have him limp about like a clumsy toad and get himself killed anyway. Such a blunder would put all their lives in danger.

Shaken, she ran to the nearby wood and searched for him in the deepening gloom. Maybe he had staggered out here and passed out again.

No, she didn't see him.

Gwyneth hoped MacGrath was already on his clan's land. Perhaps he'd been wise to leave. At least she wouldn't be found guilty of harboring the enemy.

But she would miss the charming way his obsidian eyes sparkled when he was thinking of a bit of devilry. It had been years since a man had teased and complimented her as he had.

I am a daft woman, always a fool for a handsome man. They were all the same—pretending to be considerate one moment, and lapsing into hatefulness the next.

"'Tis better that he's gone." She strode into the byre again to clear away the last traces of his presence—the blanket and herbal supplies.

Rory skipped in, halted and scanned all the corners. "Where'd he go?"

"Home, I hope."

"Oh." A glum expression weighted her son's features. And in the deepest part of herself, Gwyneth felt the same.

"I wish he'd stayed," Rory said. "He was going to teach me to be a warrior."

No, he will not! She glared at her son. With the education she was giving him, he would become a learned man, perhaps a scholar, steward or merchant. She wanted him to live a long and happy life. Not be killed in some senseless skirmish.

It was best for them all that Angus MacGrath was gone. And since no one else had known he was here, they'd be safe now. At least she didn't think anyone else knew.

"You didn't tell the boys at Finella's about him, did you?"

Rory's eyes widened. "Only Jamie. But he's my best friend, and he won't tell anyone."

Dear heavens! What have you done?

◦◦◦ ◌◌ ◦◦◦

Crouched behind the rock, hiding from the MacIrwin clansman stalking him, Alasdair tightened his grip on the spear. In his other hand, he picked up a stone the size of his fist and waited.

Strength infused his muscles as it did when he charged into battle. The pain slid away and his attention focused. He gauged the horse's distance by the sound of its hooves among the rocks.

He sprang upright, aimed at his enemy and hurled the rock. It hit the hulking man on the side of the head with a thwack, toppling him from the horse.

The horse whinnied and scuttled sideways.

Alasdair prayed he hadn't killed the man, but he had no time to find out. Pain lancing his foot, he limped forward. This MacIrwin was out cold, certain sure. Alasdair tossed his primitive spear, snatched the man's basket-hilted sword, which he was far more skilled with, and heaved himself into the saddle. The animal shied from an unfamiliar rider. Alasdair controlled him with the reins, his legs and murmured Gaelic words.

He kicked the horse into a gallop across the moor and headed toward MacGrath land. No time to tarry. The MacIrwins would find their injured kinsman soon enough. The thin, cold mist dampening his face smelled of soggy peat and freedom. The horse's gait over the uneven terrain snapped Alasdair's teeth together. Clenching his jaw, he leaned forward.

Too late, he glimpsed a group of what appeared to be MacIrwins on a nearby trail, some on horseback. By St. Andrew, they'd already spotted him. His only option was to race toward his own land.

The men called out and charged forward on their horses. The wind whipping his hair into his eyes, Alasdair glanced back and counted five in pursuit. "God's teeth!" He dug in his heels, urging his mount to a full run.

Two shots exploded behind him. He lay over the horse's neck, expecting the lead balls to tear into him…but he felt nothing. Thank God the MacIrwins were bad shots and pistols were not as accurate as they should be.

A good warrior he was, but not against five, and him injured besides.

The horse beneath him was sweating and near winded. He hated to push the animal more, but his own life depended upon it.

He darted another glance back. The cursed MacIrwins advanced from the white mist, their swords poised to run him through.

"Iosa is Muire Mhàthair!" Kicking his mount's flanks, he held his own pilfered sword at the ready. He could off two or three of them before they dealt him fatal injury. But the last two worried him.

They yelled curses, taunts and threats meant to undermine his courage. He oft used the same tactic himself.

Alasdair peered back and found one of the horses breaking away from the others, surging forward like an Arabian. The bearded, yodeling devil of a rider waved his broadsword overhead.

The fog thinned and the distant hills of his own land came into view. But he wasn't there yet. The MacIrwin knave bore down on him. Alasdair easily understood the other man's murderous threats, called out from a few paces away. The breath of his mount huffed within earshot.

His pursuer drew almost even with him on the left. Alasdair thrust his sword at the man's abdomen in a quick, precise stab. The pressure on the blade's point told him he'd struck his mark. The other man growled an oath and lashed out with his own sword.

Alasdair dodged away, guiding his mount to the right.

"A mhic an uilc!" the man bellowed, dropping back.

The renewed thunder of hooves approached. Alasdair glanced back to find the other four MacIrwins at twenty paces and gaining ground.

A hill lay before him. The horse beneath him would be hard-pressed to climb it. One thing stood in his favor—it was his hill on his lands.

Up ahead, battle cries rang out through the dusk. Through the drifting clouds, the faint light of the moon glowed off the pale shirts of a half-dozen of his clansmen descending the hill, some on foot and others on horseback.

He called out to them, slowed his horse and turned about to face the nearest MacIrwin. Alasdair raised his blade to deflect the enemy's first blow. Metal clanged against metal. He struck out again and again at the other man with thrusts and slices.

"Alasdair!" His kinsmen joined in the skirmish. They unseated two of the MacIrwins and sent their mounts galloping. The remaining two swung their horses about and raced away, back down the hillside. The two on foot fled.

He'd made it. He released a shout of victory in the wake of the retreating MacIrwins.

His clansmen surrounded him and called out greetings. "Chief! You live!"

"We thought you dead for certain sure," his cousin, Fergus, said.

He laughed. "I would've been without your help."

At the hilltop lookout, he dismounted and slapped his borrowed horse on the haunch, sending it back to its owners. He would not be accused of horse thievery. A lone torch revealed a dozen of his clansmen gathered here, but some were missing. "Who died in the skirmish yesterday?" he asked, thankful to see his cousins Fergus and Angus hale and hearty.

Fergus named five men. Good, strong, noble men, the lot of them. Men he had grown up with and fought beside many times.

"*Muire Mhàthair!*" Alasdair felt responsible, for he should never have trusted the enemy's word on anything. Tomorrow, he would visit their families and offer what help he could. But nothing would replace a husband and father gone forever. One way or another, he would see the MacIrwin pay.

"Glad we are that you made it back." Fergus slapped him on the shoulder.

"No more glad than I. My skull was near bashed in." Alasdair limped forward. "And I broke a toe. Smarts like the very devil."

Despite the gloominess of the situation, they chuckled at him.

Two hoisted him atop another horse.

He smiled at their good-natured ribbing about their formidable chief being brought down by his toe.

"Where's Lachlan?"

"At the tower," Angus said. "Hatching up a plan of attack on the craven MacIrwins. He's madder than hell itself, thinking you dead. We all were. But I've never seen the lad so intent on revenge."

Lachlan was the merry sort, and Alasdair hated to see him fash himself so. As second in command, he would be next in line to inherit the titles of chief and earl if something happened to Alasdair. Lachlan hated responsibility or being tied down and would likely find the position difficult to grow accustomed to.

"I must see him. I thank you for coming to my rescue."

The men laughed and slapped the rump of his mount. The horse trotted forward, carrying him toward his tower, Kintalon Castle. Mist had risen from the loch and now cloaked the castle.

Inside the high walled barmkin, he dismounted and handed the reins to a stable lad who gaped at him slack-jawed.

Shouts of "Alasdair!" and "Laird MacGrath!" rang out around him. He smiled and greeted his clan.

Several of his overjoyed clansmen lifted and carried him up the spiral stone staircase in the attached round tower.

Once inside the candlelit great hall, they set him down. The familiar smells of baking bread and spiced ale calmed him. Home. He limped to a chair and stood behind it. The room of thirty or more people fell silent. He scanned the pleased faces of his kinsmen and women before him. Gratitude and pride in his clan tightened his chest.

"I'm thankful to be home this day. I have a few minor injuries, but I'm alive."

Their boisterous cheer resounded off the two-story high ceiling.

His brother, Lachlan, descended the stone steps. His gaze lit on Alasdair, and his face paled. "By heaven! Alasdair? You live!" He rushed forward and pulled Alasdair into a rough hug. Lachlan, the same size as him but two years younger, did not realize his own strength.

Pain shot through Alasdair's chest and abdomen, but he didn't even grunt. "Aye, *mo bhràthar*."

Lachlan pulled back. "Thanks be to God. We thought you dead and buried in a bog, or sunk in the loch."

Alasdair grinned. "A bonny MacIrwin fairy saved my life."

The men's laughter bounced off the stone walls. But concern for Gwyneth weighed heavily in Alasdair's mind.

Would Donald MacIrwin find out she'd saved his life? He'd been nowhere near the cottage when he'd been spotted, so surely they wouldn't make the connection.

Unless they backtracked him.

ഇ ഇ

The entry door of Irwin Castle burst open. Chief Donald MacIrwin glanced up from his wooden bowl containing his meager supper of bland porridge, annoyed they were near out of oats and ale or anything else to eat. He hesitated to have more of the cattle or sheep butchered, else they'd have none. They'd need to raid a nearby clan soon.

"What is it?" he demanded of his four clansmen striding forward, their wild hair windblown as if they'd ridden hard, and their plaids askew. He'd set them to guard the border betwixt his land and MacGrath's. "And more importantly, what the devil are you doing away from your posts?"

"Alasdair MacGrath was here, m'laird," Burgin, one of his best guards, said.

Donald bolted up from his chair, rage blazing through him. "Alasdair! The chief? Where?" He reached for his sword at his side, then realized the weapon was in the armory, being cleaned and sharpened.

"Aye," Burgin said. "He knocked Charlie out and stole his horse. Then he fled across the moor onto his own lands. We tried to stop him but Charlie's horse is fast. He had reinforcements waiting at the border."

"Damnation! What was he doing here? The chief would not come alone."

"He must have been here since the other skirmish. He'd been hiding in the wood, waiting to attack one of us and make good his escape."

"That whoreson." Donald felt like overturning the whole table, but held his temper. How could MacGrath have hidden in the wood that well for almost two days? "Was he injured?"

"He did not appear to be injured as he fled but mayhap he was. We thought we'd seen him fall during the first skirmish. Red John remembered striking him, but then we couldn't find his body."

Something strange was going on. Had a member of the MacIrwin clan helped this MacGrath bastard?

"At first light, find out where he was hiding in the wood. Edward is a good tracker."

∘◦◎ ◎◦∘

The next day, Gwyneth set down her herb basket at the crest of a hill and once again murmured a prayer that Rory's little friend would not mention the enemy warrior to anyone. Rory assured her he hadn't said the MacGrath name to the other lad or that the man had been hiding in their byre. Still, Gwyneth's stomach had been upset all night and she had gotten little sleep.

She inhaled the calming scents of the pungent herbs from her basket and the clean breeze as she gazed out over the rolling brownish Cairngorms toward the east. The sheep and cattle dotting the lower green hills were not MacGrath livestock. Their holdings lay beyond the meager wood and beside the loch in the distance reflecting the blue late afternoon sky. Apparently the high mountain blocked her view of their castle.

Though she did not want to admit it, she'd spent the day missing the big, teasing Scot. His devilish smile and lingering midnight gaze had disrupted her mundane life. Now, her only entertainment was her memories.

And the memories did crowd in on her. He'd said she was lovely as a spring morn, and he'd looked at her as no man had in years. As if…had he not been injured and they had been at a banquet, he might have asked for a dance, or a walk in the garden. Or a kiss.

Imagining what his lips might feel like on hers—warm, firm and smooth, she realized she had taken too close a notice of his mouth.

She pressed her eyes closed. *I'm a wanton. No wonder I'm stuck here in the godforsaken Highlands.*

But it wasn't just his dark good looks that appealed to her. He appeared to have a good and compassionate heart.

She had to believe he'd made it home, where he would be safe from Donald and his men. Home, where he would heal and live to fight another day.

Yes, it was best he'd gone. She hated war, but that was his life.

From the small pouch attached to her belt, she withdrew her only remaining memento from England—her mother's pelican-in-her-piety pendant.

Just before Gwyneth had left her father's house, over six years ago, her mother had slipped this piece of jewelry into her hand as she'd embraced her the last time. The pendant was pewter and not

35

very valuable except for the small ruby at the pelican's breast. Legend said that if the pelican was unable to find food for her young, she would peck at her own breast and draw forth blood with which to feed them.

At first Gwyneth had thought her mother had given it to her as a reminder of her faith, the pelican representing Christ. But years later, she came to realize that perhaps her mother's message meant something else—that as a mother, Gwyneth must be willing to sacrifice all for the sake of her son.

And if she had to, she would.

She closed her fingers over the worn surface of the pelican and her three chicks. She missed her mother terribly, but her father would not allow them contact. What would her mother think of Rory? Surely she would love her grandson, born in shame or not.

Gwyneth returned the pelican to her pouch and picked up her herb basket. *I will not dream of things I cannot have.*

"Come, Rory," she called to her dawdling son. "Tell me, what is this herb?" She bent and fingered the rough green leaves.

He frowned. "I do nay ken," he said in a strong accent like MacGrath's.

"Where did that Scots brogue come from?"

Rory shrugged.

"I think you spent too much time with Master MacGrath."

"You mean Angus?"

"You are not to call him by his first name. 'Tis not respectful."

"He said I could."

"I do not care what he said."

Rory pouted. "I wish he would come back."

She knelt before Rory. "Listen, son, you are not to mention Angus MacGrath's name to anyone else. Do you understand? Donald will kill Master MacGrath if you do."

Rory's eyes widened.

So she'd told a little fib. In truth, Donald would kill Gwyneth and Rory if he knew.

"I can keep a secret," Rory said with a solemn expression.

"Good." She hugged him, kissed his forehead and straightened. "Time to go home. Evening will be upon us soon, and we must milk."

He found a short stick and, as if it were a pistol, pretended to shoot at birds with it.

She shook her head. The boy would make anything into a

weapon.

When they rounded the hillside, the stench of smoke met her nose. She grasped Rory's hand and pulled him along with her. Shouts and a scream in the distance chilled her.

Forcing herself to move forward, she cut through the trees above the cottage. Flames devoured the thatched roof.

Mora!

"Where is Mora?" she whispered, ran several paces, then halted. Her dear friend lay face down in the dirt yard, a sword protruding from her back. "Dear God." She felt as if a dagger had struck her own heart.

Donald's men milled about around Mora.

Murdering fiends!

Horror crumpled Gwyneth's body and she fell to her knees among the rocks. "Oh, dear heaven, Mora, what have I done?" she sobbed, pressing a hand to her mouth to hold in a scream.

"Ma, I'm scared," Rory whimpered.

"Shh. You must be quiet." She turned Rory away from the carnage and held him tight in her trembling arms.

Donald must have found out about Angus MacGrath. Was it because of Rory's friend, or had MacGrath been captured when he was trying to escape?

Either way, Mora was dead and Gwyneth took full blame because she'd insisted on helping him. Mora had cautioned her against it.

I'm so sorry, Mora. I will never forgive myself.

Gwyneth wiped her eyes and stood. "Come. We must hide." She shoved her herb basket under a short bush, grabbed Rory's hand and they ran through the wood, slipping on leaves and pine needles.

Two of her kinsmen appeared some distance away, headed to the left of them.

Freezing, she glanced about frantically, and then spotted a ditch behind a rock. She dragged Rory toward it.

"Lie down, and don't make a sound," she whispered. When he wadded himself into a ball on the ground, she covered him with soggy leaves and twigs. Hiding herself would be more difficult. She amassed a large pile of leaves and burrowed beneath. She laid a hand on Rory to keep him calm. As a mere babe, he had learned how to be quiet when it was important. Baigh had made sure of it. He'd hated a crying child.

The MacIrwin men walked by, talking. Panic quickened her

blood.

Please God, don't let them find us.

She couldn't believe sweet, kind Mora was dead. A plague upon Donald! She would see him pay for this. Mora had done nothing wrong.

The men's voices moved further away, and silence returned. Gwyneth concentrated on Rory's warm, trembling hand within her own. The rocks on the ground beneath her jabbed into her shoulder and hip. She found the scent of moldy leaves and damp earth comforting because they hid her, and kept her and Rory safe.

Night descended, the temperature cooled and two owls hooted. She would not be helping Mora milk her cows this day, or ever again. They would never share another meal or work together delivering bairns. Dear Mora, a good woman. A strong woman. But not stronger than Donald's gang of murderers. Tears streamed from Gwyneth's eyes and dripped into the stony dirt.

Her only hope now was to flee with Rory, try to make it to MacGrath land and hope Angus MacGrath would ask his laird to give them safe passage to the Lowlands, or someplace away from here.

Donald's men would undoubtedly be posted at various points to watch for her during the night. The MacGrath holdings were a long distance away, perhaps five miles.

⁂

Gwyneth and Rory stayed that night in the wood, hiding beneath the soggy, rotting leaves. The next morn before daybreak, Gwyneth pushed herself up, wincing at the pains that radiated from her stiff back and legs. A chill breeze penetrated her damp clothing, and she shivered. Quietly, she woke Rory.

Holding his hand, she led him a short distance through the wood. Using her dirk she dug roots for them to eat. Mora had taught her well which wild plants were poisonous and which ones might serve as food. Gwyneth's eyes burned and her throat closed each time she thought of her dear friend.

Mora had been the only one to help her bring Rory into this world during a difficult birth. In truth, Mora had been like a second mother to her.

"I don't like this." Rory grimaced as he gnawed on the crunchy silverweed root.

"I know. I'm sorry, but it's all I could find. Later, we will look for berries. You like those."

He nodded, but his eyes were red and moist. She felt like bursting into tears herself, but couldn't. She had to stay strong for his sake.

"Did Laird MacIrwin kill Mora?"

"Yes, he or one of his men did."

"Because we helped Master MacGrath?"

"Yes."

Rory dropped his gaze to his lap. "Was it my fault because I told Jamie?"

"No, Rory. It wasn't your fault." *It was mine.* "But I hope if Master MacGrath made it back to his clan, his laird will help us now in repayment for the good deed we did. He told me the laird was his cousin."

Gwyneth held Rory's small hand, and they slipped further through the wood. From her cover behind thick bushes, she spied one lookout during the day. He was near the trail she usually took. *In faith, Donald will not give up until we are dead.*

At dusk, Gwyneth quickened their pace and eventually they left the trees and came upon bush. Bilberry and gooseberry grew thickly. She and Rory ate their fill of the unripe, tart berries and waited for nightfall. When darkness surrounded them, they left the cover of the bushes and set out across the damp moor.

They were headed toward MacGrath lands—that much she knew. She prayed, if he was there, Angus MacGrath would return the favor of saving his life. But what if he turned out like so many other men she'd known and betrayed her at the last moment? Pains gripped her stomach, both from anxiety and hunger.

Rory was all she had—the most valuable thing in her world. For him, she would go to the MacGraths and beg assistance. Protection.

But first, they had to safely cross the moor.

༄༅ ༄༅

For hours, Gwyneth and Rory trudged through darkness, with only the moon for light, and picked their way through the gorse and heather not yet in bloom. A movement up ahead at a lone tree caught her attention. She recoiled, breath held. In the dimness, her eyes strained to identify the movement—a horse swishing its tail. Where was the rider?

"Shh," she hissed at Rory, and gave the tree a wide berth.

The horse snorted and stamped its hooves.

Gwyneth's skin prickled. She crouched and pulled Rory down beside her.

A man grunted, groaned, then strode out into the moonlight to relieve himself. Once finished, he returned to the shadows, and a screeching birdcall sounded from the tree. Some distance away, an answering call responded. Her blood chilled. The men were communicating. What were they saying?

Gwyneth and Rory sat hunched for an immeasurable time, until her legs cramped. If they moved now, the watchman was certain to see and capture them. Vigilant to all the sounds and movements around her, she seated herself into a more comfortable position upon the damp ground and waited for the man to fall asleep.

A mist floated above the ground like a giant cloud, obscuring the moon, and the first glimmer of dawn brightened the horizon before her. Indecision tormented her. They had to leave now or be discovered in the daylight. If only the mist was lower it might conceal them.

"Shh," she whispered to Rory. "We must move quickly but quietly."

Rory blinked sleepy eyes at her, seemingly half aware of where they were.

"Are you awake?"

He nodded. Her poor, sweet child. She hated that he had to go through this.

She rose and tugged him along with her. They slipped toward a distant hill, her skirts snagging on heather and gorse. Cold water from the peaty soil seeped through her rawhide slippers. The cool, damp air around them vibrated with tension. She tried to ignore the knotting pain in her stomach and the weakness of her whole body from lack of food.

She had no notion where the border to MacGrath holdings was, but surely they would reach it soon.

The birdcall echoed from the tree behind them. But this time the sound was different—an alarm. *"Jesu!"*

A horse galloped forth, a menacing black silhouette advancing from the white mist in the distance.

"Run, Rory!" She tugged her skirts off her shoes and broke into a sprint.

He dashed several paces ahead of her.

"Faster!"

She glanced back. Two horsemen thundered close behind, one chasing on her heels. *Oh, dear God, protect us!* She switched directions, gasping, lungs burning, desperate for more air.

Where is Rory? Her legs wouldn't move fast enough. The air around her thickened like water, and she couldn't get through it.

Spotting Rory, she chased after him. "Run!" She slipped in a puddle but righted herself before she fell.

They will kill us. They will kill my precious Rory.

More horses joined in the chase. They surrounded her, their demon riders yelling in Gaelic. Two hemmed her in. Trapped, she dashed headlong between them. Something caught her by the belt and yanked her into the air. Her legs flailed on nothingness. She landed hard on her stomach across the front of a saddle. The breath whooshed from her constricted lungs.

"Ma!" Rory yelled.

CHAPTER FOUR

"Rory!" *God, help me, I must get to him.*

Gwyneth's vision grew fuzzy. How could she free herself from this rider without getting herself killed? She gasped for air that refused to enter her lungs.

The ground beneath the horse hurtled past at dizzying speed. She fought to escape, tried to grab her captor's sword or dagger.

The kilted Scot—probably one of her own clansmen—shoved a strong hand against the back of her neck, restricting her movements. She couldn't reach her own dirk either. Her throat tightened and tears streamed from her eyes.

Where was Rory? He still screeched nearby, though she couldn't tell where with all the jostling. If one of these brutes hurt him, she'd take her dirk to the blackguard and damn the consequences.

The bare, hairy leg of the Scot flexed in front of her face. She could bite him. But this would only anger him, and he might toss her from the galloping horse.

More hooves pounded close-by, and eerie war cries resounded. Her captor yelled in Gaelic. The ding of clashing metal rang out.

What's going on? The MacIrwin men wouldn't fight amongst themselves. Were the MacGraths challenging them? Had she and Rory made it to MacGrath land? A ray of hope lit the thick blackness that had near smothered her.

Gwyneth turned her head and, upside down, watched the men slashing at each other in the misty dawn light. The pop of a pistol shot echoed. Her captor jerked and growled a curse.

He slowed the horse and unsheathed his sword. Steel blades clanged over and behind her. The man's body tensed. The muscles of his legs under her bunched and flexed hard as iron as he engaged in swordplay with someone she couldn't see.

The horse beneath them danced about, reared. Gwyneth's head spun in the turmoil of movement.

Her captor shrieked. His body convulsed. The horse reared again. She slid with the man, but tried to grab onto the saddle. Her hands clasped air. With a scream, she tumbled over the animal's hindquarters and hit the ground.

The hard impact jarred Gwyneth's teeth and every bone in her body. Pain radiated from her left side. At least the man had broken her fall a bit.

The horse fled. She scrambled away from her captor—one of her distant cousins with red hair, a bushy beard and a grimace such as she'd never seen. He grabbed at his neck where blood gushed.

Glad to be free, but at the same time, hating to see anyone die, she rose and stumbled further away from him.

Pausing a short distance from the main skirmish, she frantically scanned the turmoil for Rory. The meager light revealed less than a dozen men on horseback and some on foot. They cut and jabbed at one another.

A man on foot, a good friend of Donald's, spotted her and stalked her way. He wielded a claymore, bloodlust gleaming in his eyes.

Panic spurred her into a full run.

Where is Rory? Where is Rory?

A horse approached, chasing her. *God protect me.*

Yet again, a rider grasped her belt and yanked her off her feet. She screamed. Her new captor slammed her across his saddle. Pain throbbed in her abdomen.

She struggled to draw breaths. Her black-speckled vision cleared by slow degrees. This man's kilt was of an unfamiliar tartan. She prayed he was a MacGrath.

Her strength drained away. Her whole body trembled with

weakness.

I must find Rory.

The Scot urged his horse up an incline. They were not traveling toward Donald's holdings. This territory was foreign to her.

"Ma! Ma!"

"Rory!" she yelled. Thanks be to God, he was alive. She glanced about upside down, but couldn't see him.

At the top of the hill, the man slowed his horse. Other men surrounded them.

She squirmed, attempting to escape. "Let me down!"

"What do you have there, Fergus?"

"He's gone out and captured himself a bonny bride."

Masculine laughter erupted around her.

Her captor grasped her belt and dragged her backward. "Hold her."

She slid toward the ground, flailed about, but strong hands caught her arms.

The blood rushed from her head. Dark spots obscured her vision, and she grew lightheaded. She swayed and jerked against the hands that held her. They tightened like ropes.

"Ma!" Rory called yet again.

Her vision cleared, and she glanced around in the pale dawn light. The man who'd snatched Rory handed him down to another.

Rory kicked, punched and screamed like a wildcat.

"Rory!" she warned, not wanting the man to hit him. With a trained eye, she searched his body for blood or wounds and thankfully found none.

Her son stilled, looking about wide-eyed.

"Shh," she said when his gaze met hers. She turned her attention to the men around her. "Are you MacGraths?"

"Aye."

She almost collapsed with relief and gratitude, but she still didn't know what kind of reception she'd get.

Her rescuer, the one they'd called Fergus, dismounted and faced her. "Are you MacIrwin?"

His appearance startled her for an instant. He held a strong resemblance to the man whose life she'd saved days ago. His long dark hair reached his shoulders. He had a clean-shaven face and a square jaw, but his eyes were of a different shape and light color.

"I'm Gwyneth Carswell, and this is my son, Rory. The MacIrwins are trying to kill us. We seek refuge."

"And why would they be wanting to kill you, Sassenach?" he asked in a derisive, disbelieving tone.

"They learned that I helped save the life of one of your clansmen, Angus MacGrath."

Fergus frowned and glanced at another man. "Angus, do you ken this woman?"

She scanned the men standing about, expecting to see the man whose life she'd saved. Where was he? And why had he not stepped forward?

"Nay."

She didn't recognize the man who spoke. While he had the same dark hair as most of his other clansmen, he was fully-bearded and a decade older than the man she'd helped. She felt disoriented. He wasn't Angus, unless there were two men named Angus in their clan, a definite possibility. "No, not him."

"I'm thinking she means Alasdair," another man said.

"What were his injuries?" Fergus asked her.

"A large knot on his head, a broken toe, and several cuts. Did he make it back safely?"

"Aye, by the skin of his teeth. That would be Chief MacGrath you're speaking of. And grateful we are that you helped him." Fergus gave a brief bow.

"But he said…." As she'd suspected, he'd lied to her about who he was. Indeed, he hadn't trusted her. But could she blame him?

Six horses charged over the crest of the hill. Five riders sat in saddles and the sixth lay strung over his horse's back.

The men around her rushed forward to meet them, and the one who'd held her captive released her.

"Campbell didn't make it through the skirmish." A bearded man in trews swung down from his saddle.

"Nay!" Angus yelled and pulled the dead man from the horse.

Gwyneth saw then that Campbell was very young, perhaps not yet twenty. Big, tough Angus held the young man's body and sobbed.

"His eldest son." The burly man who still held Rory glared at her.

"Oh, no," Gwyneth whispered. Because of her, someone else had lost their life. A boy who had not yet had time to live his life.

She rushed forward. "Are you certain he's dead? I'm a healer. Let me examine him."

"He was stabbed through the heart." A grim, middle-aged man snarled. "Do you think we don't ken when someone is dead? All you Sassenachs think we Scots are daft."

His words struck her like stones. "Pray pardon." She stepped back a respectful distance.

Watching Angus grieve the death of his son was horrible enough. But when she imagined losing Rory in a like manner, she pressed a fist to her mouth to quell the agony. This was why they had to leave the Highlands. She did not want to be in Angus's shoes ten years hence, grieving the loss of her son in some skirmish.

Rory broke away from the man restraining him and ran to her. She knelt and hugged him tight. It could just as easily have been her or Rory who had died at the MacIrwins' hand. Campbell had given his life for theirs.

"Take her to the tower and see if the laird kens who she is. If he doesn't, cut her throat," bellowed the grim man who had spoken last.

⋘⋙

Gwyneth waited in the quiet, dreary great hall with Rory in front of her. She prayed Alasdair was the true name of the man she'd helped days ago. If not, she and Rory had no hope. One of the men who'd marshaled her and Rory to Kintalon Castle still stood behind them, a sword in his hand. The other man had disappeared up the spiral stone steps to find his laird.

Fear constricted Gwyneth's throat. *Please let him be the MacGrath I know.*

The delicious scents of bacon and freshly baked oat bannocks drifted up from the ground floor kitchen, making her empty stomach rumble and ache, but she would willingly go hungry if only Rory could have some food.

Sunrise gleamed through the small windows cut high into the thick stone walls. No fire yet burned in the fireplace—so massive a person could stand upright within. Only a few worn and faded tapestries depicting battle scenes served to decorate the austere walls. Instead of filthy rushes on the floor, clean rush-mats lay here and there. While they waited, servants and clan members entered to set up trestle tables for breakfast, casting a few curious glances her way.

Many tense moments later, a man limped down the steps on a regal-looking cane, his kilt hastily pleated. With her first glimpse of his familiar face, she whispered a prayer of thanks and gripped Rory's shoulders. She dared not even draw breath for several seconds.

Laird MacGrath moved closer and gazed down into her eyes with solemn concern. "Are you well then, m'lady?"

"Yes. I thank you." She couldn't help the unevenness of her voice that betrayed the rush of relief flooding through her.

He glanced at the men behind her. "Aye, this is the woman who saved my life. Tell the others she and her son have safe haven here."

So overwhelmed was she by his words, she could not hear the other men's response for the blood pounding in her ears. She wanted to throw her arms around him in gratitude, press her face to his chest and cry her eyes out. But she would never demonstrate such a loss of control, no matter how drawn to him she was or how thankful for his compassion.

She swallowed against the constricting emotion. "So, in truth, you are *Laird* MacGrath?"

"Aye. But you may call me Alasdair. I found it necessary to lie to protect myself. I didn't ken whether I could trust you or not."

"And you're still not sure, are you?"

A slight smile lit his eyes. "Nay. But I'm hoping I can."

His friendliness conspired to put her at ease, but she still had to be sure of his intentions. "You will not turn me over to Donald's men, will you?"

"Nay." He frowned. "You didn't turn me over to them. Why

would I be doing anything less?"

She gave a curtsey. "I thank you, my laird."

"I'm glad you and your son are here. I was hoping to see you again…to thank you once more for saving my life." His intense midnight gaze held her. He'd looked at her thus before, days ago. Though he exuded male interest, there was naught insulting in it. Instead, she sensed deep-seated fascination, as if he were loath to glance away from her.

Rory stood silent before her, staring up wide-eyed at Alasdair. She understood her son's fascination and hero worship for she felt the same, though with a woman's appreciation.

"You are welcome, of course. I'm very sorry about Angus's son," she said.

"As am I. I must go see to them. In the meantime, break your fast." He motioned toward the trestle tables with benches where women were assembling food and wooden tableware.

She curtseyed again. "I thank you."

He bowed. "Later, I'll be wanting the whole story of how you came to be here."

Before he left, he spoke quietly to one of the women servants. She stared at Gwyneth and nodded.

Seeming much too solemn for her satisfaction, Alasdair sent her one last glance and limped out on his cane.

One of the youths of his clan had lost his life. Would he blame her for it?

⁕⁋ ◑◐ ⁋⁕

After breakfast, Rory played with the other children, while Gwyneth busied herself by assisting the servants clearing away the meal and working in the kitchen. Sunlight shining through two narrow windows near the vaulted stone ceiling and the lingering fragrance of oat bannocks helped calm her nerves. The plentiful food she'd eaten soothed her stomach.

Though her eyes were scratchy with exhaustion and her muscles sore, she was too tense to sleep. Besides, no one had offered her a bed. Thankfully, they had allowed her to wash herself up a bit before breakfast and loaned her clean clothes. Her own had been covered in black mud from the moor.

Making herself useful to the household was the only way to keep her worries, as well as her grief over losing Mora, at bay. But even washing the wooden bowls reminded her of her dear friend, because they had often shared this task.

"What's taking you so long, Sassenach?" the house-keeper, Mistress Weems, bellowed.

Gwyneth glanced up at the rotund, middle-aged woman with her snarling face. Though no longer above the other woman's social station, Gwyneth refused to be intimidated and met her gaze squarely. Weems glared for a moment, snorted, then barreled toward the other side of the kitchen.

"Pay her no mind," the girl beside her said. "She's a right auld hag."

Gwyneth smiled at the girl. A *kerch* held her red hair back, but small locks curled about her face.

"I'm Tessie." She appeared to be three or four years younger than Gwyneth's twenty-three years, and the *kerch* indicated her married state.

"Pleased to meet you. I'm Gwyneth."

"I ken it. Everyone's talking of you."

Uneasiness crept in on Gwyneth. "What are they saying?"

Tessie cast her a nervous glance. "That you're English and an enemy MacIrwin."

"I am English, true, but not an enemy." She couldn't deny her distant blood link to the MacIrwins, but she could refuse to accept them as true family. "Anything else?"

Tessie studied the bowl she was drying. "Well, some are saying if not for you traipsing onto MacGrath land, Campbell might yet live."

Gwyneth had feared as much. And indeed she carried a heavy weight of guilt for the boy's death. "I wish he had never ridden into the skirmish. He was too young. I had no other choice but to come here. It was either flee to MacGrath holdings or be murdered by my own second cousin. I had to protect my son."

Tessie nodded. "I understand, mistress."

"Please, call me Gwyneth."

"As you wish." Tessie's smile disappeared when she glanced over Gwyneth's shoulder. Heavens, what could be behind her?

She turned to find Alasdair limping across the suddenly quiet kitchen. Goodness! What did he want? Given the servants' reaction, she suspected he didn't visit the kitchen very often, and his imposing form seemed out of place.

His penetrating gaze touched upon her with much familiarity and connection. "I would have a word with you upstairs, Mistress Carswell," he said in a formal but kind tone.

"Very well." She wiped her hands on her skirts and preceded him toward the spiral staircase. She felt all eyes boring into her, speculating what their laird wished to speak to her about in private. She prayed that whispered rumors would not start. The last thing she wanted was another scandal.

"We shall talk in the library." His voice echoed when they entered the empty great hall. His cane pecked along the stone floor as he kept pace beside her.

Alone? In a private room? It wasn't that she didn't trust him. She did. But there could be much speculation from the clan.

How singular and strange this seemed, to be strolling along with such a handsome laird. She must remember her manners. "How are your toe, your head and your other injuries, Laird MacGrath?"

"Please, I would have you call me Alasdair. My foot is mending by the day, and the lump on my head no longer causes me dizziness. As for the cuts, they no longer bleed."

"I'm glad."

"'Tis to your credit I've healed so quickly."

She started to argue, but they entered the library through an impressive carved oak door, and he closed it behind them. She glanced about in wonder at the book-lined room. The MacGrath clan must've indeed been more fortunate and prosperous than most. The musty scent of books reminded her of the small library in the manor house where she'd grown up. A moment of nostalgia transported her back to a time and place where she'd laughed with her sisters and read stories.

Oh, if only she could read some of these books to Rory. She wanted to pull one from the shelf and leaf through it, but restrained herself.

"What a lovely library," she whispered.

"My thanks. Do you read?"

"Eh, yes." Although she was revealing to him her former social station—because usually only the wealthy or the titled read—it could not be helped. Her mother had educated her and her sisters.

"You may use it whenever you like."

"I thank you. I am teaching Rory to read." She was also grateful he didn't ask more questions about her past because they always led to the scandal. And that, he could not find out about.

This room was smaller than the great hall here at Kintalon, and clearly a newer addition, with a lower ceiling and chairs and benches in groupings. Her toes itched, wanting to dig into the rich plushness of the Turkish carpet spread across the center of the floor. A small fire crackled in the fireplace, topped by a carved walnut mantel. She had not seen such luxury since she'd left England. This was a fitting place for a noble laird such as he was, certainly better than a byre.

"Have a seat, if you please." His voice was but a murmur in the cozy room.

She chose a wooden chair and sat, focusing her attention on the business at hand. "How is Angus?" Her heart ached for the poor man.

"Bearing up. 'Tis no easy task to lose a son." Alasdair sat across from her.

"No, of course not." Guilt gnawed at her vitals. "I cannot tell you how awful I feel about it. I suppose if I hadn't come, Campbell would still be alive. It was my fault, I know, and your clan is right to blame me." She simply prayed he could forgive her.

"What?" He frowned. "This was not your fault, m'lady. And the clan doesn't blame you."

She kept her mouth sealed tight, wishing that was the case but....

"Do they?" he asked, his gaze sharpening.

"I'm not certain. But if they do, I can see why. In truth, I had no other choice but to flee and come here. Donald and his men must have discovered that Mora and I had helped you. When I came back from gathering herbs, the day after you left, I found them burning our cottage." Gwyneth's throat closed up and her vision blurred, but she swallowed and continued, determined that everyone know how evil Donald was. "They stabbed Mora in the back and left her lying in the yard."

"By the saints. What a barbarian he is!" Alasdair blew out a long breath. "I am sorry."

His response gratified her and, she had to admit, surprised her. She could count on one hand the number of times a man had come to her defense. "I knew if any of them saw Rory or me, they'd kill us both."

"Of course. M'lady, I'm thankful you and Rory made it here safe and sound. Don't blame yourself for Campbell's death. 'Twas his choice to ride into the skirmish. He had trained for many years, since he was a wee lad, and was as prepared as he could be, for his age. Lives are oft lost in such situations. He was a warrior, and defending the clan his job."

She nodded, though she wasn't sure she agreed.

"In fact, I must blame myself for the trouble you've had." His expression contrite, Alasdair studied the carved wooden handle of his cane, shaped like a falcon. "As I was crossing from MacIrwin land to MacGrath, they near caught me. I'd knocked out one of their men and borrowed a horse and sword. We had a wee skirmish. After that, I feared they'd backtrack me to your cottage." His gaze locked onto hers. "I ken 'tis my fault Mora was killed, and I'm deeply sorry."

Gwyneth's throat ached and tears stung her eyes, both because Mora was dead and because Alasdair seemed truly remorseful for any indirect part he'd played in Mora's death. Never had she known a man who felt remorse for anything.

"I must take part of the blame as well," Gwyneth said. "When you were hurt, I was determined to help you, even though she cautioned me against it."

Why hung in the air for a few seconds as he gave her a dark searching look laced with some emotion she could not identify. She hoped he wouldn't ask. The peace treaty—that was the reason she would give.

"M'lady, that wouldn't put the blame on you, but on me once again." His voice softened. "'Twas my life that was saved, and hers that was lost."

Renewed outrage rushed through her over Mora's death. "No. 'Tis Donald's fault. All of it. He is the very devil!" Never had she wanted to strike him down so badly. And she had never been a violent person.

"Aye, I won't argue about that." Alasdair leaned back in his chair and laid the cane across his lap.

The kilt ended at his knees, leaving a goodly portion of his legs bare. She had been in the Highlands long enough to grow used to seeing that much naked, male skin, but she took more notice than was prudent of Alasdair's golden skin, with its sprinkling of dark hairs, and his pleasantly muscled calves. She knew his thighs to be just as thick with muscle from when she'd examined his injured body.

He had succeeded in distracting her. The heat of her anger had turned into a different kind of heat, shameful and inappropriate at a time like this, when lives had been lost and her own likely still in danger. But Alasdair's vitality embodied life and passion. She could not look at him without seeing this. Everything about him, his masculine beauty, his physical power, shouted *I'm alive*. And sometimes she thought if she could only touch him, he would imbue that same strength of life in her as well.

"Tell me what happened after I left. I'm wanting all the details," he said.

Gwyneth recounted everything she and Rory had seen and experienced, from spending the night in the woods, eating roots and berries, then crossing the treacherous moor at dawn. Alasdair listened intently, nodding from time to time and making comments.

"You must be near exhausted, m'lady. You should've been sleeping, not working in the kitchen."

His concern was a novelty that caressed her like soothing fingers. "I thank you, but I couldn't sleep."

A knock sounded at the door, then it opened and a tall man stuck his head in. He grinned.

"Lachlan, come on in, then." Alasdair motioned the kilted man forward. "M'lady, I would like for you to meet my brother, Lachlan."

The man's tawny, golden-brown hair was long as a pagan's and hung halfway down his chest. His amber-brown eyes, several shades lighter than Alasdair's, held her own in a startling, direct manner. Waves of magnetism emanated from Lachlan. She suspected no lass he set his sights on would retain her virtue for long.

"Mistress Carswell is the MacIrwin fairy I told you about who saved my life."

Both men grinned at her—a devastating picture, to be sure, with their virile good looks.

Gwyneth's face heated with the ridiculous comment. *Fairy, indeed.*

She stood and curtsied. "'Tis a pleasure, sir."

"I assure you, m'lady, the pleasure is all mine." He bowed. Coming forward, he grasped her hand and pulled her upright. "Alasdair, I believe your words were 'bonny MacIrwin fairy,' and I must agree with you. Ne'er have I seen such lovely blue eyes." Lachlan kissed her fingers.

Good heavens! What silver-tongued charmers these MacGraths were. Heat rushed over her.

Alasdair cleared his throat, and Lachlan released her.

Gwyneth's gaze locked with Alasdair's, which harbored a glare, and his brother stepped away to stand at the mantel. Something unspoken had passed between the two men. And something possessive in the way Alasdair watched her now held her captive.

Oh dear.

Her knees going slightly weak, she reclaimed her seat.

"I'm forever in your gratitude for saving the life of my beloved brother," Lachlan said over his shoulder. She glimpsed a hint of a smile and wondered the reason for it, though she thought she knew.

"I assure you, it was the least I could do," she said.

"'Twas a brave thing to defy your laird in such a way."

"I'm no longer loyal to my second cousin in any way. He is a brute."

"Donald MacIrwin is your cousin, then?" Lachlan turned and studied her. "I was thinking you'd married into the clan."

"I was married to Donald's friend, Baigh Shaw."

A moment of tense silence stretched out in which Lachlan's expression turned hostile. "Baigh Shaw?" he growled, then darted a glower to his brother. "You knew of this."

"Wait for me outside, if you would please," Alasdair returned calmly, but with a hard look that brooked no argument.

Lachlan clenched his jaw, flicked another brief glare her way and stalked out.

Shock and icy fear rushed through her. "What was that all about? What did Baigh do?" she asked.

Alasdair rose and limped across the room on his cane. "'Tis of nay importance now. The man is dead."

Gwyneth sprang from her chair and followed him. "It's important to me. I want to know. Your brother had the same reaction you did when you learned my late husband's name."

"I don't wish to speak of it now," Alasdair said firmly, his back to her.

"When will you tell me? I have the right to know. I'm being judged for something my husband did."

Alasdair turned and cast her a dangerous look with ten times the potency of his brother's. Gwyneth backed away. She'd learned in recent years what pain angry men were capable of inflicting.

"Do you ken what meadow saffron is, m'lady?" he asked in a soft but deadly voice.

She blinked for a moment, trying to comprehend his unexpected change in subject matter. "A poisonous plant."

Alasdair's gaze skewered her to the spot as if he didn't care for her answer. "Do you recognize the name Callum MacGrath?"

"No." She could scarce breathe as she waited for his meaning to become clear.

"Are you certain Shaw didn't mention the name to you?"

"Yes. Why should he? He told me naught of what he did or who he had dealings with."

Alasdair paused, scrutinizing her in a foreboding manner. She had been subjected to such by her father over six years ago—the cutting gaze judging her as a lower life form, an animal with no morals.

"Callum MacGrath was my father. And Shaw murdered him."

"What?" She stiffened.

"Aye. 'Twas the meadow saffron he used. I was away at the time, but Lachlan was here. Donald MacIrwin, Shaw and some others from your clan came here for the signing of a peace treaty and a meal. Shaw was seated to my father's right during the meal. Though we have nary a drop of proof, one of the servants said she might've caught a glimpse of Shaw slipping the powdered herb into Da's drink. Needless to say, Da died the next day. I was on my way back from Edinburgh, and barely arrived in time for the funeral."

Gwyneth stood frozen. Baigh had murdered this man's father? Her mind reeled, unable to comprehend…. Maybe Alasdair was mistaken. Though Baigh had not been a pleasant man, would he have murdered someone in cold blood? A man who'd welcomed him into his home for a meal. Such treachery, breaking the Highland code of hospitality.

Or was she simply the most naive person on earth?

"When did this happen?" she asked.

"Six years ago this October."

That was around the time she'd married Baigh.

"I ken you were married to him at the time. Rory told me he'd be six next month."

Gwyneth opened her mouth to disagree, but she couldn't without revealing she'd had a child out of wedlock. Alasdair didn't know yet, and she wouldn't be able to bear the judgmental look of censure he was sure to cast her way—as everyone did.

A memory came back to her. When she still lived in Donald's home, an ancient crumbling castle, one night she'd overheard Donald and Baigh talking about some kind of bargain in which Donald would allow Baigh to marry her if Baigh came through with his part. The two had left and returned two days later. A short while after that, she had married Baigh. At the time, he'd seemed benign enough. Later she'd found how wrong she'd been.

What if murdering Alasdair's father had been Baigh's half of the bargain? Had she been payment for services rendered?

"You were going to say something?" Alasdair's words brought her immediately to the present.

"I'm sorry. I didn't know," was all she could choke out.

His gaze turned piercing. "You ken all about herbs."

Was Alasdair accusing her of helping Baigh kill his father? Prickles chased over her skin.

"Not at that time. I only learned about herbs after I moved in with Mora, three years ago. After Baigh died."

Alasdair eyed her in silence.

"Do you truly think I helped them kill your father?" She tried to keep the anger from sharpening her voice. Men were forever judging her as less than nothing. She was not trustworthy, not an honorable person. They saw her as a whore…and now a murderess.

Bastard.

She turned and strode toward the door, but before reaching it, she whipped around to face Alasdair again. "If you would be so kind as to have someone escort Rory and me to Aviemore, I will not impose upon you any further, Laird MacGrath."

"Nay, you will stay here, Mistress Carswell." His words were a gentle but firm command.

"I cannot stay in the household of a man who thinks I poisoned his father. I helped save your life—risking the life of my son, causing my only friend to be killed—and now you think I'm a murderess? You are like all other men in this godforsaken kingdom! You think women are less than human and have no honor or nobility. No morals or intelligence."

Alasdair limped forward. "I didn't say that."

Unable to bear the betrayal she would see on his face, she refused to look at him. She'd thought him a good man, the only one she'd ever met. But it wasn't so. He was like Baigh—appeared benign at first, and then his true nature emerged.

She stared at the floor. "You didn't have to say it. 'Tis very clear to me how you feel. You think I provided the meadow saffron. No matter that I wouldn't have known what it was six years ago."

"M'lady," he said in a soft, desperate voice, almost like an endearment.

She stood numb and unmoving. She did not know this man, did not understand his changeable moods. He was far more complex than the other men she knew.

"Look at me." He tilted her chin up.

The too-intimate touch of his roughened fingertip quickened her pulse. In the dimness, she stared at the white linen shirt covering his chest and the bronze falcon brooch pinning his plaid in place.

His warm fingers spread, cupping her face. He trailed his thumbs along her jaw and cheek on both sides and tingles cascaded in the wake.

Her breath halted. Heavens! He should not touch her thus. And yet, she couldn't draw away. She was trapped like a bird within his big, gentle hands.

His fingertips slipped downward to brush over her pulse and the tender skin of her neck. Something in her chest fluttered in a crazy dance of delight. *Insanity.*

She lifted her gaze to his heavy-lidded eyes. Their dark depths focused on her eyes, then shifted to her lips.

Dear lord, surely he will not kiss me.

CHAPTER FIVE

Alasdair feared he might give up the whole of his lands and title to claim one fiery kiss from Gwyneth right here, right now. Not that he would have to give up anything. But it was not something the Earl and Chief of the MacGrath clan, should do with a lady under his protection.

For a certainty, he had never felt skin as velvety smooth as that of her face. He wanted to brush his lips over her throat, her soft breasts and breathe her woman scent. Live on it.

Her eyes did not reflect fear. Instead, they glinted with waning anger, and a mixture of confusion, wonder, and excitement. Her pink lips looked innocent enough, but when she licked them—as he hungered to do himself—arousal tightened his loins.

If he were more like Lachlan, he might have her begging him to lift her skirts, here within this library, and satisfy their deepest carnal yearnings, perhaps yearnings she didn't even know she possessed until that moment.

But he was not his brother. Alasdair had to think of his position, always. He refused to take advantage of those subordinate to him, like a man of less honor would do. Though he craved her, he did not want her to think his help came with a price. Because it certainly didn't.

He dropped his hands away from Gwyneth and took a step back. "I believe you."

"Truly?" she asked in a shaky whisper. Hope shone from her eyes, blue as the cloudless sky after a fierce rainstorm had washed it.

"Aye." He turned away. He didn't believe her guilty, but something about the connection between his father, her and Baigh Shaw still irked him like a wee pebble in his shoe.

"I thank you."

The door opened and clicked closed. When he glanced back, she was gone.

By the saints, his body still tingled with rushing heat. Lust. Arousal such as he'd not felt in so long he'd forgotten it was possible to need with this intensity. He had always been faithful to his wife. Even two years after her death.

"'Slud!"

He had but a moment to wallow in longing and regret before Lachlan barged in and slammed the door behind him.

"What's the meaning of this, Alasdair?"

"She's innocent." Alasdair hoped to forestall his brother's anger, which he could well understand. He'd watched their father die of the poison.

"You're sure of this, then?"

"She saved my life."

Lachlan's eyes narrowed. "She didn't ken who you were. The men told me she was calling you Angus."

"Aye, I lied to her. I was unsure whether I could trust her at the time. Now, I believe I can. If she was wanting all us MacGraths dead, she would've finished me off when I was out, not ushered me back to the land of the living."

Lachlan's frown remained in place, and his perceptive gaze searched Alasdair's face.

"Don't fash yourself so," Alasdair said.

Lachlan's expression lightened. "Easy for you to say. You're wanting to bed her."

With his well-earned reputation as Seducer of the Highlands, Lachlan was an expert at spotting attraction from ten paces away, whether it involved him or not. There was no escaping his brother's insightful observation, and Alasdair had no intention of denying his attraction to Gwyneth. "'Tis nay concern of yours."

Lachlan smirked, half genuine smile, half derision. "I don't know whether to congratulate you on finding a wench to your liking, or warn you that lust has blinded you to her scheming ways."

"I'm not blinded! 'Tis not the way of it."

"Oh, aye." The scoundrel's grin broadened.

"She's a lady deserving of our respect."

"So you say. I've not seen proof of it, save her haughty Sassenach speech. Why, pray, would an English lady marry Baigh Shaw?"

Lachlan's doubts were the same ones that plagued Alasdair.

"I haven't figured that out, yet. But I intend to in due time."

Lachlan observed him with a calculating, devilish grin. Alasdair expected a fair amount of ribbing from him. Due in part to the fact that Alasdair had shown little interest in women since his wife died. He'd loved Leitha, and could never imagine replacing her. And he wasn't thinking such now.

In truth, he desired Gwyneth in a most carnal way, but that was not a good thing. He couldn't have her. Whether she denied it or not, her speech and manners told him she was a lady, deserving of his highest regard. He wouldn't treat her like a common wench. In addition, she was of the enemy clan, widow to his father's murderer. Nay, he could never touch her.

"Och, man." Lachlan chuckled. "I've not seen you in such a stew over a lass in years."

Alasdair rolled his eyes and wished his brother would go on and leave him be. "I'm not in a stew."

Lachlan snorted. "Forgive me if I don't believe you. Never before have you protested with such a possessive glare when I've kissed a lady's hand."

A wave of annoyance and chagrin washed over Alasdair. 'Twas true, he'd even surprised himself with that exaggerated reaction, but instinct had taken over. "I simply didn't want you seducing her as you do all the other females you meet. 'Tis not permissible for either of us to view her in that manner."

"Aye, keep lying to yourself, brother. Mayhap one day you will start believing it."

༺ঞৎ ঞৎ༻

That night, Gwyneth slept on a straw mat in a large upstairs room shared by the women servants, while Rory slept in the room next door with the children. She was not yet accustomed to the smell of so many unwashed bodies in one place. At Mora's cottage, she had grown more used to the fragrance of fresh air, drying herbs and peat smoke.

Alasdair had offered her a private room in the newer wing, reserved for special guests of the nobility when they visited. She'd refused. Most of his clan already disliked and mistrusted her. If she placed herself in such an exalted position, they would undoubtedly hate her.

Best to stay in the class she'd sunk to, rather than pretending to return to her former station. Likely, she wouldn't catch a wink of sleep on a soft featherbed, anyway. She didn't allow herself such

61

flights of fancy. She had lost all comforts and luxuries when she'd given up her virtue to that titled, villainous knave in London.

Regrets proved useless. She focused on Rory, as she always did, and said a prayer of thanks for him. He truly was a gift, and she would never regret having him.

Thoughts of Alasdair shoved sleep away. When she imagined him, his dark eyes and big gentle hands, a thrill spiraled through her. Why? She did not know. Was he a man of honor, or was he concealing his true nature from her?

She couldn't forget the way he'd caressed her face, as if she were made of precious glass. Her breath hitched even as she remembered the compelling, seductive look in his eyes. She'd thought, with fear and longing, that he might kiss her. Heavens! What would she have done if he had? When he had released her from his spell, she felt as if she'd been freed from the effects of a drug.

I am foolhardy for thinking of such matters.

She barely noticed the quiet footsteps padding in her direction, the squeak of a floorboard, and assumed one of the women was headed to the garderobe privy. A thump sounded and a woman's grumble floated in the darkness. Gwyneth turned her back to the commotion, wishing instead to secretly drift off to sleep amongst dreams of Alasdair.

But the footsteps drew nearer and a sudden hot pain pierced her arm, radiating outward. Gwyneth cried out and rolled into one of the other female servants to escape further injury.

Dear lord, someone is trying to kill me!

Screams and yells erupted among a tussle.

Panic quickened her movements as she crawled over the other women.

A candle flared to life, and the darkness retreated. She rose and clasped her bloodied upper arm. Pain sliced through her.

She surveyed the chaos of the room around her, trying to discern who had the weapon. Some of the women stood, while others sat or remained lying. Rush mats and plaid blankets were strewn about, no bloody daggers in evidence.

"Gwyneth, you're bleeding!" Eyes wide, Tessie crossed over several people and grasped her arm.

One of the men, named Busby, stuck his head in. "What's the ruckus about?"

"Someone cut Gwyneth."

Feeling strangely suspended, Gwyneth held her arm and prayed the pain would lessen.

Busby waved her forward.

Tessie guided her toward him. He ripped open her sleeve and eyed her wound. "'Tis deep. Laird MacGrath will be wanting to know about this. Follow me."

"No. Not now." Gwyneth hung back, not wanting to cause a scene. "He's asleep. I can take care of it myself."

"Go on now, Gwyneth," Tessie urged but stayed behind.

Busby pulled Gwyneth through the doorway, down the spiral steps, then up a different stone staircase. "Someone's wanting you dead, lass. And I won't be responsible for leaving you in a den of female vipers."

Holding the candle aloft, Busby rapped at an ornate, carved door.

She squirmed in both pain and unease about disturbing the laird. Men did not like their sleep interrupted.

After a moment, Alasdair, wearing a long-tailed shirt, opened the door and squinted against the candle's flame. His gaze locked on Gwyneth's. "Aye? What's wrong?"

"Mistress Carswell has been hurt. One of the women stabbed her in the arm."

"In truth?" Alasdair's frown deepened. "Let me see, m'lady."

She took her hand away from her now-bare upper arm and blood trickled from the throbbing, burning wound.

"By the saints! I'll have somebody's head for this!"

"No, Laird MacGrath." She'd known he'd be angry, but she hadn't been sure it wouldn't be directed at her. Now she feared he'd kill one of the women.

"Who did this?" he demanded of her.

"I know not. The room was dark."

"Rouse everyone within these walls," Alasdair commanded Busby. "Have them assemble in the hall, forthwith."

"Aye, m'laird." Busby trotted away, yelling for everyone to proceed to the great hall.

"I don't wish to cause an uproar," Gwyneth said.

"You're not the one causing it. I'll find out who did this and see her punished." His Scottish burr grew more pronounced than usual. "*Iosa is Muire Mhàthair,*" he muttered, along with other Gaelic words.

"I need to clean the wound and apply some herbal ointment, but I don't have any with me." Lightheadedness snatched her equilibrium for a moment and she caught herself against the wall. She hadn't lost much blood and had endured far worse pain than this in the past. She simply needed to sit down for a minute.

"Saints! You're about to keel over." His words, which sounded like *ye're aboot t' keel o'er*, didn't make sense for a moment. He gently caught her good arm and her waist, then led her into the darkness of his room. "You must lie down. I vow, whatever crook-pated wench did this will regret it."

How could he see anything? 'Twas dark as pitch. But his musky male scent permeated the room in a disturbing way. That, coupled with his strong hands upon her, was near too much.

"I am fine now, truly. A chair will do," she assured him. She simply could not lie upon his bed. Not only would the whole of the clan be gossiping, but she would find it too disconcerting.

He seated her in a padded chair by his bed. "*Uisge-beatha* is good for wounds. I've used it for cuts on the battlefield." Alasdair lit a candle on the mantle, then pulled on a pair of trews beneath his long-tailed shirt.

Gwyneth yanked her gaze from the appealing sight of him to stare at the elaborately carved headboard to her left. She could not watch something so intimate as Alasdair dressing, even if she had seen him close to naked during his illness. And what a vision that had been, all those firm muscles.

I should not be here, in this room.

She should be focusing on her wound and the dire situation she found herself in. But heavens, his bed was big. And soft-looking. The white sheets and counterpane twisted and thrown back. They were probably still cozy and warm from his body. How would it feel to lie there with him, his body warming and protecting her?

"I'll send Busby into the village, and he'll bring back what you need from Tessie's mother, Seri."

Gwyneth shoved her foolhardy thoughts away to think about what he'd said. "Tessie's mother is the healer?"

"Aye. In the meantime, we'll clean the wound with this." Alasdair snatched a flagon of *uisge-beatha* from a chest. While holding her arm lightly in his hand, he dribbled the strong-smelling whisky onto her wound.

Her arm burned with liquid fire. She jerked away and sucked in a hissing breath.

"Pray pardon. I ken that smarts like the very devil. I'm not such a gentle healer as you are." He set the whisky on a table and searched about inside a chest, then came back and wrapped a white linen cloth around her arm. "There, now. Better?" His tone sounded so hopeful, how could she disagree, though the wound still pained her greatly. After all, it was a stab wound rather than a cut.

"Yes. I thank you," she said. Why was he so kind to her? Maybe it was all pretense, because he somehow perceived it would knock down her defenses. But to what end? Perhaps he was scheming to use her against Donald for revenge. Or did he want her in that illicit way that a man wants a woman? Hot shame washed through her, for she was not immune to his appeal. She feared she might want him in the same illicit way.

"I'm sorry this happened." Alasdair put the whisky away. "Without doubt, you don't feel safe anywhere. You'll stay in one of the guest rooms like I suggested afore, and I'll post a guard outside. Rory can stay with you if you'd like."

"Yes, I think he should." Rory liked staying with his new friends, but he might be in danger as well.

"Are you feeling well enough to go to the hall?"

"I think so." She stood, discovering she was very steady and clear headed. The dizziness had left her.

She preceded him out. Cane in one hand and a candle in the other, Alasdair limped forward and ushered her along. He didn't allow the steps leading down to slow his pace.

Once in the noisy great hall, he motioned to Busby. "Go into the village and get the herbs Mistress Carswell requires."

Gwyneth relayed to Busby what she needed, the bare essentials—royal fern, comfrey, vervain, and a couple others—in case he couldn't remember detailed instructions.

When he hastened away, Rory tugged at her skirts. "Ma, what happened?"

She knelt and hugged him. "I am well, but someone cut my arm." She pointed to her bandage. "You will stay with me the rest of the night."

"I would have your attention," Alasdair called with echoing voice to the teeming group of servants and other clan members— between twenty and thirty people—gathered in the candlelit hall.

Silence descended and all eyes turned to him where he stood, tall and commanding, upon the dais.

"Someone has injured Mistress Carswell." He motioned to her, standing a few feet to the side. All eyes shifted to her, and she stiffened. Now they would hate her even more.

"First, I would have you ken that Mistress Carswell well and truly saved my life a few days past, when I was injured on MacIrwin land," he said. "If not for her kindness and healing skills, I would be dead now. For me, she put her own life in danger, as well as that of her son and her friend. Because of this, she deserves the highest regard and gratitude from us all."

Bless him. Tears pricked her eyes.

He glared at the rapt crowd. "Now, tell me. Who took it upon themselves to stab Mistress Carswell in the arm? I require that you step forward now." Alasdair's gaze raked over the group of women servants who had been in the room with Gwyneth when she'd been injured.

Everyone stood frozen. Her own elevated pulse thumped in her ears and shot pain through her wound.

"I didn't expect that you would. If anyone kens who did this, speak up now!"

The long moment of silence stretched Gwyneth's nerves to near breaking point. Who wanted to kill her and why?

"Well then, you're protecting someone with nary a qualm about murdering. I have no choice but to release the lot of you from your positions within my home."

Gwyneth frowned. Was he mad? His household could not function without the female servants.

"Nay!" several women cried. Much jostling and whispering ensued. They shoved a thin young woman forward. "'Twas Eileen," they announced.

Gwyneth didn't recognize her.

"Eileen MacMann, why would you want to harm Mistress Carswell?" Alasdair asked.

"I didn't want to, Laird MacGrath. Mistress Weems forced me to. She said I would lose my position if I didn't do as she bid."

This bit of news didn't surprise Gwyneth in the least. Weems had not liked her from the moment she laid eyes on her. She suspected the housekeeper saw her as a threat to her position. Gwyneth couldn't believe how far the other woman would go to see her gone.

"Nay, the wench lies!" the housekeeper bellowed.

"Silence!" Alasdair thumped his cane on the floor, his expression hardening. "Weems, step forward."

The housekeeper waddled forth and blinked her beady black eyes at Gwyneth, then turned her full attention to her laird.

"Why would you want to injure Mistress Carswell?"

"I don't want to, Laird MacGrath. Eileen is lying. 'Twas all her doing, alone."

Eileen shook her head, tears dripping from her red-rimmed eyes.

Alasdair scrutinized Weems for a long moment, then turned his attention to another servant. "Tessie, what do you think?"

"Me, m'laird?" The girl swallowed hard and her gaze searched out Gwyneth. She nodded at Tessie to give her a bit of courage. Both Alasdair and Weems could be intimidating—Alasdair put her on the spot and Weems could make her life miserable.

"Aye. The truth please."

She flicked a nervous glance at Mistress Weems. "I think what Eileen says is true."

The housekeeper turned and glared at her.

"Do you now?" Alasdair asked.

Tessie nodded.

"Does anyone else agree with Tessie? Raise your hand if you do."

Several hands went up tentatively.

"They're liars, the lot of them," the housekeeper yelled.

"Mmph." Alasdair stepped down from the dais and limped toward Gwyneth. "Has Mistress Weems shown any ill will toward you?" he asked in a low tone.

"A little. But I don't know why."

He paced before the servants again. "Very well. Mistress Weems and Eileen, both of you will spend some time in the dungeon until I decide what to do with you. I won't tolerate such aggression within my own household. If you wish to wield a blade, you can ride into battle with the men during the next skirmish."

The male servants and clan members cackled at that. The wide-eyed females whispered amongst themselves. Eileen covered her eyes and cried, while Mistress Weems, with her red-faced snarl, appeared angry enough to slaughter ten warriors. Her glare bore down on Gwyneth, but she again refused to look away. She would not be intimidated by the bullish woman. Not that Weems could do much damage to anyone while in the dungeon, except Eileen.

"Laird MacGrath," Weems said, drawing his attention again. "The MacIrwins killed my husband years ago, when you were no more than a wee bairn. And she's a MacIrwin." Weems pointed a condemning finger at Gwyneth.

Low mutterings and grumbles issued forth from the crowd, and a cold surge of dread arose within Gwyneth.

"Silence!" Alasdair demanded. "Weems, you may be older than me, but I'll tolerate no insolence from you!" He paused and let his glare slide over the people. "Most of us here have had a loved one killed by the MacIrwins. But Gwyneth Carswell didn't do any of that. She grew up in England and has only lived in the Highlands a short time. Because she helped me, the MacIrwins want to kill her, too. That puts her on our side."

The room remained quiet.

"Now, does anyone else have any ill will toward Mistress Carswell?" he asked. "Anyone else here going to pin all the MacIrwins' misdeeds on her?"

Several heads shook negatively in response. And a few murmured, "Nay, m'laird."

"If you do, you'll have me to answer to, and I won't be so lenient with the next offense." He turned toward two men, guards carrying swords and outfitted in metal studded leather armor, and spoke quietly to them.

Now that she was fairly certain the clan wouldn't lynch her, Gwyneth tried to calm herself, despite her knees being a bit unsteady. She was most thankful to Alasdair for defending her. Still, she was concerned for Eileen and bewildered by her. She feared the girl wouldn't be safe in the cell with Weems.

The two guards escorted the women through the ranks of the silent clan. And Alasdair headed toward her.

"Come with me, m'lady," he murmured as he passed her. She could not fathom the way he switched from calling her 'Mistress Carswell' in front of his clan, to a more elevated form of address in private. He had deduced too much about her, insisting on using a form of address she no longer claimed. But because of the way he said it, almost as a friendly endearment, she could not bring herself to ask him to stop.

Urging Rory before her, she followed Alasdair up the stairs and down a short corridor, past his room. He flung open a door. "You'll both use this room. 'Twas cleaned earlier today. I hope you'll find it to your liking." Without waiting for her to answer, he limped in and lit a candle with his own.

The meager light revealed a spacious room with a large, heavily-draped poster bed in the corner and a thick Turkish carpet before it.

"Oh, I cannot take this room," Gwyneth said, taken aback by

the finery. "Don't you have something smaller, less ornate?"

"What's wrong with ornate?" An almost imperceptible grin quirked his lips. "I would wager, m'lady, that when you lived in England, you had a room far grander than this one."

She stared at the floor, refusing to reveal a glimpse of her past to him. What he said was too close to the truth, and she did not wish to take a step back in time. Rising above her station for a brief time and enjoying such luxury could only be more painful in the end, when she had it no longer.

"Did you not?" Alasdair asked.

Gwyneth was glad when a panting Busby stopped in the open doorway.

"Mistress Carswell, I have the herbs. Seri was out birthing a bairn, but one of her daughters said these would be what you're wanting."

Gwyneth rushed toward him and took the tiny sacks of crushed herbs. She sniffed them, their distinct pungent or bitter aromas confirming their identities. "I thank you. If you would be so kind, could you ask Tessie to bring me some fresh, clean water and whisky?"

"Busby, also please tell MacDade to come up as well. I would have him guard," Alasdair said.

"Aye, m'laird." Busby scurried away.

Alasdair stood at the mantel, his back to her. "You'll be needing a fire in here. 'Tis chill." He set about building one himself. Why would he not have a servant do that?

Gwyneth turned down the fine linen and wool covers on the bed. "Get in, Rory."

Her sleepy son complied.

Minutes later, she wondered how long Alasdair would stay. Did he want to oversee the care of her wound?

He stood, his attention still cast toward the small fire he'd built. "If you should require other clothing, you shall find some in that trunk in the corner." He nodded to his right, still without looking at her.

"You are too kind. Whose clothes are they?"

A long moment of silence stretched between them, and she thought he wouldn't answer. The fire caught the tender and popped.

"They were my wife's," he said in a monotone.

"Your wife's?" He'd never mentioned a wife before. Was this the Leitha whose name he'd murmured in his fevered sleep several nights ago?

"Aye, she died two years past. She was a wee lass, much like you are, so I'm thinking the clothes may fit. Anyway, you came here with naught more than the clothes on your back. You'll be needing something else to wear."

"I thank you."

"'Tis the least I can do."

Gwyneth wanted to disagree. What did this cost him? Had he loved his late wife so much that giving away her clothing pained him? Or did he have no emotional attachment to her?

At any rate, he was far more generous than her father or her late husband had ever been, but discussing such matters did not seem appropriate. The atmosphere of the room already felt too intimate by far. She stood in a bedchamber, in the middle of the night, with a handsome man who dangerously lured her without even trying. One glance from him could draw forth the sensual side she tried to keep bound and hidden.

Her son snoring in the bed, along with the pain in her arm, kept any shameful thoughts at bay.

"Have a seat, m'lady, afore you fall down. You're pale as a specter." Alasdair motioned toward a chair, then paced to the door. "Where is Tessie?"

Gwyneth sat. "I'll wait for her. Please, you should go back to bed. It is late."

"Nay, I cannot sleep now anyway." He rubbed the back of his neck. "I should've let Mistress Weems go years ago. She's a right *olkeyr*."

Gwyneth wasn't sure what an *olkeyr* was, but it didn't sound pleasant.

"She was in the employ of my father," he continued. "I feared she wouldn't be able to find another position at her age. I've a feeling she's terrorized more than one of the maids." He was silent for a long moment. "What she had Eileen do is unforgivable."

Unforgivable? Did he mean to have Weems killed? And Eileen—she'd practically been forced into her actions. In Gwyneth's experience, men often judged women too harshly.

"What will you do to them?" Surely he wasn't the sort of man who would execute women for injuring someone.

"Let them stay in the dungeon for a few days while they worry about what I *might* do to them. As for after that, I haven't decided."

"I think Eileen is as much a victim as I am." Gwyneth hoped he would show her some mercy, at least.

"In a way, aye. But she should never have carried out the stabbing. She should've come to me instead of believing Weems. And if any of the other servants or clan members get it in their heads to stab someone, outside battle, they will know I'll dole out a just punishment."

Tessie trotted into the room with the water and whisky, then upon seeing Alasdair, halted and bobbed a curtsy. "M'laird. Mistress, I'd have been here sooner, but I had to draw fresh water from the well."

"It's all right."

Tessie helped her clean the wound again with the whisky. Gwyneth mixed the herbs with the water and applied a paste, and then a bandage, while Alasdair watched from the background. She could scarce believe he had so much interest in her wound. The concern in his eyes made her feel self-conscious. She was afraid his clan would notice and whisper speculations behind their hands. That was all she needed, to be the focus of another scandal.

Once Tessie finished and left, Alasdair glanced into the corridor and spoke to the large, dark-haired man who waited there. "MacDade, you are to guard Mistress Carswell and her son. Don't let anyone pass through this door without checking with me."

"Except Tessie," Gwyneth said.

"Aye, if you trust her."

"I do."

"Very well, then. I'll be next door if you should need anything."

"Many good thanks, my laird."

He gave a brief bow, and his troubled gaze lingered on her until he closed the door between them.

His kindness confused her. Was he simply repaying the favor since she'd helped save his life days ago? Or was it something else? She didn't know how to interpret his actions. In her experience, men were only kind to women in the presence of others, or when they wanted something. Such had been the case in her parents' marriage when she was growing up.

Gwyneth paced to the bed and observed Rory sleeping. He looked pale and exhausted after the turmoil of the last few days. The dark circles beneath his eyes concerned her.

She was not the least bit sleepy. The sharp pain in her arm remained strong.

In the dim candlelight, she glanced around at the luxurious

room. Green velvet curtains draped the bed. Indeed, the featherbed was the softest she'd ever touched. Rory had never slept on something so fine. If the man who'd sired him had taken responsibility, Rory would have slept on a bed soft as this from the time he was a tiny babe. And she would've been a marchioness. But such things were of no significance now.

She shivered and climbed into bed. During the next few hours, sleep eluded her. Despite the extra blankets she piled on the bed, she only grew colder.

⁘⊙⊙⁘

"Laird MacGrath."

Alasdair roused from a fitful sleep he had just fallen into. Thin dawn light strained through the window.

Trained as a warrior who had to be ready for battle at any moment, he sprang out of bed and bumped his sore toe against the floor. Pain shot up his leg. "*Iosa is Muire Mhàthair!*" he rasped, along with a few more words he wouldn't utter in mixed company. "Aye, what the devil do you want?" he demanded of Busby when his breath returned.

"Pray pardon, m'laird. MacDade says Mistress Carswell is worsening with fever."

"Damnation!" He pulled on trews and a shirt, grabbed his cane and hobbled into the corridor. "I should string Weems up for this," he said between clenched teeth, pain still emanating from his abused toe.

"Would you be needing some help with that?" Lachlan asked behind him.

Alasdair turned. "Where have you been?"

"In the village with Celine a good part of the night. I just heard what happened to Mistress Carswell."

Well, that didn't surprise him. Lachlan was usually in the bed of one wench or another. Alasdair rapped on Gwyneth's door. It inched open, revealing the wee lad standing there, big-eyed.

"Good morrow, Rory. How's your ma?"

"She's sick," he said in a small voice.

Leaning on his cane, Alasdair limped forward to the bed. Gwyneth shivered beneath the covers.

"Not feeling well, m'lady?" As gently as he could, he touched her face. By the saints, she was burning up. He'd seen more than one person die of a fever, and he did not want to consider such a fate for his bonny Sassenach angel.

"No," she whispered on an uneven, intake of breath. "Would you have Tessie bring me willow bark steeped in hot water?"

"Aye, that I will." Thanks be to God, she was well enough to ask for whatever medicine she needed. He instructed MacDade to fetch Tessie along with the willow bark tea. Something could be done to help her and she would be well soon. Alasdair willed it to be so.

Rory stood by, squirming. His wide blue gaze darted back and forth. The appearance of the tiny boy, so silent and alone reminded Alasdair of how he'd felt as a child when his own mother had been deathly ill.

"Come here, lad." If he couldn't do anything right away to help Gwyneth, he'd do what he could for her son.

Rory hung his head and crept forward.

Alasdair bent, picked him up and held him on one arm. The lad weighed no more than a full-grown squirrel.

"Don't fash about your ma. She will be well soon."

Rory nodded and buried his face against Alasdair's neck. He hoped to God the lad wouldn't cry. He didn't think he could abide it with a dry eye.

Lachlan sent him a curious, lifted-brow look, along with a tiny grin.

"Rory and I have been friends since I awoke mangled up in the cattle byre, have we not?"

The child nodded and lifted his head to peer around with watery eyes. Saints, the lad near broke his heart.

"Rory, this is my younger brother, Lachlan. He's a right nice sort of fellow most of the time. But sometimes he's a pain in the rump."

"Och. My thanks to you, dear brother," Lachlan retorted.

Rory allowed a tiny grin.

"A pleasure to meet you, Rory." Lachlan shook his hand.

The lad averted his gaze, then glanced at the bed where his ma lay, worry again paling his face.

"Lachlan knows a fair bit about swords, daggers, claymores and such, do you not, Lachlan?" Alasdair asked.

"Aye."

"'Haps you could show Rory your collection."

Lachlan frowned.

"Rory has a fondness for such things." He gave his brother a meaningful look.

"Ah, very well then."

Alasdair set Rory on his feet. Lachlan took his hand and led him from the room. Lachlan looked right at home, leading the lad around. He had two sons of his own he carted about on occasion, when he brought them up from the village. Bastards to be sure, but Lachlan claimed them as his own and loved them.

Alasdair turned back to the bed at the same time Tessie rushed into the room with the willow bark in hot water.

"Good, I'm glad you're here."

"M'laird." Tessie gave a brief curtsy.

"This will help her recover, I'm certain," he said with the strongest conviction he could muster.

The girl turned wide eyes on him. She looked no older than a child, herself. "I pray it will."

He nodded and forced himself to rebuild the fire when all he wanted to do was touch Gwyneth, hold her hand.

"Here, Gwyneth, drink this," Tessie whispered behind him.

He prayed that another woman he was getting used to having around wouldn't desert him.

CHAPTER SIX

Gwyneth awoke with a start and a clear mind. Her sweat-dampened clothing clung to her skin. Overheated as if she lay in an oven, she shoved the covers down. Claws of soreness sank into every muscle of her body. She stilled, praying the pain would go away. Her gaze landed on the sole light in the room, the fire in the hearth. The faint but bitter scent of peat and wood smoke filled the room. Heavy rain blew against a glass window.

Where am I?

The glow from the flames revealed the carved bed draped in velvet. Alasdair's guest room.

She glanced aside and found him sitting in a chair by the bed. Good heavens! What was he doing here? All her muscles tensed with shooting needles of pain. Then she noticed his eyes were closed, and his head rested against the back of the chair. It reminded her of the eve she'd found him injured on the battlefield, passed out. Somehow, she'd known then he was an unusual man. A leader who craved peace had to be a caring man. She could never grow tired of looking at him. Long dark hair framed a ruggedly appealing face. His jaw clenched hard, and she thought she heard his teeth grinding together.

But this was no romantic interlude. Danger and treachery lurked about everywhere, in her clan as well as this one. Someone here had tried to kill her after all. Ignoring the soreness, she sat up and glanced about. Rory wasn't in bed beside her. Where was he? Maybe Tessie was watching after him. She slid toward the edge of the bed to find out.

At her motion, the bed creaked.

Alasdair awoke and straightened. "M'lady?" His gaze searched her face, then dropped to her arm. "How are you feeling?"

"Better." She gently touched her injured arm. "But still sore. Where's Rory?"

"My cousin's wife is caring for him. No need to worry. She's very trustworthy."

"Good. I thank you." A bit of relief eased her tense muscles.

Leaning forward, he examined her closely in the dimness. "The fever is gone, then?"

"Yes." Tugging the coverlet up again in modesty, she realized she needed to change out of her sweat-drenched smock.

Before she knew what he was about, he reached out and placed his hand on her forehead. He skimmed warm, raspy fingertips down to her cheek while his sharp, observant gaze searched her face. His frown remained in place a long moment.

She forgot to breathe beneath the caring, yet seemingly desperate, ministrations of his hand.

"Thanks be to God." He shoved himself out of the chair and grabbed his cane. "Are you hungry?"

Before she could answer, he wrenched open the door and bellowed a command to someone in the corridor. "Have Tessie bring porridge and milk." He eased the door closed and sent Gwyneth a sheepish glance.

Milk? What was she, a child? And his order had made the food sound like a life or death necessity. She hid a smile behind the coverlet and her drawn-up knees. She had never encountered a man such as Alasdair.

He poked at the fire and added a bit of peat. Long moments passed while he stared at the flames, the only noise the popping of the sparks. Finally, her curiosity overcame her.

"What are you doing in here?" Without doubt the clan would gossip about their chief's highly unusual activity of caring for a sick woman of the enemy clan.

He cast a dubious look over his shoulder. "Making sure you were recovering. Did you do any less for me?"

She shook her head, remembering the night she'd lain in the byre beside him when he'd had a fever. Surely it wasn't the same. She was a healer; he wasn't. Had he applied a cool cloth to her hot forehead? She could not imagine it.

He seemed intent on coaxing the fire into throwing off more heat, though the room was sweltering.

"What of the two women in the dungeon?" she asked, hoping he hadn't done something drastic.

"They remain imprisoned," he said in a hard tone. "I held off deciding their fates until I knew you lived."

A knock sounded at the door. When Alasdair opened it, Tessie entered with a tray of food.

"I'll be next door if you should need anything," he said.

She didn't know whether she was glad or disappointed that he'd suddenly decided to take his leave.

"I thank you," she told him before he disappeared. "And I thank you as well, Tessie. You are a blessing."

"You're welcome. I'm pleased to see you feeling better." She set the wooden tray laden with food on Gwyneth's lap. The delightful smells made her stomach grumble.

"I'm sorry you've had to fetch me so many things."

"Nonsense. I would do naught less for a friend such as you are."

Gwyneth took a spoonful of the warm oat porridge. The slight sweet flavor surprised her. "Did you put honey in this?"

"Aye. 'Tis the way the MacGrath eats his porridge. Do you like it?" Tessie plopped her thin frame down onto the chair by the bed.

"It's delicious."

The girl grinned.

"How long did I sleep?"

"Since early this morn when I gave you the willow bark. 'Tis now close to midnight. More than eighteen hours, you slept." After glancing at the door, Tessie leaned forward and lowered her voice. "The MacGrath refused to leave your side, except for a few minutes at a time. He is fair taken with you."

Another type of fever washed over Gwyneth. She cleared her throat and stared into the cup of milk. "You must be mistaken."

Tessie giggled. "Nay. I've worked here in the castle for more than four years. He's shown no interest in women since his wife. And believe me, more than one lass has tried to catch his eye."

Goodness. He'd said his wife had died two years ago, hadn't he? He must have indeed loved his lady a great amount.

"Please, tell me about her...his wife."

"Leitha was a right sweet lady with red hair and green eyes—a Lowlander. 'Twas a love match, you see. It near killed him when she died of the childbed fever."

Gwyneth's heart ached when she envisioned such a scene. "How awful. Did the babe survive?"

"Nay, the poor wee laddie."

"A tragedy. I'm so sorry to hear of it." She couldn't imagine what she would've done if she'd lost Rory during the birthing.

"The MacGrath held up well afore the clan, but afterward he kept to himself much of the time. I've a feeling 'twas far harder on him than anyone kens."

"I'm sure you're right." Alasdair gave the impression of strength much like a mountain of stone. But he seemed to have a caring heart. "I've noticed how kind he is. Tell me, is he typical of the men in this clan?"

Tessie shrugged. "Some people are kind and others are cruel, in this clan as in others. My own Robbie is kind as well."

"I'm glad. 'Tis clear you have a love match."

She blushed and grinned. "Indeed. What of Rory's father?"

Gwyneth shook her head, thinking of two men—Rory's natural father and Baigh Shaw. "He was a beast. I have not known any kind men in my lifetime."

"How sad. If anyone deserves kindness, 'tis you. And glad I am that Laird MacGrath is taking to you like honey bees to heather."

Gwyneth almost choked on the sip of milk she'd taken. She sputtered but finally swallowed. "I'm sure you're overestimating his concern."

ᘛ ᘚ

"We have to get Gwyneth Carswell back, along with her bastard," Donald MacIrwin told Smitty, his sword bearer, as they leaned over the small table near the fireplace in the dim great hall of Irwin Castle. He kept his voice down, not knowing which of his clan might betray him. Donald thirsted for a mug of ale, but dared not consume too much, else they'd run out. The clan needed funds badly.

"Aye, m'laird." Smitty's dark eyes gleamed like bits of coal.

"Once Lord Darrow finds out his daughter is nay longer here, he'll stop sending the payments. But I have a plan."

Months ago, a Sassanach lord named Southwick had sent him a missive telling him to send Gwyneth's son Rory to him in London. Donald had ignored the demand, of course. He didn't take orders from the damned English and besides, Lord Darrow's money was useful to him. If the lad was nay longer here, Darrow might send less money for Gwyneth's upkeep.

But now maybe Donald could strike a bargain with Southwick. He could retrieve Rory himself...for a price. A very large price. Enough silver to support Donald and the clan for a few years at

78

least. He didn't care why Southwick wanted the lad, but he suspected the man was the lad's natural father.

"How will we get Gwyneth and her son back?" Smitty asked.

Donald darted a glance around the great hall, making sure none of the busy-body maids were close by and lowered his voice. "A surprise attack. I want as many of the MacGrath clan dead as possible. An utter sacking, I tell you. Take all their cattle and sheep, along with Gwyneth and Rory. I want them unhurt, mind you. But we will torch the rest of them. Find the clerk and the messenger for me."

"Aye, m'laird." Smitty headed across the great hall.

Donald would have the clerk scribe a fancy missive to Southwick. The Englishman would be on his way here by the time they snatched the lad from MacGrath's talons.

⋅⊙ℚ ℚ⊙⋅

Guilt tormented Alasdair though he sat in a peaceful place. Leitha's flower garden was a walled, private spot to the side of the castle, with a gate, herbs and shrubs. The scent of roses surrounded him, reminding him of his late wife. But another woman, very much alive, occupied his thoughts.

He'd tried to avoid Gwyneth for the last few days, but he knew she was healing. He'd noticed she had started using her arm.

His carnal attraction to Gwyneth gnawed at his conscience, and was the reason he steered clear of her. When he was in her presence, he sometimes forgot about Leitha. Forgot he was supposed to be grieving her loss. "I'm sorry, Leitha," he murmured. "I'm the worst sort of rogue."

An appealing scent caught his attention—the lemon balm plant that his leg was brushing against. He snapped a leaf from it and chewed it. Would it ease his grief as was rumored? At least the tangy citrus flavor was pleasant and refreshing.

A soft summer breeze, like a gentle hand, touched his face and blew his hair back. After a time, a sense of peace settled in his chest.

"Oh!" a feminine voice said behind him.

Turning on the stone bench, he glanced over his shoulder and found a wide-eyed Gwyneth standing just inside the gate.

"Pray pardon. I didn't know you were here." She turned away. "I won't bother you."

"Nay. Come back." *Please.*

He was thankful for her recovery from the fever. The Almighty likely had not heard so many prayers from him in the past two years.

Though at first she hesitated, Gwyneth came forward. "I thank you for showing mercy to Mistress Weems and Eileen."

Yesterday, he'd had the two women escorted miles away to Aviemore. "The world is surely a more dangerous place with those two loose in it, but I couldn't have them roaming about the castle trying to kill you."

A faint grin lifted the corners of her lips. "I am much indebted to you for your protection. You are too kind."

He snorted. "I have never been called such afore, and I would thank you to keep it a secret. I have the reputation of being a fierce warrior."

"So, what are you, fierce warrior, doing sitting in a flower garden?"

He smiled and savored the teasing glint in her eyes far more than he should have. "'Tis the only quiet place about."

"And beautiful." Gwyneth's light blue gaze darted over the pink, white and red flowers growing near the wall. "Sometimes I come out here for a breath of fresh air and to smell the roses."

He'd always found it the best place for reflection. "Are you fond of flowers, then?"

"Yes. In England—" She pressed her lips closed, looking a bit shocked at herself, and glanced quickly away.

"Go on," he encouraged.

"We had...a garden."

He waited for her to elaborate, and when she didn't, he let it go. She didn't trust him enough yet to talk of her past. How he wished she did. But trust was something he'd have to earn.

She strolled to the wall where a climbing rose was secured against it, cupped a red blossom in her hand and buried her nose in it. "Ahh. I love roses." She turned to him with a smile more beautiful than all the flowers gathered here. So tempting. She effortlessly drew him under her spell, against his will. And he found himself wanting to grin like a fool, but controlled the impulse.

"So why do you have such a lovely garden? Was it your mother's?"

"'Twas my wife's."

Gwyneth's smile faded. "Oh, pray pardon. I shouldn't have intruded. I'm sure you want time alone."

"Nay, I'd like it if you stayed. Truly."

Leitha, if you're out there anywhere, looking down on us...this is Gwyneth. You would've liked her, I think. She saved my life.

"Did she like roses, too?" Gwyneth asked, standing a few feet away.

"Aye, she loved them. She'd wanted that particular rose to grow here. I sent one of the servants to the Lowlands to get it, but Leitha died before he returned. The servants planted the rose in the garden, then rooted another to plant by her grave at the kirk."

Gwyneth blinked quickly against the moisture that gathered in her eyes. "Oh. That's so romantic."

He shook his head, denying any emotion. "Nay, I don't have a romantic bone in my body. 'Tis only what she would've wanted."

Gwyneth glanced away and brushed a finger against her eyes.

Her response touched him. She felt his loss. He didn't know what to do with that realization, but he would like to hold her in his arms. Comfort her. Comfort himself.

"The servants attend to the garden," Alasdair said to distract himself from her. "Continuing Leitha's work." Some of the female servants knew how much it meant to him. But he would not have the men of his clan know. He was a warrior and a chief, and should not give flowers or women's feelings a second thought.

Nor, if he were wise, could he let another woman inside his heart. It would be too painful when she left him alone. The same had happened to his father. Alasdair's mother had died when he was a child, and his father had spent the rest of his life alone. Such loss painted a dismal picture.

"Tessie told me yours and Leitha's was a love match." Emotions apparently under control, Gwyneth sat on the other stone bench, opposite him, and cast a shy but curious glance his way.

Too many keen-edged feelings stewed inside him, and not wanting Gwyneth to see them, he dropped his gaze to the carved falcon's head on the wooden handle of his cane. "Aye, I did grow to love her. We met at a banquet one night at the home of a friend in the Lowlands."

"Did you offer for her hand right away?"

"The next day."

"Sounds like a romantic legend."

He shrugged, dismissing such sentiment. "In truth, 'twas for practical reasons. I needed a wife and an heir. The romance didn't last long. She died giving birth to our son a year later. And the wee bairn with her."

Gwyneth came forward, sat on the stone beside him and clasped his hand in hers. "I'm sorry for your loss." Her voice was little more than a whisper, and filled with sympathy.

"I should be getting over it by now." He stared at his large hand in Gwyneth's small, cool ones, then turned one of hers over and brushed the palm. Her hands were not like Leitha's. Gwyneth's were near rough and calloused as his own. Work worn. It wasn't right. She was a lady, and she should have a lady's smooth hands. Despite this, he hungered for her touch upon his deprived skin. Stroking, caressing, coaxing this simmering ember to life within him.

When he thought of kissing her hand the way Lachlan had, something within him riveted and burned with a flickering heat. Aye, he should—he would love to—but he feared he couldn't stop with her hand.

She closed her fingers and pulled away. "Nonsense. We never forget the pain of losing those we love."

His fingers ached with her desertion. He had not realized how lonely and deprived he was until that moment.

"You ken the pain of loss, too, for you lost your husband." The murdering bastard. Had she loved him? In truth, it shouldn't matter, but Alasdair wanted to learn more of their association.

"Yes, I know something of loss." Gwyneth stood and paced toward the bed of herbs a few yards away. Her action was nothing less than what he'd expected.

"What about you and Shaw? Was that a love match as well?"

"Heavens, no." She shook her head. "Not at all. My cousin arranged the whole thing."

Tension he hadn't realized he'd been feeling released him. His shoulders relaxed. "Why would you, an English lady, marry a course Highlander, and one who isn't a chieftain at that?" He had to know. But would she answer? She hadn't admitted to being a member of the aristocracy, but he knew from her manner and speech she had to be.

A long tense moment of silence followed. "Well, 'tis a long story, and I wouldn't want to bore you." She faced him. "I would ask another favor of you, Laird MacGrath."

"Alasdair, please," he corrected, loath to admit that he wanted to hear his name from her lips.

"Alasdair, I know you will grow tired of providing food and shelter for me and my son before long."

How could she say such a thing? "Nay, you are both welcome to stay here as long as you like. I have the room, and you both eat like wee birds."

"I thank you, but I do not wish to impose. I've been thinking I would like a position as a governess or tutor for some wealthy family in the Lowlands or in England. I thought perhaps you might know of someone who could use my services. I would need to take Rory with me, of course. I have no references, but if you could provide some sort of character reference or letter of recommendation, I would be deeply indebted to you."

He wished he could employ Gwyneth. If his son had lived, he would've one day needed a governess. Aside from that, he didn't want Gwyneth and Rory to leave. In such a short time, he'd grown fond of the lad. As for Gwyneth, he could not yet begin to fathom the impact she was having on his life. She'd saved his life, helped him heal. That was only the beginning. But now...seeing her never failed to shine more light into his day. In the most crowded of rooms, the great hall, his gaze always found her, singled her out as if she were the only person in the room.

"Would you be willing to help me find a position?" She pulled him from his musings.

"I'll see what I can do." Another idea came to him. "I ken 'tis beneath you, but I have need of someone to oversee and organize the maid servants, now that Weems is gone. I'd pay you well, of course. Would you be willing to help out in that way in the meantime?"

"I'd be glad to." Her sincere and direct gaze lit on his for a moment then slid away. "But it would only be temporary until you find someone else, because I would prefer a governess position away from the Highlands."

"I understand." But he didn't have to like it. "I'll send some letters out."

"You will?" She seemed much too pleased.

"You're surprised that I would help?"

Her gaze drifted to the flowers. "You are a kind man. Not like my cousin Donald."

"You asked for his help, and he refused, didn't he?"

"Indeed."

What a bastard the MacIrwin was. "Well, I don't ken your family's situation. Mayhap he had a reason to want to keep you on his lands."

She frowned and jammed her fists onto her hips. "That's it. My father."

"And who would he be?" Alasdair was glad for the opportunity to ask.

"'Tis of no importance."

"Is it now? Somehow I doubt that. I suspect your father is someone of much import."

Gwyneth shrugged. "I would wager—had I anything to wager—that my father is paying Donald to keep me."

"Why would he?"

"I'd rather not say, but I'm sure Donald would've wanted something for his trouble. Oh, men!" She thumped her foot against the stone-paved ground and turned away. "I detest every last one of them."

Alasdair snorted. "'Tis saddened I am to hear that you detest me, as well."

She halted by the rock wall and sent him a sheepish glance. "I didn't mean you."

"And what am I, then? A wee hare?"

In the glow of sunset, her blush deepened. "Hardly." A stiff, refreshing breeze off the loch pulled strands of hair from the knot at the back of her head.

He rose and limped forward on his cane. His gaze traveled over the tall rock wall, toward the mountains and the setting sun obscured by pink and orange clouds, but his full attention locked on this mesmerizing woman.

Gwyneth.

He passed her name through his thoughts a hundred times a day. He wanted to say her name, whisper it into her ear. But that would imply an intimacy they didn't share.

In that moment, the sharp urge to kiss her burst through his defenses. Her small yet full lips were dark-pink and moist. Last night he had dreamed of kissing her, and a lot more—removing her clothing, stroking his lips over every inch of her soft skin, sliding fully into her tight, wet depths. He had wakened hot and aroused as he had not been in years.

"What would you do, m'lady, if I kissed you?"

Her wide-eyed gaze flew to his, and she stepped back.

Aye, retreat if you ken what's good for you.

He was strong enough to resist her allure, but he didn't want to. Not anymore. Damnation, he'd tried. But each day she stole more and more of his attention, until finally his nights were filled with those heated dreams, and his days with scorching fantasies. He was a chief with no interest in leading at the moment.

Slowly, he moved toward where she stood with her back to the wall. Arms crossed, she watched him warily for a moment as if he were going to attack her. She didn't know him very well at all, did she?

He propped his cane up, placed his arm on the wall beside her and leaned casually, close to her. Closer than was proper. Her womanly essence sent his thoughts scattering. "Gwyneth, I wonder, have you ever had a kiss that near took your breath away?"

Her cheeks reddened even more.

"I confess, just the thought of kissing you the way I would like does that to me."

She swallowed hard and stared at the ground, then at the gate as if she might make a mad dash for it. But she didn't. "Oh, you are...unseemly." Her whispered chastisement sounded more breathless excitement than offended shock.

"Aye. That I am. I have sinful thoughts about you at night, in my bed," he whispered.

Her breath came out in a rush against his throat. Heat and chills chased over his skin and his erection tingled and tightened, hard as the stone wall.

He exhaled against her forehead. "God help me, Gwyneth, I want to taste your skin." *Kiss you, lips to ankle and back again, lick you in dark, forbidden places. Get drenched by your desire while you surround me and hold me tightly so deep inside you. Wrap yourself around me and moan my name.*

"Good heavens," she whispered.

"Are you wanting that, too?"

She didn't answer.

He pressed a kiss to her forehead, then drew back slightly. "Gwyneth?"

She glanced up, her normally light eyes turned dark, her lips parted. Though it might be sacrilege, he thanked Heaven for female lust. She slipped her hand around his neck. Taking that as the signal he needed, he captured her lips.

She tasted of salvation and damnation at once. No woman had ever lured him to forget who he was...forget his past, his future, and fill him with the need to have her no matter the cost to his soul.

She was more delicious than the sweetest comfit. She was honey and cream he wanted to lap up like a famished cat. He hardened so fully, dizziness snatched his equilibrium. He could not help but pull her to him, his hands at her waist dropping, caressing her derriere through the petticoats, no farthingale to hamper his progress. His fingers ached to tug up her skirts, to caress the softest skin, wet, hidden female places.

Alasdair's kiss was unlike anything Gwyneth could've expected. Never had anyone kissed her in such a fierce-tender, devouring way. The shameless movements of his tongue, flicking into her mouth, shocked her and awakened her to each tiny detail of him. He tasted faintly of lemons, delicious and tangy, and she savored him.

A moan rumbled from his throat. *"Mo dia."* A curse or prayer, she wasn't sure which.

Tingling heat covered her body and moisture gathered between her legs. By the saints! This was worse—far more sinful than anything she'd ever done, because she exulted in it. The sheer sumptuousness of his mouth obliterated all else.

Her aching nipples rubbed the hard muscles of his chest. And his hands, good lord, the places he caressed. And then she felt him— his aroused shaft stroked her belly, pressed firmly against her, as if begging to be inside. She ached. His kilt and her own threadbare skirts were almost as nothing between them. Instinct urged her to pull him down to the ground, atop her. Inside her.

She gasped, shocked at her response to him. What her father had said was true—she was a harlot, easily seduced when the right words were whispered in her ear. And Alasdair knew the perfect ones.

She jerked away from him.

In the gloaming, his face was flushed, his eyes black as midnight, his breathing unsteady. She had always thought his eyes had a sensual, lustful look about them. Now, that was multiplied a hundred times. Undoubtedly, he was a man made for the bedchamber. A man who knew everything about seducing a woman and rendering her helpless under his lascivious spell. A woman such as herself would be doomed in his presence.

"I must go." She ran back toward the door of the castle.

☙ ❧

That night, the soothing rhythm of Gwyneth's clear, animated voice mesmerized Alasdair, as it did his clan. Days ago, she'd started telling Rory and one of the other lads a story of great adventure, but within a few days she'd lured all the children. And now the bigger part of his clan, young and old, had gathered around her in the great hall after supper to hear these fantastic tales they'd never heard before—obviously English, or perhaps she'd made them up herself to amuse her son.

Her descriptions of the unusual landscapes her characters passed through and their funny adventures were indeed spellbinding. What he'd found even more enthralling was her kiss. It was a good thing she'd pulled away. He might have taken her there, against the stone wall, with no protest from her. Indeed, she had been an active participant, tugging him closer, teasing his tongue with her own. Saints! A passionate woman was a wondrous treasure. Thinking of how she had kissed him with a hunger that increased his own now made him hard with need.

It had been far longer than he wanted to admit since he'd been with a woman. He'd smothered his natural desires beneath his grief and his duty of leading and overseeing the clan. Apparently, his desires were awakened in full now and demanding release. But he could not pursue this with Gwyneth. He could not dishonor her.

He turned away from the sound of her seductive voice and strode upstairs onto the battlements. The cool night wind blew his hair back from his face. He released a pent-up breath and drew the fresh air in deep.

The high-pitched skirl of bagpipes echoed through the darkness from the village. Beautiful and haunting, the hymn reminded Alasdair of his father's funeral. The pain and confusion that came with becoming the clan's new laird was something he had finally overcome. But the grief he had not forgotten. Of course, all his life he'd known he would one day be laird, but he had not expected to be so young, twenty-three, when it happened.

He had promised himself he would avenge his father's murder, but he hadn't been able to. He hadn't told all of his clansmen who the murderer was. They simply blamed it on the MacIrwins, Donald in particular. Not long after his own father's death, Shaw had been killed in a skirmish with the Kerrs.

The matter was finished, but it didn't seem so. Donald, along with Baigh's two grown sons, had been with him that day. Accomplices. No, Alasdair didn't want revenge against them, but he considered them the lowest of common criminals.

He was sure Gwyneth had nothing to do with his father's death, but he couldn't remove certain images from his mind—images of her and her vile husband together.

"What are you doing out here moping? Did you grow tired of the fairy's tale?" Lachlan chuckled.

He turned, surveying his brother's amused and carefree expression. He envied him that. "I'm but thinking."

"'Tis the lady that's put you in this glum mood."

The truth of that prickled like a thistle in his plaid. "There is naught wrong with my mood."

Lachlan snorted. "I saw the way you were watching her. Like a juicy red apple just out of your reach."

Alasdair flicked a glare at his meddlesome brother. "'Tis hard to ignore someone who has bewitched the whole of our clan."

"Including you, first and foremost."

"As I recall, you were not immune to her charm."

Lachlan snickered. "I'm not immune to any wench's charm."

Nor were they immune to him. The lasses from miles around were in love with him. Alasdair had never had time for such frivolities. Nor did he now. Best to put Gwyneth from his mind.

"Are you certain you can trust her? She is, after all, a relation of the MacIrwin," Lachlan said in a more serious tone.

"It matters not. I'm helping her as she helped me. 'Tis all." But indeed he did trust her, no matter her clan connection.

"'Tis time you were looking for another wife."

Alasdair lifted a brow, determined to remove the focus from himself. "You're one to talk."

"I'm not the earl and chief, and don't need a legitimate heir. But you do. An heir, and a spare. And a few wee lasses." Lachlan grinned.

In truth, 'twas what Alasdair yearned for so badly his chest ached. Children and a cherished wife. But he shrugged it off. "If I don't, the clan has plenty of other lads who can step up and be chief one day. 'Haps one of yours if you marry."

"Ha!" Lachlan shook his head. "I'll never marry. Besides, Da would've wanted the next chief to be your son."

"I'm certain he would've approved of either."

Lachlan had never been in love and therefore had never had his heart ripped from his chest even as he stood helplessly by and watched the life drain from his wife and child.

Alasdair did not possess the strength to endure it again.

ঔৣ৾ঔৣ৾

That night Rory was sleeping with Alasdair's cousin's family in the village, with whom he'd stayed while Gwyneth was sick. She trusted them completely, and Rory had made friends with their sons.

Lying on the soft featherbed, Gwyneth wondered what Alasdair was doing in the bedchamber next to hers. Was he sleeping? She couldn't. Her imagination worked overtime.

She could hardly believe the shocking and seductive words he had said to her. *I have sinful thoughts about you at night, in my bed.*

What sort of thoughts, precisely? And was he having them now? Her heart rate escalated.

Remembering the firmness of his lips on hers, she re-experienced his kiss in the darkness. She craved his taste, the hard press of his powerful body against hers. Never had a kiss been so intoxicating and delicious, like wine infused with herbs and honey—sweet, warm and citrusy. She smiled against her pillow, then traced her overly-sensitive lips with her fingertip.

She recalled the sound of his deep voice murmuring in her ear. *Gwyneth, I wonder, have you ever had a kiss that near took your breath away?* Oh heavens, yes, his kiss had done that and more.

She could easily imagine lying in his big cozy-looking bed she'd sat beside several nights ago. The best part would be his hard-muscled body next to hers, his skin heating hers, his mouth and hands doing wicked but exquisite things to her.

Energy tingled through her body, as if she'd been standing a bit too close to a lightning strike. What had Alasdair done to her?

She must have slept…and dreamed. The images before her and the lustful sensations possessing her body couldn't have been real life. She had never experienced such carnal indulgences before—not at her promiscuous downfall nor during her hellish marriage. Those were mere gray pebbles compared to the diamond-like sensations that sparkled through her at Alasdair's touch.

Loud shouts and running footsteps woke Gwyneth from her restless dreams. The fire had gone out in the hearth, casting the room in cool darkness. She jumped up, crept to the door and opened it a crack. She couldn't understand the shouts of alarm coming from the great hall, but something was terribly wrong. Even MacDade, her guard, was gone.

Gwyneth yanked on her petticoats, skirts and *arisaid* over her smock and crammed her feet into her leather slippers. She strode along the dark corridor and down the steps. In the great hall, the women servants scurried back and forth.

She spotted Tessie and hastened to catch up. "What's happened?"

The young woman turned panic-stricken eyes on her. "'Tis the MacIrwins. They're burning the village."

A sickening chill shook her. "Rory's down there!"

Tessie's face blanched and tears glistened in her eyes. "Oh,

Gwyneth," she whispered and shook her head.

No! Something deep inside Gwyneth screamed. Denial blocking out all other thoughts, she dashed out the door and down the stone steps into the barmkin.

"Gwyneth!" Tessie chased after her as she ran mindless toward the gate. "You cannot go down there."

No one would dare keep her from it. She stopped at the gate and faced Tessie. "I must go get Rory. Where's Laird MacGrath?"

"With the men, of course, fighting."

"Is he a lunatic? His foot is not healed."

"'Twould surprise me if he is not at the forefront. 'Tis his way."

"Open the gate!" she told the guard. Resolve tightened her muscles.

"You're forbidden to leave. The MacGrath's order." The large, battle-scarred warrior stood firm.

"Some of the men are in charge of bringing people up here from the village," Tessie said. "Maybe Rory's here."

Could it be possible? Hope making her lightheaded, Gwyneth glanced back, searching in desperation among the villagers milling about the barmkin. But she didn't see Rory or the family he was staying with.

Beyond the iron gate, fires blazed in the distance, lighting up the pitch black night. She closed her eyes and the screams of the villagers reached her ears. A shudder of revulsion and terror ran through her.

Gwyneth's throat tightened and she feared she might be sick and burst into hysterical sobs at the same moment. But she gathered her strength. "Let me pass! I must get my son."

"Nay!" the guard bellowed, his scowl and thick beard giving him an intimidating look.

"I beg you to stay here." Tears streamed down Tessie's face.

Gwyneth didn't realize she was crying until her vision blurred. She swiped the tears away and tried to think logically. How could she slip past the guard?

A group of armed men and villagers, including women and crying children, approached the gate outside. Soot and smoke blackened their faces and clothing.

Please let Rory be among them.

The guards motioned her and Tessie back as they admitted the villagers. Gwyneth searched each face.

She was devastated to see none of the four children who'd

arrived was Rory. Making a desperate decision, Gwyneth ran through the gates before they swung closed.

The guard shouted behind her, and Tessie screamed out her name, but Gwyneth didn't look back. She would find her precious child.

CHAPTER SEVEN

Alasdair rode hell-bent between the burning cottages of the village. Acrid smoke stung his eyes and congested his lungs. The intense heat seared his skin. In the bright light from the flaming thatch roofs, he searched for the thrice-cursed MacIrwins.

He would see Donald pay for this as he had never paid before. Alasdair had let things go on far too long—the murders, the ambushes. And now this, killing the innocent people of his clan...women and children.

No more. No mercy for the MacIrwins.

He prayed for rain to pour from the cloud-filled sky and death to all the murdering MacIrwin men.

He'd dispatched five of the enemies thus far himself. His men had taken out several more.

Most of the villagers had gone to the relative safety of the barmkin and tower. But some had already lost their lives in either the fires or the battle.

His cousin Fergus approached on horseback. "The MacIrwin wants Mistress Carswell and her son back," he shouted. "He claims we've taken them hostage."

Alasdair faced him, his rage escalating. "That hell-hated bastard! He will kill them if he so much as sets eyes on them. I would never make them go back."

Fergus wheeled his horse and charged a MacIrwin approaching from behind.

Pounding hooves and a war cry shot toward Alasdair from the shadows.

Determination rushing thorough his veins, he tugged on his mount's reins and turned about to meet the threat, head-on. The horse reared and near unseated him. He wrestled the temperamental animal under control just in time to strike out. The blade of the MacIrwin warrior clashed against his own.

Alasdair slashed and thrust. His spooked horse reared again, catching him off guard. He toppled over the horse's hindquarters, slammed against the stony ground but maintained a hold on his sword. Damnation! Though the pain in his hip near blinded him, he scrambled out of the path of the MacIrwin's horse.

Lachlan stormed into the fray, engaging the enemy and running him through.

"Are you all right, brother?" Lachlan called over the roaring fires of the cottages.

"Aye, just busted my arse." Coughing, he rose and turned about in search of his horse. He could hardly see through the smoke and brightness of the flames.

"You should return to the tower! You've scarce recovered from the last skirmish," Lachlan said.

"You're wasting your breath, mother hen."

Riding away, Lachlan found Alasdair's horse, slapped it on the rump and sent it trotting to him.

Once mounted, Alasdair cursed at the fresh wave of MacIrwins invading the village, on foot and horseback, slashing at anything that moved.

"Murdering bastards!" Alasdair gripped his basket-hilted sword and joined Lachlan to fight beside him.

☙ ॐ ❧

Shaking and almost out of breath, Gwyneth approached the village from the shadows. The roaring of the flames chilled her to the core. How many had already died in the fires? How could Donald do such horrid things?

Heaven help me, if Rory dies, I'll personally kill Donald myself, even should his men strike me down after I do the deed.

She'd been to the cottage where Rory was staying once and hoped she could find it again. But, dear heavens, all the cottage roofs were on fire.

The heat singed her skin. The bitter smoke choked her. Coughing, she yanked her plaid over her head and pulled the small dagger from her bodice.

Her attention ahead, her foot caught on something. Saints! A fallen warrior...three of them. Whispering a prayer, she skirted around them.

Near the first burning cottage, two men on horseback broke into a sword-slashing duel. Sparks popped off their clashing blades. She circled back and approached from the rear. In the light from the fires, she now saw that one of the men was Alasdair, his smoke-blackened face a mask of fury.

"Dear God, protect him," she whispered.

Alasdair's injuries of a few days ago hadn't slowed him down. He skillfully parried and thrust against his opponent.

A tiny child ran screaming from behind the row of cottages near her and blindly headed toward the fighting warriors. A surge of strength jolted Gwyneth. She darted forward and snatched the child from the ground. He wasn't Rory, but he was someone's baby.

A MacIrwin foot soldier wielding a two-handed sword, chased the child, quickening his pace when he noticed Gwyneth. Skin prickling, she dashed in the opposite direction, toward the tower.

I have to get Rory.

Halting, she glanced back at the same moment Alasdair struck his mark, his sword sliding with deadly accuracy into the mounted MacIrwin clansman's chest. The man shouted and toppled from his horse.

The other beast, chasing her on foot, shouting taunts in Gaelic, and waving his claymore about, didn't let up.

Clutching the wriggling child, she faced forward and ran. She would take him to the tower and come back to search for Rory, if she could get this barbarian off her heels. Hooves clattered on the earth behind her. A hoarse battle cry erupted, blades clashed.

Afraid she'd stumble and fall on the rocks, Gwyneth could spare no time to glance back. The sound of a blade slicing against bone met her ears, followed by a man's scream. She cringed.

"Go to the tower and stay there!" a man yelled. Was that Alasdair's voice?

She stopped and turned. The villain who'd been pursuing her lay in a heap on the ground.

"Gwyneth? Is that you?" Alasdair rode closer on his big black warhorse. "God's teeth, woman! Get inside the gates and don't come back down here!" His hair hung wild about his soot-blackened face, and his fierce expression brooked no argument.

"I must find Rory! He was with your cousin, Colin, and his wife."

"I sent Rory to the tower with Fergus some time ago, along with Colin's family."

Gwyneth almost sank to her knees in relief. "Is he well?"

"Aye. Go back. Now!"

"I thank you. God keep you," she called out, though it was pitifully little and did not convey what she wanted to say. She wished to drag him off his horse and bring him back to the safety of the tower with her.

"Don't worry. Now go!"

She turned and climbed the road up the hill even as the first drops of cool rain fell. When she glanced back, he was still watching her, guarding her.

Once she was inside the gates, Alasdair wheeled his horse about and galloped away.

May God protect him.

Still carrying the screaming child, she glanced about for Rory inside the barmkin. The summer rain shower increased, drenching her and everyone around her in a chilly downpour.

"Rory!" Gwyneth called. Alasdair had said Rory was here, so he had to be. But where?

"Och, wee Kean!" An elderly woman approached Gwyneth and gently took the child from her arms. "Thank you, mistress." Rain washed through the soot on the woman's wrinkled face.

"You're welcome. Do you know Rory? Have you seen him?"

The woman shook her head.

"He was with Colin and Grace."

"Mayhap inside the castle."

Gwyneth raced up the spiral tower steps. How had she missed Rory's arrival?

In the great hall, women, children and elderly men moved about or sat on benches. Her gaze searched each child's face.

"Ma! Ma!" Rory, soot-covered and ragged, dashed toward her.

Thank you, God. She dropped to her knees in relief and caught her precious child in her arms. "Oh, Rory. Sweetheart, I'm glad you are well."

Now, if only Alasdair were safe too.

෯ௐ ௐ෯

Hours later, Alasdair stood beside his horse on a small rise, overlooking the village and the activity there. He and his men had cleared the area of live MacIrwins, but several dead ones remained. Their bodies would need to be returned to their clan.

Though Alasdair had lost only two of his own fighting men in the skirmish, the loss was great to him. And he didn't yet know how many of the villagers had perished. Each member of his clan was family, whether by blood or friendship.

He still couldn't believe Gwyneth had been in the village— damn her daft hide—right in the midst of the fighting. He should string up the guards for allowing her beyond the walls. And he'd rake her over the coals as well. Of course, nothing would hold her back from saving the life of her son. Thank God she hadn't gotten herself killed, and Rory was safe, too.

The first rays of orange dawn light shone above the high mountains on the horizon. Exhaustion weighing his sore, overworked muscles, Alasdair craved to do naught more than collapse in his bed, but he well knew he would get no sleep for a while.

The belated rain had helped douse some of the fires, but all that remained of most of the cottages were the thick rock walls and trails of smoke drifting toward the purple-gray sky. The flames had quickly devoured the thatch roofs, which then caved in and burned everything inside the cottages. The villagers had lost nearly everything they possessed of material value.

Various sheep, goats and cattle milled about the cluttered and muddy dirt street. It would take a tremendous amount of work to put the village back to rights. But some things could never be replaced.

Lachlan approached, his face black and his clothing bloody. "'Tis because of *her* that they attacked."

His brother's sharp gaze and hardened jaw surprised Alasdair. "What are you blathering on about?"

"Mistress Carswell."

Alasdair drew back, frowning. "Nay, the MacIrwin's attacked because I escaped their clutches almost a fortnight past."

"Aye, you would deny it! Fergus told me of the message—the MacIrwin wants her back."

"You would have me send her to her death! Along with her innocent son?"

Lachlan inhaled a deep slow breath and continued in a calmer tone. "Nay, but you must send her away, mayhap back to England."

"Nay! Don't challenge me, Lachlan."

"Surely you see what she's bringing down on our clan."

Alasdair loved his brother, but at the moment, he felt like slugging him in the jaw. "She has nowhere else to go. Her family disowned her. Her father sent her to the MacIrwin, and the bastard will kill her if he has a chance. She saved my life and I will return the favor as many times as I must." Aye, that's how grateful he was for what she'd done for him, endangering her own life and losing a friend in the process. Gwyneth deserved someone to protect her.

Lachlan sighed. "You should find her a place far from here."

Alasdair shook his head. He knew not why, but something deep inside him said her place was with him. "We had conflict with the MacIrwins long before she came to us. In case you forgot, they killed Da six years past."

"How could I forget?" Lachlan snapped, his scowl severe. "It happened right before my eyes."

"And they burned the village once before, nine years ago. Will you blame that on Gwyneth, too?"

"Nay. I'm not—"

"Lachlan!" cried a female voice.

They turned to find an elderly woman hobbling toward them. Alasdair couldn't recognize her with so much soot on her face.

"'Tis Mary Anne! She's dead!" The woman wailed.

Mary Anne was the mother of one of Lachlan's children. A stricken look crossed his face. "Are you certain?"

"Aye." The woman wiped her eyes, smearing soot.

"Where's Kean?" Lachlan strode away with her.

Alasdair propped his hand against his saddle while the horse hung its head and nosed at the trampled grass. Then he remembered—Gwyneth had been carrying Kean last night when she'd left the village. She'd saved the wee lad's life.

What was he going to do about her?

Lachlan was right of course, Alasdair should send her away. As long as she remained here, she would draw the MacIrwin's attention. She'd said she would like to find a position as a governess. Maybe that would be the best solution for them all. Except for him. But being the clan chief had required more than one sacrifice on his part.

⁂

Sharp sunlight gleamed over the peaks of the blue-purple mountains to the east. A stiff summer wind carried away the scents of smoke and blood, of war and violence that Alasdair hated. He ignored the aches and pains of his own body, and forced himself to concentrate on what could be salvaged rather than what had been lost. He must give his clan hope of a brighter future. They looked to him for support and encouragement and he would not let them down.

While some of his men transported the bodies of the dead MacIrwins to the borders of Donald's holdings, others carried the three injured MacGrath warriors up to the tower. He'd posted several guards around the grounds in case the MacIrwins returned.

As soon as Alasdair stepped into the great hall, Gwyneth appeared beside him and grasped his hand. So thankful was he that she was unharmed, he wanted to yank her into his arms and embrace her so tightly he might crush the breath from her. But he forced himself not to and squeezed her hand instead.

"You're not hurt?" Her frantic gaze searched him, then fixed on his torso. "You're bleeding."

"Nay, 'tis not my blood. I only have a few scratches and bruises. Since you are a healer, I wondered, could you help these three men?" He motioned to the side. "Our village healer is busy with the others."

Releasing his hand, she turned her attention toward the moaning or unconscious men being carried in. She directed where they should be laid in the great hall. She then set to work examining them and telling the women which herbs and supplies she would require.

At her suggestion, Alasdair gave whisky to the ones who were awake and in pain. She removed a lead ball from his steward's shoulder, and after cleaning the wounds, stitched up the cuts and gashes of the other two men, Angus and Padraig.

Alasdair watched her work tirelessly for more than an hour and assisted by turning the men over when she asked. The blood and gore did not appear to bother her. She had a backbone of tempered steel and more courage than a lot of men he'd seen. Yet, she possessed the gentle and caring touch of a guardian angel.

The uninjured warriors ate and rested, preparing to take their turn at watch. Tomorrow, the clan would hold the funerals and bury the dead. The next day, they would look toward the future and start to rebuild the village. In the meantime, everyone pulled together and consoled one another.

"'Tis time you ate something, then rested," Alasdair told Gwyneth. The dark circles beneath her eyes showed she was as exhausted as he.

She nodded, rose and went in search of food, he hoped.

Alasdair cleaned himself up in his bedchamber, changed clothes and then found Lachlan in the great hall. He also looked a mite better without the bloody clothes and the soot.

"What is it you're wanting to tell me?" Lachlan asked in a surly tone once they were inside the library. The cheerful sunlight slicing through the two narrow windows clashed with Lachlan's dark scowl, and Alasdair's own mood.

"I'm sorry about Mary Anne," Alasdair said in a calm voice that he hoped conveyed his sympathy.

"Aye, we all are. Now my son has no mother."

"But he has a father—as we did growing up. He will come here to live in the castle if you wish it."

His brother propped his fists against his waist. "That won't change the fact that your fine Lady Gwyneth caused all this."

"Gwyneth saved Kean's life."

Lachlan looked as if someone had hit him broadside with an ax. "What?"

"Aye. She came down to the village during the fighting, looking for Rory. A MacIrwin on foot was chasing Kean while I was trying to fight off another one on horseback. She jumped out and grabbed Kean. He could've been trampled beneath the horses' hooves or killed by the enemy. I didn't ken who either of them were at first. But when Gwyneth turned back, I saw her face. And I also saw Kean in her arms."

Lachlan froze for a moment, then released a harsh breath. "Merciful God, I must thank her."

Alasdair stepped forward. "I'll go with you."

"I appreciate your trust in me," Lachlan said in a dry tone, his expression easing.

"I ken how you like to show your gratitude to the ladies."

Lachlan's abashed grin appeared, and he clasped hands with Alasdair in a quick, fierce handshake. "Aye, you ken me too well, brother, but I value my neck too highly to dally with that one."

Alasdair ignored his brother's thinly veiled reference to his possessiveness. "Later, I wish to talk to you about going to the Privy Council in my stead. We'll bring charges against the MacIrwins for the attacks."

Lachlan nodded. "'Twould please me beyond measure to see Donald MacIrwin kicking the wind."

They found Gwyneth in the great hall, again watching over the injured, seeing that they drank broth and herbal teas. He would indeed have to order her to her bed and force her to rest.

Alasdair stopped close beside her. "M'lady, if you please, we would have a word with you in the library."

Gwyneth drew back, her confused gaze darting back and forth between them. But Lachlan's slight grin must have put her at ease. Alasdair followed her into the smaller room, and Lachlan closed the door behind them.

His brother dropped to one knee and grasped Gwyneth's hand in his. He feared Lachlan went too far when he pressed his lips to the back of her hand.

Gwyneth froze, her wide eyes beseeching Alasdair.

He smiled, attempting to reassure her that his brother had not been stricken with lunacy.

"M'lady," Lachlan said. "I thank you, and I owe you a grand debt of gratitude for saving the life of my son."

She frowned down at him. "Your son?"

"Aye. Kean is my son—the wee lad you rescued from the village last night."

"Oh. I didn't know," she said softly.

"Surely, you are an angel sent from heaven."

"No, not at all." Face flushing bright pink, she gently tugged her hand from within his. "I simply acted on instinct."

Lachlan rose. "Nevertheless, if there is ever anything I can do for you, I will. Just let me know."

She curtsied. "I thank you."

Lachlan gave her a bow and let himself out.

Gwyneth darted a glance at Alasdair. "If that is all—"

"Nay." The word popped from his mouth, perhaps too quickly, but he enjoyed being alone with her too much to allow her to leave so soon. Had it only been yesterday evening when he'd kissed her? It seemed a week ago, so much had happened since.

He'd had no time to think about the kiss and what it had meant—that he was far more drawn to her than he should be. And that he wanted another kiss. Wanted more than a kiss. But aside from that, nothing else had changed. Sending her away would be the best solution for her and the clan. Besides, it was what she wished. But he wouldn't do it now. He had to find her a safe and suitable place first, and at the moment, they needed her healing skills here.

"Yes, my laird?" Her blush was still in evidence, and it lent her a charming quality.

"I wish to thank you, as well, for saving Kean's life and those of my men."

"I could do nothing less."

Though modest, she had the proud posture and regal bearing of a lady, which could not be concealed beneath her dirty, bloody clothing.

"When I saw you in the village during the worst of the fighting, I wanted to throttle you for putting yourself in such danger." He'd meant to speak the words in a harsh, angry tone, but couldn't quite manage it. Instead he simply sounded...desperate. Desperate to keep her safe.

She lifted courageous eyes to his. "And what about the danger you were in? Going into battle already injured."

"My toe is much improved. And 'twas my responsibility. Not yours."

Blue fire lit within her eyes. "Rory is my responsibility, and I would go through hell itself, if I had to, to save his life."

He nodded. "Aye, of course. You are a brave lady, to be sure. And I admire that." In truth, he admired far too many things about her.

She glanced away as if dismissing his words. He wanted to hold a mirror up to her, to show her what an incredible woman she was. He wanted to show her how she should value herself. Too many men had put her down and treated her poorly, instead of giving her the care and attention she deserved.

"You're always taking care of others," he said. "I wonder, who takes care of you?"

She looked at him straight. "I'm not too proud to accept the help of others, but I take care of myself for the most part."

Indeed, she did. She was independent, too, flexible as a willow. A survivor. He could not recall a woman he admired as much—well, except for his Leitha, of course. Still, Gwyneth was stronger. But she needed someone to take care of her from time to time. Someone to lean on and cling to in the storm.

One part of him craved to be that person. Another part of him rebelled at the very thought. He could never again be that close to anyone. It hurt too much when they abandoned him. He reinforced the icy wall around the most vulnerable part of him, but it did not stop him from craving everything about her.

"I thank you for looking out for Rory and sending him up safely with Fergus," she said.

"Of course, 'twas the least I could do."

The village had been crawling with MacIrwins, any one of whom wanted to see her dead. A careless flick of a blade and her life would've been forfeit. Drained away, as Leitha's had, leaving him regretting that he had not done more. 'Twas a tragic thing to realize you were too late.

Acting on naught more than the fierce and perplexing feelings raging inside him, Alasdair stepped forward and pulled Gwyneth into his arms. "Pray pardon, m'lady. I must hold you for a minute."

"Oh." The wee surprised sound was no more than a breath from her.

He pressed his face against her silky hair and inhaled the smoke scent mixed with a hint of herbs and whisky with which she'd medicated the injured. But most of all, her own unique female scent held him spellbound. He remembered it from when he'd kissed her and that little window to paradise had opened.

Her small frame against his own much larger one soothed his battle-ravaged soul. The vital warmth of her reassured him she was indeed alive—that they both were.

Her body was still taut with tension, but her arms crept around his waist and held him just as tightly. He savored her touch and her embrace, afraid to move. Afraid he would frighten her away. After a moment, her body relaxed within his arms. Aye, this was the way it should be. Naught had ever felt so right. Relishing the lithe, sensual feel of her, he tried to absorb her calmness and peace into himself.

Against her cool hair, his lips formed a kiss. Saints! How he treasured her and wished to kiss her all over. Without thought, he brushed his lips across her forehead, then pressed a kiss to each of her cheeks. She pulled in a shaky breath, drawing his attention to her lips he hungered to taste again.

Tilting her flushed face down and to the side, she withdrew her arms from around his waist. Disappointment besieged him, though in truth he didn't know what the devil he was doing kissing her face in such a way. Had he gone mad? He immediately released her.

With much hesitation, she glanced up at him with darkened blue eyes. "I must go see to the injured men."

Shoving away the ardent feelings that now filled him, he focused on her words. "Nay. You are to go get some sleep yourself, afore you fall down."

"But—"

"I won't be hearing an argument about it. Off with you now, to your room."

Maybe if he treated her like a child, she would lose some of her womanly appeal. But he doubted anything would cool his body's heated interest in her.

Having washed away all traces of soot, blood and grime, and wearing fresh clothing, Gwyneth paced from one end of her chamber to the other, past the ostentatious bed, where her freshly bathed son lay snoring within the downy mattress. She paused by the narrow window with its wavy glass. She was not sleepy in the least. Tired and shaken, yes, but not relaxed enough to sleep. She was glad Rory had agreed to a nap.

The events of the past few hours replayed through her mind over and over. The fires, the violence, the death.

The fear.

Fear for Rory's life and for Alasdair's.

After she'd found Rory and held him in her arms, her worries had turned to Alasdair. She'd feared his broken toe would cause him to make some small mistake in battle and get himself killed.

But he was alive, thanks be to God.

Alive and warm and strong. When he'd held her for those few shining moments in the library—*heavens!* She'd almost broken down into sobs. Why? Not sadness. No, with thankfulness, and joy and a hundred other emotions that crashed in on her when he touched her.

The intensity of his dark brown eyes and the firm grip of his arms told her he'd needed to hold her. That his regard for her went beyond a man's physical need for a woman. He had felt the same concern for her safety that she'd felt for his. And the way he'd kissed her forehead, her cheeks. With affection. With passion that went beyond the physical. She'd been near shaking with emotion for him by the time she'd left the library.

Always, he looked at her with such admiration—she could not fathom it.

He wasn't like his charming seducer brother, but Alasdair was nonetheless charming and seductive, in a more subtle way. Mayhap in a more cunning way that gave her a false sense of security, until she was well caught in his trap...and then she would be a gone goose.

"No. No, I must not," she whispered. "I must go away from here." For the sake of Rory's life and her own sanity.

But the prospect didn't hold the appeal it once did.

CHAPTER EIGHT

"May I have a word with you?" Gwyneth asked Lachlan later that afternoon when she found him in the noisy great hall. Normally she would not have asked anything of him, but she was desperate.

His brows lifted. "Indeed." He followed her to the less crowded side of the huge room where they might have a bit of privacy.

"I searched you out as soon as I heard you were going to Edinburgh," she said.

"Aye, Alasdair is sending me to petition the Privy Council on his behalf. He kens of how charismatic and diplomatic I can be." Lachlan smiled and winked.

The man should learn to rein in his effortless seductive charm. No more than a flick of an eyelid from him, and she felt like an awkward young girl. Not that she was attracted to him—certainly not in the way she was attracted to Alasdair—but Lachlan constantly left her in a state of discomfiture.

"You said if I ever needed your help to ask," she reminded him.

"Aye." He watched her warily, his countenance turning serious. "What would you be needing help with? As I said, I'm in your debt for saving Kean's life."

"I want to leave the Highlands."

He frowned and glanced about. "Aye, but I don't think you should travel with me this time. I'm in a wee hurry."

"No, not now."

He smiled. "I'm relieved. As I'm sure Alasdair will be. He would be in a foul mood indeed if I deprived him of seeing your lovely face every day."

Heat rushed over her. The implication that Alasdair enjoyed looking at her—goodness. It filled her with giddiness and sparked the memory of his wicked kiss.

"He would take his fury out on the clan—and me too, of course," Lachlan continued. "There would never be another peaceful day here at Kintalon. I wager he would follow us all the way to Edinburgh to reclaim you."

Her whole body started to sweat. She couldn't believe how he was going on about Alasdair's interest in her. Surely he exaggerated. "Please, sir—"

Lachlan chuckled, and she realized he was teasing her. The knave.

She cleared her throat and tried to remember what she'd wanted to ask him. "As I was saying, I must find a place to go in the Lowlands or England. I want to find a governess or tutor position if possible. Laird MacGrath has said he will write me a recommendation. If you should run into a friend or acquaintance in Edinburgh, perhaps you could inquire whether they are in need of someone."

"I will make every effort, m'lady." Lachlan bowed, took her hand and kissed her fingers.

She snatched her hand away. He grinned and headed for the door.

"Have a safe journey," she rushed to add.

She glanced across the great hall and met Alasdair's midnight eyes. His scowl told her he was vexed about something—surely not because she'd been talking to his brother.

⚜ ⚜

The next evening, Gwyneth oversaw the clearing of the tables after the meal in the great hall. This day had been a long, sad one with the funerals of six clan members who had died in the attack. The kirk had been overflowing with mourners. A pall of tragedy hung over the clan like the gray clouds above.

Downstairs, just outside the kitchen, Gwyneth paused upon hearing one of the female servants whisper her name.

"'Twas Gwyneth's fault the village was burned, I tell you. The MacIrwin sent a message, he wants her back."

"You best not let Laird MacGrath be hearing you say that. You'll be spending the night in the dungeon," another female voice warned.

"Fie!"

"Stop spreading rumors," a third woman said. "Mistress Carswell has saved the lives of four men including Laird MacGrath himself."

"Shh." One of the women spotted her through the doorway and they all hurried back to their tasks.

Had the woman spoken the truth? She was to blame for the village being burned? It seemed a rock had been dropped onto her chest for she could hardly breathe. Why would Donald want her back that badly? Or was it a matter of revenge?

Footsteps approached from behind and Tessie stopped at her elbow. "Laird MacGrath wishes to see you in the library," she whispered.

"I thank you." Gwyneth would ask him about this.

Determined to learn the truth, she turned and climbed the stairs. What could Alasdair want? He had not said more than five words to her all day. As was to be expected, he had given his full attention to the families who had lost loved ones. Gwyneth saw how much he cared about them all, and she admired this in him.

When she stopped outside the intricately carved oak door of the library, her palms sweated, and a sudden giddiness rippled through her. Not because she was afraid to be alone with him, but because she was looking forward to it too much. Though it was folly, she craved his complete attention. How greedy she was. Often, she did not know what to do with his attention once she had it. To feel his gaze on her and to hear his deep voice murmuring words, no matter whether mundane or scandalous, to her alone. Those were the moments when she didn't have to share him with his clan, yet also the moments that thrilled and frightened her most.

Drawing in a deep breath to calm her frantic heartbeat, she tapped her knuckles against the door three times.

"Come," said a deep voice from inside.

She stepped into the room. A small fire popped and flickered in the hearth, the glow adding further warmth to the candlelit room. The scents of smoke, melted tallow and rich spice blended into a comforting fragrance.

Alasdair stood, facing her, before the mantel, looking dark and mouth-watering, wearing a fine belted plaid and doublet. She forced herself not to stare and instead focused on the fire. The last time they'd been alone together in this room, he had held her tightly in his arms and kissed her face. How comforted and protected she'd felt, but just beneath the surface, smoldering embers of desire had near scorched her. She both hoped and feared he might embrace or kiss her again.

No, don't think such thoughts.

Risking a glance at him, she found him studying her face, then his gaze dropped to her clothing. Well, in truth, his late wife's clothing, which she'd worn today for the first time. She hoped the garments hadn't brought back painful memories for him.

"You wished to see me?" she asked.

"Aye. Have a seat, if you would please." He motioned toward one of the wooden chairs situated not far from the hearth, and she lowered herself into it. "Would you care for some clary?" he asked, pouring wine into a pewter mug.

"No, but I thank you." Though the sweet ginger scent of the mulled claret did tempt her, she had to keep a clear head around him.

Carrying his mug, he took the chair opposite her. "Glad I am to see you finally wearing the clothes I gave you. You look lovely in them."

Heat rushed over her and she was thankful for the dim lighting. Dropping her gaze and trying to think of something neutral to say, she studied the exquisite cloth of the dark gray woolen skirts. "I thank you. I wouldn't want to ruin the fine clothing in the day-to-day running of the household, but for the funerals I needed something better."

"Aye." After taking a sip, he leaned forward, propped his elbows on his knees, bare below his kilt, and frowned into his mug. It seemed the weight of all of Scotland rested upon his shoulders. "I'm grateful to you for attending the funerals and consoling the family members of those who died."

Unexpectedly, her eyes stung—a combination of having seen so many others in pain, Alasdair's own apparent depth of feeling for his people, and the fact that he appreciated her presence. And she hoped, took some comfort from it.

Though her throat tightened, she forced the words out. "I've come to care for your clan. They have treated me far better than mine own."

"I'm glad." Alasdair drank another swallow of the clary, and Gwyneth suddenly craved the taste of it. Surely the spicy sweet flavor would be as drugging as the man. But she did not trust herself to drink such an indulgent beverage in Alasdair's presence. She was certain it would drown her good sense.

"I'm building a case against Donald MacIrwin," he said. "And I would like you to testify against him if you're willing, before the Privy Council in Edinburgh."

Heavens, that could be nerve-wracking, but no question, her cousin and his lawlessness had to be stopped. "I'll be glad to."

"Good." He raised a brow. "You're willing to testify even if it means some of your cousins are imprisoned or hanged?"

A tremor of revulsion passed through her. "I hate to see anyone hanged. But they are guilty of murder. Mora's for one. As well as the defenseless people who were not able to escape their burning cottages or who were slain in the street. And I've no doubt Donald would've killed Rory and me if he'd half a chance." With great effort, she pushed away the dark suffocation of her memories and focused on the man before her.

"Aye." Alasdair blinked hard once and glared into the fire for a long moment as if deadly thoughts passed through his mind.

The accusation of the whispering women haunted her, the burden of their words increasing. "Did Donald burn the village because of me?" she asked.

Meeting her eyes, Alasdair frowned. "Nay. Why do you ask?"

"I overheard someone talking about it. I regret that I've put your whole clan in danger by coming here. First, young Campbell lost his life, and now six more of your clan. Not to mention, the village burned."

"Nay, the blame does not rest on you."

"I know how cruel and bloodthirsty Donald is. When I escaped him, it angered him beyond measure. He wants revenge, does he not?"

"'Tis but an excuse. Donald burned the village nine years past, too. And I suspect you were far from the Highlands then."

"Yes." What a monster Donald was.

"Well then. When he's furious with us, for whatever reason, he does things like this. I escaped his clutches as well, so he could just as easily be angry with me alone. I wish you would tell me who said this."

She shook her head. Though Alasdair's rational explanations made much sense, they could not calm her worries. "I also heard that Donald wanted me returned to him." Her stomach ached with anxiety. "Is this true?"

Alasdair sat back, scowling. She knew the fearsome look was not meant for her, but for her cousin. "He did send a message by one of his men. But I would never, and I do mean *never*, return you to him. 'Twould mean certain death. Or worse, imprisonment and torture."

It was as she'd feared. She had to do something. "Your clan would be much safer from Donald if I left."

"Nonsense," he muttered in a surly tone.

"How can you say that? He burned the village and killed people. What will he do next? No, it is clear to me that it would be best for everyone—your clan, Rory and me—if Rory and I left the Highlands."

Maintaining his annoyed expression, Alasdair remained silent.

"I asked Lachlan to inquire while he's in Edinburgh as to whether anyone he knows might be in need of a governess or tutor for their children," she said.

"Ah." Alasdair placed his mug on the small table by his chair, stood and approached the fireplace. After staring into the flames a long moment, he turned back to her. "I don't want you to leave."

Though his words said much, his troubled expression told her more. He wanted her to stay because—

The rest of the thought was too outrageous. Too tempting. Exciting. She studied her fingers clutched tightly together on her lap. *Heaven help me.* "I had best check the kitchen maids." She sprang from the chair and charged for the door.

"M'lady."

Though she wanted nothing more than to flee the room and the keen exhilaration of him, she halted, pulse racing.

He approached upon soft footsteps and stopped in front of her. For a moment, he studied her, his dark eyes gleaming. With gentle fingertips, he traced her jaw to her chin.

"I don't want you to leave." His raw whisper snatched her breath. Without warning, he ducked his head and kissed her. The spiced wine on his lips intoxicated her, and she curled her fingers into his thick silky hair. She was not the master of her own body when he touched her.

Wanting more of him, she opened her mouth to receive his honey and ginger flavored kisses. She should not partake…but she couldn't resist. He flicked his tongue over hers, then away in a delicious game.

A low animalistic growl rumbled from his throat, and the kiss became something irreverent and without restraint. She sucked at his tongue, famished for the male taste of him.

Muttering words she did not understand, he kissed a mesmerizing path down her chin and underneath. Closing her eyes, she tilted her head back, giving him access to her throat. He trailed his tongue down over the tender skin and pressed kisses lower, the stubble of his chin scratching beneath the neckline of her smock.

He pulled at the ribbon tie and she felt it loosen. He inhaled deeply against her skin, his lips caressing carefully now the upper swells of her breasts. "Mmmm. I could devour you."

She gasped. Her nipples tingled, yearning for his hot, wet mouth. Though her corset prevented him from moving lower, he rubbed his chin over her nipples beneath the thick material. She was certain he couldn't feel them, but he stimulated her, made her yearn to tear all the clothing from her body so she might feel the delights he would heap upon it.

A lascivious moan met her ears and she realized it had come from her own mouth.

But she was beyond caring. All that concerned her at the moment was Alasdair, his mouth, his hands.

He moved behind her, and nuzzled her ear with warm lips and tickling breath. She shivered, her body quaking with such a thrill as she'd never felt. He stroked her neck and the upper part of her chest. Upon raising her arm, she threaded her fingers into the silk of his unbound hair and he slipped his downward toward her bodice. Into her bodice, beneath her corset.

His warm fingertips glided over the sensitized, bare skin of her breasts. She had not imagined he could reach such a place. Bowing her chest inward, she invited more. Oh, how much more she wanted! Obliging her with a muffled growl, he moved lower, and his thumb and finger closed gently over her hardened nipple. His tongue circled her ear even as his fingertip circled her nipple. He whispered Gaelic words that meant sweet, beautiful.

Paralyzed with riveting sensation, she could not breathe; he had stolen her ability. He sucked her earlobe into his mouth and plucked at her nipple with his fingers.

Grasping a handful of his clothing, his wool plaid, she groaned, shocked at the wanton noise she made and the need that filled her. Her back arched, and she pushed her derriere against his hard shaft. Near out of her mind with arousal, she turned her head toward him, ready to beg, and he immediately captured her lips, sliding his tongue into her mouth.

She couldn't bear another moment of these exquisite sensations. She might well splinter like a falling star.

Something thumped, jerking her from this sensual dream and away from Alasdair—a log in the fireplace had shifted and sparks showered the hearth.

What am I doing? Her body aching, she glanced up at him from inches away.

The renewed fire illuminated Alasdair's passion-filled expression and lowered brows. He looked like he wanted to bite her, ravish her. She yearned to do the same to him but—*heavens.*

"*Mo chreach.* I swore to myself I wouldn't do that. But you're so—" He blew out a harsh breath.

I must go while I still can. While I can still make a rational decision. Stumbling toward the door, she tried to calm her ragged breathing and will some strength into her wobbly legs.

I must leave the Highlands before I become a slave to mine own desires and the drugging effects of this man.

⁂

When Gwyneth fled the library, closing the door behind her, Alasdair sucked in a deep breath, trying to drive away some of the lust engulfing him. He could not recall being so aroused in his life.

"Damnation! I'm daft," he muttered, approaching the mantel and leaning an arm upon it. He should not have accosted her with such force. Likely she would never speak to him again, and who could blame her? He was no gentleman. Nay, he was a rogue, in truth. But her sweet delicious mouth. Her soft breast...in his hand...it had fit so perfectly. Her nipple peaked, aroused. He would give near anything to taste it, draw it into his mouth. Her silky skin and her scent seduced him. Thought deserted him when he touched her. The wanting near consumed him. He turned into naught more than an animal that craved to have her beneath him. The drive to taste, to claim, to possess clutched at his gut.

Though he was loath to admit it, she was amazing to him...lovely beyond words. He could never tire of looking into her blue eyes, like the summer sky, and he could not yet comprehend all he saw there—intelligence, sensuality, caring. More. His carnal side said he could never allow her to leave. But deep in his vitals he knew if she stayed, he might well lose his heart. Again. And what if she left after that? He could not bear to give up another woman he loved. The last one had near killed him.

Nay, he must control his carnal urges. Though when he was in her presence, controlling himself was the most difficult thing on earth.

The clan...that's what he must focus on. They would be occupied for the next several days rebuilding the village, replacing the roofs. He would spend all his time working with the men, and he would have no time or energy to think about the lady who had bewitched him.

⁓᷂ ᷂⁓

Four days later, Gwyneth paused on her way into the village alehouse where the midday meal for the workers would be served. Bright sunlight gleamed down, heating her skin and brightening her mood. She had hardly seen or spoken to Alasdair during the past few days. He had kept himself occupied, and she had as well. Still, it was impossible to forget the shocking but delectable incident in the library.

Padraig, one of the soldiers who'd been injured in the attack, stood by the door, his attention focused on the men thatching roofs across the way.

"How are you feeling, Padraig?" she asked.

He jerked as if she'd burned him. "M'lady, pray pardon. I didn't see you there." He bowed, cradling his wounded arm. "I'm much better. Thanks to God for blessing you with healing skills."

"I'm glad you're recovering." She strode inside the alehouse where several female servants worked, removing food from baskets and readying it for all the workers. The stone floor and walls of the building still smelled of smoke, but the new timbers and fresh thatch overhead gave her a feeling of hope. Gwyneth put down her loaves of bread on a new table near the back which she'd covered with a cloth earlier.

"I would much rather be on one of the roofs," Padraig said behind her.

She jumped and turned. Was he following her?

"Nonsense, sir. You are not yet well enough to help with the thatching."

"But I will be soon, thanks to you," he said eagerly. His craggy face looked ruddy in the dimness. "'Tis glad I am that you came to our clan."

Good lord! Surely he was not thinking to court her.

"Would you like a piece of bread? It's still warm from the oven." After slicing a thick chunk from the loaf, she handed it to him, hoping to halt his talkativeness.

"Many thanks. You are most kind, m'lady. Most kind, indeed."

While she sliced bread, he launched into a tale about a cow and three lads. She laughed and realized Rory would love the story. Where was he? She glanced about and saw him playing nearby with

112

another boy.

Before she turned her attention to the bread again, she caught sight of Alasdair standing just inside the door, watching her. Her pulse skittered like a startled rabbit and she pretended to ignore his progress in their direction.

Her hands were a bit unsteady on the knife handle as she continued her chore. She had not talked privately to him since the library incident. Well, truly, it wasn't an incident. It was an indulgence. One she must not fall into again.

"Padraig, how's the arm?" Alasdair asked in a boisterous tone.

"'Tis improving, m'laird. I was just telling Mistress Carswell about the time the demon cow run my two brothers and me to ground."

"Indeed? I wish I could've seen that." Alasdair's gaze upon Padraig was not as friendly as it should've been. The silence between the two men extended and the tension thickened. Pretending not to notice, Gwyneth continued with her task. *Slice, slice.*

Padraig cleared his throat. "Well, then. I must find Sweeney. Pray pardon." He bowed and ambled away.

Gwyneth glanced up at Alasdair and lifted a brow. Men. Could they do naught but compete in everything they did?

She tried to pretend their kiss of a few nights ago hadn't happened. A kiss and a bit more. *Do not think of it.* He had seemed to be avoiding her the past few days.

"Glad I am to see you here." The tightness had not left his face.

She tried to think of something intelligent, yet not flirtatious, to say. "I never thought I'd be serving food in an alehouse, but in this case it seems innocent enough."

Alasdair's expression lightened. "Aye. No carousing today."

Gazing into his dark eyes was like food for her soul, but she must not overindulge even in that small pleasure.

A thick post blocked them from most of the others in the large room and created a sense of privacy. Her awareness of him intensified. He smelled of fresh wood shavings, a few of which still clung to his kilt.

"But we'll be carousing during *Feill Sheathain* a week hence Midsummer's Eve or St. John's Day to you Sassenachs." He grinned. "'Haps even a lady such as yourself will let down her hair."

Good lord, the celebration was certain to be pagan...and beyond scandalous. She had been excluded from festivities while a part of the MacIrwin clan. Donald's idea of a celebration involved him and his soldiers, food and drink, and all the whores they could find. The common people of the clan were suppressed and barely given enough food to survive, even though they were the ones who did all the work.

"I do not think so, Laird MacGrath. I'm not much for that sort of thing."

"Well, you should be." He turned his head sideways and gazed down at her. "There is a time to mourn and a time to celebrate. We should throw ourselves wholly into each when the time comes. 'Tis a part of living. If we don't enjoy life when given the chance, then the chance may never come again."

His words sounded sage enough. She longed to live her life fully and enjoy it. But she didn't know how. Her circumstance for the past few years had been too uncertain.

In the next instant, Alasdair stepped in close behind her, and her awareness of him shot upward like a flaming arrow. His breath warmed her ear, and he brushed his lips across her temple. "Don't be afraid of living, Gwyneth."

Chills shimmered through her body. The knife slipped from her fingers and clattered on the table beside the bread.

Oh, good lord. Don't do this to me, Alasdair. Don't turn my body into a traitor.

He pulled back a few inches, slid something behind her ear and stroked a finger down the sensitive skin of her neck.

"What is...?" Her words trailed off on a breath. She inhaled the scent of wild roses even as she removed the smooth stem from behind her ear. A simple white rose with only a few petals and yellow stamens in the center. Emotion caught in her throat. *Alasdair.* She closed her eyes and pressed her nose to the flower, letting its lavish scent and his sweetness wash over her.

"I thank you," she whispered, not daring to let him see the moisture in her eyes.

He stepped back. "Och! Rory, what are you doing down there?"

Her son peered up at them from beneath the tablecloth. His hair stuck out in all directions, and his curious, wide-eyed gaze darted back and forth between them.

Alasdair chuckled. "You have the look of a wee hedgehog about you, lad."

Rory grinned and crawled out. "I saw a badger yesterday."

"Did you now? What did he look like?" Alasdair winked at her before they strolled away, Rory talking as fast as his tongue would move.

Gwyneth exhaled, releasing the tension and savoring the affection he conjured in her. After sniffing the rose once more, she slipped it into her pocket. She would not have anyone wondering what she was doing with a rose behind her ear, or what secret person might have given it to her. Feeling overheated of a sudden, she wished for a hand fan.

Straightening her spine, she picked up the knife and continued slicing the bread, though her hands were less steady than before.

I cannot allow him to weaken me with a rose...with his teasing touches and hot breath, whispering in my ear. I must remain strong at all costs.

Nothing but trouble would follow if she did lose her head. And though he was kind, he was a man like all others, interested in bedding whoever was willing and available...and caught his fancy. It was simply the way of men to pursue their baser sensual instincts.

Well, she was neither willing nor available.

Truly, I am not! I will not think of him anymore.

༺ ❦ ༻

"My lord, a messenger from Scotland is here to see you."

Maxwell Huntley, marquess of Southwick glanced up at his footman who bowed then straightened. Messenger from Scotland? Could it be that the MacIrwin barbarian was finally heeding his request?

"Show him into the library and wait with him. We don't want him to stuff his pockets with trinkets, now do we?"

"No, my lord. As you wish." He bowed again and retreated.

Southwick smiled. He'd written months ago to that damned MacIrwin, inquiring about his son. Finally, a response. He'd never met his son, nor did he know his name, but he would soon. This was the only son he'd ever have, so he had no choice but to find him. All he had to do now was figure out how to make him legitimate. But first he had to gain custody of him from his whore of a mother. That should prove easy enough given he was a marquess with powerful connections, and Gwyneth was...nothing.

Taking his time, Southwick stood and straightened his green brocade doublet and his white ruffled cuffs. He proceeded down the wide, ornate stairway to the library, where a footman opened the door for him. He entered to find another footman and a shabbily dressed messenger in a belted plaid. A barbaric Scots peasant, to be sure.

"M'laird." He bowed at least.

Southwick cringed at his accent. There was nothing that grated on his nerves more.

"Are you Laird Southwick?" the messenger asked.

"Indeed, I am Maxwell Huntley, marquess of Southwick. And who might you be?"

"Robertson, sir. Chief MacIrwin sent me to bring you this." He extended his hand and in it was a dirty, bent and folded missive.

Thankful he was wearing gloves, Southwick took the paper, broke the red wax seal and flung the paper open. Perching his spectacles upon his nose, he tilted the paper to the light from the tall, heavily-draped window and read. Well, he tried to read. The handwriting was near illegible. Something about his son. MacIrwin had him and if he wanted him, he must send two hundred pounds.

"Outrageous! Two hundred pounds is an outrageous sum! He is my son. Why should I have to pay for him?" he shouted at the messenger, who stepped back wide-eyed and bowed slightly.

A hostage. MacIrwin was using his son as a hostage, and this was the ransom. Bastard! Southwick squinted down at the paper again, trying to decipher more of its words. Whoever wrote it didn't use standard spellings, and it looked more like a sheep had written it. Damned Scots couldn't speak or write in a coherent manner. He crumpled the paper. Where in blazes would he get two hundred pounds silver? Certainly he was wealthy, but he didn't keep that much silver and gold lying around. He'd borrow funds from his friends, and ask a few of them to accompany him. He'd need plenty of guards.

"You are to take me to MacIrwin, and I do mean with great haste," Southwick said.

The messenger's eyes near bugged out of his head.

"You didn't think I was just going to hand you two hundred pounds, did you?"

"Eh…nay, my laird."

"Good. We leave at first light." It would take him all day, at least, to gather all the funds. MacIrwin was a thief and an outlaw!

ॐ ॐ

Two days after he'd talked to Gwyneth in the alehouse and given her the rose, Alasdair slipped into Leitha's flower garden, hoping Gwyneth would show up again so he might talk to her in private about nothing in particular until gloaming settled over the land. Or perhaps steal a kiss. The scent of sun-warmed roses brought their first kiss to the forefront of his mind, and he indulged in a bit of daydreaming. At a noise behind him, he glanced around, expecting to see Gwyneth, but found Rory gazing up at him with a trusting look of adoration.

Och. The lad needed a father, and Alasdair did not feel worthy or capable of filling such a lofty role. But at times like this, he wanted to try.

"A good eve to you, Rory."

"Will you teach me to fight with a sword?" The boy rushed forward, a small wooden sword in his hand and anticipation brightening his eyes.

How was he supposed to refuse such an eager request? The latest attack must have spurred the lad's protective instincts. And he truly did need to learn some weaponry skills, for he'd be a man one day. And he'd need to defend himself.

"Very well. I'll demonstrate a move or two." Alasdair removed his own basket-hilted broadsword from his scabbard, held it aloft and waited.

The lad mimicked his stance.

"See, Rory, hold the hilt of your sword just this way." Alasdair showed him the correct grip. "Try it."

"Like this?" Rory adjusted his grip on the rough mock weapon that one of the older clansmen had carved for him. The hilt was actually too big for his small hand.

"Aye, very good. Now, if one of the enemy clan comes at you directly in front, thrusting straight toward your chest, deflect the blow this way." Alasdair showed him the simple defense tactic.

The child repeated the move perfectly.

"Excellent! You're a natural."

His eyes alight, he grinned ear to ear. "Truly?" He even did a little bounce on his toes.

"Aye. 'Twas perfect." Och, the lad near carved his heart from his chest at times. Maybe because he looked so much like Gwyneth, with those blue eyes. Or 'haps it was because Rory made Alasdair realize how much he missed his own son.

But he must not dwell on the past. Here and now were the important things.

Rory stood beside him, awaiting the next instruction.

Alasdair backed up to give himself room. "Now, if the enemy is slashing from left to right, trying to take your head off, you would block the blow this way." He flicked his blade at the correct angle.

"What are you doing?" the incensed female voice echoed from

behind them.

Alasdair turned. Gwyneth stood with her fists propped on her narrow hips, her brows lowered, and her mouth crimped into a thin line.

Now I've gone and done it.

"He's showing me how to use a *claidheamh mòr*." Rory proudly demonstrated his new skills for his mother.

She stiffened. "Why don't you go find Little John Ray and show him? I need to talk to Laird MacGrath."

"Aye!" The boy ran from the garden.

"Do not run with that sword!"

"'Tis not real, Ma," Rory said as if she were daft.

"I know that, but you could still fall on it and hurt yourself."

Rory let out an impatient breath and walked the rest of the way.

Gwyneth faced Alasdair again and crossed her arms over her chest. He would like to kiss the tightness and annoyance from her lips. But first he would, without doubt, have to endure an unpleasant sort of tongue-lashing. He would much prefer the other type, a flick of her tongue against his lips, inside his mouth. Saints! He could not look at her without hot arousal stirring his blood.

"I do not want you teaching my son how to wield a blade," she said firmly.

Alasdair returned his broadsword to the scabbard at his hip. "And why is that, m'lady?"

Her face darkened. "Rory will not be a Highland warrior when he grows up. You people fight over everything. It's your favorite pastime. I tell you, killing should not be a pastime."

"'Tis a matter of survival. Do you think we invited the MacIrwins to burn the village? Nay. Every man must learn to defend himself and those he cares about. I make sure all the lads are trained so that when they become men, they can protect themselves, their families and the clan. If Rory grows up without knowing how to handle weapons, he will be at a disadvantage. If he is attacked, he will be unable to defend himself. Is that what you're wanting?"

"No. I just don't want him fighting, or using weapons at all," she said in a calmer but stubborn tone.

"You're a woman, and English at that. I don't expect you to understand what it means to be a man of the Highlands. But Rory has undoubtedly inherited his interest in swords and protecting his family from his father."

"From his father? That's preposterous."

"Baigh Shaw was ever a man who relished battle and fighting."

Gwyneth opened her mouth, then closed it. Twice. For a moment she reminded him of a grounded salmon. Then the skin of her face and throat turned that adorable pink color. He wondered if her whole body blushed in just that way during lovemaking.

"The p-point is…I will not allow Rory to learn to fight or go into battle. I am giving him an education, and he will one day find a good position in a safe place. He could be a scholar, perhaps a professor at university, or even a physician."

She had a grand dream for her son, and there was naught wrong with that, except it might not be what Rory wanted. When he grew up, he might wish to join the king's army instead. But Alasdair wouldn't deepen her anxiety. "Aye, I ken your meaning. No parent wants to think of their child in a dangerous circumstance."

"You're not a parent, so you cannot grasp the import of it."

Her words flayed him like the sharp edge of a blade. "You're right. I'm not a parent because my son died before he could be born."

Gwyneth pressed her eyes closed for a moment, and when she opened them, managed to look most contrite. "Pray pardon, my laird. I did not mean that," she said softly.

He didn't respond, but tried to lock his emotions away again. He didn't like them breaking free at the least provocation, nor did he wish to speak harshly to her.

"I only meant that, I don't want anyone to encourage Rory in his interest in swords," she said. "He's always fighting mock battles with imaginary people. I usually try to divert his attention to something else."

"'Tis a good habit. But you must realize the lad has a lot of Scots blood in him, and making him lose interest in fighting or weaponry will be a task. 'Tis natural. He was born to it. I was the same way as a lad. I was always hacking away at something with a wooden sword, as were my brother and cousins."

"That's fine. I'd just prefer you didn't show him any more techniques for killing people."

"I wasn't showing him how to kill people. I was showing him how to block the blows of blades coming at him, moves that could one day save his life."

She stared at the ground in silence and rubbed her forehead. He hoped she would think that over thoroughly, because a grown man who couldn't defend himself was as good as dead.

"He but wants to protect and defend his ma," Alasdair said.

"Did he tell you that?"

"Aye. When I was hurt and in your byre, he said he would protect you from the MacIrwin."

"I see."

He wasn't sure she did. "Even then, Rory knew Donald was evil and that you were afraid of him. Rory's a bright and canny lad, m'lady, and he's but trying to develop the skills he needs to be a man."

"He's only five," she said, her voice low and vulnerable.

Alasdair restrained the urge to take her into his arms and hold her, to soothe away the tension and fear. "He'll be six soon, but it doesn't matter his age. He's a lad without his da, so he feels 'tis his job to protect the women of his family—you."

"I must take him from the Highlands." She locked her determined gaze onto Alasdair's. "I'm sure Lachlan won't be back for weeks with news of a position in Edinburgh. Have you thought of a family I might find a position with?"

Here it was again, the task he didn't want to push forward with. It created too much turmoil within him. He'd already told her he didn't want her to leave. But it would be best for Gwyneth, Rory, and the MacGrath clan if she did. Still, Alasdair knew he was a greedy, selfish bastard. He wanted...

What did he want?

"I have thought on it some. But I know very few Lowland families. None come to mind with young children."

"What about your in-laws?"

"I've had little contact with them for some time. Perhaps one of Leitha's brothers or sisters would be in need of a governess. I'll send a letter."

Her face brightened. "I would be in your debt."

And what he would like in payment was a kiss. But how ridiculous he was—like a green lad on the edge of becoming a man, gazing at a pretty lass.

How he would love to be the cause of the happiness she now showed. But it was the prospect of leaving the Highlands—of leaving him—that filled her with joy.

"I thank you for your recommendation, Laird MacGrath."

"You're welcome. And 'tis Alasdair," he corrected for the thousandth time. After the intimate way he'd touched her in the library, he couldn't believe she would address him so formally, especially when they were alone. Clearly, she was trying to push him away.

She sobered, a guarded expression falling into place. "Very well, Alasdair."

He shouldn't have said anything. He preferred her smiling and carefree. She had the look of a very young lass then.

But he did savor the sound of his name on her lips. More than that, he wanted to savor her lips, feel them open beneath his, the way they did when he'd kissed her. She had invited him inside with warmth and ardor as if unable to control herself. Would she do that again now?

His expression must have changed for when her eyes met his, a sudden look of alarm crossed her features. "I must be off to see what Rory is into." With a swish of her skirts Gwyneth turned and left.

He thought about calling her back but knew it would be folly. It was best that he not touch her again.

At midmorning several days later, Alasdair returned to his bedchamber to retrieve an old dagger he wished to let one of the villagers borrow. He halted when he found Gwyneth making his bed.

The sight of her bending over, touching the linens that had lain next to his naked skin the night before jolted him.

"You're not a chambermaid."

She spun around. "You startled me!"

"I only wished that you oversee the servants and make sure they do the work. Not do it yourself." He could not abide watching her do household chores. He knew not why, but something about that felt very wrong.

"Willamena is sick, and I've taken over her chores," Gwyneth said.

"You should've assigned it to someone else. You're a lady." He knew, without doubt, she was from the aristocratic class, though she refused to admit it. He could not fathom why.

She frowned and her eyes glinted with mysterious pain. A pain he yearned to get to the bottom of. What had happened in her past?

"I will earn my keep as well as my son's," she said with fierce pride.

"You've more than earned it with your healing skills. You saved my life and, to me, that's worth a hefty sum."

"Nevertheless..."

He paced toward the chest, trying to remember why he'd come.

His attention strayed to Gwyneth as she approached the door.

"Um," he said, hoping to stop her before she left. Why? He wanted to look at her a bit longer, listen to her soothing voice.

She turned. "You wanted something?"

Aye, I want something. Alasdair held himself back from suffocating in the blue of her eyes, bright as the loch reflecting the clear sky. "You must have been avoiding the garden of late." *And the kisses.*

Her face flushed, but she held his gaze. "I would not wish to...cause a problem."

"'Twould not be a problem, lass." The only problem was that he wanted to kiss her again, but she'd made herself scarce. He longed for her cool hands to stroke over his naked skin, both inciting and soothing at once. He yearned to know what lingered in the depths of her thoughts. What did she want and need? What did she feel when he kissed her? Did she hunger the way he did?

She swallowed hard and stared at something behind him.

"Gwyneth." Just saying her name aroused him as it would have to trail his tongue up her neck.

Her eyes darkened when she gauged his expression. He knew his desire must be written on his face. It had been a long time since he'd invited a woman into his bed, and his body was rebelling from the lack.

"What say you?" he asked.

"About...what, Laird MacGrath?"

She was attempting to remind him of his place, but he didn't want to remember. He wanted only to be a man for a few minutes, and she a woman.

"What would you say if I locked the door and—" He inhaled a ragged breath, unable to vocalize what he wanted. So much.

She gasped. "No, you must not," she whispered. "'Tis not proper."

"Nay, not proper at all." The fantasies playing through his mind threatened to render him senseless. Images of her naked beneath him, on top of him...squirming, arching bodies. The slide of her bare smooth skin across his. He was famished for the sweet, female taste of her. He wished to fill all his senses with naught but her.

"But 'tis beyond appealing to think about," he murmured.

"Appalling, you mean."

"Oh, nay, m'lady." She didn't mean that; she couldn't. 'Twas obvious she'd relished those earlier kisses as much as he had.

She eased toward the door again, but he moved quicker and closed it in front of her. *Hell. What am I doing? I should let her go.*

His hand on the door, he tried to calm his need. *Have I lost my mind?* He wouldn't do anything except touch her face, kiss her. Then he would stop. He would not dishonor her. He but wanted to cherish her for a moment. One stolen moment in time…for him and for her, amid all the thousands of hours of duty that devoured his time. Did they each not deserve a moment to enjoy something exquisite?

"Sir, this is not…this would not be wise."

She was right of course. 'Twas foolhardy and reckless. Yet it was something he had to have, and whether she admitted it or not, something she also wanted.

"One kiss and you're free to go." By the saints, he did have the same blood as Lachlan running through his veins. Alasdair hadn't used his seduction skills in so long they were rusty as a sword from the sea.

He inched closer to her, but in an attempt to restrain his primal impulses, pressed his forehead to his fist against the door. He didn't touch her, though his fingers ached to stroke her silky skin. "The kiss in the garden," he said. "And the one in the library…I cannot get either out of my head. Do you ever think of them?"

CHAPTER NINE

Gwyneth couldn't look Laird MacGrath in the eye when he said such things, reminding her of the lascivious kisses they'd shared. He stirred up a cauldron of wicked feelings inside her. Desires she thought she'd experienced before, but hadn't. Her first seduction had been nothing compared to this.

Alasdair's clean, woodsy-musk scent teased the side of her that reveled in sensuality, tempted her to press her nose to his chest and breathe him in. Clearly, he had bathed this morn in a pleasant-scented soap.

He leaned against the door as if she might escape. She should've fled earlier, just as he'd entered. The rational part of her knew this. But now a battle waged within her, and her sensual side craved naught but being pinned beneath his strong body.

"I guess you've forgotten both kisses, then," he murmured. "They were naught, aye?"

Was he mad? She could think of little else. The kisses would remain her fondest memories. She had to leave this place, leave the enticement of this man.

Though her reputation and virtue were in tatters, she had tried to gather the mended shreds about her in these last few years. But he inspired her to set a torch to them. He drew her to him like iron filings to a lodestone, and when she looked into his eyes or stood in his presence, she questioned the value of reputation and virtue. They seemed cold, lifeless companions when she faced the brilliant, life-affirming heat of him.

"I remember the kisses," she admitted, pressing her back against the solid wood of the door. "Indeed, how could I not?" *I relive them every night. And every time I see you during the busy, tiresome days.*

His eyes, black as the depths of sin, trapped her. She couldn't help but trust him, couldn't help but put herself under his control.

"Why can I not turn away from you?" she whispered.

He released a ragged breath. "'Haps the same reason I cannot turn from you. 'Tis beyond my strength."

And clearly he had impressive strength, but whatever drew them together was far more powerful.

She moved toward him. "I shouldn't do this again."

But she did.

She slid her fingers into his dark hair and met his delectable lips with her own. *Ahh.* She had dreamed of this, relived his kisses so often, it seemed Alasdair had kissed her a hundred times. But he hadn't, not like this. She had not remembered each nuance—the wet warmth of his mouth, his arousing masculine taste, the way his whisker stubble rasped her chin and upper lip, the way his big hands framed her waist and pulled her close.

She opened her mouth, hoping he'd slide his tongue inside and flick it across hers. When he did, her knees lost all strength. With a groan, he caught her to the solid muscles of his body and lifted her, stroking her over his stone-hard shaft. She squirmed and wrapped her arms around his neck. She craved him beyond all reason.

Why this intensity? She could scarce breathe. His lips ate at hers, his tongue tasted and seduced.

He kissed a teasing trail down her neck and sparked sensations through her breasts without even touching them. Oh, her nipples were hard, craving the heat and suction of his mouth savoring them.

She murmured a sound between a gasp and a moan before she could squelch it. How scandalous she was, but she could not renounce her needs.

Harsh breaths escaping him, he set her down gently and tried to hold her away from him, even as he kept pressing light kisses to her mouth. "Sweet Mother Mary, I believe you're right, m'lady. Not wise."

She didn't want it to end, this dream, this sensual haven. She had experienced what went on between a man and a woman on a few occasions, but never had she yearned for it this badly. He was like a lodestone, and she could not back away.

Already, she missed the heat and solidity of his body. She followed him when he retreated, unable to smother her wanton hunger.

"Let me lock the door." He lowered his lashes, half concealing the dark desire that burned in his eyes.

She couldn't respond to such a request, for the implications far outreached the simple statement.

I can't do this.

Yet, she had to. It was not in her power to say no. She needed him too much.

"M'lady—Gwyneth," he whispered against her ear. "I'm wanting you now as I've never wanted another woman. You have damn well bewitched me, and all I can think of is being inside you, taking you over and over."

Good heavens! Such shocking words he spoke. But, because of them, she ached.

"What say you? Do you want me as well?"

She grasped all her courage together. "Yes, I want you... Alasdair," she whispered.

"Och! Dear God, how is this possible?"

She wondered the same thing. How could she have happened upon such a treasure as him? And such undeniable passion?

With a click of the key turning in the lock, he shielded them from the intrusion of the outside world. For this beautiful moment, he was hers alone in the intimacy of his bedchamber.

He picked her up, flush against his body, and kissed her...a deep devouring kiss. She perceived that he withheld nothing, but infused this kiss with his soul, and all his hunger. So fogged was her rationality, she didn't realize they'd moved across the room until he lowered her to his bed.

He drew his shirt over his head, removed his sporran, but left his kilt belted at his waist. Viewing the sprinkling of dark hair over the battle-honed muscles of his chest and abdomen was a wicked indulgence. His eyes gleamed with seductive promises, anticipation, but what she treasured most was the care and compassion she saw there. This was a man such as she never knew existed. He would not selfishly take from her; he'd give her what she craved, generously.

Standing at the edge of the bed, watching her with eyes near dark as onyx, he gently pushed up her petticoats and skirts. His rough hands smoothing up her thighs above the tops of her stockings sent chills over her body.

"Mmm...Gwyneth." He crawled onto the bed, between her legs, and kissed her neck, licked a trail down toward her breasts where they were pushed up by her corset.

With a muttered Gaelic word, he pressed kisses to the upper

swells of her breasts and slid his tongue along her cleavage.

A sharp yearning speared her, and she mindlessly thrust her hips toward him where he hovered over her. "Oh," she gasped.

His hand beneath her skirts, he caught her and cradled her derriere. At the touch of his warm palm rasping her delicate skin, she grew impatient and pulled him closer.

Gazing into her eyes, he stroked gentle fingers through her moisture, parting the sensitive lips of her sex. Drawing air between his teeth, he hissed, his eyes almost closing.

Such forbidden cravings that he elicited stole her thoughts and reasoning. "Alasdair?"

"Mmm, I wish I had time to take off every stitch of your clothing. But I'm on the edge. I cannot take another minute of your tempting."

He couldn't be talking about her. Yet when he gazed at her with such raw intensity, she knew he told her true.

Shifting, he brought her hand down to his sleek hard shaft. Fever-hot and generously proportioned. She wrapped her fingers around him, marveling at how exquisitely made he was.

His eyes drifted closed and his jaw tightened at her touch. Though she should be embarrassed, she wasn't. The feel of him was heaven. And she wanted him, that part of him, inside her. She squeezed and stroked.

"You're amazing," she whispered and couldn't help the way her voice trembled.

"Och, lass." He shook his head, his hair tickling over her face. "You're the one who's amazing. You're my undoing."

"I want you now," she whispered, unable to tolerate the aching need any longer.

"Aye." Drawing near, he kissed her, flicked his tongue between her lips in an erotic echo. "Guide me into you," he murmured against her mouth.

"Yes." How he aroused her and empowered her, giving her control over their lovemaking. She stroked the broad tip of his shaft through her moisture. "Oh. That feels…" *Splendid.* Her yearning for him magnified. She positioned him just where she wanted him.

His muscles bunched, and he slid in, slowly stretching her with sublime fullness. "Beautiful," he moaned in an awed tone against her ear, blocking out her own frenetic sounds. "You are so…beautiful. Gwyneth. Mmm." He inched slowly deeper.

Yes, yes! She wanted to give herself over to him completely. She wanted him to pin her down, thrust hard, fast and without restraint. Instead, he held himself still and rigid within her, scarcely breathing, as if savoring their erotic bond.

"Please," she whispered. "Alasdair."

"Aye, *m'eudail.*" In that moment, he seemed to understand what she needed for he withdrew and plunged in deeper, again and again, becoming slicker, sliding easier each time. His movements came faster, more forcefully.

Oh, she could scarce believe what carnal bliss.

"Saints!" he growled.

It seemed she had never experienced this before, because never had the joining given her such an upheaval of pleasure. But not just pleasure—magnitude, a depth of meaning. Something this thrilling had to be sinful, but she felt no shame.

Her body burned where it joined with his. She couldn't discern her own breaths from his against her lips. She was as close to him as she could get, yet she grasped him to her, wanting closer, more, wanting to touch all of him at once. Her clothing was a hateful barrier between them. Craving his naked skin against her own, she wrapped her legs around his, and her arms around his neck.

And the way he moved, undulating. He slid in a fluid motion, thrusting to her depths and away, fast and powerfully. What magic.

"*Mo dia,* Gwyneth," he rasped between kisses. "You're so lovely." He watched her, gazed into her soul. As if he understood and felt what she did. As if he was wholly there with her, drowning in this ocean of madness. He was. He had to be; she saw it in his eyes.

Her corset turned sweltering and constricting. She couldn't breathe deeply enough.

A hot tingling began in her center where he slid. It gathered speed and intensity. A breathless sensation gripped her and the pleasure crashed in on itself, magnified, seized her thoughts.

What's happening? I'm dying! She screamed, but Alasdair closed his mouth over hers, muffling her sounds. She pulled him harder against her. She wanted him all the way inside. More, more, more.

She reveled in a moment of reckless abandon such as she never allowed herself. And if she truly were dying, there could be no better way to go.

But she didn't die. She'd never felt more alive. Joy bubbled up inside her, and she laughed. The pleasure flowed away from her in little waves. Alasdair chose that moment to growl, drive himself to the hilt and pour into her. From his fierce expression, he seemed in pain. But she knew he was experiencing the same rapture she had. She had only thought men did that. She had not known a woman could find her release, or enjoy this act so thoroughly.

Just as he withdrew, someone pounded at the door of the bedchamber, shattering the sensual spell woven around them.

"Oh, no." Gwyneth struggled from beneath Alasdair. She yanked down her skirts, stood and adjusted her clothing. "No one must find me here."

Not yet recovered from his climax, Alasdair glared at the door and muttered Gaelic words amid harsh breaths. "Don't fash yourself, lass," he whispered, then yelled *"Fuirich mionaid!"* at the person on the other side of the door. Breath calming, he lazily stood, pulled his shirt on over his head and moved toward the door.

She scurried behind it. "Do not let them in."

He shook his head and opened the door a crack to peer out. "Aye?"

"Is everything all right?" a man outside the door asked.

"Aye. I was but changing my shirt."

Alasdair closed the door and approached her. He stroked his fingers beneath her chin and pressed a sweet kiss to her lips. "Gwyneth," he said as if the word itself were sacred. "You're a treasure more fine than ever I touched."

Vulnerability rolled through her and threatened to fill her eyes with tears. She had made her own choice, and she was glad.

I refuse to regret it.

"Are you well?" His dark brows furrowed with concern.

She nodded.

"Did I hurt you?"

She shook her head. What he'd made her feel was far from pain, but now...

His worried gaze lingering on her, he stepped away and stuffed his shirttail beneath his kilt and fastened the top portion with his brooch.

She faced the door and waited for him to finish. *Upon my faith, what have I done?* Any woman who followed her body's urges was full of folly, was she not?

Alasdair moved in front of her, tipped her chin up and studied her. "I'll tell no one. 'Tis our secret, aye?"

She nodded and said nothing, though inside she was screaming, *I should not have.*

He pressed a quick, firm kiss to her lips, then stepped back. "I'll check the corridor and if no one is about, you can slip away to your bedchamber."

He peered out, then motioned to her. She slunk along to her room, feeling like the lowest of thieves.

⚜

That afternoon, the sun beamed down brightly as Alasdair oversaw the thatching of the last roofs of the villagers' cottages. He stood aside, away from the crowd, watching his strong clansmen on the roofs, working hard, but laughing and joking as was their habit.

But neither thatch nor jokes could hold Alasdair's attention. His mind drifted back to three hours earlier, in his bedchamber.

Gwyneth.

How lush and lovely she was. Eager and sensual.

Saints! He hadn't expected to bed her today. Or ever, in truth. He'd thought her resistance would prove unmovable. Not so. 'Twas a flood of the best luck he'd ever had.

His erection swelled, tingling for her again, and he was glad for his sporran, preventing his plaid rising in front. She was an astounding woman. So sweet and passionate. The way she'd wanted him so badly compounded his own desire. He had always loved bringing a woman to the height of ecstasy. That Gwyneth had responded and experienced it so quickly had taken away the last vestiges of his control and he'd gone hurtling over the edge of delirious pleasure.

Though he could never give his heart to another woman the way he had to Leitha, maybe taking another wife would not be such a bad idea, as Lachlan had suggested. Perhaps Alasdair should propose a hand-fasting to Gwyneth. He needed an heir after all, and Gwyneth was obviously fertile, given that she had Rory.

Planting his seed within her would be no duty, but boundless pleasure. Och! He would relish bedding her every night, and sometimes during the day, to make sure she was pregnant. Imagining her carrying his child within her stirred up all sorts of primal urges and he craved her again. Now.

⚜

Heaven help me, what have I done?

Gwyneth paced from the window to the cold hearth in her room. She had fallen for a man's charming seduction yet again. She felt seventeen, just as vulnerable and stricken with panic.

What if someone finds out? What if I'm with child?

Only this time she had no naïve, romantic illusions. She knew there would be no offer for her hand, and she didn't want one. She rather looked at it like England's former queen, Elizabeth—Gwyneth would never again subject herself to the whims of a man.

Likely Alasdair would turn his back on her now and treat her like so much gutter rubbish. It was the way of men. Once they had their physical release and their curiosity satisfied, they were off to more interesting, prettier women.

She had not even been able to keep her despicable husband's attention—which she was heartily glad of. After three times, Baigh Shaw had shunned her and searched out his favorite village whores. She imagined they'd shown far more enthusiasm toward him in bed than she had.

But with Alasdair, she was afraid her enthusiasm had been abundantly clear. How she had wanted him! She could've eaten him up like a honey drenched comfit. Hellish heat burned her cheeks at the memory of her wanton abandon. She'd been possessed of a wicked pleasurable release for several moments. Oh, the noises she'd made. He would think her the most lurid of whores.

Yet, she couldn't forget the way he'd looked into her eyes as he drove into her over and over, giving her ecstasy so profound she must have imagined it. Unearthly. Magical.

He'd been fully present with her, fully aware it was she whom he was bonding his body with. His attention to her own pleasure demolished all her feeble expectations. He was a man who knew how to make love to a woman. A man who knew how to make said woman daydream about him all day, wondering when she might let herself be seduced again.

I'm a harlot. Not in name only this time, but in truth.

She strode quickly to the village kirk and prayed earnestly for forgiveness, her tear-stained cheeks burning with mortification. Though when she returned to the castle an hour later and saw Alasdair crossing the barmkin with a stranger dressed in the English style, she knew she truly wasn't sorry for her sin. The temptation of Alasdair gripped her anew and refused to let her go. Her body heated and she craved him.

I've gone mad.

Surely she had. What other explanation could there be for repeating the same behavior that had destroyed her life six years ago?

What devastating effects would it have on her life this time? If she already carried Alasdair MacGrath's babe within her, what would he do? Shun her? Take his child from her and send her away? Would looking at her disgust him? He wouldn't marry her—that much she knew. He was an earl after all, a peer, though not as stuffy as those who lived in London. A nobleman didn't take a fallen woman to wife.

Do not even think of it. He will turn his back on you. He will have no respect for you. You are a weak, sinful woman.

ೂ೭ ೨ಎ

"My good man, your cook is improving." Edward Murray, Earl of Hennessy, sat to Alasdair's right during the evening meal. The squat man, a Lowlander who fancied himself English, had attended university with Alasdair in Edinburgh. Edward had holdings in the Highlands and was passing through on his yearly inspection of them.

"I'm glad to hear it." In truth, Alasdair was so distracted he could hardly hold a coherent conversation, or taste the delicious beef roast Cook had prepared. His encounter earlier in the day with Gwyneth was still impressed like a searing brand on his memory.

The moment she entered the great hall, he knew it, and his eyes followed her with a will of their own. How lovely she was, enigmatic. Innocent-looking, yet with a depth of passion he could hardly fathom. Small and soft and affectionate but with an inner strength of steel.

He yearned for her by his side, now and always, to take her meals with him so that he might enjoy looking into her eyes and talking about nothing in particular. He wanted her close enough that he might touch her anytime he wished. He would make her smile and laugh as she had during their lovemaking. She needed happiness and he would do everything in his power to provide it.

"I say, is that Lady Gwyneth Carswell?" Edward watched her with bulging eyes, his jaw slack. "What is she doing here?"

Alasdair experienced a moment of silent shock. Edward knew who she was? "She is in my employ. Why? What do you ken of her?" He hated the way Edward gaped at her.

The man covered his mouth with a napkin and coughed as if the astonishment of seeing her had near strangled him. He took a long swig of ale.

"I know her family well."

Alasdair sensed he was about to learn more about Gwyneth than he'd ever expected to. "Is that so?"

"Indeed." Edward lifted thin brown brows. "I wonder, did she ever marry?"

"Aye, to Baigh Shaw." *The fiendish whoreson.*

Edward's pale eyes rounded. "So she found someone to marry after all. Shocking."

Alasdair frowned. "Why would it be shocking that she marry?"

"You don't know?"

"Mayhap you should enlighten me." Alasdair ground his teeth, his mood growing darker.

Edward leaned forward and lowered his voice to a near whisper. "Well, you see, a few years ago at a masque in London, she placed herself in a most compromising position with a higher up peer, the marquess of Southwick to be precise. He escaped to the continent, and she was left carrying his bastard." Edward cringed melodramatically.

Numbness settled over Alasdair. It was much better not to think or feel.

"A tragedy really," Edward went on. "Her father disowned her and sent her, I believe, to live with relatives here in the Highlands. But that would not be you, would it? I had no idea you were related to the Earl of Darrow."

Alasdair barely shook his head, unable to comprehend what all of this meant. Rory was not Baigh Shaw's son, but some English marquess's? Of that he was glad, strangely. Why had she not told him? And Gwyneth was the daughter of an earl? He had been right about her noble upbringing, but he hadn't imagined the rest of it. No-nonsense, uptight Gwyneth, who blushed at a mere glance or a smile…ah, but she was indeed a sensual woman, and tempting to any man. Perhaps a rogue much like himself had seduced her. He couldn't imagine her as the butt of such a widely known scandal. How painful that must have been for her.

"Alasdair, are you quite well?" Edward glanced over his shoulder. "Do not tell me a specter has passed behind my chair." He laughed.

Alasdair's mind worked overtime, trying to put together all the missing links. "I am providing her protection from her cousin, the MacIrwin. He's trying to kill her because she saved my life. I was wounded in battle on MacIrwin land. She is a healer and came to my rescue."

"My lord, man. Damned astonishing! Are you fully recovered?"

"Aye. I owe her my life, so I will provide her and her son protection as long as needs be."

"Her son, yes. Is that him there?" Edward pointed toward the table in the far corner where servants and children sat on benches. Gwyneth placed a bowl of food before Rory.

"Aye. He's a fine lad, sharp and canny. He'll be good with a sword one day."

"'Tis indeed fortunate for her that scandal doesn't carry this far north."

"I don't care what kind of scandal is attached to her name. She is a good woman who saved my life." Annoyance simmered in his blood.

Edward seemed impervious to his brusque tone. "And you are a good man, Alasdair. A noble man. Would that there were more like you in Scotland. And England."

Alasdair didn't know if Edward was being sincere, nevertheless he had to treat him as an honored guest. "How long will you be staying with us, then, Edward?"

"If you wouldn't mind, I'd like to stay tonight and be on my way in the morn."

"You're welcome to stay as long as you like, of course, beyond Midsummer's Day if you wish it."

"Highland hospitality is always impressive, especially yours, Alasdair. But I have business in London, and I must hie back as soon as I can. You must come to visit sometime. I daresay you would enjoy London."

"No offense, but 'tis doubtful." Alasdair forced a dry smile. There was naught he hated more than the stench and crowds of big cities. The fresh, crisp Highland air and beautiful scenery were what he loved.

Edward laughed and clapped him on the shoulder. "I know— you prefer the rustic life up here in the middle of nowhere."

"God's country," Alasdair corrected.

"True, true! But you must remember, our own king is of Scottish birth, and he much prefers London."

"Our own king lacks a certain fondness for Highlanders. He would have our Gaelic tongues ripped from our mouths if he had his way."

"Indeed, but that, my friend, will never happen. Highlanders are far too stubborn to give up something so important as their language. Hell, they will not even give up a dram of whisky."

"Och, there you're wrong!" Alasdair grinned. "I'll give you a hundred drams if that's what you're wanting."

"I could accept one or two." He nodded eagerly.

Alasdair took Edward to the library, filled him with whisky and pumped him for more information on Gwyneth's family and the scandal.

"Gwyneth's father, I tell you, he is the staunchest Protestant you shall ever care to meet." Edward slumped back on the couch and gulped the whisky as if it were water and his tongue near parched. "He won't go near anyone who's been touched by scandal. And he gives the king himself a wide berth. Doesn't care for his friends and favorites."

"I don't care if I ever see London again," Alasdair said. "One visit ten years ago was enough for me."

"One visit?" Edward cackled, obviously well on his way to cup-shotten. "You are even worse off than I thought."

"Tell me more of Southwick," Alasdair said, ignoring his friend's ribbing.

"Maxwell Huntley," Edward pronounced in a haughty tone. "*Sixth* marquess of Southwick, mind you. As pompous as a prince. Got most of his money from the duke of Watley's daughter, whom he married shortly after the scandal. She died several months ago. I assume he is sniffing out another heiress to refill his coffers and provide him an heir."

"Sounds like a right whoreson bastard."

Edward burst out laughing. "Indeed! Indeed, my good man!"

So what had Gwyneth seen in Southwick? Had she been in love with him? Or was she a light-skirt and he particularly persuasive. He hated thinking of her with a horse's arse like Southwick. This was almost as bad as imagining her with the murdering Shaw.

He would get to the bottom of her lies and deceptions soon enough. And he would not suffer her to hold anything back from him.

⁊◉ ◉⁊

The next evening after dark, Alasdair paced before the cold fireplace in his bedchamber. Only a tallow candle on the mantel lit the room to a dim gloom. Before Edward's revelation, Alasdair had near decided to ask Gwyneth to marry him, or at least hand-fast. No doubt of it, he'd compromised her, and a bairn might be the result. He would protect her and provide for her, and Rory as well. He didn't truly want to get himself into the position again of having a wife he could come to love and then lose. But, unthinking, he had followed his own instinctive urges. Urges he could not resist when she'd shown she wanted him as much as he'd wanted her. Their

135

attraction was irresistible and spellbinding.

Why had Gwyneth not told him about Rory's natural father? Was it because she was ashamed of the scandal, or did she not trust Alasdair?

Something else still nagged him in the back of his mind. Her situation with Shaw matched up too conveniently with Alasdair's father's murder. What was it? He had a gut feeling something wasn't right. He must ask her.

He strode out of his chamber and down the corridor toward the room Gwyneth used. He pounded a fist against the door.

After a moment, Tessie opened the door, and her eyes near popped out of her head. "Laird MacGrath!"

"Aye." He spotted Gwyneth in a wooden bathtub set before the fireplace. "Leave us." He strode forward, inhaling a whiff of the floral and herb scented steam that arose from her bath.

Gwyneth gasped and started to sit up, but then grabbed her smock and spread it over the water to further shield herself. He didn't know why. He'd been deep inside her yesterday morn. And he wanted that again. Now. Arousal flooded him, heating his blood.

He glanced back and found Tessie fidgeting in the doorway.

"Tell no one I'm here."

"Aye, m'laird." At his stern glare, she scurried out and closed the door with a click.

After locking the door, he dropped the key into his sporran and turned his attention back to Gwyneth. He would not have her leaving before he had his answers.

"Won't you at least allow me to dry off and dress properly?" She sat, red-faced and huddling beneath the smock.

"No need. I but want a minute of your time."

Her ice-blue eyes glittered. Good, he liked getting her passions worked up.

Moving closer, he placed his hands upon his hips. "Why did you lead me to believe Baigh Shaw was Rory's father?"

Her mouth dropped open. "What? How did you—?" Her eyes narrowed. "That Englishman who left this morn, earl of... something."

"Aye, Hennessy. Edward Murray. He's a Lowlander."

"Well, I assume he told you everything, so there's nothing left for me to say," she stated in her haughty Sassenach accent. "I shall leave in the morn."

"What are you blathering on about? You'll be staying right

here." The mere thought of her departing twisted his gut.

"I will be an embarrassment to your clan."

"No one knows, save me. And even if they did, what of it? The Highlands are full of bastards. So is England. Some even accused your former queen of illegitimacy, aye?"

Gwyneth's face reddened. "At least Rory has a name besides mine own," she said softly.

"Your name would be preferred to Baigh Shaw's," Alasdair growled.

"You are a man. You cannot understand what it is like for a woman in my situation."

"Nay, but I'm not daft. Why Baigh Shaw?" *Why not anyone but that outlaw whoreson?*

Gwyneth stared down into the water. "He was the only man willing to give my son a name. I didn't marry him until Rory was three months old."

"And exactly how old is Rory now?"

"He will be six next month."

Alasdair did the calculations in his head. If Rory had been born in July, and he was three months old when Gwyneth married Shaw, that would've made it October. Shaw had murdered Alasdair's father that same month.

Shaw was naught but a commoner and an assassin. And he would not have been worthy enough for Gwyneth to wipe her slippers on before she was expelled from her family and social position for her indiscretion. Gwyneth was a beautiful woman. Shaw likely lusted over her and, of course, had no concern for any scandal in faraway London. To marry so far above his station would've been an added reward.

"Tell me," Alasdair began, "how did your marriage to Shaw come about?"

"What do you mean?"

"You needed a name for your son. And what did Shaw need?"

She pressed her eyes closed and clenched her jaw. "What do you think? Someone to…warm his bed, of course."

The image revolted Alasdair. He couldn't fathom this woman, whom he craved and dreamed about, in bed with the man he'd hated most in the world. Unable to look at her another moment, he turned away and gripped the back of the chair by the bed. The hard oak wood bit into his palm. He felt as he did when ambushed—he wanted to destroy something.

He pulled in a deep, cooling breath. "And Donald, was he involved in the marriage arrangements?"

"Of course. I was his ruined cousin, and he wanted to get me married off. He didn't care whom I married. The fact that his friend and most loyal follower wanted me pleased him."

Alasdair forced himself to look at her again.

Her wide blue eyes were deceptively innocent, her lush lips alluring. Her bare shoulders above the water, and the knowledge she was naked beneath, aroused him fully. He imagined the rosy tips of her breasts, yearned to see them peeking from the water. The urge to yank her from the bath and drape her wet body over his near overpowered him. He hoped she couldn't see how he trembled from the waning rage and the burgeoning desire. His reaction shamed and alarmed him. No woman took his control. None! He'd come here for answers to his questions, and he would have them.

"Precisely when did the marriage take place?" he asked with considerably more calm than he felt.

"October in the year of our Lord 1612."

"What day?"

She frowned. "The twenty-fifth. Why?"

God's bones. This was no coincidence. A cold frisson spiraled down his spine. "A week after my father's murder. Do you not think it strange that the two events happened so close together?"

"Yes, I do." She stared down into the bath for a moment, then lifted her open—dare he say trusting?—gaze to him. "You think I was Donald's payment to Baigh for murdering your father, do you not?"

"Were you?" He managed not to growl the words…just barely.

"Possibly. I heard the two of them talking one night about some kind of bargain. Donald told Baigh he could marry me if he followed through with his end of it. They didn't say what the task was, but they left the castle and returned two days later. A few days after that, Baigh and I were married. Nothing about the bargain was ever mentioned again."

"I see." It was true, then. Everything he'd suspected. Yet, what did it matter? Even if she was payment, Gwyneth was still innocent of any wrongdoing. Baigh was still the murderer… a dead murderer. There wasn't enough evidence to implicate Donald, even if he did hire someone to kill his enemy and used a woman as payment.

Alasdair's anger at Gwyneth drained away and left him feeling raw. She had done naught wrong—not to him or his father, only to herself.

"Rory doesn't know Baigh isn't his father, and I would appreciate it if no one tells him," she said in a vulnerable tone.

"Your secret is safe with me. I ken your father is an earl, and that your correct title is indeed 'lady'. Why do you not use it?"

She shook her head, sadness in her eyes. "'Twould be a mockery."

His chest ached at the pain and humiliation she must have suffered, all because she'd trusted the wrong man. "Why did your father not force the scoundrel Southwick to marry you?"

Her blush reappeared, and she stared into the flames of the fireplace. "He fled to Spain or France. Besides, I had already told him of my condition, and he wasn't willing to do the right thing. He wanted someone more beautiful, someone with a much larger dowry."

Alasdair couldn't understand a man like that. He'd never seen a woman more beautiful and appealing than Gwyneth. How could a man abandon her when she carried his child? "'Twas utter lunacy," he muttered. But he was glad for it now. Else the tempting fairy wouldn't be sitting in his castle, in her bath before him.

Naked.

Time for talking was past.

CHAPTER TEN

Gwyneth didn't care for Alasdair's mood in the least. Pacing by the bath tub, he seemed to be barely suppressing his rage. But he had a right to it if Baigh had murdered his father.

Alasdair's eyes had been cutting in their intensity while he'd questioned her. Now they darkened and strayed to the water of her bath. Despite the flickering dimness of the firelight, maybe he could actually see through the thin white smock that floated over her. She did not want him to see her naked. Did she?

No, indeed.

On the morrow, the whole of Kintalon Castle would likely be wagging their tongues over what their laird had done, barging in on her bath. They might even surmise what had happened yesterday—a quick shocking tryst in his bedchamber.

"Would you be willing to step outside while I dress? The water is turning cold."

One corner of Alasdair's lips lifted, and his eyes turned devilish. "I was hoping you'd invite me to join you."

"No!"

Clearly, he now thought to make free use of her body any time he chose. He no longer respected her, and why should he?

"I'm in need of a bath." He unfastened his bronze brooch and let the upper portion of his plaid fall behind him. His hand went to his leather belt. She closed her eyes before he unclasped it. A buckle thudded upon the floor. His linen shirt brushed over his skin in a whisper.

Oh, good lord, I'm trapped, naked.

Covering her front as best she could with the sodden smock, she pushed to her feet in the center of the tub. Water sluiced down her body and from her hair. The cool air sent chills and gooseflesh over her skin.

She snatched a brief glimpse of Alasdair standing nude a few feet away. He was built like a pagan deity and displayed a full erection. Though she'd touched him there before, and had his raw power inside her, that didn't stop her from wishing the room was dark. Now, she didn't have the fog of arousal to dull her inhibitions.

Trying not to look at him, as well as keep herself covered, she stepped from the tub. Water drained from her smock onto the carpet.

Alasdair moved toward her. She scuttled away and retreated behind a wooden screen.

Please don't let him follow.

His brief, low chuckle echoed off the stone walls, and water splashed.

He took supreme delight in her discomfiture, didn't he? *I'm the greatest fool.*

She peered around the edge of the screen and found him sitting in the tub. While it had almost swallowed her whole, he fit into it perfectly.

"This water isn't cold," he said. "I'm thinking you've never bathed in Loch Morlich."

No, indeed. She didn't bathe in lochs.

She dressed quickly in a clean, dry smock and dressing gown. Both were too thin for her comfort. Determined not to tempt him or fall for his seductive charms again, she also put on her *arisaid* and belted the bulky, woolen plaid about her waist.

"M'lady, I wonder, would you be willing to help a man with his bath? I cannot reach my back."

She stiffened her spine and stepped from behind the screen. *I'll be strong. I won't let him affect me.* That was easy to think, but harder to achieve, she realized once her gaze ran over Alasdair's powerful shoulders and chest above the water. His predatory gaze tracked her movements, and she gave him a wide berth.

"Who usually washes your back?" She could well imagine any number of female servants enjoying the task.

When he didn't answer, she slid her gaze to him. He reminded her of an amused scoundrel, wicked and dark. "I've had no one in my bed, save you, for a good long while, if that's what you're asking," he said.

Her face flushed and she shrugged, trying to pretend it mattered not. That hadn't been what she was asking, but the information surprised her, relieved her, though she shouldn't even care. They had no attachments or bonds between them. Yet she found cutting jealousy edged along her nerves when she imagined him with another woman.

"I won't bite you, m'lady—" He chuckled. "Well, I would like to, but I promise I will only do so if you ask."

Heavens! Such outrageous remarks he made—she supposed she deserved it. She had certainly asked for what he'd given her yesterday, and reveled in the wild, thrilling abandon of it. But now, she was not proud of her recklessness.

She should take the key from his sporran, unlock the door and leave, but he'd likely follow. Naked. Another spectacle was the last thing she wanted.

"I have it on good authority that a woman likes a man with a clean body and a dirty mind."

How ridiculous he was. She bit back a grin. "And who told you that?"

"Lachlan, of course."

"I wager Lachlan doesn't know as much about women as he thinks he does."

"I'm thinking you're right." Alasdair smiled. "'Haps even I ken more than he does about women."

Likely he did. Certainly he appealed to her with his clean, hard-muscled body. As for his mind, she would not call it dirty, though he did know well how to seduce her with his sensual, lascivious words and scorching kisses.

"You don't wish to help me? Stubborn, aye?" He winked. "'Tis only fitting. You have a fair bit of Scots blood in you."

Trying to ignore his teasing, she strolled away, searching for something with which to occupy herself. But she slipped secretive glances back at him. Using the soap, he lathered her cloth and stroked it over his powerful chest and sculpted arms. His slow movements were beyond enticing.

She would mend a pair of trews one of the women had given her for Rory. That should take her mind off the tempting man in the tub.

No, it wouldn't, but she could pretend it did.

With a sloshing sound, Alasdair slid down and dunked his head beneath the water, then sat upright again, water streaming down his face and off his long black hair. He rubbed the chunk of soap over his hair, making a miserable attempt to wash it.

He reminded her of Rory, who couldn't wash his hair, either. Impatience overcame her. "Here, let me." She moved in behind Alasdair, then realized she'd have to remove her bulky *arisaid* to avoid getting it wet. That done, she rolled up the sleeves of her smock and dressing gown and took the mushy soap from him.

"I thank you, m'lady." His voice was deep and tantalizing.

"You won't when I'm done with you." She suppressed a small grin. "Rory always complains when I wash his head." She lathered Alasdair's hair and briskly rubbed. She scratched her short, blunt nails against his scalp, careful to avoid the spot where he'd had the injury.

"God's truth, 'tis the most thorough head-washing I've had in all my days."

"Are you complaining?"

"Nay. Never has anything felt so good." He released a brief chuckle. "Well, I take that back. One thing does feel better." He sent her a potent look over his shoulder.

Needing to get away from him, she rose. "There, I think you're ready to rinse."

"Would you wash my back first?" He gazed up at her, more innocently this time. "If you please."

What a manipulating scoundrel he was. "Very well." She took the soapy cloth and stroked it over his broad back.

Aside from a couple of scars from knife or sword wounds, his back was smooth and sleek, hard with muscle and ribs. He straightened his spine and the muscles rippled. His low back tapered in toward his hips in a most appealing way, drawing her gaze downward.

Wonder struck her again—how could a man be so beautiful? He was a marvel of creation. She found herself recalling all too vividly their encounter yesterday in his room, the dangerous and sensual magic that had drawn her to him against her rational will. She had given herself to him fully. That same magic crept into her bloodstream now, the tingling warmth flowing down toward the V of her thighs. Such delicious sin she craved with him.

She stood abruptly and laid the cloth on his shoulder. "There, it looks clean to me."

"Many good thanks." Even his deep murmur threatened to seduce her.

She wiped her hands on her dressing gown and stepped back.

Feeling completely bereft, she fought down the treacherous sensations humming through her that urged her to watch him, touch him. Invite him into her bed.

He slid down again, his knees coming up, and dunked his head beneath the water for a rinse. Coward that she was, she shifted her gaze to the fire before she could see whether his position exposed his most masculine parts. When he surfaced, water poured from his hair.

He flung it back from his face, spattering the floor with droplets, took up the rag again and flicked an amused glance her way. "Would you be willing to help me wash something else?"

Good lord. Ignoring his chuckle, she turned her back on him and paced to the opposite side of the room. No wonder he treated her as he did—she'd practically dragged him to his bed yesterday. Clearly she had no shame when Alasdair touched her.

She turned the wooden chair by the bed, sat with her back to him and took up her mending. Anything to keep her mind and eyes off his captivating naked form.

Minutes later, water splashed, and she imagined him standing. Oh, what a sight that would be. Bending, she focused harder on her task. Almost no sound came from behind her for a long, tedious moment. She squeezed her eyes shut and listened. Imagined. Soft, dry linen cloth whispered over wet, bronzed skin.

I hope he will go now. Yes, her conscious mind did, but her body tingled with anticipation.

He padded closer on the Turkish carpet.

"You should dry your hair beside the fire, m'lady." He burrowed his hand into her long hair. She'd forgotten it was wet. He stroked her neck with his warm, moist fingers.

"'Tis drying." She prayed he'd go and spare her further temptation.

On one knee, he knelt beside her chair. "Gwyneth," he murmured in a rough, intimate voice she would dream about.

He'd wrapped the linen cloth low about his hips, so that he was barely decent. His muscled shoulders, chest and arms were just as appealing and arousing as the rest of his body. He should cover himself entirely. Beads of water dripped from his hair onto his chest. She tried not to drink him up with her eyes. But when their gazes met, his dark intensity penetrated her defenses. She knew he saw the truth in her eyes, the truth of how he disturbed her, of how she was vulnerable beneath his touch.

He rose, took the mending from her hands and placed it on the bed. "Come." When he held out his hand in invitation, no part of her could've refused him, even though she was unsure what he intended. His hand warm around hers, he pulled her up. "We shall dry your hair."

Impulses warred inside her—to flee...or press her face to his chest. Resisting both, she let him lead her to a chair by the fire.

"Do you have a comb?" he asked.

She shook her head, feeling every bit the penniless pauper she was. "I'll borrow Tessie's tomorrow."

He sat in the chair first and startled her by pulling her down onto his lap.

Heavens, he was practically naked. She stiffened and tried to rise again. "No, I should not. It is not..."

"Proper? I ken 'tis the truth. Nothing about us is proper, m'lady."

And he didn't care one whit. But she did. No matter her past, she could not be a man's paramour.

He seated her firmly on his thighs and pulled her hair over the wooden chair arm. "Your hair is very long and beautiful." He combed his fingers through it, loosening the snarls. Her scalp tingled.

Oh, do stop. Her hair was mousy brown and straight as a spear. No one with an eye for fashion or beauty would find it appealing.

She tried to ignore the clean, masculine scent of him, which the light floral and herbal soap could not disguise. His face was another enticement, as were the sensual, hard curves of muscle that formed his chest.

When she shifted, his aroused shaft straining against the linen nudged her hip. He was so hard, he would feel glorious sliding into her. Moist heat prickled between her thighs and she squeezed them together.

"Relax," he murmured, working gentle fingers through the wet strands of her hair. "London society, your da, nor anyone else is here to judge you."

Her chest tightened and guilt surged through her. "You're a man. You cannot possibly understand what it is to disgrace yourself before God, your family and your community."

"'Haps not, but 'tis done. You cannot go back and redo your past."

"No, but I can behave better in the future."

"And you will, I've no doubt."

"Now. I must do better now. I must resist the temptation of…"
She let out a breath, hardly able to believe the sharp, conflicting
feelings within her.

"Of what, m'lady?" His whisper in her ear sent a tingle over her
shoulders.

"Of you." Never had anything or anyone enticed her as much.

A smile played upon his lips. "I'm not a temptation to you." He
stroked a finger down her neck. "I'm but a Highland barbarian, and
you a lady of fine breeding."

She shivered at the sensation his calloused finger wrought.
"You are no barbarian. You're an earl and a chief."

"Aye, but compared to you, I'm not very impressive."

How could he be so daft? He was the most impressive man
she'd ever met—honorable, trustworthy…tantalizing. "Oh, you
don't know." Yearning to nuzzle her face against his chest, breathe
him in, and taste him, she resolutely covered her face with her hands.
She could not believe the liquid desire aching low in her belly. How
could she turn into such a brazen wanton in his presence?

"Don't know what?" His breath, warm, sweet and ginger
scented, fanned against her ear.

"How I feel."

He stroked his mouth and nose against her hair, inhaling her
scent. "You smell prettier than a flower, and more delicious than a
strawberry."

"You see? You shouldn't say things like that." She lowered her
hands and risked a glance at his playful, inviting expression.

"Why not? 'Tis the truth. Would you have me lie?"

"No."

"Would you have me lie and say I hope to never to kiss you
again? Would you have me say I never want you in my bed again? I
don't hunger for the taste of your mouth and your skin. I didn't
spend half the night last night remembering our spellbinding
encounter in great detail, wishing you were there with me so we
might do it again and again. Do you believe those lies?"

Oh, heaven help me. "You should not, sir." She tried to pull away
and get up, but he placed a strong arm across her lap, his hand
cupping her hip, spurring even more instinctive urges.

"Why? What is so terrible about telling the truth and speaking
my mind?" The edge of passion and irritation in his voice alarmed
her.

In defense, and to still the trembling deep inside, she crossed her arms over her chest. "You want the truth? Here it is—you are a laird. And I'm only a disowned woman my family is ashamed of. The very things you speak of are what make me thus. I admit I have a shocking hunger for sensual pursuits. They are my downfall. If they weren't, I wouldn't have been banished."

"Och. 'Tis only nature, m'lady." His tone softened. "Your society would say men are different from women in their appetites. That 'tis acceptable for men to feel desire but not for women. But that is a lie. Both men and women have desires and urges. 'Tis the way God created us."

With his explanation, lovemaking sounded so simple and reasonable. Acceptable. But she still couldn't convince herself to believe it. Too many years and too many people had drummed a certain way of thinking into her—that women, especially ladies, were supposed to be above those carnal urges and immune to them.

She shook her head. "No, we must resist our human nature."

"Why must we resist the way God created us? He gave us the ability to feel these desires."

"No, you don't know what you're talking about. What we did yesterday was bad."

"You must call it what you will. But I won't call it bad. 'Twas beautiful beyond measure."

He released her and she sprang from his lap. Indeed, their lovemaking had been beautiful. The most exquisite thing she'd ever experienced.

"I must go now." He rose, threw the articles of his clothing over his shoulder and moved toward the door.

He was going? It was exactly what she wanted. Yet not.

A few feet from the door, Alasdair stopped and turned. "Would you gift me with a wee goodnight kiss?"

Heaven help me. A kiss? Before she knew what she was doing, she stood before him. *I am too eager,* she realized too late. Her skin heating, she dropped her gaze to the floor. He took her face between his hands, tilting it upward, and kissed her in a lingering brush of his warm lips and tongue against hers. Oh, she had forgotten how his kiss could seduce her in an instant. She opened to receive his tongue and her own licked against his, with a will of its own. A well-spring of hunger rose up from her chest and spurred her into action. She consumed his delectable mouth as if starved.

"*Iosa is Muire Mhàthair*," Alasdair growled and pulled her tightly to him as if control had slipped from his fingers.

Desire possessed her, shut down her decorum. Her arms closed around his naked lower back, and she stroked her hands down to his waist. The linen cloth fell away, and his trim hips were bare beneath her hands. She knew she shouldn't touch him, but she did. She remembered squeezing the powerful flexing muscles of his buttocks when he'd made love to her yesterday.

He moaned, his bare erection prodding her belly. Wetness tickled between her thighs.

His clothing slid from his shoulder. He coaxed her dressing gown from her, then gathered up her smock around her waist, even as he kissed her throat and breathed his hot breath on her. He lifted the garment farther, drawing it off over her head, and took her nipple into his mouth.

Sparkles of delight shimmered through her. "Oh."

"Mmmm." He suckled her other nipple. "I have craved these."

He walked her backward a few steps. Her thighs bumped into the bed, and he gently pushed her down upon it.

"By the saints, Gwyneth, you tempt me to near lunacy."

She squirmed, restless on the bed. Guilt ambushed her and she squeezed her eyes shut. She should fight this, resist her own desires.

"Look at me," he murmured.

She did, but seeing him in all his naked glory was a pleasure near too keen to bear. Her gaze dropped, tracing the line of hair down his flat hard belly that led to that most fascinating and masculine part of him. The act of simply observing him filled her with hunger.

She realized she had never been fully naked in the candlelight before a man and tried to yank the linen coverlet over herself. He would surely find her lacking.

"Nay." Alasdair stayed her hand, and his gaze stroked over her like a physical caress. "You cannot hide from me, Gwyneth. You're the most beautiful sight I've ever seen."

She believed him—his sincere, lust-filled eyes couldn't lie. He didn't seem to mind that her breasts weren't large and full like those women deemed most attractive. Her figure was too slim to be called voluptuous. Yet the way he looked at her, with hunger and yearning, made her feel as if she were the most desirable woman on earth.

He lifted her foot and kissed her ankle. With a sigh, she let her eyes drift closed. His lips and beard stubble tickled and scratched, sending a thrill up her leg. He trailed kisses up her calf and flicked his tongue at the back of her knee.

He pushed her legs apart, but she resisted and clenched them tightly together. He shouldn't look at her there!

"Gwyneth," he breathed against her bent knees. "Open for me."

She opened her eyes and found him hovering there, so gorgeous and scandalous, the stubble of his chin rasping and stimulating the sensitive skin of her knees.

"I meant...open your thighs," he said.

She burned from the inside out, embarrassed more by her own curiosity and a desire to comply than the request itself. "Oh, you are shameless."

"That I am." He grinned as if proud of that fact.

And she was shameless too, for her gaze dropped again to his shaft. She studied the thick, erotic shape and sleek, velvety texture of him.

"If you will but open your legs, I shall show you something you'll never forget."

"You already have." Certainly she would never forget how he'd made love to her yesterday.

"I wish to give you another pleasure." He straightened her legs and laid them flat on the bed. Determined to hold onto a speck of decency, she kept them pressed together.

He kissed her abdomen, her stomach, flicked his tongue into her navel. Tingles spread outward and the heat intensified in her lower belly. He moved in that direction, trailing his lips even into her hair.

"Oh, you cannot," she gasped and covered her face with her hands.

"I'm wanting to taste you, m'lady. 'Twould be a great pleasure for me."

He pressed open-mouthed kisses to her mound and upper thighs. *Good lord, he did not mean—*

When he nudged her thighs apart, she allowed it. Keeping her eyes closed, she felt him crawl between her legs.

The stimulation on her most sensitive flesh was not anything she knew. She opened her eyes and found his head between her legs. In truth, he was licking her. Good heavens! She attempted to close her thighs but this merely locked his head in place. He moaned. Oh, he had no modesty.

And neither did she, for she could not pull away. Could not

make him stop.

"You are sweeter and more delicious than pure honey," he whispered.

His tongue stroked flames of pleasure, such as she'd never imagined, over her, throughout her entire body. She could not break away from the sinful, divine burning, nor did she want to.

With heavy-lidded eyes, he glanced up at her just before he slid his tongue inside her. Blissful agony twisted through her as her yearning for him magnified. His moan vibrated against her. She couldn't believe what he was doing…and apparently enjoying it as much as she was. He then flicked his tongue briskly against an especially sensitive spot, where the tingles focused and flowed from.

That breathless, impending *something* she had experienced for the first time yesterday seized her again. She grasped onto the bed linens and cried out when the overwhelming sensation claimed her. Her body was not her own at that moment, but possessed by Alasdair and some instinctive rapture that frightened her. Yet at the same time, the spasm of delight was one she wanted again and again.

When she opened her eyes, Alasdair rose onto his knees between her legs, wiped his lips and gave her mischievous smile. "Did you enjoy that?"

Though somewhat shocked at herself, she nodded. Happiness germinated and flourished inside her. In that moment, all she needed for completion was his smile, his gaze, his touch. His lovemaking.

"'Twas one of the most enjoyable things I've ever done." He moved closer, positioning himself, and an eager thrill spiraled through her. He paused, searching her gaze. "Are you ready for more?"

"Yes. Please."

"Mmm." An impassioned frown crossed his features. When he nudged into her, his jutting erection felt hard as sun-warmed marble. A wild need for him rose up, and she thrust her hips toward him. He lifted her feet to his shoulders and pulled her closer. Slid deeper. She hungered for the long, thick shape of him.

The fluid, slick rocking motion of his body into hers and away was the most captivating sensation on earth. Even better than the ecstasy that had crashed over her. She knew she was making wanton noises, moans and little cries, but could not quiet herself. He overwhelmed her.

He licked her ankle, first one, then the other, his mouth, teeth and beard stubble grazing her skin. His magnetic black gaze penetrated her defenses, reached into her soul and made love to it. His eyes said he knew her, accepted her, wanted her.

His gliding movements accelerated and the excitement that swept through her was something she could not get enough of.

After placing her feet on the bed, he lowered himself over her and whispered in her ear. "How does that feel?"

He expected her to describe it? There were no words. "Wondrous." It was the only word that came to mind.

"Aye." He took her mouth in a devouring kiss that touched her deepest level. She feared he would taste and feel her adoration—something she wished she could hide. But he lured it from her so effortlessly.

He pounded himself into her with primal male power, his wet hair brushing her face. His chest hair rasped her nipples, stimulating them to hard pebbles. His harsh breathing and rough Gaelic murmurs in her ear were an arousing accompaniment. She reveled in each moment, each second his body worshiped hers.

With a growl, he slowed and lifted up slightly. She was surprised when he slipped his hand between their bodies and stroked her. Sparks seemed to jump from his fingertips, igniting that obsessed fire within her. It flamed higher and again consumed her. He took her mouth in a deep kiss before she could cry out at the burst of pleasure.

Finally, her breathing resumed and she opened her eyes. His were closed, seemingly in bliss. He hardened his jaw, drove to the hilt and, with a loud groan, shot his seed deep within her.

Watching him, experiencing him, sent joy bubbling up inside her. Never had she met or imagined a man such as him.

"By the saints," Alasdair gasped and drew in a chest-full of much-needed air after his explosive and maddening climax. Gwyneth's soft, wet woman's body astounded him. The power she held over him—damnation! He might well give his soul to lie with her every night.

He collapsed beside her, let his breathing calm and cradled her against his chest. She slipped an arm around his waist and caressed his back with her fingertips. Mmm, she fit into his arms perfectly, and felt just right. He had not experienced such satisfaction or contentment in many a year. Her presence soothed him, made him feel peace and happiness might be attainable. When he found his release with her, it seemed he released all the worrisome, painful things inside him as well.

"Gwyneth, I don't think I can get enough of you," he said, already craving her again.

"I know I shouldn't say so, but I feel the same," she confessed in a whisper.

He smiled, gratified and elated. He loved it when she told the truth. It was so much more refreshing than the lies she told herself and him when trying to be good and ignore what she truly wanted.

She threw herself onto her back away from him. "Oh, what am I doing? I should not have done that."

In a rare moment, he let dangerous, vulnerable emotion wash over him. "To appease your conscience, there is but one solution, then." His heartbeat thumped like a drum.

"What?"

"Marry me." There, he'd said it. He grinned.

She jerked back and stared at him with a wide-eyed frown, as if he'd suggested she kill him.

"Or we could hand-fast in the Highland way if you prefer," he rushed to say. Though he had no idea why he'd thought in that moment of madness hand-fasting would be more appealing. A legal marriage was far more secure.

She leapt from the bed, found her smock and yanked it on.

He sat up. "What's wrong?"

"It is cruel to jest with me so."

"'Tis no jest. I wish to marry you, Lady Gwyneth. Would you do me the honor of becoming my bride?" She would say no, he knew, somehow. Despite the impending disappointment, he could not help but make his wishes known.

Her eyes searched his. "Alasdair, you cannot mean it. You're a laird, an earl for heaven's sake, and I'm..." She covered her mouth.

"A lovely, sweet lady who happens to be a widow and mother. This would be a good arrangement, I'm thinking. 'Tis beyond clear we enjoy each other in bed. I would provide you with anything you should want or need, including protection. You would provide me with an heir. You've already admitted to being an earl's daughter, which means we are of the same social station."

She pressed her eyes closed. "I cannot."

"Why?" He wanted to shout the word, but managed to restrain himself.

She opened her eyes and observed him with a stricken look. "What about Rory?"

"I would treat him as mine own."

She shook her head vehemently. "You said yourself, you make sure all the lads are trained for battle. I cannot allow Rory to be trained to such barbaric violence. I must take him from the Highlands to some place safe where he'll never have a chance to fight and get killed."

Had she gone daft? He frowned. "That's your reason for refusing me?"

Her hands turned to fists. "It's important to me. Rory is the most precious person in my life. When I had nothing else, I had him. He was all I had to live for. And if he were to die…" Tears sparkling in her eyes, she pressed a fist to her mouth.

"Och, I would protect Rory with my life, as I would you. How can you doubt it?" Did she have absolutely no confidence in him?

"That's not going to stop him from fighting alongside your men one day," she said. "You know how he is drawn to the sword."

"If that is the case, it won't matter where you take him. When he's old enough, he will join the king's army."

"He will not!" She looked determined enough to take on the king's army herself.

Alasdair wanted to seal her mouth and make her understand. "M'lady—"

"No, I will not hear it. I could not live with myself if he rode out and got himself killed like that young boy, Campbell, when first I arrived. What a waste of precious life. He had not even begun to live. I cannot withstand that nightmare."

Trying his best to reason with her, he softened his voice. "Gwyneth, at the very least you must realize I've compromised you. And that you may be already carrying my bairn."

Her face reddened. She touched a hand to her flat belly, and he wanted to do the same, for he hoped it was so. More than anything, he yearned for her to have his child.

"But I may not be." Her look of defiance raised his ire.

He shoved himself from the bed. "Very well then. Do what you must." *Damnable woman.* He snatched up his long shirt, yanked it on and flung his plaid and belt over his shoulder. "But if you're carrying my bairn, you won't be leaving!" He stalked out, slamming the door in his wake.

CHAPTER ELEVEN

Dear God in Heaven, what had Alasdair meant? Gwyneth trod a path from the bed to the door and back again. He wouldn't let her leave if she was already carrying his child. She would be trapped again. Because of her thoughtless, wanton actions she would again have a man telling her where she could or could not go.

"I'm a widow, free to do as I wish," she muttered. "I do not have to stay here and be ordered about by him. If I but had a position...." *Could I find one myself?* Maybe she wouldn't need Alasdair's nor any man's help in becoming a governess.

She would swallow her fears and write to her eldest sister. Margaret might be persuaded to inquire in Cornwall, near her and her husband's summer estate.

I'll be an embarrassment to her.

Especially if Gwyneth now carried Alasdair's babe. If that was the case, she'd raise it on her own, the way she had Rory. It would be possible if she could move to an area which was both peaceful and no one knew her, save her sister. None of them need know how long she'd been a widow. She would earn wages and support her child or children that way. They wouldn't have much, but they could survive as they had for the last six years.

If she could leave soon, Alasdair would never learn whether she carried his child or not. Unless he searched her out. Then he'd surely take the babe from her.

Goodness, why am I thinking this way? I am not with child.

Disheartened, she slumped onto the chair. Months would pass before she'd receive a response from Margaret, if at all. If she did carry Alasdair's child, he'd find out by then. Perhaps Lachlan would return with good news sooner.

But what would she do in the meantime?

°o℗ ℗o°

The next evening, Gwyneth dragged herself up the stone steps leading to her bedchamber. With all the preparations for the upcoming Midsummer celebration, and guests arriving, she had not seen Alasdair all day. She and the women had gathered herbs and flowers, created colorful, scented garlands to decorate the great hall, and cooked special dishes in the kitchen.

Along the dimly lit corridor, she passed the open doorway to Alasdair's chamber. He was likely in the library talking and drinking sack with the loyal neighboring clan chieftains who had arrived that day.

"M'lady."

She jerked back and glared at the darkness of the doorway.

The lone sconce further down the corridor provided little illumination. Alasdair stuck his head out, glanced about, then locked his gaze on her. "I've something I'm wanting to give you."

Surely he did not mean a kiss. She felt giddy and flushed of a sudden.

Stepping into the hallway, he presented her with a parcel wrapped in a deep burgundy silk handkerchief and tied with a ribbon. The richness of the wrappings surprised her. "No, I cannot accept—"

"You don't yet ken what it is. Open it."

She couldn't decipher his expression, but he seemed hopeful, his anger from the night before not in evidence.

Gwyneth glanced behind herself to make sure no one watched, then tugged gently at the bow. She parted the silk and found a tortoiseshell comb within the folds. "Goodness, I cannot possibly take such an expensive—"

"Aye, you can. I didn't buy it. It used to be my mother's, and now 'tis yours. You need it…for your hair."

His mother's? That made it an even more extravagant and sentimental gift than if he'd bought it new. How could he part with such an item?

The fact that he didn't ply her with false and flattering compliments shattered her defenses. Last night burst into her consciousness—he had combed her hair with his fingers.

No one had given her a gift such as this in many years. His thoughtfulness overwhelmed her to the point of near tears. "I thank you, my laird."

"You're most welcome. And I pray you will pardon my harshness of last night. Can you forgive me, m'lady?"

"Yes." She swallowed. "Of course."

"I'm glad."

Though his gift meant more than she could express, she knew it was a courtship gift, just like the rose he'd tucked behind her ear…and which she'd pressed into a book so she might keep it forever.

Obviously, he had hatched up a new plan to draw her under his power and trap her and Rory in the Highlands. Fool that she was, she was sore tempted.

Wishing to escape before Alasdair could cast his spell upon her and seduce her yet again, she curtseyed. "I thank you and I bid you good evening, sir." She hastened to her room.

Once inside, she closed the door and glanced toward the bed where Rory slept. Cradling Alasdair's gift in her hands, she seated herself before the small fire in the hearth and examined the brown tortoiseshell comb more closely in the light.

How she wished things could be different, wished Alasdair was not a Highland laird and enemy of Donald MacIrwin. Wished clan warfare did not rule the Highlands.

ℴℯℯ ℊℯℴ

"We have a visitor," one of the maids announced, entering the busy kitchen the next day just after midday meal. "Some fancy Sassenach lord. He and his men will be needing trenchers."

Turning from her task of kneading bread dough, Gwyneth dabbed a sleeve to her sweaty forehead. The heat of the ovens and huge arched fireplace was getting to her. She wondered whether Edward Murray had returned so quickly, perhaps for the Midsummer's Day feast. No, probably another of Alasdair's old schoolmates.

A second servant trotted down the steps and into the kitchen. "The Sassenach's asking for Lady Gwyneth Carswell, he is," she said in a dramatic whisper, and her round eyes lit on Gwyneth.

"Faith! Me?"

The maid placed her hands on her round hips. "Well now, you're the only Gwyneth Carswell what lives here."

Dread rose up within her. "What is his name?"

The other woman shrugged. "Something Southwick."

Gwyneth's breathing ceased. "The marquess of Southwick? Maxwell Huntley?"

"Aye, I believe 'twas." The servant bustled to the other side of the kitchen.

Rory's father. "Oh, dear heavens!" What could he possibly want? A thousand questions streamed through her mind.

Where was Rory? She ran to the back doorway and found him playing in the kitchen garden with other children.

Alasdair stalked into the kitchen. "Someone, please bring Lord Southwick some food and wine. I won't have him spreading rumors that we lack manners or hospitality here in the Highlands." He turned his fierce midnight gaze to Gwyneth and lowered his voice to a murmur. "Why are you doing this kind of physical labor?"

"What? I'm making bread...the festival."

"I would have a word with you in here." Frowning, he motioned toward one of the pantries.

She blinked. Her world had just somersaulted and nothing made sense. "In there?"

"Aye."

She preceded him into the small windowless room, and he closed the door. She found it hard to breathe with the dust of flour and scents of spices thickening the air, not to mention the near pitch blackness.

She wiped her sticky hands on her skirts. "What is Southwick doing here?"

"I was going to ask you the same question."

"Did he not say?"

"Nay. Only that he wishes to speak with you."

"Oh, heavens! I never thought to see him again. I'm not sure I can face him." She concentrated on evening out her breathing and calming herself.

I have survived six years in the harsh Highlands. I can face one whey-faced English lord. He's a coward who ran from responsibility. Not worthy to be called a man.

"What if—saints!" Alasdair muttered.

"What?"

He yanked her to him and took her mouth in a hard-driving kiss—one that plunged down to her very soul. As if to say to her, *you're mine, and don't be forgetting it.*

Just as abruptly, he drew back. Gwyneth swayed, trying to regain her equilibrium within the maelstrom of emotions.

Alasdair steadied her. "Beware the fancy Sassenach. He has the look of a poisonous viper about him."

She grasped his sleeve. "Would you come with me?"

"To talk to him?"

"Yes."

He took her hand and kissed the back. "Aye, I would be honored." He opened the door, allowing light to flow in. "You might don some of the clothing from the trunk."

She glanced down at her bodice and skirts. What a sight she was with flour and dough covering her faded and near threadbare dress. What did she care? She had no more pride. Southwick had striped it from her six years ago, just as he had taken everything else.

"'Twill increase your courage," Alasdair said.

She nodded, taking in his beloved visage and his caring dark eyes. The reverent way he looked at her gave her far more courage than any clothing could. "I thank you."

He gave a short bow.

Though Alasdair wanted nothing more than to spend the afternoon kissing Gwyneth in the pantry, he knew he must deal with Southwick in an appropriate fashion and find out what the devil he wanted. Alasdair would not have allowed Gwyneth to visit with the snake alone, but he was glad she'd asked him to accompany her.

He watched Gwyneth scurry up the back stairs before he returned to the great hall.

With a stiff posture, Southwick sat at high table with two of his men. The skinny, weak-looking Sassenach picked at his mutton stew with formal preciseness.

"How are the food and wine?" Alasdair asked, forcing himself to be hospitable to the loathsome man. He'd finished his own meal with the rest of his Highland guests a half hour past.

Southwick glanced up with icy gray eyes. "They will suffice." He smirked and pushed the trencher away. "I did not come here to dine. I am here to see Lady Gwyneth Carswell."

Partly fueled by jealousy, Alasdair's temper ignited like flame to straw, but he held himself in check. "And you will in due time. If you're finished eating, we can wait for her in the library."

Southwick and one of his cohorts rose and followed Alasdair to the smaller, book-lined room.

"Have a seat." Alasdair motioned and the two men perched on a long bench.

He studied Southwick. The frail-looking man's skin was bright pink, obviously from unaccustomed sun exposure, and he reeked of some sort of flowery, musky perfume.

What did he want to talk to Gwyneth about? The dolt couldn't want to marry her now, six years after the fact. *Too late, you bastard. Gwyneth is mine and I won't be giving her up.*

"Would either of you care for sherry, sack or whisky?"

"No, thank you," Southwick answered with a sniff. "So, why did you take Lady Gwyneth hostage?"

Alasdair forced himself to remain rooted to the spot. "Where did you hear such a lie?"

Southwick let loose a soft snort and exchanged a look with his friend. "Do you deny it?"

"Aye. She came here of her own free will. Donald MacIrwin was trying to kill her."

"How preposterous! He is her blood relative. He would not want to kill her. And what of her son? Is he here as well?"

Hellfire and damnation. It wasn't Gwyneth he wanted, but Rory. She would be thunderstruck. A sick feeling twisted Alasdair's gut. "And why would you be caring where he's at?"

The marquess leveled a superior but menacing look at Alasdair. "He is my son, and I will see him now."

"Nay. You will not!"

Southwick's mouth firmed and his face mottled. "Dare you tell me *no*, you—"

"*Cùm do theanga, a mheapain!*" Alasdair stepped forward and barely suppressed the urge to fling his newly sharpened *sgian dubh* at the whoreson's throat. "You filthy Sassenach. Don't think to come into my home and order me about! As a marquess, you may be one step ahead of me, but you're in the Highlands now. And we hold no fondness for the English."

Southwick's face paled, and his eyes narrowed. "Are you—" He cleared his throat. "Are you threatening me?"

"Nay." Alasdair couldn't help that his mouth formed a smirking grin. "Just stating the facts," he said in his most civil tone, yet he was sure his glower told them something altogether different. He would protect Gwyneth and Rory with his life.

Southwick clenched his hands together and glanced about. "I will be sure King James hears of this."

"'Haps I will scribe a missive and tell him myself." Keeping the two knaves in his peripheral vision, Alasdair poured himself a dram of sherry and sprawled in the chair behind his desk. Though he wanted nothing more than to slice Southwick limb from limb with his claymore, he held his temper in check and affected nonchalance.

Perhaps Southwick hadn't heard tell of the Sassenach lordlings who'd been known to disappear without a trace in the Highlands.

With a little help from Tessie, Gwyneth put on an outfit from the trunk that held Alasdair's wife's clothing. Gwyneth's thoughts flew and scattered in all directions. Her fingers trembled so badly she couldn't manage to tie anything. She only noticed the clothing was green and gold and of fine material. It shouldn't matter what she wore, but she didn't want Southwick to know she was indeed penniless. It would put her at a disadvantage.

"Will you watch Rory?" Gwyneth asked Tessie.

"Aye, of course."

Minutes later, her drumming pulse drowned out all other sounds when she knocked at the library door. Finally, Alasdair opened the door for her. She focused on his familiar form for a moment, tall and dark, clothed in a belted plaid. She hoped he would be her calm within the windstorm. And indeed his presence allowed her a small measure of comfort.

Two men, dressed in English hunting clothes, rose when she entered. Her gaze locked on the hateful visage of Maxwell Huntley, marquess of Southwick. What struck her immediately was how much he had aged since she'd seen him last. Though his normally pale skin was bright pink, he appeared sickly, with sunken eyes and hollow cheeks. The malicious gleam in his frigid gray eyes caught her attention. How could she have ever imagined herself in love with this man? Had he changed so much, or had she?

"Lady Gwyneth, I am pleased to see you." Southwick stepped forward, took her hand and kissed it.

Though she wore gloves, her skin chilled. Genteel manners deserting her, she snatched her hand away. His strong, familiar perfume—a blend of musk, rosewater and civet—mixed with his sweat odor, nauseating her. The last time she'd seen him, to tell him she was carrying his child, he had slapped her down and called her a lying whore.

"Lord Southwick," she forced herself to say. "Are you well?"

"Indeed, I am." He sent her a tight-lipped grin, then gave a deep bow. "And I pray that you are."

Nodding, she studied his eyes and the deceit behind his facade.

"I'm glad you agreed to see me so that we might talk privately." When no one moved, Southwick cut a brittle glare at Alasdair.

"Laird MacGrath stays," she said.

"Ah." Southwick lifted his thin blond brows as if reading something lurid into their association. "Well, if you insist, *my lady*." Southwick's gaze trailed down over her as if she were a woman of ill repute. He stroked his pointed, thinning goatee. "I've come to talk to you about my son."

His son?

"I want to make you a deal," Southwick continued. "You have taken care of him these last few years alone and with little funds. Now, I would propose to take him off your hands for the duration."

CHAPTER TWELVE

The walls of the library shrank in on Gwyneth. She could not comprehend the meaning of Southwick's words. *I would propose to take him off your hands for the duration.*

He would take Rory away?

She felt as if someone had struck her chest with a hammer. Alasdair grabbed onto her before she realized she'd swayed.

She pulled away from him and steadied herself, called upon some reserve of strength deep within. "Have you gone mad?"

"Hardly." Southwick lifted a brow. "He is my son, is he not?"

She shook her head, denying he had any right to call Rory his son. Denying Southwick could touch him. Denying....

"I am offering him his heritage. He will one day be the seventh marquess of Southwick and he requires a proper education."

"But he is illegitimate. He cannot inherit—"

"That is but a formality." His sharp tone gave her pause.

"Why are you doing this?" she asked, desperate to make sense of it all. "Have you not married?"

"I did marry—the duke of Pembley's daughter, but she died six months ago, barren." His expression remained impassive.

"So marry someone else!"

"I think I've had enough of marriage. And since I already have a son, I don't need to marry again. I don't intend to take him away from you. You may visit him anytime you wish."

Visit him. Visit? "No!"

"You cannot deny me my son."

Desperate, Gwyneth grasped at the threads of control. "He is not your son. I visited with another man a few nights after

162

our…meeting."

"You lying whore!"

"Southwick, you forget yourself," Alasdair growled and stepped forward. "You will show respect to Lady Gwyneth in my home or you can leave now. Because of your actions, she lost everything."

Southwick glared at Alasdair. "Pray pardon."

As if those two insincere words could undo all the damage he had wrecked on her life. And continued to wreck.

"I'm merely trying to get her to see reason," Southwick continued in a milder tone, but malice still gleamed in his eyes. "If only her small mind can comprehend—"

"'Tis time you were leaving," Alasdair said in his laird and commander voice. He stood over the two Englishmen and pointed toward the door.

"I will give you money," Southwick said to Gwyneth.

"How dare you try to buy my son? You are the lowest —"

"Southwick, you are overstaying your welcome." Alasdair's voice held an Arctic chill. "Here in the Highlands we don't take insult lightly."

Southwick's face turned crimson, but he remained silent and exited with his cohort.

"I will return." Alasdair followed them out.

Her trembling legs no longer able to hold her up, she slumped onto a chair in the silent, empty room.

Dear heavens, what am I going to do?

What was Southwick scheming? She would be glad for Rory to be the next marquess of Southwick, but an illegitimate child could not inherit his natural father's English title. Clearly he had something illegal and nefarious in mind. Either that or he'd turned lunatic.

In any case, she would not hand her son over to the abusive knave at such a young age. Rory was *her* son, and *she* would be the one to raise him. She would not want to jeopardize his future, but she couldn't let him go now. She loved him more than her next breath and must always see that he was safe and happy. Education was not the issue. She was already seeing to that, and he was too young to be sent away to school.

Alasdair returned and slammed the heavy door. "What a vile whoreson he is. I told the guards to keep them off MacGrath land."

"He's come to finish destroying my life." Gwyneth sprang to her feet. "I cannot believe after he's cast us aside for six years, he now wants Rory when it's convenient for him. Rory cannot legally inherit his title, can he?"

"Nay. Unless Southwick's title is Scottish and you marry him."

"His title is English and I would never marry him."

"Or he might petition the king. How many people in London know for certain of Rory's existence?"

"My family." Suddenly too exhausted from the tension to stand, she dropped to the chair near the hearth. "Father didn't want word of my disgrace getting out so he sent me away. Because he had three other unmarried daughters at the time, he didn't want the family name sullied. Since Southwick and I both disappeared, I'm certain people surmised the worst."

Alasdair nodded and took the chair opposite her.

"What if he doesn't give up on trying to take Rory? Will the law be on his side?" Gwyneth asked, pressing a hand to her nauseated stomach.

"I don't ken precisely how the English courts work in this situation, but it doesn't sound like what he wants to do is legal anyway."

The jaws of a trap sprang shut on Gwyneth. Her mind struggled for an escape. Men held all the power over women and children, no matter the situation. And even if Rory couldn't legally inherit a title, Southwick could still take her son on a whim. "Dear lord, what am I going to do? He has a vicious temper when he's angry. When I—" She pressed her lips closed, shame devouring her composure.

"Go on."

"When I told him I was with child, he slapped me and I fell."

Alasdair's face tightened and the warrior in him emerged. "Why did you not tell me this afore? I would've bashed in his head on first sight!"

"You cannot do that." Although she appreciated his protectiveness, she would not have him assaulting people on her behalf. "I also heard he beats his servants and may have killed one, though no one could prove it. I cannot allow him to take my son."

"God's wounds!" Alasdair shoved to his feet and paced to his desk and back. "'Haps if you would marry me and become a countess, you would hold more power in the event Southwick tries to take Rory."

Marry Alasdair? Good lord!

Was that the only alternative?

It had been hours since Alasdair had sprung his latest

"proposal," but Gwyneth could think of nothing else—save the nightmarish Southwick situation.

She stood beside Rory in the shadows and gazed out over the bustling activity in the great hall she'd helped decorate with herb and flower garlands. Their sweet, pungent scents blending with all manner of meat, onion, and bread aromas now sickened her.

Alasdair had forbidden her to return to the kitchen or to help with the final preparations of the feast. Her fidgety hands craved something to do. But she was glad for the time to spend with Rory, simply to watch him play with his small friend. Just to make sure he was safe and still here with her.

She would have no life without her son and could never let him go.

But to marry Alasdair in the hopes his position would hold some sway with English courts didn't seem the answer. Nor would it be fair to him.

She didn't know how much influence Alasdair had with King James, but everyone knew the king, though Scottish, held no fondness for these wild and rebellious Highlanders. In all likelihood, if she did marry a Highland laird, the king and courts would have even less sympathy for her plight. Since Southwick was English, they would want Rory raised on English soil.

Gwyneth's gaze shifted to Alasdair, striding across the great hall, clothed in his finest apparel—a newly woven kilt of blue and black tartan, crisp ivory linen shirt and deep blue doublet.

He approached her through the throng of people that milled about between the two long rows of tables weighted down with food.

Please do not let him propose again.

Alasdair stopped before her and Rory. "M'lady." He bowed, then stroked an affectionate hand over Rory's head, but his focus remained on Gwyneth. "Would you do me the honor of sitting with me at high table?"

His clean scent with a trace of lavender reached her, teasing her senses. The dampness of his hair told her he had bathed recently. His eyes were dark seduction, even now. She was tempted to say *yes* to anything he asked.

"I thank you, but I cannot." Her gaze dropped to her son and the look of wide-eyed hero-worship he cast up at Alasdair. Why couldn't Alasdair have been Rory's natural father, instead of Southwick?

Alasdair let out an impatient breath. "You are a noble guest just as the laird and lady of Clan Grant are."

"No, Laird MacGrath, I am but your temporary houseckeeper. I would not care to explain to them why I am given the honor of sitting at the laird's table."

"You're an English lady, daughter of an earl. That's the only explanation you need. Besides, 'tis not their concern. I am but providing you and your son protection."

"I'm sorry." His guests were sure to assume the worst—and the truth—that she and Alasdair had been lovers. She couldn't bear any more looks or words of censure this day. Southwick's visit had been more than sufficient to destroy her composure. Aside from that, she would make a silent dinner companion.

"Very well. I proclaim you are no longer my housekeeper. You're an honored guest, and you are not to lift another finger to help."

Was he serious or teasing her? At times his mysterious eyes were impossible to read.

"Then I will be forced to leave."

"Humph. You are the most vexing woman I have ever dealt with." His grumpy proclamation was laced with humor.

She noticed a few guests nearby staring their way and grinning.

"I'm sorry not to be more agreeable, my laird," she said in a low tone.

"As well you should be."

Why in heaven's name was he talking so loud? She focused on Rory's fine hair, wishing to escape this conversation. She didn't want to draw attention to herself or more specifically, to Alasdair's interest in her.

His warm fingers underneath her chin, he tipped her face toward him, and a tiny grin formed on his lips. "I swear I shall have you eating at my table afore the year is out."

He should not touch her thus, with such boldness and possession, before anyone who watched.

"And if you do not?" she asked.

His smile widened. His eyes took on that look he always had just before he coaxed her into something delicious yet shocking. "I'm said to be most stubborn and determined."

⋙ ⋘

"You lied, MacIrwin!" Southwick shouted, his reedy voice echoing off the rock walls of Irwin Castle's great hall. "You do not have my son as you claimed in your missive. And MacGrath refuses to release him."

His muscles tense and his hand on his sword hilt, Donald MacIrwin restrained his bloodlust and surveyed his clansmen. Each of them glared at the English whoreson but held their tongues. He must do the same if he wanted the two-hundred pounds.

"Dare you call me a liar, you stinking Sassanach?" And he did reek. His perfume was enough to knock a strong man flat.

Southwick extended his arms, indicating the great hall around them. "I do not see him here in your possession. And yet, you said in your missive that you held him. That you wished me to pay a monstrous and outrageous ransom for my own son."

"That's because the bitch Gwyneth took him and fled. When I get my hands on her I'll..." *kill her.* But nay, he couldn't say that now. First, he had to separate Southwick from his gold and silver.

"I don't care what you do to Gwyneth. I want my son." Southwick's tone reminded Donald of a petulant, spoiled bairn.

"I have a proposition," Donald offered. "I'll retrieve the wee lad from MacGrath and you pay me the two hundred pounds."

Southwick's eyes narrowed as he considered. "I must have my son in hand first. Completely unharmed and healthy. Yes, you go get him, hand him over to me, and I'll give you the money."

Triumphant victory burst through Donald. He would have the money soon. "Very well." Donald stepped forward and extended his hand. Southwick, wearing brown gloves, finally took his hand and shook. Och, what a weak handshake the Sassanach had. Donald and his men could easily overpower Southwick and his lordly friends, kill them, and take the money, but he did not wish to anger King James.

"Now, me and my men must go make plans for the lad's rescue. Have supper while you wait," Donald said.

If Gwyneth or any of the MacGraths got in his way, he would not be so careful of his actions.

◈◈◈

During the *Feill-Sheathain* feast at Kintalon Castle, Gwyneth sat at a table toward the back with Tessie and some of the lower ranking clan members and children. She had nothing to celebrate and no appetite for the fine foods laid out before her—roast beef, mutton, lamb, fine yellow cheese, leeks, parsnips, cabbage, oat cakes—the list went on. Here sat more food than she'd seen during her entire stay in the Highlands, and Alasdair did not deprive even the lowest servant from partaking.

What if Southwick pursued custody of Rory? That was all she could think about, and nausea replaced her appetite.

"Is all well, then?" Tessie asked beside her.

Gwyneth nodded and forced herself to eat.

"What did the fancy Sassenach want?"

Those sitting closest to Gwyneth cast inquiring glances her way. "Nothing of importance," she said for all to hear, then lowered her voice for Tessie's ears only. "I'll tell you later." She didn't want anyone else to know her connection with Southwick, especially Rory.

After dark, music and dancing commenced around two large bonfires outside the barmkin walls on a hill overlooking the loch, the village and the fields. Gwyneth went only to watch Rory as he joined in, dancing and cavorting with the other children.

Smoke from the wood and peat fires burned her lungs when the wind shifted. She coughed and moved further away.

Small blazes, like torches, in the fields and pastures below caught her attention. Outsiders. Dear lord, was Southwick returning? Donald invading? Strangely, the torches were not moving in their direction but around toward the right in large circles.

"'Tis to bless the crops and cattle, for a fruitful harvest and many calves," Alasdair said close behind her.

She spun to face him. "In truth? Do you believe that?"

He shrugged. "Aye, why not? Our clan has been prosperous for two hundred years. You cannot argue with success. But I'm not a heathen if that's what you're thinking." His wicked grin and wink had the disturbing effect of negating his words and raising her awareness of him.

What had he meant, anyway? He wasn't a heathen, yet he believed the heathen rituals worked? In most other ways he appeared to be a Protestant, but the Highlanders held to their superstitions. Besides, something more urgent worried her.

"Are we safe out here?"

"I have posted armed guards all around, very close together. Don't worry about it. Remember, this is a celebration." He bowed. "Would you give me the honor of this dance, Lady Gwyneth?"

Heat rushed over her face. "It has been ages since I've danced. I'm sure I would make a mess of it."

"That matters not. Come, m'lady. 'Twill be fun." Brows lifted with an expectant look, he held out his hand. "You do remember what fun is, aye?"

No, she scarce remembered it at all.

"If not, I'd like to remind you."

She took his hand. "Oh, very well. But if I tread on your injured toe, you must not blame me."

"My toe is full recovered and can withstand your wee foot upon it." He led her toward the other couples already dancing. When they joined in, she was glad to see he had not lied about his toe and seemed light on his feet.

Gwyneth made a misstep and almost toppled sideways. Alasdair caught her and chuckled. Her own laughter surprised her. How long had it been since she'd laughed and danced? More than seven years?

"I have forgotten how to dance," she confessed.

"Nay. Merely out of practice, I'm thinking. But I ken well how to remedy that."

A prickle of worry returned. Where was Rory?

She glanced aside and saw him jumping around with the other children, ashes from the bonfire smeared on all their foreheads. She smiled and returned her attention to Alasdair "Someone has rubbed ash on Rory's forehead."

"Aye, 'tis for blessings as well."

More superstition. Well, what could it hurt?

"'Haps you would like me to smear ashes upon your forehead, m'lady."

She laughed. "I think I prefer a clean face."

"You are a lovely lass, but a hundred times more beautiful when you smile and laugh as you are now."

Such outrageous compliments. And the way he looked at her, with rapt attention. Her face felt as if it glowed fiery red, and not just from the heat of the bonfire.

"Promise me, every day from now on, you will smile at least once, and I must be witness to this action. Laughter is required five times a week."

Gwyneth snickered. "I can make no such promises. You are naught but a charmer."

"I have never been accused of such." His smile was indulgent, full and without restraint, reflecting her own feelings—happiness such as she had not felt during the whole of her life.

In truth, he was a charmer, and how would she resist him this night?

⊱❦⊰

After two dances, Gwyneth was both relieved and disappointed when Alasdair bowed, kissed her hand and went to talk with his

169

guests—the other chiefs and their families.

When he led one of the young, unmarried ladies out to dance, jealousy swooped in on Gwyneth.

She focused her attention on Rory and was surprised to find him twirling in circles with a small girl in fine clothing. After a couple of minutes, Rory's hands slipped off hers. She tumbled onto her rump and turned a backward flip.

"Good heavens!" Gwyneth strode forward. "Rory, you will hurt the little lady. Now, help her up."

"Pray pardon," Rory said, reaching his hand down to her.

"My, what a mannerly young sir he is," said one of the ladies as she dusted off the girl's skirts. "You are fine, are you not, Millie?"

She nodded emphatically and dragged Rory out for more dancing and horseplay.

"Well, he's already popular with the lasses." The short, round woman laughed. "I'm Alice Balfour, Lady Grant."

"'Tis an honor to meet you, my lady. I am Gwyneth Carswell."

"Oh, you're English. 'Tis clear in your speech."

"Yes."

"And how did you come to be all the way here, in the Highlands?"

"I was married to a Highlander but am widowed now. At the moment, I am the MacGrath's housekeeper but I hope to find a position as governess or tutor and go south before winter."

"Indeed? The long winter nights and deep snows of the Highlands were the hardest thing for me to grow used to. I was born in the Lowlands, you see, some miles from Dunbar."

Could this be an opportunity? "Would you know anyone in that area who is searching for a governess?"

"My brother just hired someone new for his eldest son, but they have five more, all under seven, one set of twins. I told him to give his poor wife a wee break." She chuckled. "You're serious about this, then?"

"Yes, very. Does he live in a peaceful area?"

"Indeed."

"Laird MacGrath has promised to provide me with a reference."

"His word is gold. I will send a missive to my brother upon my return home. If you have a letter of reference from Laird MacGrath, I will include that as well."

"That would be wonderful."

"The MacGrath's first wife was my distant cousin, and he is well respected and liked in our family."

Gwyneth felt like an interloper, even though she herself had asked him if his late wife's family might be in need of someone.

"Clearly you're well educated. Are you of noble birth, then?" Alice asked.

Gwyneth usually felt it best not to mention her background, but in this case it might prove helpful. "My father is an English earl."

Alice's eyes flew wide. "In truth?"

"Yes, and he provided all of us, including my five sisters and one brother, with proper educations."

"Goodness, I wish we were in need of a governess. You impress me greatly. Millie is our youngest, and Paula, our eldest." She smiled toward the twirling couples. "Dancing with the MacGrath as we speak. Oh, wouldn't they make a lovely pair?" She sighed. "I would give my eye-teeth to have him for a son-in-law."

Though she did not wish to, Gwyneth turned to follow her gaze. The young Paula, of no more than eighteen years, beamed up at Alasdair. Her long, dark hair flowed down her back. They matched in coloring and her tall height complimented his. He focused on her, to the exclusion of all else, and laughed at something she said.

"I'm thinking he'll become smitten with her. What do you think?" Alice whispered eagerly. "Look at how he smiles at her."

"'Tis possible." Gwyneth looked away. The sight of them hurt her eyes. And her heart. "I thank you for inquiring with your brother. I shall ask Laird MacGrath to write the reference missive before the morrow. Pray pardon me and enjoy the rest of the celebration."

Lady Alice bid her good evening, and Gwyneth moved toward the shadows to try and soothe her aching heart. Good lord, why had her reaction to seeing Alasdair dancing with the pretty lass struck her so?

Gwyneth couldn't marry him, so she should want him to find a suitable wife. But some part of her deep inside couldn't understand the logic of that.

Was it possible that a woman and man could love each other equally and forever? Or was it a fable? The love she'd thought she felt for Southwick years ago was but delusion. Upon much reflection, she'd come to the conclusion that her parents didn't share love, nor much warmth or fondness.

Of course, Gwyneth had never loved Baigh Shaw. She had come to believe love between a man and a woman didn't truly exist.

Was it a fantasy some poet had dreamed up to mislead people into thinking such lofty love and passion were possible?

The only love that she knew existed between people was that of a parent for a child, and vice versa, along with love between siblings and friends.

But the wondrous emotions that grew and expanded within her for Alasdair were unlike anything she had ever experienced. They near took her breath and her reasoning. She did not trust herself, nor her feelings—which were not warm and comforting, but hot and disturbing. Mayhap the Gaelic words he'd whispered in her ear during their lovemaking had been an incantation that had drawn her under his control. Or mayhap real love could exist between a man and a woman and that's what she felt for him.

Trying to keep her attention off Alasdair and any female who might be touching him or gazing at him with adoration, she focused on the male clan members who were setting a blaze to a giant cartwheel of straw. Once it was well afire, they rolled it down the hill toward the loch below. When it reached the bottom, still burning, a cheer went up. "A fruitful harvest!"

Did their superstitions know no bounds?

A short time later, a few of the older clan women started rounding up the tired and yawning children.

"'Tis time for stories and bed," Great Aunt Matilda said.

The children whined and moaned.

"'Haps we will even find some comfits inside."

The promise of sweets hastened their steps.

"I'll come with you," Gwyneth told Matilda, glad for the excuse to avoid watching Alasdair court any more ladies. She helped herd Rory and the other children toward the barmkin and castle.

"You cannot be going in now," Alasdair said behind her.

Surprised, she stopped and turned.

"You're not one of the children. And you're far too lovely to not enjoy a night like this."

She fought down her unreasonable irritation at him for the attention he'd shown the young lady. "I've enjoyed it, but I'm tired."

"I was hoping for another dance or two, if it would please you." That wicked gleam in his eye was too charming for her comfort. 'Twas time for her to face reality—nothing could ever exist between them. Nothing but the secret trysts...all in the past.

"As I said, I'm tired, but there is something I wish to speak to you about."

172

"Very well." He watched her with curiosity.

"I'll return after I make sure Rory is safely inside with the other children."

He bowed. "I'll be waiting."

She expected to find him dancing with another lass when she returned, but he stood alone just outside the barmkin gates.

"I'm glad you came back," Alasdair murmured.

Glancing around, she noticed that fewer people were present around the bonfires. "Where is everyone?"

"The women are most likely running naked through the heather." He grinned. "Will you be joining them?"

Naked? Through the heather? "Certainly not!"

He laughed. "Jumping the balefire, then? A wee bit more dangerous, but arguably more effective."

"Oh, gracious! No." She stalked toward the barmkin.

He followed. "Are you not wanting to strengthen your fertility?"

No, indeed, she did not want strengthened fertility. Trying to ignore his teasing, she focused on the reason she'd wanted to talk to him. But now that it was time to ask for the letter of recommendation, she hesitated to speak the words that would take her away from him forever.

"'Haps I can do it for you, then," he said.

"What—"

He smiled like a devil bent on sensual mayhem. No, she didn't want to know what he'd meant. She turned to go.

He grasped her hand, stopping her. She didn't even know where she'd been fleeing to. The barmkin was almost empty, though she did see a couple kissing in the shadows.

Before she could determine who they were, Alasdair tipped her face toward him. "I'm hoping you won't leave me out here alone, Gwyneth. 'Tis too early to go to sleep." With his fingers, he traced her cheek and chin. Tingles spread in the wake of his touch. "Do you ken, tonight is when fairies roam the earth, looking for mortals to pull mischief on."

She shook her head, suppressing a grin.

"Don't tell me you don't believe in fairies, for I won't be hearing it."

"Are you never serious?"

"Aye, 'tis serious I am about wanting to kiss you," he said in a deep, low tone.

Heavens! Could she not find the strength within herself to resist him? She put her hands before her, to ward him off, but he pressed firmly against her with his hard chest. Her fingers yearned to stroke over him and beneath his clothing, to absorb the feel of his muscles. But she couldn't.

"What of Paula?" she blurted.

"Who?"

"The young lady you spent so much time dancing with." *And laughing with. Oh, I am daft. I should not have said anything.*

He lifted one brow and stared at her for a long, tense moment. "I don't want to kiss her."

Did he mean it? She concentrated on his ornate falcon brooch near his shoulder, the blue and red jewels sparkling in the dim light.

"Gwyneth, 'tis glad I am that you're jealous."

"I am not jealous!" How mortifying he saw through her words.

"Och, nay. You're not." He grinned and held her with one hand around hers, his grip gentle, his thumb rubbing her palm.

She could've easily pulled away, but his warmth, the way her whole body and mind focused on the spot where his skin stroked hers, gave her pause.

"Will you not gift me with another kiss in the garden?" He advanced, and she retreated.

She did crave the profane decadence of his mouth upon hers. Her lips burned in anticipation. Her breasts tingled, craving his attention, before the hot excitement slid down through her body.

When her back came up against the garden gate, he unlatched it. She stumbled backward through. With quick reflexes, he caught her against his body, so hard and solid. A buzz of spellbinding need swept through her.

A groaning sound came from the garden. "What is—"

"Shh," Alasdair breathed against her ear, and she shivered. After their entrance, he eased the gate closed and urged her behind an evergreen shrub. The balefire lit up the sky and reflected off the gray stone castle wall to cast a soft glow down into the flower garden.

The sounds came again, a soft male groan. Was someone hurt? And then an answering giggle. Oh, dear lord, two people were...making love in the garden. Gwyneth's face grew hot as the fire crackling outside.

"We must go," she whispered.

"Nay. They will leave soon enough."

His hand rested heavy on her waist, his fingers stroking through her corset. Her nipples peaked and ached for his touch, for his wet mouth, licking, sucking.

She tried to draw in fresh air to clear her mind, to fight the effects of the spell he cast over her, but instead inhaled the smoke that had seeped into his clothing along with his clean male scent.

His hot breath fanned her hair. He sucked her earlobe into his mouth. She gasped but he placed his thumb over her lips. The thrill of him coursed through her, possessed her. She flicked out her tongue against his thumb, then surprised herself by sucking it into her mouth. She didn't know why she yearned to do that, but she wanted some part of him within her. Wanted to taste him.

Alasdair hissed against her ear, moaned her name. Shocking herself, she wondered what that other, very hard part of his body would feel like against her lips.

Though she could scarce think, she knew the other couple nearby in the garden continued with their mating, oblivious that anyone was near. Their sounds of pleasure escalated. The woman cried out. Was that how Gwyneth sounded when Alasdair made love to her? She could only remember experiencing him in a most earthly, carnal way that sent her flying toward the heavens.

As the man in the garden groaned with his release, Alasdair pressed his lips against Gwyneth's throat and trailed his tongue downward to her collarbone. The way she had taken to sucking his thumb put lascivious images in his head. Moving his sporran aside, he pressed his erection firmly against her stomach.

He craved the woman in his arms more than he craved spring in the midst of winter. And though it made him a traitorous Scot, he yearned to cast his gaze upon her more than the bonny hills surrounding him. He wanted to savor her and drink her slowly like the finest whisky.

Her skin smelled of smoke and woman. Her hands, fisted on his doublet and tugging him closer, spoke of unfulfilled hunger. He knew of hunger, aye, indeed. The kind that made his soul yearn and set his body afire.

The other couple in the garden finished their tryst and left, but he was happy to see Gwyneth hadn't noticed. He enjoyed being the sole focus of her attention. And he reveled in her earlier jealousy.

She melted and swayed against him with sighs, inciting his arousal to yet a higher level. Taking his thumb away from her mouth, he kissed her, full and deep, fed her erotic kisses, and she ate. She flicked her tongue against his. Her whimpering little gasps and moans made the aching pleasure in his erection intensify, and he wanted naught more than to slide into her tight, wet heat.

Loving the way she held him close, he yanked up her skirts and petticoats. With his fingers, he relished the softness of her thighs, the curve of her hip. Her silky skin stole the last of his rationality.

Discovering the stone bench nearby, he sat and tugged her to him, straddling his lap, facing him. He raked her skirts up to her lap.

"Oh, Alasdair, I cannot," she whispered in a desperate tone.

"You must only do what you wish." *Please let me make love to you right here.* "I'm dying to have you, *a shùgh mo chrìdhe.*"

He spread his hand on her thigh, above her stocking, and stroked it upward. He rubbed his thumb across her mound, her soft curls and lower, gently through her moisture and swollen female lips that made him ache. She gasped and jerked against him.

With his thumb he massaged her wet, swollen nub. She fell to his shoulder and moaned incoherent words. Aye, she was loving that. But no more than he did. He was ready to ignite like gunpowder.

She strained toward him, closer to his shaft. He yearned to bury himself forcefully deep inside her, but he wanted her to be the one to initiate the action, so she could not deny how much she wanted him.

She tugged at his kilt beneath her, then lifted herself off his lap, shoved his kilt up and captured his hard shaft in her cool hand.

"Oh, saints, Gwyneth!" He barely curbed the primal urge to thrust. "Take me inside you," he whispered against her lips.

By slow degrees, she lowered herself onto him. Trembling with restraint, he forced himself to remain still as he slipped deeper into her hot, drenched passage. Had he made that growling animal noise? She took his humanity and control. He wanted to ravish her like a rutting beast takes its mate, with wild immodecary.

She covered his face with kisses. Emotion ached in his chest, and suddenly with bright clarity, he knew what it was.

Mo dia, I love her.

He froze for a moment, savoring the realization. How had that happened? He knew not. The only thing certain now was he would never let her go. *Never.*

He drew her upward, then lowered her again. Her tight body clenched and caressed him.

Watching her eyes, drifted closed in bliss, he taught her the rhythm. She placed her feet on the ground and rode him with eagerness and abandon as if she could not stop. Sweet heaven, she desired him.

Marry me, Gwyneth. Nay, he could not say the words again. Not now. Her mouth would tell him *no,* even as her body said *yes.*

When she cried out in release, she squeezed him so tightly he near lost his mind. He took her mouth with a deep kiss.

His patience and control at an end, he picked her up easily. Still buried inside her, he wrapped her legs around his waist and leaned one arm against the high rock wall. His other hand beneath her hips, he held her steady and thrust up into her, slow and gently at first, but with increasing need and strength, as his body demanded. Waves of heat and pleasure coursed through him.

He breathed against her mouth, watched her eyes half-closed with female bliss. She gasped and whimpered her encouragement. When she flicked her tongue against his lips, he lost himself. His release crashed down upon him with the force of a boulder. But instead of unbearable pain, unimaginable rapture sang along his nerve endings. It went on and on, spun out and ricocheted in echoes.

For a moment, he feared they might both sink to the ground. Still holding her, he stumbled backward and dropped to the bench. "Dear God, Gwyneth, you have taken away my strength."

She held his face between her palms and, in the dimness, gazed into his eyes with a most solemn expression. "And you have taken away my control."

He smiled.

"Give it back," she whispered.

"Nay. Never."

"Then I shall keep your strength."

"Delilah."

Loving the affectionate grin that spread over her face, he kissed her once again, slow and deep and sweet.

Shouts, running footsteps and a commotion erupted outside the garden gate.

"What the devil is going on?" Alasdair helped her stand, and their clothing fell back into place. Taking her hand, he led her to the small garden gate and opened it.

All manner of clan members ran through the main barmkin gate.

"Alasdair!" Fergus shouted and strode toward him. "Some MacIrwins slipped in, but we don't ken to what purpose."

"Where were the guards?" he asked.

"I'm thinking there were too many people here for the festival, strangers and people in costume."

"We caught this one, trying to escape!" Angus and Busby dragged a struggling captive through the gates and into the barmkin. They threw a hood back to reveal a woman.

"They took Rory!" Matilda shouted from the castle portal. "'Twas one of the mummers in a mask."

CHAPTER THIRTEEN

Someone took Rory? Cold steel scraped down Alasdair's spine.

Gwyneth looked like a lost specter. In a trice, she dashed out the barmkin gate.

"God's wounds. Gwyneth!" By the time he reached the open gates, she approached the hill's edge. "Crawford, stop her!" he yelled to the guard. But she had already passed him.

Thank God, Crawford caught her halfway down the hill. Gwyneth screamed. Her arms and legs flailed as she fought and kicked. Damnable woman! Could she not think before she acted? The burly guard hauled her off her feet and carried her back toward Alasdair.

"No! They took Rory!" Gwyneth screamed.

The guard set her on her feet. Alasdair grasped her upper arms with a strength he feared was too harsh. She, at least, was safe. If Gwyneth ran onto MacIrwin land, death was sure to follow. He could not lose her.

She jerked against his hands. "Bastards! They took Rory!" The tears streamed down her face.

"Gwyneth. Listen to me."

She latched her fists onto his doublet and tugged. "They're getting away! We must get him back!"

"And we will. Just calm yourself." In truth, he wanted to charge onto MacIrwin land himself and bring the lad back, but he had enough rationality about him to realize it would be suicide without a plan and a large force of men.

"We don't ken yet who took him, Donald or Southwick."

Gwyneth sagged against him and sobbed. "Southwick," she said almost incoherently. "I wager it was the knave."

"If Southwick took him, he won't kill him. He's wanting an heir."

"He's my son! Not his! He will hit Rory. I'll kill that bastard if he harms my baby."

"Aye, and I'll help you. But first, we must go back to the tower and question the MacIrwin woman who was captured. Then we shall round up a party and go after him."

She nodded and wiped her eyes.

Guiding her steps, Alasdair helped Gwyneth back to the barmkin. Every ten seconds she glanced back over her shoulder through the darkness toward MacIrwin land. His soul ached for her for he knew what it was to lose a son, and he intended to do everything in his power to return hers to her arms.

They passed the still-burning balefire, then strode through the gates. Gwyneth tore herself away and ran toward the MacIrwin woman, whom Angus and Busby still held near the castle wall. Alasdair caught up with her.

"Who took my son?" Gwyneth demanded.

The woman hung her head.

Gwyneth grasped her hair, yanked her head up and stared into her face. "Ruth? Your name is Ruth, is it not?"

"Aye."

"Who took my son?"

"Answer!" Alasdair bellowed at the woman when she remained silent too long.

She shrank back and gaped at him, mute and wide-eyed.

"Do you ken what it feels like to have a noose around your neck?" he asked.

The woman's face scrunched into a horrid expression, and she collapsed into blubbering tears. "'Twas the MacIrwin. Don't kill me! I beg of you, don't kill me."

"Why was he taken?" Alasdair demanded.

"A fancy Sassenach lord said the lad was his son. He paid us to rescue him."

"Oh, dear lord!" cried Gwyneth.

"Southwick. 'Tis as I suspected. Where are they meeting the Sassenach with him?" asked Alasdair.

"At the south border. He was wanting to be away, toward London, afore the morn."

"London. I will kill him." Gwyneth wiped a hand over her tear-drenched eyes.

"How many men were traveling with the Englishman?" Alasdair asked.

"A half dozen or so."

Alasdair glanced around to find most of the clan gathered behind them. "I need five able-bodied men ready to ride south within the hour to recover Lady Gwyneth's son."

He was proud to see two dozen of his strongest men step forward.

"I cannot believe you would do this, Ruth," Gwyneth said. "You have a son of your own. How would you feel if a vile man stole him away from you?"

Ruth hung her head.

"Take her to a cell below," Alasdair told Busby. "Tell the guard to give her bread and water twice a day until I return." He turned to the group. "I need to see all the men in the hall now."

Once inside, he noticed Gwyneth disappearing up the stairs. Where the devil was she going?

When the clan was assembled, Alasdair motioned his cousin onto the dais with him. "Fergus, I'm leaving you in charge."

Fergus nodded and gave an abbreviated bow.

Alasdair turned his attention to the rest of the men who packed the great hall. "'Tis possible Donald MacIrwin will think I have followed the Englishman with a large company of men. He will assume he has an advantage for attack here. But he doesn't. I will only need five to ride with me. The rest of you will stay here. Be vigilant, armed and ready for battle."

He glanced at the men in front who had volunteered. "To ride with me, I will need Padraig, Angus, Boyd, Tomas, and Sweeney. As for the rest of you, I'll need your skills here to defend the clan and Kintalon. I thank all of you for your willingness to help."

He stepped off the dais and found Gwyneth descending the stairs from her bedchamber. She had changed back into her old clothing.

He narrowed his eyes and tugged her toward a corner to talk privately. "You'll stay here. We will return as soon as we have Rory."

"I must go with you." Steel resolve echoed in her quiet tone. She threw the large sack she carried onto her shoulder. What was that, her clothes?

"Nay, 'tis too dangerous."

"He's my son. I have to be there."

"You'll slow us down. If there's a skirmish, 'twill be difficult to protect you."

"If that happens, I'll hide and use my *sgain dubh*. And I'm a good rider, either sidesaddle or astride. What will you do if Southwick gets all the way to London with him? I am Rory's mother. I have legal rights to him. You do not."

He could see it was no use to argue with her. If he didn't allow her to go, she'd likely find a way to follow, alone. That would be far more dangerous for her. She had slipped by the guards before.

"You're to keep up on your own. 'Tis for your son we do this. If you hinder it, 'twill be your own fault."

She stood straighter. "I will not hinder it."

"Very well, then. I'll have one of the grooms saddle a mare. Be ready within the hour."

"I thank you, sir." She curtseyed.

Alasdair strode away from her to give separate orders to each of the five men and have Fergus convey his apologies to the visiting clan chieftains and other guests for his absence.

Gwyneth wanted to thank Alasdair a hundred times over. Indeed, she could never show the depth of her gratitude for his willingness to help her to this extent.

She glanced around at the milling crowd, then a second later, realized she was looking for Rory. The hollow pain in her chest widened. *Oh dear God, help me.*

This was her own fault. If she had been with Rory, telling stories, instead of with Alasdair, cavorting in the garden, this wouldn't have happened. She had been wallowing in the depths of carnal pleasure at the same moment her son was stolen away. *I am a horrid mother.*

๏๛ ๛๏

We will find Rory.

In the pre-dawn moonlight the seven of them raced south, over moors and between mountains.

We will find Rory. Gwyneth ran the words through her mind, silently repeating them, like an incantation or prayer.

The horses' hooves, rumbling against the ground like never-ending thunder, combined with the rhythmic movement, threatened to mesmerize her. But the cool, fresh air, along with the scent of horses and leather, kept her grounded in reality.

Her first instinct was to believe God was punishing her for her sinful behavior. Yes, maybe He was. But her regard for Alasdair was not evil. Her emotions were not evil; they just *were*. Those same emotions had given rise to her desire for the man riding before her. And that desire had allowed her bright moments of joy such as she had not known possible.

Joy and love were not evil.

Love? Do I love him?

Yes, some jubilant part of her wanted to shout. But she couldn't allow him to find out, because her love for him would change nothing about their present situation.

~ ~ ~

"Halt!" Maxwell Huntley, Lord Southwick drew up in the darkness before a rushing stream.

His son, whom the other men had bound and tied across one of the saddles, screamed and yelled. He called for his ma and for Alasdair; he screeched out insults that would scorch the ears of most soldiers. What the devil had Gwyneth been teaching him? If the loud and obnoxious little terror was not his son…he could not think of it. The lad simply had to be his.

"We don't have time to stop now, Southwick," Lord Peterson said. "If we do, the MacGraths may catch up to us."

"I must see if this irritating little rascal truly is my own flesh and blood," he muttered, dismounting. If Gwyneth had lied to him that day six years ago, he would be murderously angry. "Bring the torch here. And take the lad off the horse." Once his guard had set the boy onto his feet, Southwick yanked the sack from his head.

The boy's hair was blondish-brown and straight, much like his own.

"Take me back to my ma!"

"Rory. Is that your name?" Southwick asked.

"Aye."

He sounded like a damned Scot, and had a Scots name besides. Southwick ground his teeth. He'd see about changing both.

"What is your mother's name?"

Rory struggled against the guard holding him. "Gwyneth."

"How old are you?"

"Almost six. Let me go, you toad-spotted whoreson!"

Southwick clasped his hands tightly behind his back. He was sore tempted to slap some sense into the lad, but not in front of his men. "Cease! You will be quiet and mind your manners. Has your mother taught you nothing?"

Rory merely narrowed his eyes and produced a malicious glare. He would have to whip some respect into the little hellion.

"When is your birthday?" Southwick demanded.

"Why are you asking me daft questions? I want to go home."

"That's exactly where we are going—home. Now tell me when your birthday is."

"July tenth," he ground out between clenched teeth.

That would put his conception at the time when he and Gwyneth had a tryst. The boy looked like Gwyneth for the most part, but he had the narrow, refined Huntley nose and chin which gave him an aristocratic air, just as Southwick had himself. The boy was dirty, with soot and ash on his face and worn clothing.

"Let me see your hands and feet."

"Nay." The lad stood sullen.

Southwick bent to remove a primitive leather shoe himself.

"Nay!" Rory kicked Southwick's shin.

He grabbed the child's chin. "Listen to me, Rory. You will show me respect. I am your father."

"Nay, you're not! My da is dead!"

"That wasn't your real da. I am. You may call me *Father*."

"Nay! I won't."

Rage crawled along Southwick's nerve endings. And then he realized Rory was acting like a Huntley. Most of the men in his own family were stubborn and determined to get their way. Quick tempered. They hated being taken advantage of.

Smiling, Southwick drew in a deep breath, calming himself. Indeed, this barbaric wild child was his son. In London, when the boy was cleaned up, Southwick would teach him about manners and respect.

"Put my son back on the horse. We ride."

A few hours after daybreak, Alasdair, Gwyneth, and their party reached Aviemore. The muddy streets were filled with Scots dressed in their Midsummer finest, plaids of every description. She searched throngs of people for Rory and Southwick. Her anxiety vibrated to a higher pitch with each minute that passed.

"Did you see a half-dozen Englishmen and a lad ride through this morn?" Alasdair called to a grizzly-faced man in front of the livery stable.

"Aye, nay more than three hours past. They traded for fresh horses."

Good lord, a three hour lead! How will we catch up?

They quickly left Aviemore behind. Gwyneth rode in the middle of the group, beside Padraig. This trip through the countryside reminded her too much of when she'd first arrived in Scotland, alone and terrified, six years ago. The fear was worse now, despite the fact she was no longer a naïve girl.

Long before they reached Pitlochry, sunset gleamed over the land in bright orange rays. The gently sloping land here was not as majestic or dramatic as the Highlands.

Alasdair slowed his horse to a walk, and the rest followed suit. He stopped in a secluded spot near a stream and swung down from his bay. "We wouldn't be able to catch up to them even if we were to ride all night. And 'tis apparent Lady Gwyneth may fall out of the saddle soon."

"No, I will not." She had promised him she would keep up with the men, and she meant to do it—even if it should kill her.

"The horses need rest as well."

She was disheartened that they hadn't yet spotted Rory or the knaves who had abducted him. How far would they have to ride to catch up to them? All the way to London? She prayed that would not be the case.

The other men dismounted and started unloading the pack-horse to make camp.

Alasdair approached and stroked her mare's muzzle. "Are you ready to dismount?"

"Yes."

He reached up to her, placed his hands at her waist and lifted her from the sidesaddle. Her feet ached and prickled once set firmly on the ground. She wiggled her numb toes within her leather slippers.

Sunset lit the depths of Alasdair's eyes to rich brown. "Are you well, then, m'lady?" His low, intimate tone turned her insides to sweet plum pudding.

"Yes. Are you?"

"Aye."

Awareness of him threatened to fluster her. "I thank you for doing this favor for me. 'Tis a grand service, indeed."

"You have done more than this for me." He cupped her neck and stroked a thumb over her ear. "You risked your life to save mine when you dragged me off that battlefield."

Alasdair's eyes grew too intense, and she dropped her gaze to that vulnerable, sensual hollow at the base of his throat. Had she ever kissed him there? No, she didn't think so, but she wanted to.

Nonsense. I must not kiss him anywhere, ever again. She glanced aside. *I must think only of Rory and getting him back.*

She had to believe he was safe. Surely Southwick would not injure his son, though he might not treat him well. He might hit him or starve him as punishment. Rory was a little warrior and he might anger Southwick with attempts to escape or fight back. Southwick probably had him tied up and thrown across a saddle. Her sweet child was likely terrified beyond reason.

She wanted to take her dagger to Southwick.

჻ఆౖ ౖ

Later that night, Alasdair lay in his bedroll looking up at the stars, thankful it was not raining. Except for Boyd, who took his turn at watch, the other men snored nearby—as well they should. It had been hours since they'd all gone to bed.

Rory and Gwyneth disturbed Alasdair's thoughts. He prayed the lad was unhurt. No matter what it took, he would return him to his mother.

And Gwyneth…by the saints, at some point, she had become as important to him as his next heartbeat. It had nothing to do with her saving his life over a month ago, and everything to do with the way she'd burrowed into his soul.

In truth, he was the greatest imbecile for letting her steal his heart away. He'd never wanted to feel such depth of emotion for a woman again. When Leitha died, he'd almost died with her. A long time passed before he'd felt alive again. Maybe he hadn't truly reclaimed his life until Gwyneth saved it.

To look at her was to want her in every way—in his bed, in his life, in his heart. Though he knew he was foolish for wanting her love, that was the thing he craved most.

"Alasdair," Gwyneth whispered in the darkness, almost as if conjured by his thoughts.

He sat up. The dim light of the dying fire revealed her standing in the opening of her tent, not twenty feet away. She wore a glowing-white smock with her *arisaid* draped over her shoulders. She looked like a dream come to life.

"Aye. What is it?"

"I cannot sleep."

"Nor can I."

She shivered and rubbed her arms. What was on her mind? Did she want to talk? Or something else?

"Come. Cover up here." Alasdair lifted the edge of his woolen

186

blanket.

He would welcome her into his bed by any means, fair or foul. He craved the softness of her skin and the whisper of her words.

She glanced at the men lying closer to the fire.

"They're asleep." Alasdair darted a look toward Boyd where he stood watch on the far side of the small clearing. His back was to the fire, and none of them moved.

Now that the tempting idea of her sharing his bed had invaded his consciousness, Alasdair had to fulfill it, whether she wanted innocent sleep or something deliciously naughty.

Gwyneth crept toward him and slid beneath his plaid. Happiness and arousal flowed through him with the warmth of fine whisky. She snuggled up against him, pressed her face to his chest… and burst into tears.

Damnation.

Alasdair wrapped her in his arms. "Och, Gwyneth, I ken how hard this is on you."

"Yes."

After a few moments, she wiped her eyes and nose on a handkerchief she'd brought with her and apparently tried to calm herself with deep breaths—warm breaths that fanned against his bare chest and teased him.

He didn't know whether he was relieved or irritated that he now wore trews. 'Twas more convenient if he had to rise in a hurry. But not convenient for spontaneous lovemaking.

Gwyneth was an emotional woman needing comfort and reassurance that her son would be safe. But he was an aroused man wanting the woman he cared deeply for—nay, indeed, the woman he loved.

"'Twill be all right." He stroked a hand over her back and up into the silkiness of her loosened hair. "I'll make sure of it."

"We must get Rory back. He's all I have."

"Aye, and we will. You're needing a wee bit of faith." Though he was certain Rory meant more to her than anyone or anything, he wasn't *all* she had. *Can you not see that you have me as well? If you would but open your eyes.*

"What if we don't? Southwick is a powerful man. The courts will always side with the man."

"But Rory's illegitimate. 'Haps that will give you the advantage." Alasdair hoped what he said was true. Regardless, he needed to reassure Gwyneth and take away some of her worries.

"Why can Southwick not simply marry someone else and have legitimate children?"

"'Twould be the best solution. But mayhap there is a reason he didn't tell us."

"He doesn't even know or love Rory. I've raised him almost single-handedly. He's *my* son. The reason I push forward every day." Her whisper held the fierceness of a tigress protecting her cub.

"You're a good mother," Alasdair murmured. *Aye, why could you not be the mother of my own children?*

"I wager you're the only one who thinks so."

He kissed her forehead. "It doesn't matter what other people think. We both ken the truth. You're the most devoted mother I've ever seen." He stroked his fingertips over her cheek and chin, relishing the feel of her velvety skin. "Aside from that, you're a healer. You oft ignore your own needs to care for others. Even strangers, like me, when you saved my life. You didn't ken whether I would be friend or enemy when I awoke, but you didn't let that scare you. You're a strong woman, Gwyneth. The bravest I ever met."

"You had a peace treaty, so I knew you would be kind. I had a feeling, even before you awoke, that you were a good man."

"Och, I'm not that good." If he were such an angel, he wouldn't be thinking of ravishing her right here and now, outside on the ground with several other men within speaking distance.

His body tightened and yearned for her, but alas he must fight his urges.

Through her thin smock, her breasts pressed against his bare chest, near stripping away his sanity.

She kissed the base of his throat, and pleasure flowed through him like melted butter mixed with honey.

"You're warm," she whispered.

Either he was daft or that was an invitation. "And you're soft." He stroked his palm up from her waist and over her breast through the material. Her nipple hardened. "Except right here," he murmured and rolled her nipple beneath his thumb.

She gasped. In the abandon he loved, she thrust her breast into his hand. When she lost control, he couldn't help himself. He moved down and licked her nipple through the fabric, plucked it between his lips. The earthy scent of woman with a hint of green herbs filled his senses. Lust washed over him. She lay flat on her back and buried her hands in his hair, embracing him close.

He glanced around and found that none of the men had moved.

"Hold onto my shoulders." He lifted her as he rose and carried her to the tent. Inside, he lowered her to her bedroll and woolen blanket.

Once he'd covered them again, he kissed her, deep and thorough, relishing the wet, hot feel of her mouth and her unique taste. He loved the way she followed his mouth and sucked at his tongue.

What a rogue he was for taking advantage of her vulnerable emotions. But he wanted her. Forever. And he would use any means to tie her to him. He wanted his bairn growing in her belly. Not just because he needed an heir, but more, he never wanted her to leave him. He would have an excuse to make her stay. That probably made him a desperate bastard and a barbarian, but he didn't care. His clan, his lands, his title—those were his duty. But Gwyneth was his delight. His reason to smile.

He kissed a trail down her neck and plucked at her nipple through the material again. She whimpered and arched her back. He would have this wretched garment off her.

Stroking a hand up her thigh, he pushed the linen upward to expose her hips. She lifted her upper body, and he pulled the smock over her head.

So much silky, bare skin. The allure near made him dizzy. He didn't know where he wanted to touch her first, so he touched her everywhere, smoothing his palms along her feminine curves. She purred against his lips. When he grazed his fingertips between her legs, he found her wet. She moaned, and he ached to plunge to her depths.

She was the most eager lover he'd ever had. Surely, she craved him as much as he craved her, by simple touch or look. After he unfastened his trews and pushed them off, he parted her legs and rolled between them.

Maybe if he got her with child, she would be forced to marry him because of her blessed conscience. It was not trickery because she well knew the risks of lovemaking.

He suckled her breasts and rubbed his shaft lightly against her mound. With delirious moans, she arched and tugged at him.

"Alasdair?" she begged in a breathy tone.

"Aye." He could wait no longer to join his body with hers. Savoring every delightful inch, he slowly slid into her tight, wet heat and growled at the euphoria that dazzled him.

Gwyneth uttered beautiful quiet groans and pants. He kissed

her mouth, flicked his tongue in and out as he mimicked the motion of his shaft. Locking her legs around the back of his and meeting his hips, she shoved him to the brink of release too soon. Though it had been only a day since their last encounter, he hungered for her hourly.

Holding his weight up off her slight frame, he thrust himself into her, gently over and over. And then faster with more urgency. She tilted her hips and met his thrusts just as her climax grasped hold of her. She squeezed him and near took his sanity. With his kisses, he tried to muffle the cries coming from her mouth so she wouldn't wake the others. At the same time, his own impending release charged in on him, replacing his rationality with a pleasure so sharp it stole his breath.

Though he tried to stifle his own moans, he was too far drowned under the influence of ecstasy to control anything.

When his reasoning ability returned, he sucked in deep breaths.

He placed soft, lingering kisses to her mouth. Nay, he could never let her go.

༝ঌ ঌ༝

Gwyneth awoke sometime later, feeling a rough, hot hand stroking up her leg, over her derriere, across her belly and up to her breasts. She immediately remembered where she was. And what they'd done. Sweet heavens! She had not meant for this to happen.

Well, maybe she had.

She had but wanted someone to hold onto, someone to talk to. *Alasdair.* She was not strong like he'd said, but weak, especially in his presence. He was her weakness, but at the same time, her strength. He made her believe anything was possible, indeed, that he could accomplish anything.

With him lying close behind her, she snuggled her naked bottom to his hard body. He felt delectable. His erection prodded her. A warm tingling swirled through her belly and moved downward in a wet, itching sensation. She was his puppet.

"Gwyneth," he breathed into her ear and suckled her earlobe.

"Mmm, yes."

He lifted her leg back over his and spread her thighs in a most unusual way. With his fingers, he teased her, stroking between her legs. The pleasure was so immobilizing, all she could do was slide her hand backward around his neck, into his hair and hold on.

Then he did something she didn't expect—positioned himself and thrust into her. Surely this was a scandalous and forbidden way to make love. She had not even imagined it would be possible. This was the way animals mated. And at the moment, she felt like an animal—she wanted to bite him.

"Shh," he whispered in her ear, and she realized she'd cried out. His clansmen slept outside. She was momentarily shocked at herself. With a fingertip, he continued to rub her in a scandalously erogenous spot while he glided into her depths, slowly at first. Then with more demanding insistence.

The magical tingles centered there. She arched her back and pushed her rump against him. Wanting more, wanting him deeper, wanting all he would give her with his forceful body and powerful movements. She shoved the wadded up plaid into her mouth and bit into it to muffle her cries as rapture claimed her. Oh, her body wanted to hold onto his and never let him go.

He grasped her to him tight and slid to the hilt. There he shuddered into her and moaned.

"I want all of you," he breathed into her ear. "*Tha gràdh agam ort.*"

She knew what those Gaelic words meant—*I love you.*

Conflicting emotions besieged her. Instantaneous joy, over-shadowed by deep sadness. Rage and helplessness.

Dear God, I love you too, Alasdair. But too many things prevented her saying the words.

Their love could never be.

CHAPTER FOURTEEN

When next Alasdair became aware, men's voices echoed back at him from some distance. He opened his eyes to firelight and early dawn glowing through the tent. God's bones, summer nights were too short. He had not wanted to be caught in Gwyneth's tent, for her sake. He had meant to return to his own bedroll long before now, but he'd found it nigh impossible to leave her.

Gwyneth lay sleeping, cradled in his arms, her nose pressed to his chest and her soft breaths tickling his skin.

She was still naked, as was he. Closing his eyes, he savored this moment as one that neared perfection. If he could but wake every morn ensnared in her arms, he would be a happy man.

Would she ever consent to marry him? He would not ask her again until he was sure. She had cried last night after they'd made love the second time. Perhaps she had understood his words spoken in Gaelic. One part of him wanted her to know he loved her, but another part didn't, because she might not feel the same.

It wasn't over yet. He was nothing if not determined. Once he rescued Rory, Alasdair was certain Gwyneth would agree to marry him. He would somehow convince her Rory would be safe growing up in the Highlands. And if he could achieve peace, once Donald MacIrwin was arrested, there would be no more feuds and skirmishes between the MacIrwins and MacGraths.

His clansmen talking and laughing outside drew Alasdair's attention once more. They had to be on their way soon if they intended to catch Southwick. Alasdair gently disentangled his limbs from Gwyneth's, stroking his hand over her silky skin in the process. Such temptation. If he didn't stop touching her, he would emerge from the tent with an erection his trews couldn't hide.

He turned to his back, found his trews beside him and struggled into them. After kissing Gwyneth's forehead, he braced himself to face his men.

He crawled from the tent, stood and closed the flap behind him.

When he turned, the gazes of the five men gathered around the fire locked on him. Tomas, Boyd and Sweeney smirked. But Angus and Padraig scowled at him.

"Good morrow."

They murmured greetings in response.

He didn't care whether they approved or not. Ignoring them, he strolled toward the bushes to relieve himself, then to the stream to wash his hands and face in the cold water. That brought him awake with refreshing clarity. Upon returning to the campsite, he found his gear on the ground near his bedroll and dug through his possessions for a shirt.

He slipped the garment on and sauntered toward the fire. Angus handed him a pewter cup of ale and a warm oat bannock.

"I thank you." He sat on a rock by the fire, while the others stared anywhere but at him. "A fine morn, aye, lads?"

"Aye," they chorused.

"We shall make much progress this day and cover many miles. I'm hoping we'll be arriving in Edinburgh afore gloaming."

"Are you wanting to run the horses into the ground, then?" Angus asked, staring at the fire.

Alasdair stiffened. He hated his authority questioned, but Angus was his cousin and ten years his senior, so he oft spoke his mind.

"Nay," Alasdair said with obvious patience. "If we don't make it by then, it cannot be helped."

He ran his gaze over the men. When they looked him in the eye, he dared any one of them to challenge him. He would not have them passing judgment on something they knew nothing of—his feelings for Gwyneth and what existed between them. Best to face the issue head on.

"I can see you're all wondering what the hell I was doing coming out of Gwyneth's tent. In truth, 'tis none of your concern. And I won't tolerate your judging her for it. She is a lady now and always, deserving of our respect."

"Forgive me, Alasdair," Angus said. "But are you sure *you're* showing her respect?"

"Aye, though I ken you don't see it that way." He refused to explain his relationship with Gwyneth to them. He would not have them know he'd proposed but she'd turned him down. He was not yet done convincing her to change her mind.

"Do you care for her, then?" Angus asked.

Padraig's arrow-sharp gaze cut through Alasdair.

Boyd, Sweeney and Tomas cleared their throats, rose and drifted away to saddle the horses.

"Aye, that I do," Alasdair admitted.

"Have you thought of marryin' again?"

Alasdair tried to hold back his grin. "Don't fash yourself, cousin. I'm working on it."

Padraig clenched his jaw so hard, he was certain to crack a tooth. And his glare only intensified.

"Do you have something to say, Padraig?" Alasdair asked.

He shuffled his feet and lowered his eyes. "Nay. Just that… Lady Gwyneth is kind, and she's been through hell. You shouldn't take advantage of her weakened state, m'laird…with all due respect."

Alasdair knew Padraig was a wee besotted with Gwyneth, but he did not know the extent. He couldn't speak harshly to the kind-hearted man who had been loyal to him, and his father before him, for many years. As well, Alasdair couldn't tell them Gwyneth had sought him out last night.

"'Haps 'tis true I'm a rogue, but I have the best of intentions. Just give me a few days."

※◦❀◦❀◦※

Gwyneth awoke to daybreak and the rumble of male voices. She couldn't understand their exact words, but she recognized Alasdair's voice among them.

Alasdair. Oh, goodness!

She covered her head with the blanket and recalled the details of their encounter. The way he had given her comforting kisses and seduced her, body, mind and soul so that she forgot her troubles. Forgot her darling Rory within the clasp of a London knave.

Oh, dear lord, I am a weak wanton. She knew she shouldn't have gone to Alasdair last night. She had been safe in her tent. Safe and good and afraid…but most of all, lonely. She had craved holding someone in her arms. And needed someone strong—Alasdair—to hold her. She didn't normally accept comfort from anyone, but he had been out there, so close. She had needed his deep voice murmuring in her ear, words of reassurance that everything would be all right. She believed him; she trusted him. His hands, so warm and comforting, smoothing over her. That's what she had wanted.

But the rest—the carnal bliss that he unleashed on her—was part and parcel of their connection. Something she needed like her next breath, yet at the same time, she knew it was folly. She could not seem to learn her lesson. Sensuality was to be her downfall, her most horrid sin.

But then he'd said he loved her in his lilting Gaelic tongue. The beauty of the roughly whispered words had shattered her composure. No man had ever said those words to her. As well, she had never loved a man. But she did love Alasdair, with her whole being.

Why did this have to happen to me?

Their lives were on different paths, going in opposite directions. They could not have a love match, no matter how much she dreamed of it. She had to think only of her son and his future.

I must stop!

She threw back the covers and dragged her clothing onto the pallet. She shoved her head and arms into her smock—which Alasdair had so hastily removed the night before.

No, I will not think of last night and the forbidden, delightful things he did to me.

She put on her corset and fastened up the front with ties. Her breasts were tender where he'd nibbled at them. His mouth had been a tempting torture.

She blanked him out of her mind and struggled into the rest of her clothing. With the comb Alasdair had given her, she removed the tangles from her hair, recoiled it, then tied a *kertch* on her head.

She emerged from her tent to find Alasdair sitting with his cousin by the fire. Alasdair's sleepy but intent gaze lit on her and lingered. He had the look of a dissolute debaucher with his midnight beard stubble and his tousled mane. She had run her fingers through it numerous times the night before and knew well how soft and silky his hair was.

I am not embarrassed.

Well, maybe a little. She glanced at Angus, and he dropped his gaze to the fire. Did he suspect anything had happened last night? She hoped they had not wakened anyone.

"Good morrow, m'lady." Alasdair grinned. "Angus reheated some bannocks—if you can stomach them."

"I didn't force you to eat them," Angus grumbled.

Alasdair laughed and slapped his cousin on the shoulder.

"Indeed, they're gusty as ambrosia."

"I must excuse myself first." She gave a shallow curtsy and headed toward the bushes. The scent of horses and fresh horse dung was strong in the air as she passed their mounts. When she heard someone following, she glanced back to find Alasdair behind her.

"I will stand guard. If you require assistance, call out."

She nodded. "I thank you."

Once she was finished, she found Alasdair with his back to her, staring off into the distance and whistling. Hiding her smile, she washed her face and hands in the cold water of the stream, then dried them with the only thing available, her sleeves.

With a bow, Alasdair motioned for her to precede him.

Trying to fight back the memories of last night, she sat down on a rock by the fire. Alasdair gave her a warm bannock and cup of ale. The wholesome oat scent gave her hunger pains of a sudden.

"We must be on our way quickly if we are to catch up with Southwick. I'm hoping we'll be arriving in Edinburgh afore nightfall." Alasdair glanced at Angus. "'Twould give us about eighteen hours at this time of year."

"Do you think Southwick stopped in Edinburgh with Rory?" she asked.

"'Tis possible." Alasdair seated himself opposite her. "But the city is so large, 'twill be hard to find them. Once we're there, we must find Lachlan and have him join our party. He has spent more time in London than I have and will be much help to us if we end up having to go there."

"I see." Lord! She didn't want to go to London. Not only would Rory be harder to reclaim there, the mere thought of running into people who knew of her disgrace took her appetite.

But she would go through the fires of hell if required, to save Rory and have him back beside her. What significance were a few stares and snide remarks in the grand scheme of things? She would survive them as she survived everything else.

"Is anything the matter?" Alasdair asked.

When she glanced up, she found herself sitting alone with him. Angus had taken himself off somewhere.

Alasdair's gaze fixed upon her with concern. "Of a sudden, you're pale as a banshee."

"I was thinking, I won't be happy to have to see my father and some of those other Londoners who have told many a lurid tale about me. All true, of course."

Alasdair's face darkened, and his gaze grew sharp. "If they insult you, they'll regret it, I vow." His brogue intensified, and he muttered a few Gaelic words of dubious meaning.

"I thank you," she said, trying to keep the wistfulness out of her voice. He was as chivalrous as an old-fashioned armored knight. "But their words can no longer hurt me. The only thing that will hurt me is to lose Rory to an aristocratic beast who would abuse him."

Indeed, that would be like death to her.

"You won't be losing him to anyone. Trust me on that." Alasdair rose, strode toward where his bed had been last night and rolled up his plaid.

His determined tone gave her pause. She didn't doubt him. No, indeed, she trusted him to the depths of her soul. Adding a silent prayer for her son, she choked down the remainder of the bannock and a few sips of ale. By the time she arose, the men had everything packed, loaded and were ready to mount.

She joined them. "I thank all of you for your help."

The men murmured responses and bowed slightly.

Angus stood closest to her. "You should marry the lad," he said in a low tone. "Alasdair, I mean to say."

"What?"

Angus sent her a wise but fleeting glance. His cheeks above his dark beard were ruddier than normal. Good heavens, he knew she and Alasdair had spent the night together.

What had Alasdair told him?

She glanced at Sweeney, not far away. The young man, close to her own age, averted his gaze but she did not miss the grin he tried to hide. She scrutinized the other men. They all knew. She could see it in their mock blank expressions and lips, tight or clamped between their teeth to hide their snide smiles.

Mortified, she turned her back on them and focused on her saddle—not hers, but Alasdair's late wife's. A woman who had lain with him without shame, without the smirks of others lashing down at her.

Leather and harness squeaked and jingled as the men mounted.

Alasdair approached, stopping close behind her. "'Tis time to mount."

Angus and the other men walked their horses ahead, giving them privacy.

"What did you tell Angus?" she asked.

Taking her arm, Alasdair gently urged her to face him and

shielded her from the others. "What do you mean?"

"He told me I should marry you."

"Damnation," he muttered and darted a glare in his cousin's direction.

"Did you discuss it with him?"

"Nay more than I had to. He was wanting to ken what I was doing leaving your tent this morn." Alasdair shrugged and kissed her hand. "Don't pay him any mind."

Easy for him to say that. He was not the whore in this equation. Still, she couldn't stop herself from savoring the softness of his lips on her skin as he kissed the back of her other hand.

Because she had little choice in the matter, she allowed Alasdair to assist her into the sidesaddle. She tried not to think about his hands gripping her waist. Or the way the other men watched them.

She would not be spending the night with Alasdair again.

*

A mist of cool, drizzling rain greeted them the next evening as they reached Edinburgh. All was gray and drab in *Auld Reekie*—the grimy streets, the tall buildings, the sky with its low-hanging clouds. Even Edinburgh Castle on the steep hill above them looked mournful and bleak with its gray stone walls. The foul air of the smoke-filled city and its sewage near turned Alasdair's stomach. He glanced back at his drenched and bedraggled party. The rain matched everything else on this miserable trip.

His men thought him a heartless rogue, bent on torturing horses and debauching women. He had done neither. And it irked him like a thistle between his trews and arse that they would believe such of him.

Angus had been right; they couldn't reach Edinburgh as quickly as Alasdair had hoped. Which meant, in all likelihood, that Southwick now had an even greater lead.

Alasdair drew up at a coaching inn on Grassmarket and dismounted.

Since yesterday morn, Gwyneth had avoided him. She was polite and civil but not receptive to any private conversation or intimacy.

He'd told Angus he shouldn't have said anything to Gwyneth about marriage.

"Someone needed to tell her," his obstinate cousin had replied. "As much swiving as the two of you are doing, you need to be getting hand-fasted or married. What'll you do if a bairn results?"

"Let me handle it. 'Tis not your concern," he'd said.

Now, neither Angus nor Gwyneth was very friendly toward him. He would not propose to her again until he was certain she would say *yes* and until Rory was safe, but if she wanted him in her bed, he would readily comply. Betrothal or not, each time he made love to her, he further tied her to him. Perhaps she didn't realize that.

He would prove to her he could straighten things out with Southwick, and recover Rory. Though he didn't yet know how he would do it, he had to. He refused to let her and the lad down.

Alasdair approached Gwyneth sitting atop her mare. When he reached up to help her dismount, it was obvious she was trying to avoid looking into his eyes. She didn't want even that small connection, but he felt her body tremble when he touched her.

By the saints, I shall have you, Gwyneth, body and heart. Don't doubt it.

But he would not tell her that; he would show her. He would prove they were right for each other.

As he lifted her down, her narrow waist and slight weight within his hands bombarded him with instinctive urges, to hold her close and protect her. Comfort her. To carry her to the nearest bed for a repeat performance of two nights ago. Deep pleasure and devotion. He would show her a love so pure as to be blinding, if only she would let him.

Instead, he set her to her feet and pulled away to instruct two of the men to take care of the horses.

Within the inn's dining room, their party ate decent mutton stew, cheese and bread. The men shoveled the food in as if they had not eaten in weeks. Alasdair noticed, however, that Gwyneth picked at her food. Hating the worried slant of her brows, he vowed to take it away and set everything aright. Vowed to make her smile. Deep down, he prayed her lack of appetite and her bout of sickness early that morn signified something else—that she carried his child.

A half hour later, after he had handled the business of accommodations for their party and sent two of his men to find Lachlan, Alasdair climbed the narrow, dark stairway and knocked at Gwyneth's door.

"Who is it?" she called.

"'Tis me."

She opened the door slowly and stepped back.

Her vivid blue eyes, wide with caution, provided the only bright color in drab Edinburgh, but he forced himself to look away, toward the newly kindled blaze. He approached the small fireplace, hoping the heat would dry his clothing a wee bit.

"I'm thinking you would like a bath after being on the road so long, m'lady." He admitted he was trying to get back into her good graces.

"That would be lovely." Gwyneth cleared her throat. "Are you...staying in this room as well?"

He glanced back at her, for a moment perversely enjoying her discomfort. "I told the proprietor we were married."

Her mouth dropped open. "Why? Why did you do that?"

"You're a woman in the company of six men. 'Tis better this way. No one will question your position."

She frowned, apparently mulling that over. He was right, and she knew it. He hated the mockery of pretending to be married to her when he wanted it in truth.

"You mean to sleep here, then?" she asked.

He couldn't tell whether she hoped he would or wouldn't sleep there. How could she look so innocent, virginal and demure of a sudden, when she had been such a wanton in his arms? Wallowing in every carnal thing he'd done to her.

An image came to him, of her on top, riding him into the mattress, her eyes closed, head thrown back. Almost as she had done in the garden, but this time she'd be naked. Her creamy skin lit by the sun and her long, unbound hair tickling his legs. Her expression naught but pure rapture. He hardened instantly, wanting the image to be true so badly, sharp desire trapped his breath.

"'Haps I will sleep here. 'Tis not as if we haven't shared a bed afore."

A pink flush crept over her face and her jaw hardened. "I owe you more than I can ever repay, so if you want me to...warm your bed in exchange for getting Rory back, I will comply."

How could she think him so low? He had asked her to marry him twice. What more did she require to know he was honorable?

"What are you blathering on about? You saved my life, m'lady! I'm the one who's owing you, and repaying you. And even if I didn't, I would still help you recover Rory. Aside from that, you won't be warming my bed in exchange for anything, except the mutual pleasure between us."

Damnation, he'd let his anger get the better of him. His tone and glare had surely been harsher than he'd intended. Drawing in a deep breath, he tried to swallow his irritation.

"Well, I have no money," she said. "I cannot even pay for this room and—"

He stepped before her and tilted up her face, stroking his fingertips over her blushing cheeks. "Listen to me, Gwyneth," he said in a rough whisper. "I would give you anything I have. Can you not see that?"

Beyond a trace of tears, the blue flame of her eyes burned into his. Her small hand fisted in his doublet, tugging him closer. He lowered his head and brushed his lips across hers. Slowly he tasted her lips, and between. Such female temptation she was. Luscious torment. He wanted to lick her head to toe, devour her in a few hungry bites. Hands at her waist, he pressed her close, against his hard shaft. He could not overcome his obsession to have her. In every way.

Loud pounding on the door startled them. Gwyneth jumped back and pressed a hand to her lips, her darkened eyes filled with guilt.

"*Muire Mhàthair*," Alasdair muttered, turned his back to her and sucked in a deep breath. He tried to shut down his arousal and think of something unappealing. Damnation. Nothing was coming to him.

The knock sounded again.

Thankful his doublet was long enough over his trews to hide his erection, he wrested the door open.

Lachlan stood there, grinning like a mouse in a loaf.

"*Ciamar a tha sibh, mo bhràthair?*" Alasdair clasped his hand.

"*Glé mhath.*" Lachlan came in and bowed to Gwyneth. "Lady Gwyneth. Don't be worrying your pretty little head about Rory. We'll be getting him back afore long. Aye, brother?"

"That we will." Alasdair wondered at the way Lachlan addressed Gwyneth. Their clansmen must have filled him in on all the latest, including her appropriate title. And, no doubt, that Alasdair had spent a night in her tent. He dreaded the teasing Lachlan was sure to have in store for him.

"Have you any inkling where the scoundrel is what snatched him up?"

"We haven't seen a sign of Southwick or Rory since we left Kintalon. All we ken for a certainty is that they passed through Aviemore three hours before we did. After that, they must have ridden like the devil. They may be here in town, or proceeded on to England."

"They may have taken a ship to London. 'Twould be the fastest."

"Aye, and 'haps we should as well."

"We'll go arrange it." Lachlan faced Gwyneth. "You'll be happy to know I've found you a governess position here in Edinburgh."

Nay! The feeling of a large stone smashing into Alasdair's stomach near knocked him flat.

CHAPTER FIFTEEN

Gwyneth's face brightened. "Surely you jest, sir. A position for me? Here in Edinburgh?"

"Aye. Just outside the city." Lachlan said. "Alasdair, you remember George MacAvoy, Baron Lunsford. He's on the Privy Council now. He and his wife have three small lads and they're wanting someone to tutor them."

Alasdair wanted to punch Lachlan in his smiling mouth.

"They're right good people, and I'm thinking 'twould be perfect—" Lachlan frowned at Alasdair. "What's wrong?"

"I would have a word with you downstairs," Alasdair growled.

"I thank you, Lachlan, for your help," Gwyneth said.

Lachlan bowed and opened the door.

Alasdair followed him, then turned back. "I will have a hot bath sent up for you. Other than that, don't open the door for anyone."

"I thank you." She smiled—devil take it—because of Lachlan and the position.

Alasdair slammed the door closed behind him.

After speaking to a chamberlain about the bath, he followed his brother to a dim corner of the inn's sparsely populated public room. Lachlan ordered two tankards of ale for them.

"I ken what you're snarling about," Lachlan said. "But let me explain. As I told you afore, 'tis safest for everyone—Gwyneth, Rory, and the entire MacGrath clan—if she leaves the Highlands."

"You shouldn't have gotten involved in this," Alasdair snapped. "I'm having a hard enough time as it is, and you go and make it worse."

"'Twas because of her the MacIrwins burned the village."

203

"She saved your son's life." Alasdair wanted to smash his fist onto the thick planks of the oak table but restrained himself.

"Aye, and now I'm showing her my appreciation by helping her get something she wants. 'Twas what she asked of me in repayment."

Alasdair shook his head and stared into his ale. Hellfire, now what was he going to do? Even if he did recover Rory, Gwyneth would likely never marry him. Damn his lack-witted brother.

"I ken you have seduced her, but you can find another lass to warm your bed. A less dangerous one."

"You have no inkling what you're talking about!" All Lachlan knew of women was bedding them. Beyond the physical, he'd never had any feelings for one.

"Sweeney and Boyd told me you stayed in her tent one night." Lachlan sent him a devilish grin.

"If you were not my brother, I would kick your daft arse all the way back to Kintalon and beyond. Hell, I might anyway."

Lachlan studied him with narrowed eyes. Then shook his head. "You've gone soft-pated over her."

His muscles tense with restraint, Alasdair hoped his glare would burn a hole through his brother. Lachlan wouldn't be so damned cheerful if he'd just lost the person who brought his life into sharp, colorful focus and provided fuel to his soul.

"She's a bonny lass, to be sure. And if not for Donald MacIrwin, I'd want you to bring her back to Kintalon with you. Once Donald is arrested—if that ever happens—then you could come to Edinburgh and ask her to marry you."

"You're naught but a lunatic. If she gets settled in Edinburgh with a family, she'll not be interested in me anymore."

"Then you're better off without her. If you must marry, you want a woman who is completely devoted to you."

"You ken muckle about marriage, so don't be giving me advice on it."

Lachlan shrugged. "Very well."

Alasdair shoved his anger away for the moment and focused on another important issue. "Did you get an audience with the Privy Council yet?"

"Aye." Lachlan kept his voice low. "They are sending someone out with a message telling Donald MacIrwin and his son to appear before them here a fortnight hence."

"Good. I must schedule time to give my testimony as well."

"'Twould strengthen the case against them."

"As will the testimonies of other members of the clan."

Alasdair caught Lachlan up on the happenings at Kintalon since he had left, and they discussed the MacIrwin situation for the better part of an hour.

"More ale," Lachlan called out to the tapster, then turned his attention back to Alasdair. "I'm sorry about the predicament with Gwyneth. 'Haps 'twill work out in the end."

"No thanks to you."

"If you keep sending her hot baths, flowers, comfits and such, I'm sure she'll change her mind." Lachlan smirked. "You have the sensibilities of a gentleman-husband."

"She got very wet and muddy in the rain. I wouldn't want her to catch an ague."

Lachlan chuckled and raised his tankard. "Since most people think baths cause agues, 'tis a flimsy excuse to have a woman in your debt."

Alasdair sent his brother a hard stare.

"Aye, I can see you're calf-eyed over her."

"I cannot wait for the day you meet a lass who ties you up in so many knots you'll never be free again."

"Och! How can you place such a curse upon me?" Lachlan's expression was one of exaggerated insult and shock.

"'Tis only a matter of time, I wager."

"Never mind that. There is something I've been wondering about. This knave who took Rory, am I to understand that he is Rory's natural father?"

"Aye."

"What of Baigh Shaw?"

"Gwyneth married him after the fact, to give her son a name."

Lachlan raised his brows. "Ah. 'Tis not a terrible situation, then, is it? He may gift Rory with property one day."

"Aye, but 'tis likely Southwick will mistreat and abuse Rory. He slapped Gwyneth down once. I'm tempted to strangle him for that. She also said she has heard of him beating his servants and 'haps even killing one, but no one could prove it."

"Hell, you're right then. The lad shouldn't be with him, especially since he's so young."

"I cannot let her down."

"You would do anything to make her happy, aye?"

"I'll do what I can. Southwick is a vile serpent. In truth, I cannot stand for him to take custody of wee Rory. I was tempted to sever Southwick's limbs from his body when first I met him."

Lachlan snorted. "Mayhap you will get your chance. In the meantime, I will ride to the Newhaven docks and talk with some people I know to see if Southwick and his party have boarded a ship of late."

"I'll go with you. How far is it?"

"About two miles north. But what of the lady in her hot bath? Do you not want to check on her?" Lachlan winked.

"Nay." Alasdair stared into his ale, remembering the last bath of hers he had intruded on. She was temptation itself, her skin warm and damp, scented like flowers. Again, he would need to taste her essence, sweeter than honey, drugging like lotus. Och! He was daft, in truth.

He wouldn't impose upon her, mentally or physically, anymore.

"And why not?" Lachlan asked.

"All she will be thinking of is the damned tutoring position you've found for her."

"I'm sorry I've made your task harder, but I'm thinking you're up for the challenge. A good swiving does soften up the lasses and make them look at you with dreamy eyes."

"You're a goat."

Lachlan laughed and rose. "We should be on our way—if you're certain you'd rather visit Newhaven than the room above stairs."

※ ❧ ❧ ※

In her room, Gwyneth savored the warm bath water and the soothing fragrance of the chamomile, bog myrtle and wild thyme soap she'd brought with her. A thrill trailed along her nerves. Lachlan had found her a tutoring position. Thanks be to God. Now they had only to recover Rory, and she would have what she wanted.

They would get him back. There was no other alternative.

She imagined herself teaching three small boys, along with Rory, at a beautiful country estate just outside Edinburgh. It would be a good life.

But Alasdair's absence would linger like a great, dark cloud in her bright day. She would miss him. She would have to lock her heart away in a chunk of ice. But she must, for Rory's sake.

She lathered her hair. What other man would have sent her up a bath? None.

He was willing to risk life and limb to help her recover Rory, even willing to pay for this trip, their lodgings and food. If they took a ship to London, that would be another cost. Perhaps it was nothing to him, being an earl. But she cringed, thinking of the money he was spending on her account. She felt an obligation to repay him the money, and she would once she earned wages.

Unlike Donald, Baigh, or her father, Alasdair supported her emotionally. He did not wish to strip away her strength, but reinforced it with his own. This was something completely foreign to her. And because of it, her gratitude ran so deep it hurt her not to be able to give him everything he asked of her—and she would, if it were in her power. But it wasn't. Her responsibility to Rory superseded everything, even her own heartbreak.

After her bath, she dried her hair before the hearth, recalling the night she had sat on Alasdair's lap while he combed his fingers through the snarled strands.

How tempting he was.

How I love him.

Tears dripped onto her cheeks. She wished he would knock on her door.

She waited what seemed like hours, her hair long since dry, then finally crawled beneath the covers of the bed. She was alone. It was no more than she'd asked for. She didn't have Rory nor Alasdair to hold. Her throat ached, and her tears soaked into the pillow.

When next she became aware, knocking sounded on her door. Dawn light filtered through the small window.

"Gwyneth?" The voice belonged to Alasdair.

She rose, wrapped her *arisaid* about her and opened the door.

He stood in the corridor, his large frame overpowering the small space. Even in the dimness, the dark circles beneath his eyes told her he probably had not slept last night. "We need to board ship within the hour. Southwick and his party, including Rory, sailed day before yesterday."

⊷⊙ ⊙⊷

Two days later, Gwyneth stood on the threshold of Southwick's London residence. Alasdair's presence behind her did little to calm her nerves.

"La—" Gwyneth swallowed past the constriction in her dry throat. "Lady Gwyneth Carswell and Laird Alasdair MacGrath, Earl and Chief of MacGrath, to see Lord Southwick, if you please." Not for more than six years had she called herself *Lady*. And she felt like a fraud doing so now.

The stuffy, gray-haired steward in blue and gold brocade livery gave a curt bow and widened the carved walnut door.

Because Lachlan had several friends and connections in London, he'd soon learned Southwick was at his home and an unidentified boy with him.

The steward ushered them across the pale gray marble floor, opened a door off the main hall and motioned them inside. "Pray, wait here. I will notify his lordship of your presence," he said in a nasal voice.

Gwyneth stepped into a huge book-lined library, three times the size of Alasdair's cozy one at Kintalon. With its gilt furnishings, tapestries and dark wood furniture, the room had a regal quality that further increased her jitters. The scent of musty, leather-bound tomes usually calmed her, but this time the smell reminded her she was back in England. Back where she'd made the decision that had forever altered her life.

Wearing his finest blue and black plaid kilt, along with a midnight blue doublet, Alasdair stepped close to her. "I still say we should've stolen Rory back." His eyes gleamed dark and dangerous.

"No. I would not have this lead to bloodshed. We must work this out civilly."

"As you wish." His hand rested on the shining silver basket-hilt of his sword at his left side. A sheathed, brass-hilted dirk hung from his belt, and he had a smaller *sgian dubh* hidden inside his doublet. The tension emanating from his body told her he expected trouble and was ready for it.

"You do not think civility is possible, do you?"

Alasdair lifted a brow and let his gaze wander over the ornate furnishings and along the bookcases. "I wouldn't hazard a guess."

After the whirlwind of travel they had engaged in for the last week, the room around them was too still and quiet.

She glanced up and found Alasdair watching her.

"I thank you for coming with me."

"I wouldn't want you to arrive here alone. No telling what Southwick will do."

I must see Rory. Was he terrified? Hungry? Hurt? Her gaze kept darting to the door. She crossed her arms over her queasy stomach. She had been truly sick with worry since they'd left Edinburgh and had not been able to keep a bite down.

"You're lovely as heather in full bloom," Alasdair murmured.

His impulsive compliment created a burst of heat in her chest. She caught the longing in his eyes. It too closely matched that in her soul.

"Oh, heavens." She surveyed the emerald damask skirts and bodice she wore, pilfered from Alasdair's wife's trunk. "I thank you." She should say something to him in return, to let him see a touch of the esteem and admiration she held for him. "And you, sir, look very handsome and noble."

A half smile tugged at his mouth. His eyes gleamed with amusement and warmth.

What was Alasdair doing flirting with her? Trying to distract her, help her relax? She appreciated his efforts but she wanted this meeting over with. She wanted her son back.

"Good lord, I wish he would hurry." She paced across the multicolored Turkish carpet and back.

"If we don't emerge within the hour, Lachlan and the other men will be barging in."

"I hope it doesn't come to that."

The paneled oak door opened, and the steward showed in Gwyneth's father.

She snapped her gaping mouth closed and tried to gather her composure in the face of Lloyd Carswell, Earl of Darrow. She had never thought to see him again after he'd disowned her with scathing insults and glowers of pure loathing. His hair had turned a paler gray in her absence, and the bitter lines about his eyes and mouth were deeper.

"A good day to you, Father." She curtseyed.

"Gwyneth," he said in a sullen tone. His gaze darted over her shoulder to Alasdair.

"How are you? How is Mother...and everyone?"

"Very well."

The door swung open again and Maxwell Huntley, marquess of Southwick pranced in like a peacock in bright turquoise and yellow. "My most humble apologies for my late arrival." He gave a flourishing bow.

Gwyneth wanted to leap forward and strangle him, but restrained herself. "Where is Rory? I must see him at once."

"He is well and fit." Southwick's gaze strayed to Alasdair. "I see you have brought your mastiff along."

"You stole my son!"

Southwick smiled, resembling a blond, pointed-chin weasel. "Ah, my lady, do calm yourself, if you please."

His disregard for her wishes to see Rory magnified her anger. *I'll kill him!*

"You have developed a bitter tongue, Gwyneth," her father chided.

I have every right to my bitter tongue, Father, she wanted to shout. But doing so would not help her cause. She must play the part of a 'Lady.'

Her father's gaze raked her in a disdainful way, then shot to Alasdair. "And you must be MacGrath."

"Alasdair MacGrath, Earl and Chief of MacGrath," he said in a commanding voice. He came forward and shook her father's hand.

"A Scottish earl?" Her father frowned. "You neglected to tell me this, Southwick."

Alasdair released Lord Darrow's hand and stepped back beside Gwyneth.

Southwick blew out a puff of air and flung his hand upward. "It is of no import. As you can see by his apparel, he's a Highland barbarian."

"He is no barbarian," Gwyneth said with an intentional bite to her genteel tone. "He is a far more civilized gentleman than you."

"Well, I'm sure you know how very *civilized* he is." Southwick sniffed.

She glanced aside and found Alasdair's fierce gaze stabbing toward the smaller man. She sensed the tightening of Alasdair's muscles, as if he were barely restrained from launching himself at Southwick, blades flying.

"Let's get to the point," her father interrupted. "I must be on my way. Shall we sit down, Southwick?"

"By all means." With much drama, he waved them all toward a sitting area. His strong, perfumed sweat odor wafted to her, and she wanted to hold her breath.

Alasdair claimed the high-backed bench with Gwyneth. The other two men occupied individual leather cushioned chairs.

Gwyneth's father glared at her. "Against my sound advice, Southwick wishes to claim and support your bastard."

She fought back the flush of mortification that crept up from her chest. She would not let her father's judgmental disdain affect her. "I know that, and I have nothing against Rory inheriting if you wish to give him property, but he is too young to leave me now. I propose that I raise him until he is at least twelve, then he can go to boarding school."

"Twelve? Good lord." Southwick snorted. "That would be much too late to begin his training. He is no longer a babe. And indeed he has shocking and ghastly manners and speaks like a barbaric Scot. He requires a proper education if he is to live up to my expectations."

His expectations? As if *his* expectations were the only ones that mattered. What about her expectations of him, which he'd miserably failed in, abandoning her to poverty like the coward he was.

"I'm providing Rory with an excellent education. When he is old enough, he will be prepared for university."

Southwick smirked. "That is simply not enough. He requires proper clothing and such."

"I have provided for him for almost six years. And as you can see, he's in fine shape. I can continue to provide for him until he is older. I have full legal rights to keep him until he is at least seven."

"A future English marquess should be raised in England, to learn the English way of life. He cannot learn that in Scotland."

What could she say to that? She wanted Rory to be raised in England, but not by Southwick. How could she extract herself from this pit?

Gwyneth's father snorted. "Southwick, I daresay you will have a devil of a time convincing King James to accept your bastard as your heir."

"Do not worry over that, Darrow. Rest assured I have the king's ear." Southwick turned to Gwyneth. "I understand you are a widow now. Did your husband leave you any money or property?"

She almost gave a bitter laugh at that ridiculous notion. "No. The point is not what material possessions I can give my son, but the love and care I can give him. Which you cannot."

"My lady," he said in a condescending tone and flicked a piece of lint from his sleeve. "I have enough money to hire ten governesses to care for him if that is what's required. You would have him grow into a tender mama's boy."

"No, he is strong and brave. Laird MacGrath has provided him with swordplay lessons." Though she'd hated the lesson she'd interrupted, she felt at liberty to use it now to plead her case.

"Of the barbarous Highland variety, no doubt. That will not serve him well when he is marquess of Southwick. He must learn the skills and manners of an English nobleman."

She clenched her fists on her lap. No argument she had was sufficient for them to see her side. "Rory is illegitimate. Therefore you have no say over him! You didn't claim him when he was conceived, and now it is six years too late."

"Well." Southwick lifted his pale brows and smoothed his slim fingers over the turquoise silk taffeta of his sleeve. "You could marry me."

CHAPTER SIXTEEN

"*Marry you?*" Gwyneth couldn't believe what her ears heard coming out of Southwick's mouth.

"Have you lost your senses, Southwick?" Lord Darrow demanded.

Her father hated her. He believed her such a horrible person that he would question the marquess's sanity for wanting to marry her. She couldn't stand to look at her own father a moment longer, and switched her gaze to Alasdair.

He had turned to a statue of marble beside her, and yet through his eyes she saw a destructive storm rampaging inside him. She feared he might slay Southwick where he sat.

"My wife died six months ago," Southwick said, eyeing Alasdair with a bit of concern. "I don't feel like marrying a flighty young chit. Gwyneth, you are my son's mother. It is only right."

"Why did you not do this six years ago when I told you I was with child?" She could not comprehend how different her life would have been. Not better, but different.

He shrugged. "It did not suit me at the time."

Such was the marquess's good fortune in life. He did not even feel compelled to come up with a decent excuse for his cowardice.

"You were greedy, wanting a duke's daughter instead."

Southwick sent her a smirking half-smile. "Yes."

"Marrying me now will not make Rory legitimate."

"I'm aware of that."

Of course she wouldn't marry the snake. But what would he do about Rory if she refused him?

Gwyneth slid another glance toward Alasdair where he sat in silence. This time his gaze locked upon her. The full impact of how he felt was clear on his face. He had asked her to marry him. In his native tongue, he had told her he loved her. She loved him, as well.

Of course, she had never loved Southwick. That had been a stupid, childish infatuation. But the emotion Alasdair stirred up inside her had a life of its own. He loved her in truth. Not just in the heat of passion.

"It will do you no good to look to your lover for his approval. He will not want to share you, I don't imagine."

Alasdair turned his cutting glare toward Southwick. "The lady is capable of making her own decisions."

"I thought you worked for him," her father bellowed, his glare filled with disdain.

Whether she was Alasdair's paramour or his servant, she knew it was all the same in her father's eyes. She could sink no lower.

"I did. I was his temporary housekeeper. And I'm grateful to him for allowing me to earn my keep."

He grunted with disgust. "You should've stayed put at the MacIrwin's holdings. He is your blood kin, and that's where you belong."

Dare she say she didn't belong anywhere in the Highlands? She belonged here in England with her family. But no, that was her fault. Everything was. "Your illustrious cousin Donald wanted to kill me, and Laird MacGrath provided me protection."

"Why should MacIrwin want to kill you? I'm paying him for your upkeep."

"I knew it!" Why else would her barbaric cousin allow her to live on his lands? He would do anything for coin. The money was likely from her dowry.

"And you're showing precious little gratitude for it," her father grumbled.

Gratitude? Why should she be thankful for being outcast and exiled to the remote and barbaric Highlands, never to be seen again...at least she was certain he'd hoped never to see her again. She was equally certain he'd hoped she would die from the elements or starvation and her bastard with her.

"What did you do to enrage MacIrwin?" her father asked.

"I saved the life of his mortal enemy, Laird MacGrath. After Donald and his men left him for dead."

Her father's glare shifted to Alasdair.

"Ah. How sweet," Southwick mocked. "They've saved each other's lives. I do believe they are in love."

Gwyneth dropped her gaze to Alasdair's fist, clenched by his leg, and tried to fight down the embarrassment that both her father and Southwick knew the true nature of Gwyneth's association with Alasdair.

"'Tis not your concern," Alasdair seethed.

"It is my concern if my future wife now carries a Scots bastard. And she better hope she does not, or she will never see Rory again."

How dare Southwick say such? "I do not! I am not with child!" Gwyneth said.

Alasdair's fury became palpable, his muscles tense and his breathing faster. She was thankful for his control but feared he might lose it at any moment.

"Good." Southwick's speculative gaze darted back and forth between her and Alasdair. "If you want to be with Rory, you will marry me," he said nonchalantly. "I will be petitioning the king to claim Rory as my heir and to obtain full legal custody. You had best cooperate because you do not have a leg to stand on, my *lady*."

"You cannot mean it!" Even her arms and legs ached with the emotion and denial. "He is my son alone! You disowned us both. You would have nothing to do with us. Not until it's convenient for you. You destroyed my life, and now you want to take the last thing I have left! The *only* thing that matters to me."

Southwick steepled his fingers before him and observed her with urbane coolness. "I do not think Rory is the only thing that matters to you. If he was, you would be falling on your knees at my feet, thanking me for proposing."

"What have I ever done to cause you to hate me so? I refuse to marry you because you have treated me lower than gutter trash. You cast me aside when I needed you most."

He released a long-suffering sigh. "Such is the lot of women."

Alasdair shoved to his feet. "'Tis time to go!" he growled and stomped across the floor.

Rooted to her chair and feeling torn, Gwyneth shook her head. "I cannot leave Rory."

His back to them, Alasdair halted and clenched his fists at his sides. "M'lady, if we don't leave now, I won't be responsible for my actions!" His accent thickened.

A knock sounded at the door, and the steward poked his head in. "My lord, pray pardon. We have more visitors. Scotsmen to be sure."

Alasdair strode into the entry hall, the steward scuttling out of his way.

Oh, please don't leave me with these wolves, Alasdair.

"What a ruffian," Southwick muttered with a grimace. "The choice is yours, Gwyneth. If I see fit, I can provide for you beyond your wildest imaginings. You would never want for anything. Perhaps we could even have a few more children."

She quaked with revulsion. If he saw fit? He would like as not send her to Bedlam to get her out of the way.

"Humph," her father said. "Everyone knows you cannot sire any more children since your *illness*."

Southwick glared at Darrow. "How dare you, old man?"

"Oh, I dare. I dare! You wretched little peacock."

"Upon my faith! That's why you want Rory." Gwyneth leapt to her feet, but the arguing men ignored her. Rory was Southwick's last chance for an heir of his own loins. And she knew his pride demanded nothing less.

"You two deserve each other." Her father shoved himself to his feet. "The whore and the unmanned peacock. Perfect!" He strode from the room.

Red-faced, Southwick flicked his hand. "What of it? I don't need the crusty old earl's backing. King James is right fond of me."

In the foyer, the Earl of Darrow strode past Alasdair and his men without so much as a glance. The crotchety buffoon disappeared out the door.

"That bastard is Gwyneth's father," Alasdair muttered to Lachlan in Gaelic. "But Southwick is a thousand times worse. I swear, I want to kill him. He is naught but sheep *caochan*."

Never had he been so possessed of a killing fury and yet unable to act upon it. If he said or did the wrong thing, he could ruin Gwyneth's chances of getting Rory back legally. He was willing to restrain himself for her alone.

"You must remain calm," Lachlan said.

"Aye." Alasdair tried to shake off his anger. "I must go back in there. We will be out in a short while."

After Lachlan and his men retreated out the front door, Alasdair returned to the library.

Southwick jumped to his feet. Alasdair almost smiled at the fear that shone on the Englishman's face.

Aye, you'd best fear me, for I have plans for you. How dare the whoreson treat Gwyneth with such scorn?

216

When Southwick had mentioned Gwyneth carrying his Scots bastard, he'd wanted to strangle the swine. Aye, most likely she did carry his bairn, but it would not be a bastard. He would marry her before long, of that he was determined.

Gwyneth's face was pale as blanched linen. Wondering what had been said in his absence, Alasdair strode forward and stood beside her near the fireplace. She darted him a glance of gratitude. He hoped his presence made her feel marginally safer.

Gwyneth crossed her arms over her chest. "I want to see Rory now," she said in a strong voice. Alasdair was glad she was holding up so well.

"I will have your decision first," Southwick demanded.

Her decision? Was he back to the ridiculous proposal of marriage? She had already told him she wouldn't marry him. He prayed she hadn't said something to give the knave hope she might change her mind. Alasdair's own helplessness infuriated him. He couldn't command anyone to do anything, as he was used to. Gwyneth had to make her own decision. And her only consideration was Rory. Not Alasdair.

He hated himself for his selfishness. But he couldn't make himself stop loving her.

It seemed Gwyneth had been holding her breath when she inhaled deeply. "I will give it to you tomorrow."

Tomorrow! Damnation, you will tell him "no" tomorrow!

Southwick sighed. "Very well. You can see my son now, but I'm staying in the room."

Gwyneth glared at Southwick as if she would kill him herself.

Would you like to borrow my dagger, m'lady?

Southwick opened the door and murmured a few words to the steward. Two armed footmen entered, eyeing Alasdair with trepidation, and stood guard. He sent them a snarl-like smile. Southwick then sauntered across the room and poured himself a drink.

"Would either of you care for sherry?" he asked Gwyneth and Alasdair.

They both declined.

But I will be happy to shove the bottle up your arse.

Southwick raised his small crystal glass to them and downed a large swig.

Gwyneth pressed her eyes closed and held her face in her hands as if she had a terrible headache.

"Are you feeling well?" Alasdair murmured to her. Of course she wasn't, but he wanted her to know he was there for her. Though he could do naught at the moment like he wished to, he understood what she felt.

Her eyes met his. Her raw fear showed through clearly.

"You two stop whispering and making moon eyes at each other. You sicken me!" Southwick said.

"*A mhic an uilc,*" Alasdair said, wishing he could tell him exactly what he thought in the tongue he understood.

"I allow no swine language spoken in my house."

"*Cac. Bidh ceannach agad air.*"

Before Southwick could whine any further about his use of Gaelic, the door creaked open and Rory stuck his head around the door. "Ma!" The wee lad bounded forward and leapt into her arms.

"Oh, Rory, I missed you so." She caught and held him tightly. Tears glistened on her cheeks.

Fortunately for Southwick, the lad, dressed in English style garments, didn't look any worse for wear.

"I missed you too, Ma! I want to go home." Rory then noticed Alasdair. "Laird Alasdair!"

He moved toward the lad.

Rory clamored into his arms, and Alasdair held him like he might his own long lost son. He fought back the tightening of his throat. "How are they treating you, lad?"

"I don't like it here," Rory declared in his high-pitched voice. "I want to go home, back to Kintalon."

That the lad considered Kintalon his home clutched at Alasdair's heart. "Aye, I know you do." *And I will be taking you, all in due time.*

Rory glared at Southwick. "I don't want him to be my da. I want it to be you, Alasdair."

"Och." The tenderness he felt for the lad intensified. Rory liked him that well? This was almost more than he could comprehend.

"Why, you little—" Southwick slammed down his glass and took two steps forward.

Rory tightened his arms around Alasdair's neck.

"You won't hurt the lad!" he warned, just wishing the weasel would try it. That would give him a good reason to finish him off now.

"Or you'll what?"

"He'll run you through! You English whoreson!" the lad said.

"Rory!" Gwyneth gasped.

Southwick's face turned purple. "I see what the fine Scot is teaching him!"

Alasdair bit back a grin at the lad's courage. "Nay, he taught me that one."

Rory smiled at Alasdair and the first ray of happiness he'd felt that day shined through him.

He mussed Rory's hair. "He's a good lad. The best I've ever seen."

"Put my son down," Southwick commanded, but Alasdair ignored him.

"He does not know you," Gwyneth said.

"Well, I intend to get to know him. That's why I'll have custody. To teach him some manners. And teach him how to be English."

"He has manners. But you've scared him. You haven't treated him with kindness, as Laird MacGrath has."

"We are good swordsmen, are we not, Rory?" Alasdair asked.

"Aye." The lad beamed at him. "*Cho luath ri seabhag.*"

As fast as a hawk, indeed. Alasdair grinned.

"I will not have my son talking like a filthy, heathen Highlander!" The words exploded from Southwick's mouth.

Rory jumped, his wide eyes focusing on the marquess.

And you are a dung-covered mongrel, Alasdair wanted to retort, along with several other worse insults, but 'twas best to hold his tongue in front of the lad.

"I will have your answer to my marriage proposal in the morn. Come, Rory." Southwick held out his hand. "And why the hell did you give him such a name as *Rory?*"

Gwyneth narrowed her eyes at the man. "I was banished to the Highlands, and I wanted my son to fit in."

Alasdair set Rory on his feet, but the lad clung to him, then hid behind his leg. "I don't want to go with you. I want to stay with Ma and Alasdair."

"Rory, do not make me angry." His face red and jaw clenched, Southwick gave a false smile.

"Come, we will take you to the room you've been using. Show us the way." Gwyneth held out her hand to Rory.

He refused to release Alasdair's hand and the two led him from the room and across the foyer. They climbed a wide oak stairway to the second floor.

Alasdair felt he had a family of his own—Gwyneth his wife and Rory his son. He couldn't let Southwick steal them away from him when he'd only now realized they were a family.

"I slept here last night." Rory released their hands and opened a wide door. The bedchamber was so large it would stretch half the length of the library they had been in. And the monstrous four-poster bed was sure to swallow the lad.

"'Tis a fine room, Rory." Alasdair tried to sound happier than he felt.

"I don't like it. There's naught to play with and I can't go outside."

That reminded Alasdair...he dug into his sporran and pulled out a small wooden horse. "I carved this for you."

Rory beamed and took the animal. "Oh, I thank you, Alasdair." He bounced on his toes, then knelt and galloped the wee horse across the floor.

Gwyneth glanced back at Alasdair, affection and raw emotion in her eyes.

He shrugged. He'd needed something with which to occupy his time the last few nights, when all he'd wanted to do was sneak into her bed. As well, he had worried about the lad and how he was faring.

"I'm going to name him Tasgall," Rory said.

Gwyneth faced forward again, and Alasdair clasped her shoulders in his hands. He had yearned to touch her for two days but had refrained. Now, his hands savored the delicate feel of her. She was too thin, her shoulder muscles too tense. Gently, he dug his fingertips into them. A quiet sigh escaped her and she dropped her head forward. That she allowed him access, silently asking for more, made him feel even more possessive. *You are mine, Gwyneth, whether you acknowledge it or not.* He caressed the sides of her slender neck, wishing he could kiss her there instead. Her skin was smooth as finest ivory silk...beyond tantalizing.

"Can you carve a warrior to ride on Tasgall's back? Holding a sword?" Rory's words jolted Alasdair from his reverie.

He stilled his hands but left them lying on Gwyneth's shoulders. He could not yet bear to break the contact. "Aye, that I will, lad."

Rory stood before them, his innocent yet wise gaze darting between Alasdair and Gwyneth. "You like my ma, do you not?"

Now what was he about? Playing the wee matchmaker? "Of course, I like her." *Indeed, I love her.*

220

"You could be my new da, could you not?" The lad's tone of voice, hopeful yet so vulnerable pricked at Alasdair's heart.

"Rory, I would be honored to call you my son, but 'tis up to your mother."

Within his grasp, her shoulders shook, and she pressed her hands to her face. Perhaps what he'd said wasn't fair, considering how Southwick had her suspended over an abyss. If she would but give Alasdair the word, he would take command of this situation and Southwick would regret having ever come up with the idea of stealing Rory away.

"Don't cry, Ma." Rory stopped in front of her. "You like Alasdair. And you could let him be my da, 'cause I never had a real one that I can remember."

God's teeth. If the lad didn't close his mouth they would all be blubbering into their sleeves.

Gwyneth sniffed. "It isn't that simple, Rory. I'm sorry."

Rory hung his head.

Gwyneth knelt. "How has Southwick treated you? Has he struck you?"

The lad shook his head. "I don't like him."

"Why?"

"He talks mean and yells," he said on a sullen tone.

"Did he give you enough to eat?"

Rory nodded. "But I didn't like it."

A footstep sounded outside the door, and Alasdair glanced around. One of the marquess's men stood out in the gallery, guarding Rory from the background.

"I must talk with you alone," Alasdair told Gwyneth.

"Rory, we will be in the gallery having a discussion," she said. "Leave the door open, and I'll be back in a moment."

"Very well." He knelt and resumed playing with the wooden horse.

Once in the gallery, Alasdair discovered that Southwick had sent three guards this time—armed footmen of short stature. He could take them all if he wanted.

He guided Gwyneth away from the men, then stopped her before a tall, stained glass window. Afternoon sunlight blazed through. The colored glow lit the shimmering, golden-brown highlights in her hair and lent unnatural azure tones to her pale skin. Anguish shadowed her eyes.

"You cannot marry Southwick," Alasdair whispered

"I do not want to!" she said in a low but firm tone. "But if he won't release Rory into my custody, what are my choices? I have no means. I have nothing. Only Rory."

"Gwyneth—" He shook his head. How could he make her see?

"My own father won't help me," she whispered, her eyes pleading with him to understand. "I have no pull with anyone else. Except you. And I hate to say it, Alasdair, but we both know King James does not hold Highlanders in high esteem."

Indeed, he did not, but Alasdair's family and the whole MacGrath clan had always been on decent terms with the Stuarts. And there was something Gwyneth had forgotten—Highlanders were resourceful, tenacious survivors. One did not thrive in the rough Highlands without being so.

"This is a very delicate situation," Gwyneth said. "I would not want to ruin Rory's chances of possibly inheriting property or even a title, but I cannot leave him alone in the care of that snake."

Aye, Rory's future, that was the stumbling stone. Otherwise, Alasdair could steal him back and be off to Scotland. Since the situation was so complicated, he would have to think on it more and come up with a strategy. He would engage the help of Lachlan and the other men. Surely together they could find a way to free Rory and Gwyneth from Southwick's filthy talons.

Regardless, Alasdair had to make Gwyneth understand some things. "There are two reasons you cannot marry him."

She looked startled and perplexed. "What are they?"

"He doesn't love you like I do. And I won't allow the bairn you carry—my son—to be raised by a Sassenach bastard."

CHAPTER SEVENTEEN

Gwyneth's mouth dropped open, and her lips worked as if she had forgotten how to speak. "Good heavens. Have you lost your mind?" she whispered. "I'm not carrying—" Her words came to a strangled halt, and her face turned the color of Highland snow.

"Aye, you are with child. I ken the signs." One part of him rejoiced, while another part stood frozen with fear. Fear that she would reject him and refuse to see reason. Or that she'd ignore his help and let Southwick dictate her future. "The past few days you've been sick more often than not."

"Because I was so worried." Her words rushed out. "And…and seasick."

Must she always deny the truth? "Can you be certain of that?"

"Well—" She frowned and pressed a fist to her mouth.

"What if I'm right? You cannot marry Southwick if you carry my bairn. Not only will I not let it happen, Southwick won't marry you if he kens of it. We must find another way to fight him. Will you agree to it?"

"If I cause Rory to lose his inheritance, I will never forgive myself. That's his future. He would never have to go hungry in winter. Or be cold. He would have incredible freedoms and anything he wants, his whole life. And he wouldn't have to ask anyone for it. It would be his alone. He could easily provide for a family of his own one day."

Certainly Alasdair understood that. He would not want to part with his title and lands, either. Not because he was greedy but because his possessions gave him power over his own destiny, as she said.

223

The situation was murky. But his feelings for her were clear as a summer's day. "M'lady, I'm wanting to hear how you feel about me."

She pressed her eyes closed. "Please do not pressure me any more than Southwick is. I cannot consider more than one thing at a time."

"Well, you must, because there's more than one thing at stake here. When we made love, a new life was created. We both knew it could happen. And I hoped it would, because I want you for my wife. I love you, Gwyneth. He doesn't."

"I cannot leave Rory alone with him!"

Alasdair pulled her into his arms. "I'm not planning to."

She gazed up at him. "What will you do?"

◦৹৩ ৩৹◦

A seething rage possessed Alasdair at his own helplessness. And yet he couldn't let his men see his desperation and vulnerability.

Lachlan followed him into his room at the inn. Alasdair slammed the door. "*Mo Dia!* I cannot believe she's spending the night with that whoreson!"

"She's staying to be with Rory, not Southwick."

Something about Lachlan as the voice of reason didn't fit, but Alasdair didn't let that stop his diatribe. "She's considering marrying the pile of *cac!*"

"What?" Lachlan frowned. "Why didn't you tell me this?"

Alasdair lowered his voice marginally. "I don't want the men to ken of it. Southwick is forcing her to marry him if she wants to be with her son."

"God's teeth, man, you cannot mean it."

"Aye. Never should I have imagined a future with her. Hell, she should marry him—the father of her child. She's English like he is. 'Tis where she belongs!"

Lachlan gave him a long, skeptical stare.

Alasdair turned away. Something fierce and rebellious tore through him. "But I cannot let it be so! She will be miserable with him. He will beat her and mistreat her. The son of a bitch! He is a coward of the first order."

"*Muire Mhàthair!* For a wee bit there, brother, I thought you'd gone daft. Glad I am that you're not giving up."

"Why do you care?" Alasdair growled. "You found her employment. Either way she isn't with me."

"Marrying this hell-hated Southwick is far worse than her becoming a governess in Edinburgh, because you might be able to marry her one day, if Donald is imprisoned or hanged."

"It matters not. She can marry a murderer like Baigh Shaw and 'haps even the cowardly bastard Southwick. But I'm not good enough. I'm but a fool." How could he have let a woman delve so deeply under his skin? Even into his very bones. He had lost control...of everything.

"We must think this over rationally, brother," Lachlan said in a calm voice. "Southwick is forcing her to marry him. 'Tis not her choice. If she had a choice, I wager she would marry you."

"She wouldn't when I asked her at Kintalon, before Rory was stolen away. She wishes him to grow up in England or the Lowlands, far away from the Highlands and the feuding. And me."

"Damnation."

"Another thing I haven't told you, I think Gwyneth is carrying my bairn. And if she is, I won't allow her to marry anyone but me. Southwick already suspects it, and has said if she is, he won't marry her and will not let her see Rory."

"What a gnarled mess you've gotten yourself into."

Alasdair glared at his brother. "Are you thinking I don't ken that?"

Lachlan lifted his brows. "Well, 'tis not over yet. We will think of something." He poured wine into a pewter goblet. "Sack?"

"'Twill suffice, but I would prefer whisky."

"Aye, but we must think clearly." Lachlan handed him the wine, then took a chair by the cold hearth.

"'Haps Southwick isn't as upstanding as he appears," Alasdair said.

"'Tis rare to find anyone who is. I have acquaintances, contacts here in London. Some in high places...and some not so high. Mayhap Southwick has enemies."

"He must, considering how cruel and full of himself he is. A man who ran off to France to avoid marrying the lady carrying his child must have done other dishonorable things."

"Aye." Lachlan looked abashed for a moment. "Hell, I'm as bad as he is."

"What?"

"I didn't marry the lasses who carried my bairns."

This was the first time Alasdair had seen his brother in a fit of conscience. "'Tis not legal to marry two women at the same time in this kingdom."

Lachlan's brows lifted. "That's a right good excuse. 'Twas

impossible to choose between them."

Alasdair drank a long swallow of the wine. "I wager, one day 'twill come back and bite you on the arse." Or at least he hoped it would. He'd relish seeing Lachlan lovesick, considering the number of hearts he'd broken.

"Forsooth."

"I hope you don't have to endure the pain of love lost. 'Tis worse than any battle wound." Aye, he hoped if Lachlan did find love, he would be happy.

"Aye. Which is why I'll never fall in love."

Alasdair snorted without humor. "If it happens, you won't be able to stop it. You don't get to choose. Either it happens or it doesn't."

Lachlan grimaced. "I don't care for this subject. And you haven't yet lost Gwyneth's love. Now, about Southwick, I shall go visit some friends. Are you with me?"

"Aye."

⁘

Gwyneth trusted Alasdair and believed in his ability to get things done. But what would he do? Would it be legal? Would anyone get hurt? She lay in the huge bed and held Rory's hand. Her son snored in the darkness but she had not closed her eyes in this malevolent place. She stared through the shadows at the canopy overhead.

At least she had gotten to tell her son a story this night. And she made sure he ate well and then gave him a hug. Yet, despite this small comfort, she felt emotionally drawn and quartered.

If she now carried Alasdair's babe, Southwick would not let her stay with Rory. She would do almost anything to avoid marrying Southwick...except give up Rory.

She loved Alasdair, but she couldn't let him know that. That would make it all the harder for them both when she had to let him go.

Alasdair had not wanted her to stay here the night, but she had insisted. Surprisingly, Southwick had let her. Of course, he'd left four guards stationed in the gallery just outside the door. Several more probably lurked outside the window in the back garden.

And this way, the knave could harass her for her answer to his proposal first thing.

Dear lord! What if I have to marry Southwick? What if Alasdair didn't come through with his miraculous solution?

Though she was certain she couldn't sleep, she must have. A banging noise woke her from a nightmare.

A pistol fired downstairs. Running footsteps and shouts moved toward her. She sprang upright in bed, her pulse thumping in her ears.

What in heaven's name?

Someone burst into the room and slammed the door. Chills covered her body. She pulled her sleeping child close, her gaze darting about. The darkness prevented her from seeing who'd entered. Breathing loudly, the person dragged a heavy piece of furniture in front of the door, the wooden legs screeching over the floor.

"Who's there?" she asked.

"Is Rory awake?" Southwick's voice was high-pitched, panic-stricken.

"Why? What's happening?"

Something pounded against the blocked door. "Open up, Southwick! I ken you're in there!"

Alasdair?

"Stay back or I'll kill Gwyneth!" Southwick shouted.

Survival instincts kicking in, Gwyneth dragged Rory toward the edge of the mattress, onto the floor and pushed him under the bed.

"Ma?"

"Shh, you must be quiet," she whispered. The dust beneath the large bed irritated her nose as they crawled toward the center. But if Southwick had a pistol, hiding under the bed wouldn't benefit her or Rory. He surely wouldn't risk killing his son by shooting at her. She put Rory behind her and lay facing outward.

All remained quiet out in the gallery. What in heaven's name was Alasdair doing? Why was Southwick running from him and threatening her life?

"Gwyneth," Southwick muttered through his teeth in the darkness. Something thumped. "Oomph. Devil take it!" He hopped across the floor.

Weak light from a freshly lit candle illuminated sections of the wooden floor and Turkish carpets in her narrow range of vision.

"Where are you, wanton whore?"

A crash exploded at the door, as if it had been knocked from its hinges. She jumped, her heart rate accelerating. The large piece of furniture slid aside, tipped over and slammed onto the floor.

Be careful, Alasdair.

"Scots swine!" Southwick shouted.

"Where is she?" Alasdair strode across the floor.

Blades clashed with deafening clangs.

Rory clamored from behind her. "That's Alasdair. He came to get me. I knew he would."

"Shhh." She grabbed Rory and pulled him into her arms. They watched the feet of the two men in the throes of swordplay. Dancing back and forth, advancing, retreating. They hurled insults at each other in both English and Gaelic. She covered Rory's ears, lest he hear more curses and insults he might use.

Another piece of furniture smashed against the floor. Metal objects from it clanged and slid across the room. Glass shattered.

"Coward! What did you do with Gwyneth, *a mhican uile*?" Alasdair yelled out the window. "*Iosa is Muire Mhàthair*," he muttered. "Go after him while I look for Gwyneth and Rory."

"Aye!" Two of his men, whom she had not noticed standing near the door, ran into the gallery.

Alasdair strode across the room and threw open the dressing room door. "Gwyneth? Rory?"

Loosening her paralyzed limbs, she scooted to the edge of the bed and found Alasdair alone in the room. "We're here."

"Thanks be to God!" He sheathed his sword and pulled her to her feet with a strong grip that bit into her arms.

"What is happening?"

"You and Rory are free." He grinned in triumph. "I told you I would find a solution. With plenty of help from Lachlan, of course."

She could scarcely breathe, fearing this was a dream. "But—how?"

"That mongrel Southwick is at the center of a conspiracy to assassinate the marquess of Buckingham, George Villiers." Alasdair laughed as if this were the best news in the world. "When we informed the king of it, he sent his best guards to bring Southwick in. And Southwick ran because he's guilty, of course. I don't ken what else King James will do, but 'twill not be pleasant, considering Buckingham is the king's favorite courtier. I expect Southwick will be hanged or beheaded for a traitor if he's caught."

"Oh." Shock and disbelief froze her to the spot. Gwyneth could not even imagine the ramifications. Would Rory lose his opportunity to inherit a title or property? Had he ever had the opportunity to begin with or had that all been Southwick's grand delusion? Either way, thank heavens, they were safe from Southwick and she would not have to marry the viper. "I thank you."

"You're welcome." Alasdair surprised her by kissing her. Though the kiss was brief, it was warm, potent and delicious. It made her recall with vivid clarity all the things she loved about him. He then picked Rory up. "Are you all right, lad?"

"Aye." Rory grinned ear to ear. "I wanted to see you in a real sword fight, but Ma wouldn't let me."

"She had to keep you safe. Come, let's go." He headed toward the door.

"Wait! I must dress." Wearing only a smock, Gwyneth grabbed her armload of clothing and ran behind a screen. "Where will we go?"

"Back to the inn until Southwick is captured. You and Rory are not safe until he is. In the morn, Lachlan and I shall meet with the king."

ᴏᴡᴏ ᴜᴏᴏ

Gwyneth was in the midst of telling her son a story when a fist pounded on her door at the inn in London the next day. Maybe Alasdair and Lachlan were back from Whitehall Palace.

Though the meeting with the king concerned Rory's future, Alasdair had not allowed her to attend. It was common knowledge King James did not look favorably upon women, especially ones of questionable morals and character which, though she hated to admit it, described her reputation.

She rushed to the door but didn't open it. "Who is it?"

"There is someone here to see you, m'lady," Angus called from the passage. Alasdair had left the five clansmen to guard her and Rory until Southwick, Maxwell Huntley, could be captured.

Well, who was it? She unlocked the heavy door and yanked it open.

Her gaze fell upon her mother's face. *Heaven help me!* Gwyneth clutched at the door for support, her vision blurring with tears.

"Mother?" she whispered, almost afraid the dear woman was an illusion.

"Gwyneth." Her mother smiled, came forward and tugged her into an embrace. "Oh, child, how I have missed you."

Gwyneth squeezed her mother, though not enough to hurt her fragile frame. For six years she had feared she would never see her mother again. "Thanks be to God for this blessing."

Her mother pulled back and placed a palm against Gwyneth's cheek. "Indeed. I'm so glad you have come home."

229

"You are?" Gwyneth's throat tightened when she noticed her mother's hair had turned gray and wrinkles creased her face.

"Of course. I never wanted you to leave."

"None of us did," another female voice said.

Gwyneth glanced over her mother's shoulder and found three of her sisters standing in the passage, smiling.

"Margaret, Elizabeth, Katherine!" She hugged each of them in turn.

Two small boys ran past Gwyneth, almost tripping over her skirts.

"Boys!" Margaret scolded.

"It's fine. Come in." Gwyneth backed up and allowed them all to enter. Angus entered also, obviously still guarding, and closed the door.

"This is my son, Rory." *Please God, let them accept him and love him as I do.*

Gwyneth's mother knelt and touched Rory's hair. "Hello, Rory. You are such a handsome young man. He favors you, Gwyneth."

A ray of hope shone through her fear. "Rory, this is your grandmother."

He frowned at her and she realized he didn't know what a grandmother was.

Gwyneth swallowed back the constriction in her throat. "She's my mother and that makes her your grandmother."

"Oh." He smiled and hugged her. Gwyneth introduced everyone else, and each of her sisters complimented Rory and seemed sincere in their acceptance of him.

"Your father is an imbecile and we have shown him the error of his ways," her mother said. "We've made him promise to beg your forgiveness."

Father will never do such a thing.

"And we heard Maxwell Huntley, Lord Southwick has been arrested," Katherine said.

"He has?" A spurt of gladness shot through her.

Her sisters nodded. Another knock sounded on the door. Angus opened it. Alasdair waited in the corridor. His gaze flew past his cousin and scanned the people in her room.

"Laird MacGrath, please meet some members of my family," Gwyneth said.

He entered and she introduced everyone. Alasdair employed his most genteel manners in greeting them.

"We have heard Southwick was captured," Gwyneth said.

"Aye, not three hours past. Pray pardon, m'ladies." He bowed. "I'm needing to speak with Lady Gwyneth about a matter of much import."

She turned to her family. "Will you watch Rory for me? I'll return forthwith."

They nodded, their wide eyes curious.

Alasdair left Padraig and Angus guarding Rory.

Once inside his room, Alasdair turned to her. "'Tis a surprise to see your mother and sisters here."

Gwyneth smiled. "A very pleasant surprise. I never thought I would see them again."

"I have news. Indeed, Maxwell Huntley has been arrested as a traitor to the crown and his titles and property stripped from him. Therefore, he is no longer marquess of Southwick and the title is forfeit. As a reward to us for uncovering the conspiracy, King James is creating a new title for Rory, that of Viscount Mackem, and granting him the former Southwick's estate in the north of England."

Gwyneth felt suspended, as if the floor had disappeared from beneath her feet. "Surely you jest."

"Nay. 'Tis true." Alasdair grinned. "His Majesty was feeling rather generous and created another lesser title for me as well, for my future heir."

"In faith! Are you saying this estate in the north is Rory's now?"

"Aye, though His Majesty will watch over it until Rory is old enough to manage it himself. It is a working estate with a steward and full staff to run it. And income."

"I cannot believe it." Chills coursed over her skin. "So, if I choose, Rory and I can live on the estate?"

Studying her for a long moment, Alasdair stiffened, his expression darkening. "Aye, if you so choose." He paused. "But you need not if you don't wish it. They will be his even if you both come back to Kintalon with me."

Oh, good lord! Now the terrible choice confronted her. She had only thought she was in a quandary when faced with the possibility of having to marry Southwick. Now she had to choose between what she'd wanted most for six years, to take Rory from the Highlands…or to marry a man like no other. A man she had fallen in love with so effortlessly and deeply, she'd had no defense against it.

Guilt assailed her when she realized how selfish her love for him was. If she chose him, surely she would be punished for her greed, for wallowing in the sensual pleasures of him. She must not think of herself. She must do the right thing—what was best for Rory.

Her sacrifice would rip her heart out. "Alasdair." She swallowed hard, then forced the words to form on her tongue. "I pray you will forgive me. Since Rory was born, I wished to take him out of the violent Highlands, and you have allowed me to do that. I can never thank you enough."

"You wish to stay in England?" His tone deepened, just shy of a growl.

"I don't want to; I have to. Rory will be much safer here."

He regarded her as if she were his worst enemy. Though Alasdair had never struck her, other men had. She backed up a step, then two.

"For Rory. Not for myself. You have allowed him to have everything I could've ever hoped for and more. I never dreamed he would have property. And now all this—a title, an estate. It all astounds me. But to be an English lord one day, he will need to live here, in England. My family has been kind enough to welcome me back. And your clan could never be safe from Donald if I were there. He might burn the village again, or worse, in an effort to retaliate against me."

"Don't worry about Donald. He will be taken care of in due time." More controlled anger seeped into Alasdair's tone. Her words had caused him to transform into the fierce warrior she had only glimpsed on a few occasions. "Gwyneth, I've told you before, and I'll tell you one more time—I love you. And I wish to marry you. You are most likely carrying my bairn. Possibly my heir! Are you thinking I'll just go back to Kintalon and forget about all that?"

She could not look him in the eye when he glared with such rage. It was almost impossible to believe he was the same man who had looked at her with kind regard in the past. "No. I don't know. I must think of Rory right now. Do you think I like making this decision? No. You and I...we are adults. We must learn to deal with the sacrifices."

His eyes narrowed. "I ken all about sacrifices, m'lady! But I won't allow my heir to grow up in England."

"If I am with child, which has not been proven yet, it could be a girl. And if that is the case, she would not be your heir. Unless you imagine a female can be chief of your clan."

"I don't care if the bairn is a lad or a lass. I won't have him or her grow up in godforsaken England!"

"You are the same as Southwick!"

"Nay! How can you speak thus? I would never abandon you."

"You would take our child away from me. Or force me to marry you in order to stay with him or her."

"But there is one major difference." He pointed a threatening finger at her. "I love you. And I was thinking you might feel the same, but 'tis evident you don't give a damn about me."

"Alasdair, yes, I do care for you but—"

"Hold your tongue. I don't want to hear how you *care* for me. I care for everyone in my clan, but I don't want to bed them or marry them. You have deceived yourself. You think Rory and his future prevents you from being with me. 'Tis not true, so stop blaming him."

"He will be an English lord! And for him to be well-respected, he must learn the English way of life."

"Because the Highland way of life is inferior and barbaric, aye?"

"No. Just different. Violent."

"Don't lie to me. I ken well what you're thinking. You're like the rest of these damned Sassenachs. All you care about are luxuries and respect. You must impress the other lords and ladies. The murdering fiend, Baigh Shaw was good enough for you to marry, but I am not. Tell me, m'lady, what is wrong with me?"

She shook her head, tears flooding her eyes. He was perfection to her. When she looked at him, no other man existed in the world. *God, why must I make this decision?*

"Alasdair, you are a far, far better man than Baigh was. You must know I realize that. As for marrying him, I did what I had to do to survive. It was not my choice. Please believe me when I say I do care about you."

"Nay! I don't want to hear of your bland, mediocre regard for me," he said with disgust.

"Oh, dear God, Alasdair, it is not bland! I love you!"

"Nay, you don't. You don't ken what love is. If you feel anything for me, 'tis not love. 'Haps you enjoyed lying with me, but in truth, you have no heart."

Rage and denial lit within her. "Don't tell me I don't have a heart! You haven't listened to a word I've said. And you don't know anything about me."

"Nay, I don't ken you at all."

"I love you, but I cannot be selfish right now."

"'Haps for you 'tis selfish. But not for me. Is it selfish to want air to breathe? That is what you are to me."

He ripped her heart from her body with that. She covered her eyes and the tears burst forth. She had never imagined such fierce passion existed. And indeed, she felt the same for him. That's why it hurt so much. But just as the pelican would sacrifice her own blood to feed her starving chicks, so must Gwyneth sacrifice her heart for her son.

Alasdair stood in silence and did not make a move toward her. Once she had calmed herself, he asked, "Is that your final answer, then?"

She wiped her eyes and nodded. "I'm sorry. Alasdair, please understand."

"Very well." Pain glinted in his eyes before a wall of ice went up between them. "Southwick and his cohorts are imprisoned, so you are safe. You are to take Rory and appear before the king tomorrow. I'm sure he will have someone assist you with whatever arrangements you need to make. As for me, I am needed at Kintalon. Fare thee well." He bowed.

She moved toward him. "I'm sorry, Alasdair. I—"

He held up his hand and backed away. "I'm thinking you've said enough."

CHAPTER EIGHTEEN

Three weeks later, Alasdair stood in Leitha's flower garden. The hard stone wall of the castle behind his back was cool and rough. The sunset glowed orange and pink over the rugged Highlands. This was the first time he'd allowed himself to come here since his return to Kintalon. Though this was Leitha's flower garden, the place brought Gwyneth full into his mind, especially when he smelled the strong scent of roses here in the garden, as he had when he first kissed her.

He'd tried to numb himself against her rejection. But still, the memories mocked him and stabbed at him.

Gwyneth loved England more than she loved him. Nay, she did not love him at all. Only cared for him a wee bit. Such minuscule feelings were without doubt snuffed out by now. If not for his bairn, she likely wouldn't remember him at all. He prayed each night she did carry his son. 'Twould be his last tie to her. A tie he would never let go. Whether she liked it or not.

Instead of clearing the way for Gwyneth to marry him, all he'd done by helping uncover Maxwell Huntley's conspiracies was help her attain a grand home in England where she might live. She no longer needed Alasdair. And it was beyond clear she didn't want him or love him.

He had forced himself to leave London. Great dread of the dire and gloomy future had weighed upon him during the journey north. Once he and his men had arrived back at Kintalon, he had thrown himself into work. He could drown in either work or drink, and he had never been overly fond of the drink. That would show a distinct weakness. He refused to be weak.

Lachlan had remained at court in London, but had promised to return before the first snow.

While they'd been gone, Donald MacIrwin, his oldest son, and several of his men had been arrested and awaited trial in Edinburgh a month hence. Apparently, Donald had gone so far as to murder the messenger who'd brought the subpoena ordering him to appear before the Privy Council. This act had raised his noose several inches higher. Once the lairds who sat on the Privy Council heard of it, they'd thirsted for blood. Several of the MacGraths and MacIrwins were planning to testify against them.

Though Alasdair was glad to be home, this place was not the same without Gwyneth and Rory. If the sun shined, he didn't know it. He was there for his clan. They needed him. He liked being needed. That was one thing he understood.

If she didn't love him, he would teach himself not to love her.

◌◌◌◌◌

Gwyneth stood gazing out the tall windows into the evening. Birds flitted across the rain-drenched English moor. The mist rolled, thick and gray, as if it had come down from the Highlands to haunt her. The hilly landscape here reminded her a little of Scotland.

It had been over a month since she had last seen Alasdair. And each day one thing became more and more clear to her—though she had made several mistakes in her past, turning away from Alasdair was the biggest.

He had been right about many things, including the fact that she carried his babe. But this was not the reason she missed him. Indeed, Alasdair had burrowed his way into her soul.

She had thought sacrificing Alasdair's love for Rory's sake would sustain her. She had thought she could accept life without truly living. But she'd been wrong. Alasdair occupied her mind, morn 'til dusk. And after, in the darkest night, she would wake from disturbing dreams and wonder if he were near, protecting her from the nightmares. Sometimes he was so vibrant and alive in her dreams that he seduced her and made her yearn for him to make love to her. She swore she could smell his enticing male scent and hear his Gaelic murmurs. How many times had she reached for him in the darkness only to find the bed empty and cold?

She now realized she was the one who'd been selfish. She'd wanted all these material things for Rory. But what benefited Rory also benefited her. Now, they both had far more monetary possessions than she had ever wished for. And it did not complete either of them. Rory's future was like the dawn of a clear day, brilliant and full of promise, but the present was gloomy as the rain-gray moors outside.

"Do you think Alasdair carved a warrior for the wooden horse?" Rory asked.

Gwyneth turned from the window.

Her son slumped back in the chair before the table covered with books. He asked her that question every day without fail.

"I don't know," was always her answer.

"He said he would. And he doesn't lie."

"No, he does not."

And, dear God, the things Alasdair had said to her. Not lies, but truths so beautiful she was almost overcome every time she recalled them. Words of profound love and fierce passion such as she had never imagined. Words she did not deserve. Her eyes burned with regret.

"I want to go see him," Rory said.

"So do I, sweetheart. But we cannot right now."

"He said he would be my new da if you would let him."

Oh, goodness, that again. "Rory, someday you will understand."

"I don't like it here!" he snapped. "There's nobody to play with."

She sighed. They were wearing each other's nerves thin. In truth, he could not play with the crusty old steward. And none of the servants brought their children to the house.

"I have to go to Edinburgh at the end of the month to testify against Laird MacIrwin. To tell them about the horrible things he did when he killed Mora and burned our cottage."

Rory jolted upright, and his eyes flared wide. "Will Alasdair be there?"

"I think he will."

Rory leapt to his feet and hopped across the floor toward her. "I want to go! I want to go!" He waved the wooden horse about. "Can I go, please? Ma! Please!"

"Yes, you may."

Rory dashed toward the door. "I'll go pack my trunk!"

Goodness, the trial wasn't for three more weeks. Anticipation energized her at the thought of seeing Alasdair again. "I think I'll start packing, too," she murmured into the silence and rushed toward her bedchamber.

Alasdair sat with Fergus at a small table in the public room of a coaching inn in Edinburgh, the same one they'd stayed at two months before, on Grassmarket. Candles lent the room a dreary atmosphere. The scents of ale and roasting mutton were thick in the air, but he had no appetite for them. His clansmen, scattered about the room, and the inn's other patrons produced a murmur of conversation around them.

The trial they would testify at tomorrow would lead to the one thing Alasdair had wanted his whole life. Indeed, what his father and grandfather had wanted their whole lives as well. Peace between the MacGraths and the MacIrwins. He and Donald's second son, Carbry, who was next in line to become chief, had already come to a genuine peace agreement—one he had confidence in, because Carbry was of a completely different nature than his father.

Aye, this was what Alasdair had dreamed of, yet he felt no happiness. No satisfaction. Those things he had not experienced since he'd left Gwyneth in London two months past. Now, each night was too long. And once he slept, the morn and the memories arrived too soon to once again cast bleak clouds over his day.

He'd had his steward send her a missive about when the MacIrwin trial would be. He'd had no response and didn't expect to see her face again outside England.

The possibility she carried his child was a double-sided coin—one side agony and the other joy. He would see her again; he promised himself that much.

The wide door to the inn opened with a loud squeak, and he glanced up. The vision he saw there was both too beautiful to believe and too painful to look at. *Gwyneth.* Dressed as he had never seen her, in fine fabrics sewn into the latest fashion. Her hair styled to perfection. The epitome of a stunning English lady. And with her, three servants—a middle-aged maid, a snobbish-looking graying man, and a tall younger maid carrying the sleeping Rory. His gaze locked on Gwyneth, talking to the chamberlain about rooms for her party. She seemed a dream-like illusion. He could not draw breath.

"What is it?" Fergus glanced behind himself toward the door. "Och, good lord."

Indeed.

Fergus gauged his reaction. "Are you going to go speak to her?"

Speak to her? Hell, he wasn't even certain he could stand or form a coherent sentence. He stared at the tankard of ale between his hands. "Nay." He had tried to tell himself he'd only imagined how much her rejection had hurt. But it was not his imagination.

A moment later, rustling silken skirts stopped by the table. Shimmering blue fabric and the scent of fresh flowers. But even those things did not dazzle him. It was Gwyneth's smile and the vague hint of moisture in her eyes. "Laird MacGrath." She curtseyed.

God's teeth, man, say something.

"M'lady." He gave a mock bow but remained seated. He did not trust himself to stand without overturning the chair or some other such blunder.

"It is good to see you again," she said with extreme politeness.

"Likewise." Though in truth, this was not good for his heart since it now refused to beat properly. And his soul shriveled into a tight ball against the torture of looking at her.

"Could I speak with you?"

Though he was determined not to have a conversation with her, curiosity won. "Aye. Here?"

She darted her gaze about the crowded room. "In private."

Hell and the devil! What is she up to? He could not tolerate much more of her torment.

"Come." He rose from his chair, and without waiting for her, proceeded up the narrow stairs. One part of him prayed she wouldn't follow, that she'd find him crudely insulting and scurry the other way. Another part of him waited, breath suspended, as if it would suffocate without her presence.

Along the dimly lit corridor, he opened the door to his chamber, stood back and waited for her to enter.

She swept past him. Her wide skirts brushed silk against his legs. Refusing to think or feel anything, he followed her inside and closed the door.

Her French perfume overcame his senses. And yet she did not smell like his Gwyneth of smoke and sex, making love to the glow of a balefire. She was a different Gwyneth. English Gwyneth. The woman she was meant to be from birth. A woman who knew how to wear privilege and wealth like the finest clothing.

It was easier to think of her as a stranger. Perhaps then the abyss that always yawned before him would be a little further away. But she spoke.

"I missed you so." This was his Gwyneth's voice, the Gwyneth he knew in the Highlands. The one who saved his life and made his bed. Before he took her upon it. And her eyes, vivid blue as a clear spring day when the snow melts, they were his Gwyneth's eyes.

He looked away. "Indeed?"

"Yes. I've come to say how sorry I am."

Sorry. Aye, he kenned it well.

"And I wanted to tell you—" She wrung her hands and then crossed her arms over her breasts. "Goodness, this is harder than I'd thought."

He was in no mood to wait upon the delicate sensibilities of a woman. Especially one who had hacked his heart from his chest with an ax.

"Just say it." *So we can both go about our lives again.*

"Well, Alasdair…"

Good lord, she was getting intimate with his name. Perhaps his glare had not been cold enough.

"You were right about everything."

What the devil was she talking about? He watched her carefully. Her gaze darted about.

"And I realized I was afraid to take what I wanted…which was you." Her eyes softened upon him. Her lips lifted a wee fraction.

A twinge of warning shot through him.

"From the moment I saw you lying on that battlefield with a peace treaty, I knew you were something else. Something I had never encountered before. I feared to hope for anything. I never—" Her voice caught, and she swallowed hard. "I never believed a man like you could love me," she whispered. "I didn't believe love existed. It was more a fairytale than those stories I tell Rory. And yet, you are real." She took his hand, lifted it to her face, and kissed his palm. Her warm tears wet his thumb.

His ears would not listen to her words. He was afraid he might misunderstand them. "What are you saying?"

"I'm saying I love you, Alasdair MacGrath. And the love I have for you is not bland or mediocre. It is a love so grand it consumes every part of me. I have not lived for the past two months. I have existed in a world of gray mist and nightmares, with nothing but the memory of your face to sustain me."

Was it really him she was talking to? "Forsooth. Am I dreaming?" Maybe he missed her so bad, he'd lost his grip on reality.

She smiled, and yet tears streamed unchecked from her eyes. "Can you still love me? Will you marry me?"

He took her face between his hands, stepped close and ran his fingers over her brows, her nose, her chin. He had to assure himself she was real. "You don't mean it."

"Yes, I do." She cupped his face in her hands in a like manner. "I love you, Alasdair. I'm asking you to marry me. I want to live with you forever at Kintalon and have your bairns."

His throat tightened. "Gwyneth, don't toy with me this way! Tell me, in truth."

She tugged his head downward toward hers and pressed her lips to his. It seemed in that moment his cracked heart shattered and fell into a thousand pieces. Yet that was only a shell around his real heart—born anew and pounding like a war drum.

"I love you," she whispered against his lips. "I want to be with you."

"But what of England and safety? What of Rory and his title?"

"Donald and his men are arrested. And Rory's title means nothing if we do not have you. I thought I would be happy with Rory safe and his future so bright with promise. I thought I could sacrifice my heart, my love for you. I knew it would be painful, but I thought I could withstand it. I was wrong. Rory and I were both happiest at Kintalon, with you and your clan. That was home to us both. As for living in England, it doesn't matter if Rory behaves like an English lord fifteen years hence, if he is so miserable now he cannot drag himself off the chair."

A ray of hope shined into the bleakness of his soul. "Rory missed me?" For some reason, it was easier to believe Rory had missed him. Maybe because he'd convinced himself Gwyneth hated him.

"Yes, but not as much as I did." She stroked his face, his chin, with gentle fingers. "Do you believe me?"

"Aye. But you must understand you ripped my heart out by the roots."

Tears filled her eyes again. "Pray, forgive me. I will make it up to you, I swear, even if it should take years to prove to you how much I love you."

"You'll never abandon me again?"

She shook her head. "I won't. I promise."

With his thumb, he swiped the tears from beneath her eyes. "I believe you." Indeed he did, though it might take time for it to sink in. He still felt this was all a dream. "And I love you," he said on faith that she would never smash his world again.

She took his hand and drew it down to stroke over the silken fabric covering her flat belly. "I carry a part of you within me."

Elation filled him like a warm summer breeze. "Och! I knew it!

Did I not tell you?"

She chuckled. "Yes, you were right."

He dropped to his knees before her and pressed his face to her belly, as if he might feel his child within. She felt so good in his arms, he wanted to absorb her into himself.

"Thanks be to God. And I thank you, Gwyneth, for coming back to me. I was not sure I could exist another day without you."

Gwyneth sank to the floor beside Alasdair, and they clung to each other. Exultation whirled through her with such intensity, she laughed and wept at the same time. Oh, how delightful and stirring his big, hard body felt against hers. "Thank you for giving me another chance. I was so afraid you would hate me forever."

"Nay, I couldn't stop loving you. Hell, I admit I tried." He shook his head. "But I couldn't." Bending closer, he placed cherishing kisses over her face. His lips tickled her skin and felt like paradise on earth—soft, warm summer rain.

Rising, he lifted her into his arms, carried her to the bed and lay her down upon it. His dark gaze, solemn and fathomless, trailed over her face and delved into her eyes with such intensity, as if he still searched for the truth. As if he still needed reassurance that she loved him.

"You have not given me your answer," she said.

"Aye, I will marry you. Will you marry me as well, Gwyneth?"

"Aye, that I will, lad," she mimicked his Scottish burr and laughed, joy infusing her, head to toe, as it never had in her lifetime.

He chuckled. Then kissed her fierce and deep. The way he kissed her in memories and dreams. A kiss that possessed her mouth as his body would possess hers, with sensual power and driving force.

❦ ❦

Donald MacIrwin couldn't believe his and his clansmen's cell door had just swung open, with a soft but ominous screech, in the middle of the night. It could not be morn for he had slept none, and only a few hours had passed. He arose from the filthy, damp, packed-earth floor. Were they to be hanged tonight? Icy fear washed over him, and his empty stomach ached. He turned and glanced through the dimness at his eldest son, in his mid-twenties, young, strong and fit. Donald was proud of the fearsome young man, cut from the same fabric as his da. If he couldn't escape the hangman's noose, he hoped John could. Though Donald had other sons, John was his favorite and would make the strongest leader for the clan.

"MacIrwins, come," the guard whispered, holding a lantern aloft.

"What's happening?" Donald asked. And why would the guard whisper?

"'Tis your lucky night. Someone has paid for your freedom. Keep your mouths shut," he warned. "Or 'twill be declared a prison break, and you'll be killed on sight."

Someone paid their way out? How and who? Someone must have bribed the guards with a goodly amount of coin. Well, he wasn't going to turn down such a generous offer.

"Come," Donald whispered to his men, then crept from the cell. His clansmen silently followed him along the dank prison passageways and down stone steps. Finally, they arrived at a metal gate with bars. Another guard swung it open, and the MacIrwins stepped out into the cloudy night. A mist of rain hissed through the air, but the cool air smelled of freedom. He could barely contain his joy.

Southwick—or rather, the dispossessed Maxwell Huntley—stood nearby, holding a lantern.

"I thought you were in the tower, in London," Donald said, approaching him. The Englishman did not appear as arrogant and flamboyant as he had on their first meeting. Now, his clothing was little more than grimy rags.

"Indeed, but my good friends helped me escape, just as they've helped you. In case you didn't know, money will buy anything."

Donald grunted. "Well, I must thank you for saving our lives."

"Not yet. You are to earn it. I want my son back."

Was the man a complete lunatic? "Why? You have no title or property."

"I don't give a damn. He is my son, and I will have him back."

"You're an outlaw, just as we are."

"I want revenge." Huntley said through clenched teeth. "I want that whorish Gwyneth dead, and her damned lover, Alasdair MacGrath. They have destroyed my life."

"I'm in agreement on that." Rage seethed through Donald's veins when he thought of the two of them. "Revenge would be sweet right now." Because of MacGrath, Donald had lost everything, and soon stood to lose his life, as did his oldest son.

"I know which inn they are staying at," Huntley said. "We'll slip in, kill them, grab the boy and leave. I'll take you all to the continent with me. I have friends there who will help us."

Sounded like a right pleasant alternative to being hanged in the morn. "Very well, my good man. Point the way."

⚬⚬⚭⚬⚭⚬⚬

Gwyneth lay wrapped in Alasdair's arms, dreaming of fairytales and happily-ever-after when something woke her. A sound that prodded her to full alert. The candle on the bedside table flickered low. She tried to sit up but Alasdair's heavy arm prevented it.

"What was that?" she asked.

He shifted. "What?"

"I'm sure I heard something. Rory." Icy fear poured down from her head to her ankles. "Rory called my name!" She struggled naked toward the edge of the bed and shoved her arms into her smock.

Alasdair yanked on a pair of trews. Bare-chested, he unsheathed his sword and strode toward the door. Hands trembling, Gwyneth snatched the *sgain dubh* from her corset lying on the floor and followed. *Oh dear heaven, please let Rory be well.* She never should've left him with the maid in a room down the hall.

"Stay behind me," Alasdair whispered.

"Yes. Hurry."

A pistol fired and a section of door around the lock splintered. They jerked back. The surge of fear near chocked her.

"Get down!" Alasdair urged her backward. "Stay in the corner."

Who was that, and what was going on? With her back against the wall, she gripped the knife, her pulse roaring in her ears.

The door swung back. Her distant cousin John MacIrwin stood in the opening, sword raised. *Good lord, he's escaped!* He was supposed to go on trial tomorrow, along with Donald—his father—and several other clan members. Where was Donald? *Please God, don't let him hurt Rory.*

John's wild blue gaze lit on Gwyneth. "Da! The whore is in here!"

Alasdair darted forward and knocked the broadsword from John's hand, then bashed his hilt against John's head. He crashed against the wall and slid to the floor. Another kilted MacIrwin leapt into the room and engaged Alasdair in swordplay. Steal clashed and tinged, deafening in the close space.

Alasdair faked out his opponent and stabbed his blade into the MacIrwin clansmen's gut. "Omach!" The man doubled forward, and pitched to the floor, howling.

John finally recovered his sword, pushed to his feet and launched an attack against Alasdair. The whacking blades smashed

244

into each other by the second as the two men thrust and blocked.

John's blade nicked Alasdair's forearm and blood ran forth. Clearly, it was more than a nick.

No! *God, I beg of You, protect Alasdair.* Near frozen in place, Gwyneth bit into her fist.

John's foot bumped into his dying comrade on the floor and he wavered, almost losing his balance. Alasdair took advantage of this weakness and sliced his blade across John's throat. Gwyneth closed her eyes against the spurting blood.

Swords clanged out in the corridor, amid a din of shouting, cursing and crashes.

"Stay here!" Alasdair leapt over the two dying men and charged into the corridor.

Had he gone mad? Rory needed her. She jumped over the MacIrwins lying in pools of their own blood and chased after Alasdair.

"Ma!" Her son's cry sounded as if it came from the same room where she'd left him with the maid earlier. She prayed no one had gotten to him.

"Rory?" She tried to dash past Alasdair.

He flung his arm out and held her back. "Wait!" He darted a quick glare of warning her way, then faced the enemies again.

In the dim corridor before them, lit only by two near burned-out candles in wall sconces, Padraig fought a MacIrwin she'd seen but didn't know. Further along, Angus rained a flurry of sword strikes against Donald's blade.

She had to move past them to reach Rory.

"MacIrwin!" Alasdair yelled in a dangerous tone of challenge.

The enemy closest to them faltered and cast a glower at Alasdair. In that instant of distraction, Padraig's blade struck the man's chest. Blood spread through the white linen of his shirt.

Cursing, he attempted to block Padraig's next blow, but the move was useless. Padraig's sword shoved through muscle and ribs with the sickening sound of bone breaking. The man screamed out and slid to the floor.

Gwyneth covered her ears, hating violence as much as she always had. "I must get to Rory!" she told Alasdair. "Will you help me?"

"Out of our way, MacIrwin." Alasdair advanced.

"Go to hell! And take that traitorous whore with you!"

Alasdair raised his sword and drew a small but threatening circle in the air. Donald's eyes widened when he realized he was blocked, with Angus behind him and Alasdair in front.

"'Tis not a good time to be insulting my future wife. Would you rather hang tomorrow or die by the sword tonight?"

Madness entered Donald's eyes. He rushed Alasdair, shoving his sword upward and knocking Alasdair's blade aside at the last moment, though he retained his grip on it.

Gwyneth flattened herself against the wall. Donald lumbered past her. Alasdair switched places with her, and faced Donald again.

Seeing her chance, she darted along the passage. "I'm going to Rory."

"Let me finish him, lad." Angus stalked forward. "I've wanted to do this for your father since the day the MacIrwins murdered him. And I owe this pile of *cac* for the death of my son."

"Aye, me, too," Padraig seethed, his arm and chest bleeding.

"See that you do the job well." Alasdair's footsteps thumped behind Gwyneth as she dashed along the corridor.

Rory's shrill cry sounded behind the door where she'd left him earlier with the maid watching over him. Terrified of what she'd find inside, Gwyneth paused outside the door and grasped the knob.

Alasdair nudged Gwyneth aside and, shielding her with his body, flung the door open.

A dagger's blade glinted at her son's throat. And Maxwell Huntley, the former marquess of Southwick, held it there in a gloved hand. How could he? That was his son.

Paralysis gripped her, forcing all the breath from her lungs. Darkness threatened.

Alasdair grabbed onto her and brought her to her senses.

Rory is not hurt yet. I must get him away from that devil.

"Ma! He killed Anna!" Rory pointed toward the bed in the far corner and the still form covered in a blanket.

Their maid. "God help us," Gwyneth whispered.

"What do you want?" Alasdair demanded of the knave.

"Your black heart on a golden platter," Huntley sneered.

"Let the wee lad go and I'll fight you, man to man."

"First, I want her dead." He sent a poison glare at Gwyneth. "You steal everything I have and give it to her."

"Nay, the king gave the estate to your son, as you wanted."

"It is not what I wanted now! Fifty years down the road, yes. He's still a sniveling child. Besides, my title that I wanted him to have is forfeit. And her... What a whore you are, my lady."

"Unhand Rory this instant! He's an innocent child."

"But you are not—innocent, that is. You have just come from swiving the filthy Scot."

Rory slammed his foot hard against Huntley's toes.

"Ouch! You little shit!"

Alasdair rushed forward. He grabbed Huntley's knife hand and shoved him against the wall.

Rory tumbled forward into Gwyneth's arms. *Oh, thank God.* She dragged him away.

Alasdair's sword clattered to the floor as the two men fell.

She glanced up to find them rolling on the floor, grappling for the dagger in Huntley's hand.

"Heavens!" She pushed Rory into the corner beside a chest. "Stay there."

Refusing to let Huntley have the upper hand, and with Alasdair's arm injured besides, she gripped her *sgian dubh* and moved Alasdair's sword from her pathway. She had saved his life once; she would do it again.

Rolling on top, Huntley squalled and sliced his dagger at Alasdair's throat. Alasdair held him off. Their hands on the knife bobbed in the air.

Gwyneth leapt onto Huntley's back and sliced her knife across his arm. "Turn him loose!"

With an elbow, he flung her off him. "Bitch! I'll kill you for that!"

She stumbled backward, realizing her knife wasn't big enough. She threw it down and picked up Alasdair's basket-hilted, bloodied broadsword. *Heaven help me. Can I use one of these?* It was heavier than she'd expected.

Alasdair shoved his knee upward and threw Huntley off. At the last moment, he dragged his blade across Alasdair's bare chest. Blood poured from the fresh cut. Alasdair kicked the knife from his hand.

Huntley pulled a pistol from his doublet. *No!* Gwyneth charged him with the sword. The blade pierced through Huntley's belly and drove into the wall behind him.

He screamed.

Alasdair snatched the pistol from Huntley's hand before he could use it.

Gwyneth released the sword and backed away. *What have I done? I have killed a man.*

Huntley crumpled to the floor cursing, writhing and trying to pull the blade from his belly. Blood gushed from his wound and his hands.

A sob clogged in her throat. Not because Huntley was dying. But because she had been forced to kill a person. "I had to," she told Alasdair. She'd had to protect the man she loved. And her son.

"Aye, you did good, my wee warrior." Alasdair gathered her to him and pressed her face to his shoulder. But his wound was bleeding badly.

"Your chest," she gasped. "And your arm."

"Don't worry. I'm well."

Angus barged into the room. "Donald MacIrwin is dead!"

Alasdair turned. "I thank you, Angus. 'Twas an act of justice. My father will no doubt rest in peace now."

Gwyneth whispered a prayer of gratitude that they were safe at last.

Rory tugged at their arms and Alasdair picked him up.

Tears of happiness, gratitude and a hundred other emotions burned Gwyneth's eyes.

"I knew you would come," Rory said. "I knew you would!" He buried his face against Alasdair's neck and hugged him tight.

"Och, lad. You are like a son to me." He drew Gwyneth against him once again. "My family has been returned to me."

⚬⚭ ⚮⚬

Four days later, Gwyneth rode pillion behind Alasdair, her arm around his waist. The thick cushion beneath her derriere made the ride quite comfortable.

The blueness of the sky hurt her eyes, and the crisp, hay-scented air soothed her senses. To the north, ridges and hills foretold of the majestic Highlands to come. Indeed, she was going home with the man she loved.

Home with my fierce Highlander.

When she could not contain her joy, a chuckle escaped. *I am the luckiest woman on earth to be blessed with such a man.* She slipped her fingers between the buttons of Alasdair's doublet and, below his healing wound, gently stroked his chest through the linen shirt. She could scarce go five minutes without touching him to reassure herself he was truly here with her.

He cast a sly glance back at her. "You're a naughty lass," he murmured too low for the others to hear.

A thrill shot through her. "Maybe so, but you taught me to be that way."

He chuckled.

She turned to see if anyone was watching. Rory rode with Angus. And the rest of the clansmen traveled along with them, too, some in front and some further back. She'd also brought a governess and a tutor for Rory. Losing her maid had been a terrible blow. She was a sweet woman who had been so good with Rory. When Maxwell Huntley had broken into their darkened room, he'd probably thought Anna was Gwyneth and slit the maid's throat.

With these dark thoughts, Gwyneth fought back the fear that gripped her and reminded herself it was over. Huntley could no longer hurt any of them. Nor could Donald.

It had taken four days to deal with the authorities and the dead bodies, a funeral and proper burial for Anna. None of the MacGrath clansmen had been killed, thank God, though she'd had to see to their many wounds.

Two of her MacIrwin cousins had survived the skirmish in the inn. Before they'd been hanged, they confessed that Maxwell Huntley had known Gwyneth was traveling to Edinburgh to testify against Donald MacIrwin. He knew Alasdair would be there and that this was his last chance for revenge before he planned to flee to Spain with Rory. Huntley's wealthy friends in London had helped him escape the Tower. He'd sailed north and bribed the guards to free the MacIrwins.

"And where is Lachlan?" Gwyneth asked Alasdair.

"You haven't heard?" He laughed. "You won't believe what a tangle Lachlan has gotten himself into."

"Tell me."

"Och! 'Twould take all day."

"You can tell me tonight, then, in our tent."

"I will be too busy to speak of Lachlan tonight." He winked.

She pinched him. "Are you certain? Mayhap I will be too sore from riding to move tonight."

He sent her a wicked grin. "I ken well how to soothe your aches, m'lady."

<hr />

Look for *My Wild Highlander*, (Lachlan's story) next in the series.

ABOUT THE AUTHOR

Vonda Sinclair is the USA Today bestselling author of award-winning Scottish historical romance novels and novellas. Her favorite pastime is exploring Scotland and taking photos along the way. She especially loves ancient castle ruins! She also enjoys writing about hot Highland heroes, unconventional ladies and the healing power of love. Her series are the Highland Adventure Series and the Scottish Treasure Series. Her books have won the National Readers' Choice Award, the CRW Award of Excellence, the Winter Rose Award of Excellence in Published Romantic Fiction--1st Place Historical, and an EPIC Award. She lives in the mountains of North Carolina where she is crafting another wildly romantic Highland adventure.

Please visit her website at: www.vondasinclair.com.

The Highland Adventure Series

My Fierce Highlander
My Wild Highlander
My Brave Highlander
My Daring Highlander
My Notorious Highlander
My Rebel Highlander
My Captive Highlander
Highlander Unbroken
Highlander Entangled

༄ঌ

The Scottish Treasure Series

Stolen by a Highland Rogue
Defended by a Highland Renegade

Made in the USA
San Bernardino, CA
07 February 2020